THE ROCKWOOD TRILOGY
By
Brad McCormick

COPYRIGHTS

This is a work of fiction. Names, characters, businesses, places, events and incidents are either the products of the author's imagination or used in a fictitious manner. Any resemblance to actual persons, living or dead, or actual events is purely coincidental.

Copyright © 2020 Michael B. McCormick

No part of this book may be reproduced in any manner whatsoever without permission except in the case of brief quotations embodied in critical articles or reviews.

ALL RIGHTS RESERVED.

ISBN: 9798583185740

Dedicated to the lovers of B-movies.

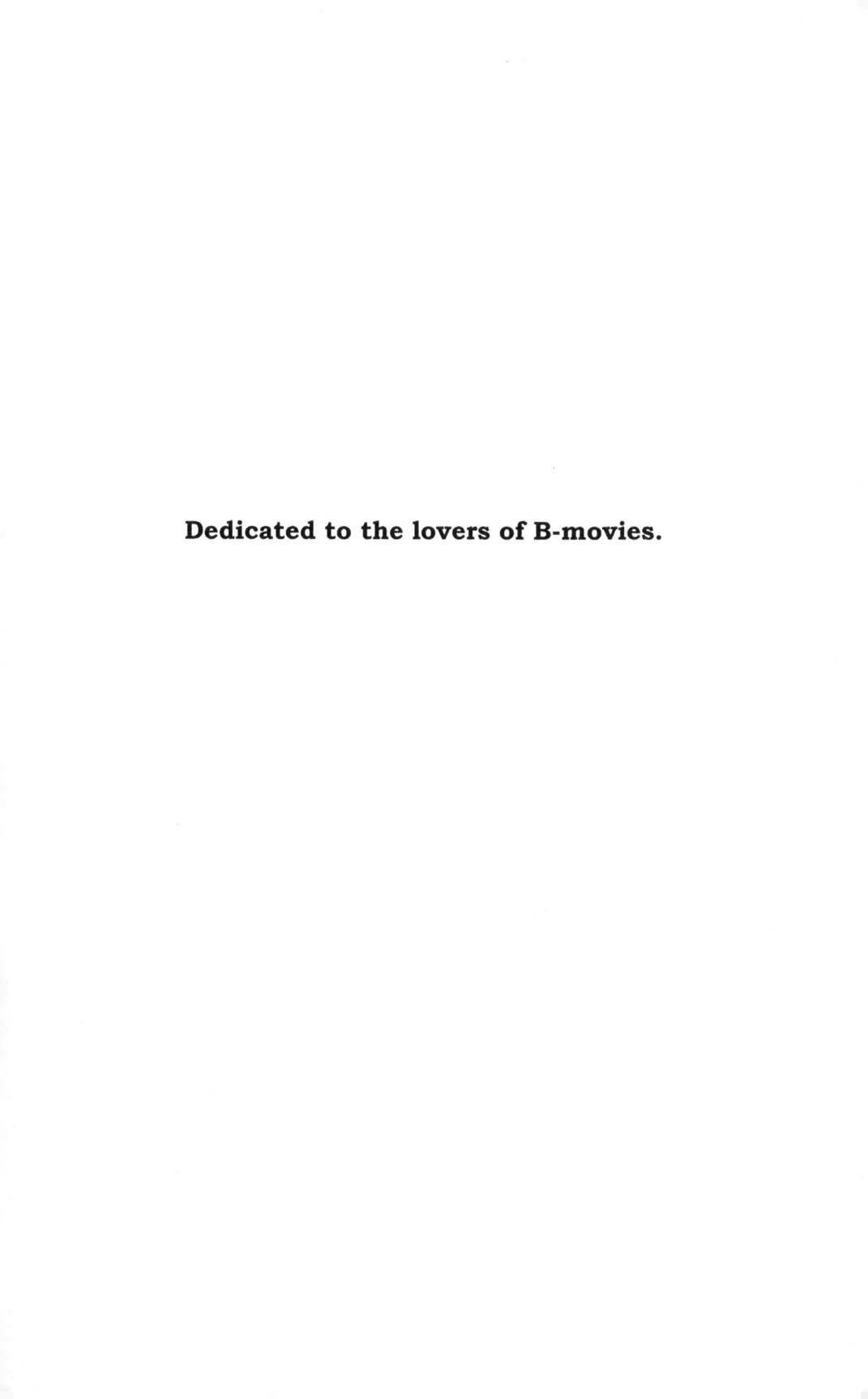

**SWITCHBLADE:
A KILLER COMEDY**

BOOK ONE

PROLOGUE

Illinois: A Simpler Time

In the moonlight, several cars were parked along Lover's Lane, overlooking a small Midwestern town. The faint sounds of Johnny Ace's "Pledging My Love" played from one of the cars.

From the glow of a dash's stereo, Greg—a local high school sports hero—sported his best letterman vest and the world's greatest parted head of hair. He kissed on the town innocent, Betty Lou. The song ended, and they separated.

"Gosh, Betty Lou," Greg said. "I don't know no girl that can kiss as good as you. I mean, gee. Would you look at that?"

Greg motioned to the hard-on trying to poke through his trousers.

Betty Lou's eyes bulged. "Gosh, Greg. What on earth is going on with your dick?"

"That's my hard-on, Betty Lou. It does that when we kiss ... when I kiss *you*, my Betty Lou."

"Well ... uh ... I just don't know what to say. What am I even supposed to do with that?"

Greg grinned.

Betty Lou quickly realized what was on his mind. "Greg Straton. How dare you? I'm Catholic, for God's sake."

"Ah, shucks. Not that again. Come on, Betty Lou. Last time we fooled around, my poor balls hurt all night. I was walking bowlegged up the stairs when I got home. Mom didn't know what to think. Shoulda seen it."

Betty Lou giggled.

"Don't laugh."

"Why on earth did your balls hurt, Greg? I didn't even touch them."

The people in the next car could clearly be seen having sex. It drove Greg crazy to see some lucky guy with a girl who had her legs up in the air like that. Poor Greg could never catch a break. He began to get defensive. "Well, that's the reason they hurt, Betty Lou. It was blue balls. You didn't touch them, and well ... you should have. They need to be touched—or else old Greg here is gonna catch a case of them blue balls again. Don't do this, Betty Lou. Not again. I know you don't want to hurt your man, do you?"

"Of course not but ... Greg ... what is blue balls?"

"Well, Betty Lou. Blue balls is when you get all worked up down there and don't release them rascals. By rascals, I mean semen. And by release, I mean come."

"Well, I ain't ever heard such a thing."

Greg grabbed Betty Lou's hand and guided it to his crotch. "Come on," he said. "Touch it a little."

Betty Lou pulled her hand back.

"Oh, come on, Betty Lou. Look. I once read that if you do it while the moon is full, then the girl can't get pregnant. Well, guess what?"

Greg pointed to the blazing full moon and then looked back to Betty Lou with a shit-eating grin.

Betty Lou gulped.

Greg's door quickly opened. The killer pulled his head back lightning fast and slit his throat, viciously sawing back and forth. Blood sprayed the car's interior.

Greg shook and twitched.

The killer held tight.

Betty Lou was frozen.

The twitching finally ceased, and Greg gurgled his last bloody breath through the hole in his throat.

Betty Lou let loose one of the worst screams in acting history. The scream continued until ...

"Shut the fuck up, bitch," the killer said.

She did.

"Worst fucking scream I ever heard in my life," the killer added. "And I've seen a lot of shitty-ass horror movies. Now, gimme them drawers!"

We have this thing in Rockwood, you see? It's called pride. It makes us who we are. When you're stuck in your ways and such, you tend to maintain a certain way of life. Rockwood, much like myself, can handle itself just fine. Well, every now and then, your ways are gonna be tested. Something new just comes out of nowhere and says, "Don't just talk about it, son. You best be about it."
—Earl Tubb, 1983

The world breaks everyone and afterwards many are strong in the broken places. But those that will not break it kills.
—Ernest Hemingway, *A Farewell to Arms*

It's fun to do bad things.
—Frank "Switchblade" Butz

7:08 a.m.

"Hey there, bitch," the killer said sporting his favorite pair of Elvis shades and a shit-eating grin. His wannabe-greaser hairstyle reached high, just like the collar on his black leather jacket. He held a massive dual-cassette-deck boom box he once claimed took fifty D batteries in one hand and a switchblade in the other. It was already popped open and ready to use.

The nurse's scream echoed the halls of the asylum as the blade plunged deep into her belly. The alarm rang out like a tornado warning over the sleepy, backwater town of Rockwood, Mississippi.

Wonk! Wonk! Wonk!

Ralph, a resident of the asylum, was sitting under the shade tree outside. He was completely lost in the latest issue of *Mad* magazine. He didn't even look up when the nurse stumbled out the front doors with a "No Sharp Objects" sign stabbed into her back. Her intestines dragged the pavement and left a red trail as she struggled to remain conscious.

Ralph, however, turned to page five.

The nurse continued her death march. She came to a stop, wobbled, fell straight forward, then slammed her face onto the concrete.

Ralph chuckled at page six. "No way."

The killer came ditty-bopping out in all his smartass glory. A true legend in his own mind, a troublemaker, a straight-up punk. He was what an old-school sheriff might refer to as a "real jokester type-a fella." Someone who downright needs a good ass whopping. That was this man, all right, and he loved that about himself. Just ask him, and he'd tell you the same. He casually walked up to the nurse as she took her final breath and placed the boom box down by her head.

Ralph looked up from his magazine just in time to see the killer pulling his blade out of the dead nurse's back. He waved at the madman. "Oh. Hi, Frank," he smiled.

The killer wiped the blood from the blade against his jeans, popped his collar, and looked over at Ralph with a friendly smile. "Aye, yo, Ralphie Boy," he said, sounding like a moronic, punch-drunk Sylvester Stallone. "Uh, how's it goin'?"

7:50 a.m.

With his trusty boom box by his side, the killer ditty-bopped the desolate back roads of Rockwood without a care in the world.

The morning heat was already baking the pavement, but it didn't bother him as he remained cool as usual. It was his thing. You wouldn't understand.

To the left, Jimmy Lee's legs were sticking out from under a black, 1974 Plymouth Duster that was hanging halfway out from a garage that seemed to be near collapse. The hot rod was straight from hell, had oversize back tires, and a dirty rebel flag license plate that was ready to piss off any Yankee boys it came across.

The killer was instantly in love. If the car were a southern belle, he'd bang the shit out of it—twice.

Inside the garage, D.J. Barnett "Pistol" Lee played from a workbench radio behind the hot rod. Proudly on display were various competition trophies, honorable mention ribbons, and a diploma for a two-week course in refrigerator repair. Dead center was a photo of the toothless Jimmy Lee, smiling proudly next to his ride, beer in hand.

Jimmy Lee continued to tinker underneath the car as he listened along to Pistol Lee's broadcast.

"Just heard a siren blast by the studio here. Must be some speeders out there or something. Well, let's move on to the next classic from Cletus Cooper with 'Nailing Jelly to the Wall.' The best song ever recorded about an impossible love. Right here on Ram-N AM."

A horrible country song began to play. It must have been karaoke hour.

The killer whipped out his comb and combed with precision, eager to make a good first impression on the ride. He walked up to the car and admired its awesomeness.

"Let's fucking do this."

Jimmy Lee stopped cold under the car. *Who the hell is that?* "Ethel. That you, Ethel?"

"Yes, dear," the killer responded in his best old-lady impersonation. He just *loved* doing impersonations.

Jimmy Lee fumed. He was disgusted by Ethel. He hated the very sight *and* smell of her. *She* was the reason he was always out here working any damn way. She might get a black eye for this one.

"Now, goddamn it, Ethel. I told you not to be coming out here when I'm trying to work on Nadine. Fuck's wrong with you, bitch?"

Ignoring him, the killer made his way to the driver's side door and glanced in.

Jimmy Lee continued. "Why don't you just take your fat ass back inside the house. Clean out my poop pan or some shit? Wash my drawers."

The killer opened the door and hopped in like a kid on a brand-new Big Wheel.

Jimmy Lee came unglued when he felt the car bump his belly. "Now you wait just a goddamn minute, Ethel. You know you ain't supposed to be up in there."

Removing his shades, the killer checked out the interior. His gaze froze when he saw the little dashboard Jesus looking back at him. He really dug that dude. Word was the killer grew up Catholic. This appealed to him on a spiritual level. He cocked his head, smiled, and gave the little guy a twinkle-eyed wink.

"Ethel. You fucking deaf? I know it's you. I can smell that gash from down here."

The keys were in the ignition. The killer fired it up.

Jimmy Lee about shit when he felt the hammer drop. "Whoa! Whoa! Whoa!" He tried to wiggle out from under the car. "When I get out from under here, I'm gonna—"

The killer hit the gas and spun out violently on Jimmy Lee's head. His legs flailed comically about, and the back tire shot exaggerated amounts of blood, brains, and skull all over Jimmy Lee's shrine. It knocked over trophies and shorted out his radio, which silenced the awful tune it was playing.

The killer yelled in joy as the garage quickly filled with exhaust, mayhem, and madness. Against his will, the dashboard Jesus vibrated in a spastic, plastic seizure until the big crunch came, and Jimmy Lee went limp.

The hot rod barreled from the garage like a beast unleashed. It sprayed dirt and gravel at Jimmy Lee's white-trash home and broke out its windows like a Wild West shoot-out. The hot rod finally hit the road, caught its traction, and hauled serious ass—straight for a little girl who was out walking her birthday present.

"I love my little Fluke," she said as she skipped along with her new puppy.

The killer jerked the wheel and quickly crunched Fluke under his tires. "Hot dog!" He sped away.

The little girl screamed, "Asshole!"

7:59 a.m.

Outside Jan's Horseshoe Inn, a young barfly was passed out cold against the building. It was unclear whether the puddle of urine she was sleeping in was her own. In the distance, the sounds of a hot rod's engine came closer and closer. The killer spotted the young barfly through the dusty windshield and chuckled like Butthead from *Beavis and Butthead*.

"Uh. Huh-huh-huh. Cool."

He pulled into the empty lot next to her and came to a slow, steady stop. The engine rumbled along. The girl would still not wake. He gave the gas a double tap.

Vroom! Vroom!

She woke, struggled to stand, and stumbled to the passenger door. She leaned in the window.

Her stench filled the car immediately.

"Hey there, Mr. Rock 'n' Roll guy."

The killer was reasonable. "You'll do."

8:38 a.m.

The killer picked a nice, secluded spot. Nothing for miles. The scene was silent except for the faint howl from the wind in the surrounding fields. The hot sun beat down on the barfly's blood-caked face. She was duct taped to a lawn chair in the middle of a long, desolate road. There was no telling what sort of things the killer had done to her. A huge gash on top of her head steadily leaked blood down her beaten face. That was until...

A switchblade jabbed straight through her bare foot. It hit the hot pavement, and the barfly sprang to life. Her bloodcurdling scream travelled and attracted a field of cows. One responded back with an enthusiastic moo.

The barfly began to frantically jerk at the tape and scream at the top of her lungs.

The killer was kneeling before her like a kid playing marbles and continued digging into her foot with his blade. A dumb smile spread across his face.

"Mister," she screamed. "What the fuck are you doing?"

"Huh-huh-huh." The killer jumped back, bloody blade in hand. He looked down proudly and smiled. "Lookie there. I stabbed your foot."

The barfly continued to scream.

The killer began to think. *Hmmm. This shit here obviously isn't working. Tough crowd, yo. Maybe she'll dig my moves instead!* He immediately broke into a Running Man dance that had zero rhythm. "You like that shit?" he asked as his legs kicked about.

"No! Lemme go! Ah!"

"You said no?" he asked in amazement, still dancing. "You don't like this? Really?"

"No!"

"Well, fuck you then, bitch," he said, sounding hurt.

He cocked back and delivered a right cross to the barfly's face, which jarred her brain and silenced her pleas. He went straight into a George Jefferson pimp strut to the idling hot rod and threw up his arms in victory like a prizefighter.

"Fuck Barber Beefcake," he yelled to his fans.

The barfly, barely mumbling at this point, tried to plead with him, unaware he had walked away. "Mister. D-duh-don't ...hurt me anymore like this. Just ... please stop."

The killer hopped into the hot rod and tossed the bloody blade on the dash. It splattered blood across little Jesus's holy robe and caused him to wiggle and dance. The killer slammed the door, checked his hair in the mirror, kicked it into drive, smashed the gas, and continued his vicious attack by pelting the barfly in the face with gravel. Ten seconds later, he shot forward into a roaring 360. He held his arm out the window and hooted, "Yee haw!"

Missing by inches, the hot rod blasted down the long stretch of road and left her to choke in a cloud of dust and exhaust.

She could barely make out the vehicle through the blood, dirt, and tears.

After two hundred feet, it spun to a screeching 180 in the middle of the road. It growled in the distance, ready to charge. But first ...

The engine rumbled.

The killer let out a slow exhale. *How's my hair?* He peeked in the mirror. *Wow! The curl coming down the front never looked more badass on me. Ever! Damn near like James Dean. Or Superman! Shit!* He winked at himself, reached in his pocket, and pulled out a white cassette with Side B written in red marker. He popped it into the boom box, slammed the door shut, and hit play. The tape's wheels began to turn. The killer popped his collar, gripped the wheel, and got ready to rock.

The boom box blasted, and Motley Crue's "Live Wire" filled the car with hair-metal chaos. Loving that Tommy Lee, drum-driven intro, he got amped and slammed the gas. His spinout sent ungodly amounts of smoke high into the atmosphere. He finally rocketed off toward his target, pedal to the deadly metal. The car's acceleration climbed fast.

The killer pumped his fist, devil's-pitchfork style, and sang along. "'Cause I'm alive! A live wire! 'Cause I'm alive! Huh-huh. That's my shit, yo."

The barfly couldn't even bring herself to look up.

The killer squeezed the wheel for impact. "This shit might sting, bitch!"

Blam!

"Woo-hoo! Ten points!"

The hot rod was gone in a flash.

Moments later, the barfly came straight down from the heavens and hit the hot pavement—still attached to her chair—with a messy splat.

9:52 a.m.

I am so not in the mood for this stupid-ass horseshit, Yancey Wallace thought. The stocky, weathered, tough-as-nails, redneck sheriff drove his dusty Lincoln Town Car to the scene of the crime. His large cowboy hat allowed very little headroom, and the morning heat, which was rising fast, was causing murder on his hemorrhoids. To say he was pissed for being called in on his day off would be putting it mildly. Sheriff Wallace was not a happy man.

Pistol Lee kept him company through the stereo. "Word is, Jimmy Lee done went up to Sutter County and snatched another honorable mention on that Duster of his. Way to go, Jimmy Lee! Well, let's move on to what I like to call good music. Here's Bill Dollar with 'My Favorite Satin Jacket,' a personal favorite."

The song began to play.

The sheriff turned it up and sang along with the upbeat Bill Dollar. "Well, my favorite jacket has a long black stripe that's going down the sleeve tonight, all right. Its color is maroon, come feel on it soon. We'll undress by the light of the moon. Yee-haw."

Wallace hocked a loogie out the window. "Goddamn. It sure is one hot, miserable-ass, bullshit day. Hell with this shit."

10:10 a.m.

The barfly was dead in the middle of the road. A pile of broken body parts attached to the busted lawn chair. Flies had gathered in the heat and buzzed what was left of her face.

The scrawny junior deputy, Lester Boone, walked the crime scene.

Twenty feet away, Sheriff Wallace was chewing out the ass of the other deputy, an overweight slob with little intelligence on his face. There were numerous food stains on his uniform and his crooked name tag read: E. Tubb. He stood before the sheriff at a half-assed attention while the sheriff continued to bark at him like it was all his fault.

"Nobody—and I mean *nobody*—is gonna come into my town and start no kinda shit like this." He spit his tobacco juice with a splat. "Nobody! Now, I don't know just what the fuck you intend to do about this, but you best do it—and you best do it quick. I want you to go out there and hang this come-fart taco to the nearest goddamn wall. Just look at that shit!" The sheriff motioned over his shoulder at the corpse. "It kinda makes me look bad."

"Ah," Lester yelled from the background, grossed out. "Is that ... is that a toe? Aw, man."

Sheriff Wallace attempted to calm himself. Maybe he could be reasonable for once. Maybe the deputy before him *could* handle this after all. Yes, this deputy was a full-fledged moron. The town dipshit, so to speak, but what the hell, right? This can't be *that* goddamn hard. The suspect will probably end up getting caught taking a shit in somebody's backyard anyway. These crazy types do that kind of stuff.

The sheriff spit again. *Splat!* "Now, looka here, Earl. I know I done passed you up for promotion in the past, but if you nab this sucker, then it might just change things for you. You nab this perp and maybe—*just* maybe—we'll have a talk about that little promotion of yours. How's that grab you, Earl? You the man for the job?"

The weekend volunteer smiled with a gleam in his special eye. He tried to tighten his attention and still looked like a complete slob. He opened his mouth, and said, "I have been waiting for something like this my whole life."

"Earl Tubb's on the job, huh?"

"I'm all over this, Sheriff. He's *all* mine."

"Earl, there was never a doubt in my mind ... because if you don't get your fat ass out there and find the stupid sumbitch who thinks he can just run around my town and be fucking up my folks, well, then it's gonna be on you. You understanding me, Earl?"

Earl took a long, hard gulp.

"Good." The sheriff quickly turned and walked over to his car. He opened the door and looked back at Earl. "Now, after the wagon gets here and scoops this little bitch up off my road, you and Lester getcha asses out to Jimmy Lee's. He done got his ass too."

Earl's jaw dropped.

"Oh, shit," the sheriff said. "That's right. Y'all related, ain't ya?"

"I found her foot, y'all," Lester yelled.

Wallace said, "Well, guess what then, Earl? Looks like this asshole done up and got personal with you. He done up and killed your cousin. At this point, it's like he's just throwing it in your fucking face. He's laughing at you, Earl. Laughing! Looks to me like he doesn't give one bit a shit about how you feel as a human being. He don't care, so as far as I'm concerned, neither should you. Get my meaning, Hoss?"

"Yeah, Sheriff." Earl looked down. "I think I do."

Wallace walked over and put a phony, caring hand on Earl's shoulder.

Earl slowly looked up.

The sheriff's eyes locked with his and started burning straight into Earl's soul, bringing him back to the mission at hand. "No," Wallace said calmly. "You *get* my meaning?"

Earl turned red, balled up his fist by his sides and began to perspire. The morning heat mixed with the hate he had for any and all lawbreakers, especially ones who would have the damn nerve to kill his cousin. His family. Earl loved his cousins, especially Marybeth. She was his second cousin and the cutest one he had. So, in Earl's mind, doing certain "things" with her was A-OK.

The sheriff said, "Well, let's have it, son."

Earl had plenty of vengeance in his voice to go around. "For Earl Tubb, failure is not an option. I will crush this man's nuts and eat 'em for lunch. You can just about guaran-goddamn-tee that shit."

The sheriff got excited. "Oh yeah. That's the shit I wanna I hear—right there." He slapped Earl's sweaty back. "Now go on and getcha asses to work." Wallace walked back to his car, opened the door, and hopped in. Slamming his door shut, he grimaced and moaned from the discomfort from the hot leather seat, which instantly lit his 'rhoids on fire. He started the engine and gave Earl one last glance. Earl was staring off into the horizon, contemplating God knows what. He scanned Earl top to bottom and shook his head in disgust. "Jesus God Almighty. Yuck."

He put the car into gear, pulled out, and kicked up a dust storm around Earl.

Earl was still staring off into the distance, completely stone-faced. He began to contemplate deeply on the mission. He quickly realized he had one advantage over the so-called fugitive as the dust finally began to settle. Earl knew this town like the back of his hand, and he was proud of that fact. *Knowing a town like the back of your hand is just what a "soon-to-be hero" like me needs in his arsenal. And I do. Bet your ass on that, boy. You can't hide forever. It's only a matter of time before I getcha.* This was Earl's chance to prove to the whole town that he was worthy of the respect that had dodged him in Rockwood his whole life. No friends. Bullied on the playground. Always picked last in gym. He even had to take his own stepsister to the grade school dance. He didn't think there was anything wrong with that—until they all laughed at him. No matter how hard Earl tried, no respect. Ever. But things were about to change for Earl. *That* he knew. When he does in fact bring this man down, they might even throw him a party at the VFW like they did for Cutty that one time. *That'd be great.* Earl nodded at his destiny. "Get ready to fall, you diabolical asshole," he said under his breath. "Hey, Lester!"

"Yeah, Earl?"

"Let's do this."

The officers walked to a patrol car that had seen better days. It was rusted, busted, and the magnetized antenna attached to the trunk reached high for the sky. Earl wished it had a single red cherry on top, just like Starsky and Hutch, but it would do. They climbed in and slammed their doors in unison.

All was quiet between the officers.

Earl stared down the long road ahead and began going into cop-mode. A thousand-yard stare slowly came across his face. He had been practicing his thousand-yard stare for weeks and was ready to use it with confidence.

"Lester?" he said.

"Yeah?"

"Jelly."

Lester reached in, grabbed the last jelly doughnut from the box, and handed it to Earl.

Without taking his eyes off of the road, Earl took a man-sized bite that made jelly spurt down his shirt.

"Mmmm," he chewed in ecstasy.

Not one to give a shit about jelly stains; he fired up the cruiser and pulled out onto the empty road. Their mission had begun.

10:25 a.m.

The officers cruised. Earl continued to munch away.

Lester broke the silence. "So, whatcha do last night, Earl?"

Earl took a bite. "Movie show."

"Movie show, huh? Whatcha go see?"

"*Stroker Ace.*"

"*Stroker Ace*? Hmmm. Don't think I know that one. Any good?"

Earl took the last bite of doughnut and crammed it in nice and slow. He loved to make Lester wait for his replies. It made him feel superior. He swallowed it down, turned, and acknowledged his admiration for the new Burt Reynolds film. "Best movie since *Smokey and the Bandit.*"

Lester's eyes bulged. "... No way."

Earl didn't even reply. Instead, he popped a fresh toothpick into his mouth and looked slowly back to the long, steamy road ahead.

"Better than *Bandit*?" Lester asked, still in shock.

"Better. Look, Lester. I know these things. Take this scene with Loni Anderson. She got drunk and passed out on the bed with Stroker in the room, right? So, what's Stroker do, you ask? Well, I'll tell ya what he did, Lester. I'd probably do the same thing myself. Ya see, Lester? It makes sense that I'd do the same thing since I'm a lot like Burt Reynolds. Hey! You remember that nude poster he had a few years back? I got one for Christmas. And there was this one time—"

"Earl?"

"Yeah?"

"Where you reckon this fella's at?"

Earl thought. "Who?"

"The guy. The one we're after. The one that ran that girl over back there. You know. The guy."

"Oh. *That* guy. Well, let me tell you about *that* guy. Ya see, Lester? I don't need any more abuse from our good Sheriff Wallace back there, so I guess we best find *that* guy—and we best find him quick."

"Why's the sheriff hate ya so much, Earl?"

"I don't know, Lester." Earl shook his head. "I just don't know. I do know one thing, though."

"What's that, partner?"

"He would just *love* to crucify me. 'Crucify Earl Tubb' is what he'd say. Believe me. He thinks I'm a joke. I'm not. But you wanna know what, Lester?"

"What?"

"What the sheriff wants to do to me ain't *nothing* ... compared to what Imma do to this sorry sumbitch when I catch him."

"Dang, Earl. Whatcha gonna do?"

"What am I gonna do, Lester?"

"Yeah."

Earl knew exactly what he was going to do to Puke Face when he caught him. "I'm gonna reach in real real deep ... and rip this boy's spine straight up out his own goddamn asshole."

Lester gasped. Violence scared him.

"How'd that last little statement grab ya, Lester?" Earl asked with a crazy smile. "You like that shit?"

Lester didn't.

Earl continued anyway. "And when I yank that bitch out, I'll look him straight in the eye and give him my specialized 'Earl don't give a shit' grin. Once that's done—and I'm fully confident he's learned his lesson—I'm gonna piss on the boy's battered bones. Then I might just have to hang that sorry-ass sumbitch from the highest tree in the county just so any and all who pass by can bear firsthand witness to the delivery of *true* Tubb justice. And *that* is what Imma gonna do."

Lester thought. "Hmmm. Now, Earl. You know if we find 'em, we supposed to call—"

"No," Earl shouted, not listening anyway. A better idea came. He slowly pointed his hand like a gun down the road, and his eyes went wide. "Imma get the sumbitch lined up in my crosshairs and straight blow his goddamn sick ass back to Dixieland Delight. And I don't think anybody with half a brain up they goddamn noggin would mind none too much neither. That about clear enough for you, Lester?"

Lester stared straight ahead. It was more than clear.

10:43 a.m.
Back at the scene of the crime, Earl looked over the bloody trophy display inside Jimmy Lee's garage. Ethel balled her eyes out in the background and wailed away.

"Waah! Why? Why? Not my Jimmy Lee!"

Earl shook his head in disbelief. This shit pissed him off to no end. Jimmy Lee *was* his first cousin after all. Earl even remembered being happy for Jimmy Lee when he bought that hot rod with that slip-and-fall settlement from Kmart. Jimmy Lee even promised Earl that he'd leave him that hot rod if he was to ever get himself killed in a card game gone bad or caught by some lady's husband in bed with his wife. That was a promise he'd made to Earl. Now, they were both gone. The cousin *and* the hot rod. This was some bullshit. The chunk of flesh that was stuck to Jimmy Lee's photo began to slide down his toothless grin. It fell off and hit the dirt by Earl's foot. Earl put his hands on his hips and nodded. "All right, ya goddamn sick sumbitch. Get ready to meet Earl Tubb."

Mabel called over the CB in her sweet drawl. "Base to Earl. Come back. Sheriff got something new fer y'all."

Earl stepped over Jimmy Lee's headless body and strutted out of the garage, right past Lester, who was trying to console Ethel.

She kept reaching for the sky. "Waah. Why, Lord? Why? Why? Oh shit! Oh shit! Shit! Ah!"

Earl walked up to the cruiser, pulled out the CB and stretched the cord to its limit. Nothing made him feel cooler than talking on that damn CB radio. He truly loved it. He looked left to right, brought it up to his mouth, and said, "Go for Earl."

"Uh. Yeah. Sheriff done told me to tell y'all to go out to that hospital on the edge of town and meet with a Dr. Roberts. He gonna fill y'all in on everything ya need to know about this feller ya looking fer, okay?"

"That's a big ten-four, base. En route to one Rockwood Home for the Criminally Insane. Earl and Lester out."

Earl pulled the CB, released it, and caused it to quickly *whipishhh* back into the car.

Lester was still trying to console Ethel.

Earl yelled, "Officer First Class Lester Boone."

"Yeah, Earl?"

"Better break out the funny-farm repellent, son. We 'bout to find ourselves 'round a whole bunch of crazy-ass, retard motherfuckers."

"No!" Ethel cried.

11:07 a.m.
The hot rod's gas gauge began to creep over to empty. The killer screeched a hard right into the parking lot of Clint's Gas-N-Grab: a one-pump station on the outskirts of town. It wasn't much to look at. He skidded up next to the old pump and kicked up some dust.

The tail end of Pistol Lee's broadcast filled the car as the killer fixed his hair, still in high spirits. "Apparently this fella's a little off his rocker. A real mean motor scooter, if ya know what I mean. Our good sheriff said that he probably done fled town, but just in case, be on the lookout for Jimmy Lee's Duster. It was last seen heading out toward Clint's—"

The killer killed the engine. The sounds of ZZ Top's "Tush" emitted from the shop at high volume. The killer got out with much swagger, grabbed the gas pump handle, and slammed it into his tank like a true slickster. He leaned back against the hot rod to relax as his gas pumped slowly.

Inside, behind the counter/display case that housed random-colored dildos, porn, brass knuckles, southern pride merchandise, and weed paraphernalia, the forty-six-year-old brute, Clint, yelled over the music to his sidekick, Andy, who sat on a stool with a spit cup and hung on Clint's every word. Off to the side, a porno played on a small TV. In it, a middle-aged woman was getting torn up by a little gray alien—and she was loving it. Her moans filled the shop.

Clint shouted, "So, then I told that stupid-ass bitch that I don't drank enough if you ask me! You're damn tootin', goddamn it."

Andy picked up the black dildo from the counter and began to scratch his back with it.

"I said to her, if you think you gonna be laying around the house all day taking them goddamn pills, then don't you be worrying about what the fuck I be doing. Because Imma do what I want."

Andy stopped scratching and pointed the rubber dick at Clint. "Clint Don't-Take-No-Shit Kiker ought to be your name," he said as the dick flopped about. A fly buzzed by. Andy watched it zigzag before them. When it landed on the counter, he smacked it with the rubber dick. *Splat!*

Clint shook his head. "I tell ya, Andy. This woman's nothing but trouble. And that goddamn redheaded, nigger-music-loving boy of hers."

Andy was shocked. "He likes that nigger shit?"

"Well, hell yeah! The other day I let him borrow my van to go get me a pack of smokes. He musta took one of them nigger rap tapes and left it in the tape deck. The next morning, I get in my van to come down and open up shop." Clint exhaled. "... Andy?"

Andy leaned in. "Yeah?"

"I turned that ignition on and this *nigger* was coming through my stereo—full blast! Just like this." Clint jumped into a mock, beatbox impersonation by spitting puffs of air into his cupped hands like one of the Fat Boys. "P-p-p-puhh. Puhh-p-p-puhh. Puhh-aha-aha-aha-puhh."

Andy just stared, mesmerized by the sound. He wasn't sure what to make of it.

Clint continued. "P-p-p-puhh. P-p-p-puhh. P-p-puh-p-puhh. A-ha-ha-ha. A-ha puh-ha."

Andy shook his head at the noise they called music nowadays.

Clint stopped, pointed at Andy, and tried to reassure him of the facts. "Yes, sirree, Bob. Goddamn it. He was just like some stupid nigger in a *Beat a Street* movie, Andy. That's what they do. Just like that. This is what I have to live with. I'd rather be fucked gently with a rusty chainsaw up my brown stink-hole than have to put up with this goddamn bullshit anymore."

"I'd knock the shit outta him if he did that bullshit around me," Andy said. "No joke."

The song on the jukebox ended just as the gas bell outside stopped at $6.66 with a *ding!* The killer outside noticed this and chuckled.

Back inside, Clint was watching the porn Andy had brought in. The little alien now had the woman's legs pinned behind her head, pounding away like a true stud. She grunted with every thrust. "Uh! Uh! Uh! Shit!"

Not taking his eyes off the screen, Clint motioned outside. "See who that is outside, would ya, buddy?"

And as if on cue, the shop's door flung open, slammed hard against the wall, and somehow fired up the jukebox. Robert Gordon's "The Way I Walk" blasted at high volume.

The clerks jumped.

The stranger appeared from a cloud of awesomeness and slowly strutted into the shop to the beat.

The clerks were mesmerized by the entrance with the accompanying theme music. That's never happened there.

The stranger froze, waited a tick, and then completely cut loose. He danced the shop floor like an idiot to the nasty rockabilly tune with a series of drops, pops, and spins. The bass shook and rattled the fishing lures right off the shelves as the stranger stayed lost in dance, spinning in place until the music, and him, as if somehow on cue again, stopped.

The sound of the porno woman's moans filled the shop. "Fuck! Me! Ha! Ha! Harder! Oh! Oh shit!"

The stranger instantly noticed the smartass smirk on Terry's face.

Terry decided to break the ice. "Whatcha say there, Barbarino? Flat-out loved your ass in *Grease*."

"I liked him on *Happy Days* myself," Andy said.

Clint rolled his eyes and shoved Andy's arm. "It wasn't *Happy Days*, Andy. You fucking shithead. It was *Grease*. Part II." He smiled at the stranger. "Ain't that right, boy?"

With the exception of the porno, a silence fell over the shop. The stranger popped his collar, slowly walked toward the counter, and then rudely kicked over the magazine rack.

Clint shouted, "Whoa! Fuck you think you doing, boy? Don't be kicking my shit down like that. Fuck's wrong with you? Now, Andy's gonna have to clean all that shit up."

"Me?" Andy didn't even work there.

The killer centered like a Wild West showdown.

The porno woman continued. "Ah! Ah! Uh! Fuck yeah! Fuck me, little fella! Fuck me! Uh! Ah! Shit!"

Clint cocked his head at the stranger. "Ain't it kinda hot to be wearing a fucking leather jacket?"

The killer pushed his jacket aside to make way for his imaginary six-shooter. He slowly brought his hand up, blew on his fingertips to dry any sweat for the draw, then slowly brought his hand back down. He began whistling the theme from *For a Few Dollars More*, stopped, grinned, and said, "Say when."

Both clerks were completely dazed by the look in the killer's eyes. Crazy. Scary. Creepy. Tension filled the shop—along with the sound of the alien finally coming all over the woman. "Uh," it panted. "Shit, baby."

A real silence fell over the shop. The killer fixed his gaze on Andy, playfully winked, and blew him a kiss.

Andy gulped. He had never been more frightened in his life. With a shaky hand, he tapped Clint's shoulder. "Clint? What's going on here, man? I'm getting scared."

Clint cut him off with a quick, "Shut that shit up, you asshole."

The killer hopped into a mock, Bruce Lee fighting stance, complete with under-the-breath moans and groans.

Clint just stared, speechless.

The killer began bopping back and forth, ready to strike.

Not knowing what to make of it all, Clint shrugged his shoulders and decided to make a peace offering for the first time in his life. "Hey, there buddy. We're running a special this week." He grabbed the black dildo and held it up with a smile. "Nigger dicks are half off."

The sound of the killer's blade came to life.

Snikt!

11:31 a.m.
Behind his desk, Dr. Roberts was going through a file folder with "Classified" marked across the front in big bold letters. He flipped through some pages, stopped, and read quietly to himself.

> Frank Butz's response level has been the highest on record for Serum 13B. The recipient has accelerated far beyond the others and expanded treatment has been approved by Dr. Ganipgonads. Increase doses and report back daily on progress as it unfolds.

He closed the file with a look of confusion.
 There was a knock at the door.
 "Come in."
 The secretary opened the door for Earl and Lester. "Gentlemen," she said.
 "Thank ya, ma'am." Lester took off his hat.
 Earl strutted right past, ready to get down to business. "Yeah," he said. "Thanks there, lady."
 "Rose." The Dr. held up the file. "Where did this progress folder on Frank Butz come from because it's not one of ours. Did that one group from Nevada leave it last week before I arrived?"
 "Sorry, Dr. Not sure. It doesn't really look like one of ours."
 "That's okay. Thanks, Rose. Hold my calls until I'm done here with the officers."
 Rose nodded with a smile, walked out, and closed the door.
 The Dr. motioned to the two chairs in front of his desk. "Have a seat, gentlemen."
 The officers walked over and plopped down in perfect unison. Lester quickly whipped out his mini pad and pen, ready to take notes.

Earl eyeballed the degrees on the wall. He sucked through his teeth at them. "You Dr. Bob?" he asked, wishing there were more jelly doughnuts in the car.

"Yes, but it's Dr. Roberts."

"Heard one of your boys up and got squirrelly on ya. Ran off."

"You are correct, Mr. *Tubb,* is it?"

"*Officer* Tubb to you." Earl popped a fresh toothpick in his mouth and leaned back, cool as a cucumber.

"Okay then, *Officer* Tubb. Here it is. The one and only Frank Butz has escaped and is on the loose." The Dr. waited for reactions and got none. "Does this not concern you in the least?"

"Not really." Earl began to flip the toothpick back and forth with his tongue and think. *Wish I had a matchstick to chew on instead of a toothpick. Matchstick would look much cooler. Tougher. Like Cobra! Or maybe even Clint Eastwood. I'll get one at lunch. And a candy bar. Maybe two. A Chunky, perhaps. Mmmm.* Earl rejoined the conversation. "Say, just who the hell is Frank Butz anyway?"

"Perhaps you know him by what the media called him. They called him Switchblade."

"Switchblade, huh?" Earl sat up. "Write that down, Lester. That's two words. So why the name Switchblade, Doc?"

"It stems from his obsession with the greaser culture of the fifties. He thinks greasers are 'really cool' and 'very boss.' Those are his words. Since he thinks greasers are cool and being cool is definitely a top priority for him, he naturally wants to be a greaser—or at least look like one. Given his moniker, his weapon of choice, as you may have guessed, is a—"

"Gun!" Earl jumped in.

"No," the Dr. said. "... A switchblade."

Earl leaned back and took it all in, but still didn't get it. "Well, I don't watch the news, Doc, and I sure as shit wasn't born in the fifties. I *do* know what a switchblade is though."

"So do I." Lester looked up from his mini pad.

The officers nodded proudly at one another.

Dr. Roberts looked at them. "I see. Well, time is of the essence here since innocent lives are at stake. No more beating around the bush. Look at what he did to his sister's two kids."

The Dr. tossed a crime scene photo on the desk that slid to a stop in front of the officers, revealing carnage like none they'd ever seen.

Lester gasped. "Oh my God."

"What the shit?" Earl looked away. "Man, that shit ain't right."

Lester asked, "Whatcha reckon we gonna do, Earl?"

Earl assessed the situation. *Don't lose your shit, Earl. Take control, now. Take control. You're doing great so far. Don't look scared. Don't look nervous. You're never supposed to let 'em see you sweat—just like in that one deodorant commercial I like so much. 'Never let 'em see you sweat' is exactly what they say in it too. Sure as shit, they do. I've seen it about fifteen times already, and they say it each and every damn time it comes on. And I won't. I won't let 'em see me sweat. Not today. Not ever. Fuck that.* "Calm down now, Lester," he said. "Just calm down. Take it easy. I got this. You just follow my lead like we talked about before." Earl fixed his attention back to the Dr. and leaned in. "So, what are you trying to say here, Dr. Bobby? You trying to say that old Earl Tubb here needs to be scared? Huh? Huh?! Well, lemme tell you good Dr., I am not." Earl leaned in closer. "Now, you level with me, Dr. Bob. What *is* he?"

The Dr. leaned back in his chair and began to realize just how moronic these two were, especially the fat one. He talked as if he were speaking to a confused child. "He is a complete ... homicidal ... maniac ... a killer in every sense of the word. In the past three months alone, he's murdered fifteen inmates, eight patients, the nurse this morning, *and* his last psychiatrist. And probably a few more since we've been sitting here gabbing."

"Killed his headshrinker, huh?" Earl asked. "Why'd he do that, ya reckon?"

"Well, I don't know. Because he's crazy, maybe. Like I just explained to you. Something along those lines. You know? Crazy? Crazy as in psychotic."

"What the hell is that?"

"What's what?"

"Psychotic?"

Lester chimed in, happy to help. "You know, Earl. Yeah. You know. Like that one movie *Psycho*."

Earl looked back to the Dr. "*Psycho*? You mean to tell me this asshole dressed up like an old lady and ran a motel or some shit?"

The Dr. had to pause on that one. "Out of curiosity. How many men are out looking for Frank? Is there even a manhunt?"

"Just what the hell you think me and Lester's doing here?" Earl motioned to the degrees on the wall. "Guess there's just some things ya don't get from book learning, huh?"

"Just tell your team that—"

"We *are* the team. You got anything important to say, then you can just say it to the two of us."

"Just the two of you? No no no. This is not good. Look, officers, this is not a game. This man? Well, he's dangerous. *Very* dangerous. This is what he does. He goes around and kills for fun—for 'kicks' as he puts it. He doesn't care about tomorrow, and he doesn't care about the consequences of his actions. He can't be bargained with. No amount of medication has ever worked on him, and up to this point, the only thing we can do with him is try to contain him in a strictly secluded setting for everyone's safety. You need to find him and bring him back to me—or else Frank Butz is going to rip right through your little town in no time flat. He's not going to stop until he's killed every last—"

"Um, Doc? We get the picture. Nice speech and all, but you already done said this sorta shit, and I'm getting kinda hungry. We got us a so-called wannabe badass to catch. Excuse us."

The officers stood.

"Wait!" the Dr. jumped out of his seat. "You won't be able to do this by yourself. You'll need more men."

That did it. Earl had heard enough out of this Dr.—with his plaques on the wall and his fancy little diplomas mocking Earl with his sixth-grade education. "Now, looka here, Dr. Bobby."

"It's Roberts."

"Well, look here, Dr. Bobby Robert. He's just one man. We're two."

Lester held up two fingers.

Earl nodded in approval. "Can't ya see that? Or maybe you ain't learned to count. Now, I been working for the sheriff's office going on three years now. Three! Lester here is new, but he was in the guard for two years."

Lester held up two fingers again.

Earl took a slow, steady step forward and started the speech he had waited his entire life for. "Now, you listen to me, Doc Bobby—and you listen good. We handle our own shit in Rockwood. Always have. Always will. Now, like I said before, he may have been a little squirrelly for y'all, but that don't concern Earl, ya see? Imma track 'em. And Imma find 'em. And when I do ..." Earl held up his hand and balled it into a deadly fist of vengeance, hoping to hell his knuckles would crack out loud. It would be a really cool moment for him. They didn't, but he continued anyway. "Imma gonna squash his ass. Hell. I'll chase his goddamn ass all the way up to Randolph County if I have to."

"Isn't that just twenty miles away?"

"Yep. All I need from you, Doc, is a good pic of this shithead. Let the big boys handle the rest. Think you can handle that?"

The Dr. reached in the file, pulled out Frank Butz's mug shot, handed it to Earl, and said, "Frank Butz needs *serious* help."

"Oh, we gonna help his ass all right." Earl took the mug shot. In it, Switchblade sported a busted lip, a black eye, and hair a complete mess from his apparent police beat-down. Earl was none too impressed with the punk. He shook his head in disgust. "This sick bastard knows exactly what he's doing, so don't you be giving Earl the 'he needs help and can't help it' speech. I done heard it all before, and I ain't buying." Earl held the mug shot just inches from the Dr.'s face. "Look at him, Doc. Look at him."

"I am."

"You see him, Doc? Are you looking?"

"Yes! I see it! I've seen it before! I'm the one who just gave it to you to few seconds ago, *remember*?"

Earl paused, took a deep breath, and glared into the Dr.'s eyes. He began to imagine playing in his very own movie about a cop on the edge who just couldn't take it anymore—something he felt was very true to life. He could definitely play the part himself. *That*, he knew. On the set, he could even give the director some cool suggestions. Like here. The camera could do a slow zoom on his face as he gave the badass speech. *That's what I'd do if I were the director. On this part right here.* Earl wouldn't have it any other way. This was his movie, and he went for his one take, knowing speeches don't get second takes in real life. He began slowly. "Frank 'Switchblade' Butz. Ruthless. Cold. Calculating. All the way. Shit, boy. I've seen these types before. Punk-ass youngsters with no respect for the law. Knocking over mailboxes, toilet paper in the trees, soap on *my* goddamn windows, and burning rubber in town square during bingo night. I'm flat-out sick of all this kinda shit. Tell ya what Imma do, Doc. Imma have me a little Frank Butz roast. Some barbecued bitch. All the victims' families are welcome to attend, and guess what? You're invited! Come getcha a bite, Doc. I can grill my ass off, and I fully intend to barbecue that sorry-ass sumbitch."

Lester tugged at his collar. This was a little too intense for his taste.

Earl looked over. "Lester. Let's roll!"

11:50 a.m.
The cruiser patrolled the back roads of Rockwood with Earl and Lester on high alert.

"That's what I'm trying to tell ya, Lester." Earl said. "Mexicans learn slower than whites. It's been proven for God's sake. Look, Lester. When a Mexican gets a book, the first thing he does is—"

Mabel interrupted through the CB. "Base to Earl. Ya out there? Come back."

"You still got a thing for Mabel?" Lester asked.

"Oh yeah. I fucks that pussy all the time."

"Wow, Earl!"

Mabel tried again. "Come on, Earl. Pick up. I needs to holler atcha, now. Come back."

Earl popped a fresh toothpick in his mouth and went for it, looking left to right before mashing the button.

"Go for Earl," he said.

"Sheriff wants an update."

"Update ... on what?"

"The case, Earl."

"Oh, yeah! Shit. Got that right here. Hold up." Earl grabbed the mug shot. "Got me a one Frank 'Switchblade' Butz. Some high-octane, certified psycho, Jack the Ripper, Twinkle-Dink sumbitch according to Dr. Bobby back there. You should see him, Mabel. Looks like one of them greaser types. Probably smokes pot too. An Arthur Fonsternelli shithead if I ever saw one."

"I think that's Fonzarelli," Lester said.

"What I say? Panstertelli?"

Lester shrugged and looked out at the passing cows. He smiled and waved at them.

"Well, anyway," Earl continued, "that's what I got here. Anything new on your end?"

"Yeah. Sheriff wants me to tell y'all to go out to Clint's Gas-N-Grab. Apparently, this fella done up and killed Clint and Andy."

Earl dropped the CB, and his bottom lip began to quiver. He swallowed the lump in his throat, grabbed the CB from his lap, and said, "Th-th-this man done did what?"

"You okay, Earl? You sound kinda hurt."

Earl did his best to hold back the tears. "Clint and Andy? They used to be my fishing buddies when we was little. *Sniff-sniff.*"

"Aw, heck, Earl. I'm sorry."

Earl quickly regained his composure like a seasoned professional. He spit his toothpick out and brought the CB up. "Get the darkest cell we got ready *and* a mop. We're gonna be bringing this bastard in a little messy. En route to Clint's Gas-N-Grab. Earl and Lester out."

Earl threw the CB down. He tightened his grip on the wheel and bit down on his lip.

Lester looked over. "Earl … you gonna be okay?"

"Clint and Andy used to be my fishing buddies, Lester. You take that away from a man, and it changes him … on the *inside.* When we do finally catch up with this sumbitch, I want you to do one thing—and one thing only."

"You just name it, Earl. Anything."

"Stay the fuck out of my way."

11:55 a.m.

Back at the town square, an old timer walked down the sidewalk just as carefree as a man could be for such a blazing hot day. He passed an alleyway, stopped, then pulled the handkerchief from his back pocket to wipe the sweat from his brow.

"It sure in the fuck is one hot, goddamn day. Woo-wee. Hotter than horse pussy in heat, smack dab in the middle of July. Fuck this miserable shit. Man, oh man."

Switchblade peeked out from the alleyway and whistled at the old-timer like he was a dog.

"Huh?" the old timer said. "Who's there?" He turned around, caught a switchblade to the eye, and dropped to the ground dead.

Switchblade celebrated by spinning victory 360s in place, which ended in a Run-DMC chest hug over the old-timer's body. "Fuck yeah, bitch," he shouted at the corpse.

He then moonwalked away—very, very badly.

12:07 p.m.

Back at the Gas-N-Grab, Clint and Andy's corpses were left bent over the counter naked in a homosexual pose. Both were slashed to shit. Patsy Cline's "Back in Baby's Arms" played from the jukebox.

Outside the station, Earl was down on one knee examining the hot rod's tire marks down the highway.

The shop's door flung open. Lester stumbled out of the Gas-N-Grab, coughing and gagging into a handkerchief.

Earl said, "Never let a civilian see ya puke, Lester. Go behind that Mountain Dew machine over yonder if ya gonna be ralphing." Earl shook his head in disappointment.

"I'm sorry, Earl." Lester wiped his mouth. "It was just hard to look at is all. I think I'm done now."

Earl stood and tugged his britches. "To a seasoned officer like myself, these kinda things really don't get to ya. Remember that Tastee-Freeze break-in a few years back?"

Lester tried to think. "Hmmm. Maybe."

Earl pointed at his own chest. "They called *me* in for that. Now, whatcha know about that shit, boy?"

Lester shrugged. "Nothing, I guess."

Earl knelt down, picked up a handful of dirt, and waited patiently for the wind to pick up and do its thing. When it did, he flung the dirt high into the air. The wind whooshed it down the highway in a cloud of almost mystic dust. When it was finally gone, he nodded knowingly. "You went west, didn't you? You goddamn sick sumbitch."

"You say something, Earl?" Lester said.

"Huh? Nothing. You wouldn't understand."

Lester walked over, handkerchief in hand, and began to wipe the sweat from his brow. "So, what's our next move there, partner?"

Earl stared down the long road. He stuck out his chest to try and look buff.

"Whatcha thinking, Earl?"

"What am I thinking, Lester?"

"Yeah."

"I'm over here thinking we all do bad shit from time to time. You do. I do. Hell, we all do. I'd even bet the balls on a low-flying duck that old Satan himself has a pinch of regret from time to time, but Frank Butz? This boy just has no remorse. None whatsoever. Shit, Lester. Did you see the way he left Clint and Andy? Thinks he's funny with that goddamn trickster shit."

Earl finally let his anger get the best of him. He began challenging Switchblade as if he were standing before him. Lester watched the meltdown with concern.

"Hey, goddamn it," Earl shouted, pointing at the invisible Frank Butz. "Stop right there! I'm talking to you, you goddamn cock-knock bastard! Huh? What's that? What's that you said? You want me to go fuck myself? You do, dontcha? Well, I don't do that shit, you no-law-abiding, sorry-ass sumbitch!" Earl spun around and began poking Lester in the chest. "This asshole gets no free passes with me. This asshole is gonna wish he was never born, but above all, Lester, this asshole has pissed me off."

"Calm down now, Earl. It'll all be fine. I promise. Just take it easy."

"Easy? You gotta be shitting me! Easy? I don't think so. This man done up and killed my cousin. That's family, boy. And now Clint and Andy—my fishing buddies when we was little. (Earl was lying about that, by the way.) Shit, Lester! What's this guy's fucking problem? And what about that nurse this morning? Huh? What about her? And let's not forget about that poor girl he smashed in the middle of the road back there. Easy? I think not." Earl looked back down the road and shook his head. "Damn, son. Makes me wonder what old Earl did to deserve all this mess."

12:20 p.m.

Switchblade started to get bored and desperately needed something to do. Maybe find someone he could smash into? Why not? He stopped the car, flipped on the stereo, and caught the latest updates from the day's events.

"I tell ya, folks," Pistol Lee said. "It's just nuts. Bonkers y'all. That's what it is. Bonkers. This type behavior we got going on here? Just plain sick. And the more I hear about this Frank Butz fella, the more I think he's just down right ornery. Probably on purpose. But that's what happens when you don't go to church, y'all. You up and stray from the Lord, and you go out and do this kinda stuff. Happens every time."

Switchblade looked at the Jesus on the dash who had been watching him this whole time without judgment. He loved the fact he could act any way he wanted and then just have to ask for some forgiveness from the little guy. That was pretty sweet. He cocked his head, smiled, and double-tapped its nose.

Down the street, a middle-aged woman pushed her wheelchair-bound mother out of the drugstore. Despite the heat, the old lady had several blankets around her legs and a thick scarf wrapped around her head. They began to make their way to the four-way stop.

"You get my prescriptions?" the old lady asked.

"Yes, Mom. I already told you. They're in my bag. And I'm not in the mood to cook anything too complicated tonight. We're having soup. Got it?"

"Well, I guess. It's the only thing that don't clog me up anymore."

They approached the intersection, looked left to right, and began to cross the street.

The old lady looked up. "You get my prescriptions?"

In the hot rod, Switchblade spotted the women. *Bonus points! Shit. Old ladies is worth twenty-five.* "Huh-huh-huh."

"Enough of that mess," Pistol Lee continued. "I'm no preacher. I'm a DJ. One who thinks it's time to lift your spirits with a song that's just downright good to boogie to. It'll even get your granny up out her chair—so turn it up loud."

Switchblade did as he was told. He cranked the knob and waited for liftoff.

"Here's Jimmy Knott with 'Be Nice and Flush It Twice' right here on Ram-N AM."

Fiddle music blasted, and Switchblade shot off like a rocket.

The two women heard the massive wall of sound coming, and before they knew it, the beast was on them. Instinct kicked in, and the daughter jumped back, leaving her mother alone in the street.

Switchblade slammed into her and launched her into a high arc across the sun—still in her wheelchair like some kind of blazing-hot version of ET's moon jump. Switchblade howled like a wolf man as she smashed through a storefront window.

Several men ran out of the store and quickly scanned the area. The sound of screeching tires was all that could be heard from around the corner.

The owner came running out of the store and yelled, "Who the fuck just broke my goddamn window with this old lady? This is some bullshit!"

12:32 p.m.
The weekend volunteers were still cruising on high alert.

Earl said, "Seriously, Lester. Think about it. *Me.* Earl Tubb—an ass-kicking Texas Ranger with a deadly ax to grind every week on my very own show. Best idea I've had yet. Whatcha think about that shit, boy?"

"You could come on after that *Fall Guy* fella."

"Now, *that's* a goddamn line up. I'd drive a big-ass truck. Chevy. Let all the bad guys drive them piece-of-shit Fords. Put me up a gun rack in the back window. Couple shotguns."

"Like Bert Conway?"

"*Exactly* like Bert Conway. Maybe even throw in my bow with some dynamite tips. Blow their goddamn asses right off the fucking episode."

"Have at least two fights per show," Lester pointed.

Earl held up his karate-chop hand. "I'd break their faces, Lester. It'd be my finishing move ... every time."

"Ya need a love interest of course."

"Oh yeah," Earl answered all sexy-like.

"Who would ya pick, Earl?"

"Imma have to think about that one for a while. So, what else would you do, Lester?"

"Well, shucks. I dunno. Just try and do it different from the rest, I guess. Push them boundaries some. Give us some cutting-edge stuff to watch, ya know? Why dontcha try mixing it up a little. You could make your partner black or something. Times are changing. Change with them, my granny used to say."

There was a silence.

Earl looked over. "Lester?"

"Yeah?"

"You musta lost yo goddamn mind."

Mabel came over the CB. "Ya out there, Earl? Gotcha ears on?"

Earl grabbed the CB. "Go for Earl."

"Sheriff wants me to tell y'all to come down to the station ASAP. Another murder done happened uptown, and I think the sheriff's starting to get mad about it all a little bit."

The officers could hear the sheriff throwing stuff around the office and cursing up a storm. Earl and Lester exchanged a nervous look. Earl nervously cleared his throat and mashed the button. "*Ahem-hem.* That's a big 10–4 base. On our way. ETA? Ten minutes. Earl and Lester out."

Earl put the CB back, slowly looked over to Lester, and smiled. "What else would ya do, Lester? Give the black dude a cowboy hat and let him ride shotgun in my Chevy? Who'd even believe that stupid-ass bullshit?"

12:45 p.m.

Despite his hemorrhoidal discomfort, Sheriff Wallace sat behind his desk on the telephone, kicked back with his size-thirteen boots on the desk. A big, sloppy wad of chew was crammed in his jaw. Behind him was an impressive display of southern pride items, including pistols, citations, antique shackles, and a Mississippi state flag. Wallace listened to the mumble on the other end of the phone and then gave it a piece of his mind. "And just what the fuck you want me to do, Mayor? I'm doing the best I can with what I have. How the fuck was I supposed to know some shit like this was gonna pop the fuck off this weekend? If I *had* known, mind you, I wouldn't have given Skip and Brian the weekend off to go fishing, now would I?"

Angry mumbling came through.

Wallace bolted forward and slammed his fist on the desk. "And just how the fuck am I supposed to do that? Last time I checked, they didn't have telephones on goddamn fishing boats."

More angry mumbling.

"Who'd I give it to?" Wallace took a breath and braced for the worst. "I gave it to Earl Tubb and Lester Boone. Now, I know what you're gonna say."

The phone cracked in the sheriff's ear. "Mayor? Mayor Bradley?" He slammed his own phone down. He spit at the spittoon next to his desk, missed, and hit the hardwood floor with a splat. He wiped his mouth and hit the intercom. "Mabel. Earl Tubb show up yet?"

"Not yet, Sheriff. Said he was on his way."

12:52 p.m.
Over at the Tastee-Freeze, Earl and Lester ate ice cream cones as they walked back to the cruiser.

"Ya see, Lester? Catching this guy is just a simple matter of mathematics. I can add, ya know?"

"I know ya can, Earl."

Two little girls approached the Freeze. Earl stopped, nodded, and gave them his friendly, public-servant smile. "How you girls doing this fine morning? You doing okay?"

"Don't even talk to me," the smaller one replied as they entered the shop. She turned around, stuck her middle finger up at Earl, and slammed the door.

Earl said, "Little bitch. You see that shit, Lester?"

Lester was staring at the ground.

Earl nudged him to jolt him out of his trance. "Here, buddy. Hold my cone. Shit. I just knew I shoulda got me a chocolate-dipped cone instead of a plain vanilla. Damn stupid-ass diet. Wanna trade?" Earl unbuckled his belt and trousers on the spot and tried to fix his uniform's food-stained alignment.

"Earl?"

"Yeah, buddy? Gotta fix my britches."

Lester looked out to the horizon as Earl continued to fuss with his trousers. "Ya know, Earl? We been going on being partners for about three weeks now. And I guess I just always felt that partners should be up front and honest with one another, ya know?" Lester bit into the chocolaty shell of his cone and chocolate smeared his lips. "Take this Frank Butz character. Now I know he ain't gonna shake you off your tractor none, but me? I gotta be honest with ya, Earl. I'm not sure I'm up for this. I'm kinda scared."

Earl took his cone back, smiled at his partner, and put a caring hand on his shoulder. "Lester, you have nothing to fear, my friend. He ain't gonna escape me. I got eyes in the back of my head, and they see better than the ones in the front. Believe that shit."

Lester exhaled with smile of relief. "Great, Earl. That's just great. I'm so glad to hear you say that."

The men celebrated the moment and took a bite of ice cream together.

"Mm," they said with big, yummy smiles as the hot rod drove by—unnoticed.

Inside the hot rod, The Chips' "Rubber Biscuit" blasted. Switchblade bobbed his head and sang along.

"Cow cow hoo-oo. Cow cow wanna dib-a-doo. Chicken-hon-a-chick-a-chick-a-hole-hubba. Hey fried chuck-a-lucka wanna jubba."

Driving like a maniac, he jerked onto the shoulder of the road to take out a long row of mailboxes and smashed through them with ease.

"Hi-low nay wanna dubba hubba. Day down sum wanna jigga-wah."

He smashed through the last mailbox and hopped back up on the road.

Up ahead, a scruffy man carried a garbage bag full of cans. He bent over to pick one up off the road.

Switchblade plowed right into him.

Smash! Cans exploded.

He continued without a care in the world. He made a hard right off the road, shot through the yards of a trailer park, and smashed toys and tricycles to smithereens. He continued to sing and bob his head.

"Mm-mmn, do that again. Doo doo doo boo."

He plowed through a privacy fence and then through the patio furniture on the other side of it. Keeping his foot to the floor, he began tearing up the yard with doughnuts.

An old lady watched in disbelief from her porch. She bolted from her chair, dropped her crocheting needles, and screamed, "Hey! Quit doing that! You're rutting up my yard, dammit!"

Going into his fifth doughnut, Switchblade yelled in glee. "Whee!"

"That's it," she screamed. "Imma sick my dog on ya now!"

She ran inside and slammed the door.

On Switchblade's seventh doughnut, she came back out with a double-barrel shotgun and her dog. "Get him, Bippy!"

A pissed-off Chihuahua leaped off the porch in attack mode, soared high through the air like Mighty Dog, and then landed behind the hot rod. It began chasing the car in its circle and nipped at the back tires.

"Come and get some of this!" The old lady took aim and blew out the hot rod's back window.

Switchblade laughed. "Huh-huh-huh. What a bitch. And fuck you too, dog!"

The old lady's next shot missed by inches.

He made a break for the main road. In no time flat, he was back to tearing it up. He spotted a couple of young country girls. *Might as well take them out too.* He blasted into them, launching one into a cornfield and the other onto the hood. Her face slammed the windshield and cracked it, knocking her out cold.

Switchblade began tearing up the shoulder of the road. The woman slowly woke to the wind slapping her bloody hair against her face. The blast of the engine filled her ears. Dazed and confused, she looked inside the cab at the madman, and saw her reflection back in his Elvis shades. He waved her a friendly hi, and she let loose a horrific scream.

Switchblade giggled. "Get off my hood, you bitch!"
"Stop!"
"I'm serious! Go on! Get!"
"Please stop!"
"What?"
"I said stop, fucker!"
"Uh. You want me to stop?"
"Please!"
"Okay, you dumb-ass bitch! Here!"

He slammed the brakes and sent her flying into a farmer's field. She tumbled over and over until finally slamming to a stop into the side of an old barn.

"Oh! Oopsy daisy," Switchblade said.

The hot rod slid to a stop.

"That was some funny-ass shit! Hey. Wanna see something cool?"

He hopped out of the car.

Blood, sweat, and mascara streamed down the girl's face. Long, bloody slobber dangled from her lip. Terrified, she began to cry. She tried to stand for an escape, but the broken bones in her body said otherwise. She screamed instead.

Switchblade approached with a smile.

The girl took a defensive step back, stumbled from the pain, and slammed against the barn.

"Where you going, honey tits?" Switchblade asked. "I ain't gonna hurt you. Here. Lemme help."

He gently grabbed her arms and tried to steady her.

She screamed in pain.

"Oops," he said. "My fault. That was my fault. Huh-huh. Look. Here's the thing. I'm a little shy around girls, so you'll have to forgive me for acting all silly and shit. Having said that, I need to ask you to do me a favor ... and then I'll let you go. Deal?"

"Yes, Mom," she replied, not knowing what planet she was on.

Switchblade stepped back and examined her. "Just stand straight and hold still, baby doll. I know it's tough, but you can do it. I know you can. I wanna see if I can do something. Kinda like a strength test."

"Like a what?"

"Just hold still. Can you do that for me?"

"I think so." She was numb from shock.

Switchblade quickly hopped into what looked like Mr. Miyagi's crane technique from *The Karate Kid*. He stood with one foot high and his arms spread wide like he was ready to take flight. He began to hear Mr. Miyagi speak directly to him. "Called crane technique, Frank. If do right, no can defense."

The woman's eyes began to close. Her knees buckled.

Switchblade made his move. "Hee-yahhh!" He delivered a lightning-fast kick to the woman's head and decapitated her on the spot. A huge fountain of blood pulsated from her torso, which remained standing like something out of a samurai flick.

Switchblade casually combed his hair and watched the red fountain spurt. He pocketed his comb and waited until she finally ran empty and her body dropped. "Fuck Ralph Macchio," he said. "Punk-ass muthafucka."

1:12 p.m.

Earl and Lester were jamming out to the Pistol Lee Banjo Hour, bobbing their heads in perfect unison with the beat.

Earl looked over at Lester and showed off by joining in full blast as the song's chorus took off. "He-he! Hiddle-hiddle! He-he-hawwww!"

Lester freaked. "Dang, Earl! I didn't know you could sing too."

"Oh, yeah," Earl said cocky.

The cruiser hit the sheriff station's lot and skidded to a halt.

Inside Sheriff Wallace's office, a toilet flushed. The sheriff came out of his private restroom with a *Big Black Booty* mag tucked under his arm. He walked over to the window, looked out, and spotted the cruiser. "Mabel! That worthless turd Earl Tubb out there?"

"Yes, he is, Sheriff."

"Send 'em in."

Wallace went behind his desk, tossed the swank mag in the bottom desk drawer, and kicked it closed.

Earl and Lester walked in.

"Hi, Sheriff," Lester smiled.

Keeping his hate-filled gaze on Earl, Wallace said, "Lester, my man. Do me a favor. Go outside and keep an eye on the car."

"Car's fine, Sheriff. I locked it and everything."

"Hey, Lester."

"Yeah, Sheriff?"

"Get the fuck up out of my office."

Lester quickly scurried out and shut the door.

Wallace continued to glare.

Earl attempted to make a friend. "Want a piece of gum, Sheriff? I have gum."

"... Have a seat, Earl."

Earl sat.

Without hesitation, Wallace spit at the spittoon and swooshed it with a *spat-tiiing*. He sat, adjusted the chew in his jaw, then slammed his fist on the desk. "Okay! Here's the rub, Tubb. I have a mayor up my fucking ass, and it hurts as you can imagine. Almost feels like he went up in there sideways. Gotta figure me a way to get him up outta there. Maybe you can help. Ever have a mayor up your ass, Earl?"

Sweat began to trickle down Earl's chubby cheek. The office was getting hotter by the second. He tugged at his collar.

"You hot, Earl?"

"Guess so, Sheriff. Pistol Lee said it might get all the way up to—"

"I'm hot too, Earl. Hot at you, actually. Wanna know why, boy?"

"What'd I do, Sheriff? What'd I do?"

The sheriff lunged from his chair. "Why the fuck am I getting calls about some maniac smashing old ladies through storefront windows like they was a goddamn human cannonball! Now goddamn it, Earl! I trusted you! I put you on this case! I asked if you're the man for the job, and you said, 'Yeah. Duh-duh-duh. Uhhh. Sheriff Wallace, sir. Uhhh. I got this. He's all mine.' What a goddamn load of horseshit!" The sheriff shook his head. "Maybe that talk of promotion was a bad idea after all, Earl."

"Aw, come on, Sheriff. Don't be like that."

"Well, it's something you're gonna have to earn, son. You sure as shit ain't gonna earn it by showing up after the crime done took place. What the fuck good are ya then? Why don't I just give you a goddamn mop to clean up after this prick?" Wallace slammed his fist on the desk. "You gotta be two steps ahead of this cocksucker, Earl! Now just what the hell you and Lester been out there doing? Sucking each other's dicks?"

"We don't do that, Sheriff," Earl looked down. "That's a lie."

"So, then why's your hand so goddamn sticky, Earl? That some of Lester's jizz or more goddamn ice cream? Don't tell me you stopped at that fucking Tastee-Freeze again. I'll straight-up kick your fucking ass into the next time zone."

"No, Sheriff. No. We didn't stop at the Tastee-Freeze. I swear."

Wallace grunted and sat back down. He knew how incompetent Earl was. He could possibly lend a hand but fuck that shit. It was *supposed* to be his day off. He was already steamed he missed his favorite show *Wishin' I Be Fishin'*. He wasn't about to add to that misery by going out in this heat with hellfire hemorrhoids worming their way out of his ass onto a hot leather seat. Seeing that his options were limited, he decided to take another chance on Earl.

"Fuck it." He pulled out a ring of keys and unlocked the desk drawer. "I'm about to elevate your shit to the next level, son."

He pulled out a box of ammunition and tossed it on the desk with a thud.

Earl's jaw dropped.

"You know what that is, dontcha?" Wallace asked. "I'll tell ya what it is. I'm giving you your first batch of ammunition. Congratulations."

Earl couldn't believe this shit was happening. "Thank you, Sheriff. Thank you so much. Oh my God. I won't let you down. I swear."

"Now, I know it's a small town, Earl, so it can't be that goddamn hard to find some asshole running around in a black leather jacket, sticking out like a sore thumb, racking up a goddamn body count. Now, you have everything you need. You go ... and you get 'em."

"Will do, Sheriff."

"You gonna bring that hammer down, son?"

"Better believe it. Uh. I mean yes. Yes, Sheriff. I will."

"Kinda weak-ass answer is that? You gonna bust this sumbitch or what, Earl?"

"Yes, sir."

"That's it." Wallace cupped his hand to his ear like a wrestler and leaned in. "Now let me fucking hear it!"

"Yes, sir."

"Bullshit, boy! Louder!"

"Yes, sir!"

"One more time!"

"Yes, sir!"

"Oh yeah!" Wallace plopped back down in his seat and pointed. "That's the shit I like to hear, right there!" He put his boots back up on the desk, grabbed the black booty mag, opened it to the centerfold, and took a quick sniff of the girl on the page. He looked at Earl. "Now, grab them bullets and get your fat ass the fuck up out of my office."

Earl snatched the ammo and exited faster than he'd moved in years.

"And bring me my criminal," the sheriff shouted as the door slammed shut. "Jesus H. Christ. That boy sure is one dumb-ass sumbitch." Wallace turned to the next page and smiled at 295-pound Desiree. She was bent over, trying to open a jar of grape jam with what appeared to be a hot buttermilk biscuit shoved inside her mouth, nude as can be. "Mmmm-mm." Wallace said, suddenly getting hungry.

Outside, Lester was guarding the patrol car while trying to recite the Miranda rights to himself.

"You got that right to be quiet. Hold up. That ain't it. Um ... oh! Remain silent! That's right. Y'all got that right to remain silent. Okay. If you choose not to remain silent, but you can't talk, then your lawyer could do the talking for you. But if you—"

Earl busted out of the station, happy as a boy on Christmas, skipping as he crossed the station's lot. "Hey, Lester. Get your skinny ass in the car. Just wait'll you get a load of this shit."

"Is that what I think it is?"

Inside the patrol car, Earl showed Lester the ammunition. "Check *this* out."

Lester was beside himself and beyond proud. It was as if Earl was a full-fledged cop now that he finally got some bullets. "Well, I'll be. Congratulations, Earl!"

Earl blushed. "Thank you. Thank you. Thank you."

"Let's load that sucker up."

Earl whipped out his revolver and opened the chamber with a flick of the wrist.

Lester opened the box of ammo and began feeding him rounds as he loaded his peacemaker.

"Ya know, Lester? If someone would have told me back in the day that I would grow up to be the town hero, I'd have believed it 100 percent. It's my calling, Lester. A destiny thing you really can't explain to another human being. Regardless. Now that I've arrived, I'd just like to say that I'm glad I'm sharing this moment with you, buddy."

"Gee, Earl. Thanks."

The two shared a look only they would understand. Earl shook it off and continued to load.

"This sure is exciting," Lester said. "Bullets and all. Hey. You know my cousin Bud?"

"Think so. Ain't he the one that lives behind Belmont Creek?"

"Yep. Never comes out. Son, let me tell ya. That boy right there got some firepower. So, I've heard. We ever need anything, then he's our man. You know he's a Vietnam vet, right?"

"Think I heard that before."

"Got that sucker loaded?"

"Yup."

Earl closed the chamber with a flick of the wrist and aimed out the window at nothing.

"Frank 'Switchblade' Butz," he said. "Prepare to meet your maker. I am dead on your ass and ain't about to take any of your shit."

58

After several crank attempts, Earl fired up the cruiser, pulled onto the empty road, and putted away in search of their fugitive. Seconds later, the hot rod pulled into the station's lot and came to a stop. Clueless, the boys continued down the road.

"Say we do catch this guy, Earl. What can I do?"

"I thought we covered that already, Lester."

"Come on, Earl. I'll do anything. *Anything.* Want me to hold the ammo, I'm there for you. Want me to drive, no problem. I'd love to read him his rights while you cuff 'em. Anything, Earl. Just name it."

Earl thought. "Well, Lester. I guess there is one thing you could do."

"What? What?"

"I guess you could—"

"Breaker breaker for that, Tubbster," an unknown voice said through the CB, mocking a southern accent. "Earl, good buddy, ya out there? Ya got them ears on?"

Earl and Lester exchanged a nervous look.

Switchblade changed to a thicker accent. "This is Earl, is it not? Ba-durrdy-durr."

Lester looked over. "Guess you better answer it."

"Th-th-this is Earl Tubb. And just who the h-h-hell is this?"

"I bet it's the guy," Lester said.

"I'm the guy," Switchblade said.

"Told ya."

"So, you're the guy, huh?" Earl asked.

"Yep. I *am* the guy."

Earl shook off the nervous jitters and regained his composure. He popped in a fresh toothpick, looked left to right, brought the CB up, and mashed the button. "So ... we finally meet. Good. Maybe you can explain a little something to me then, guy. Just how the hell do you plan on getting my foot outcha ass when I catch up with ya? You about ready, boy?"

"Huh-huh. Ready for what?"

"For justice delivered the Earl Tubb way, and I promise you, son, that it's gonna hurt. Right upside your goddamn head, boy."

"Got this little bitch on my end. Says her name's Mabel."

Lester bounced in his seat. "He's at the station, Earl. He's at the station."

Earl fumed. "You hurt one goddamn hair on her head, and I swear to God—"

"How 'bout a whole shitload of hairs, Earl?"

Through the CB, the officers heard the sound of a switchblade come to life and Mabel scream, "Earl! Help me!"

"Hang the fuck on, Lester!" Earl jerked the wheel and spun to a screeching 180 in the road.

Lester slammed against his door.

Earl smashed the gas. The cruiser took off slowly and backfired. "I'm coming, Mabel!"

The cruiser slowly built to a shaky forty miles per hour and backfired again. The car filled with the sounds of wet stabs, screams, and Switchblade laughing his ass off.

Lester cupped his hand over his mouth to keep from puking.

Finally, ... silence.

Earl's face went blank.

Switchblade giggled over the CB. "You can't fuck with a killer, Earl. You stupid dumb fuck."

The officers drove in a shocked, mournful silence. Earl was absolutely crushed. It couldn't be. Not this. Not his Mabel too. A single tear slid down.

Lester looked over. "He just called you a dumb fuck."

1:39 p.m.

Earl and Lester inspected the bloody scene. The station was in complete shambles. The wall above Mabel's desk had been sprayed with blood, and her scalp was rudely pinned to the bulletin board with several colorful thumbtacks.

"He sure did leave a mess, didn't he?" Lester said.

"This is nothing compared to the mess Imma leave his face when I find 'em. Now I think I might just have to ... goddamn it!"

"What, Earl?"

"That asshole shit on my desk!"

Lester glanced at Earl's desk. Next to the pile of feces was a note.

"That goddamn, nasty motherfucker."

"That a note, Earl?"

"Yeah."

"Well, what's it say?"

Earl went over, picked up the note, and read it aloud. "Earl's f-f-face looks just like this p-p-p-pile of my shit. Love, Switchblade." Earl crumbled up the note and threw it back on the desk. "That punk-ass sumbitch! Who the hell does he think he is saying that my face looks like a pile of his shit? It don't—damn it!"

"He's just messing witcha, Earl. Don't let 'em get to you like that."

Earl opened the desk drawer, jumped back, and gasped. "That sumbitch pissed in my drawer *and* broke all my goddamn pencils!"

A weak mumble came from the sheriff's office. "Earl Tubb. Front and goddamn center."

Earl ran straight for the office. "You're alive!"

The sheriff was lying in a pool of his own blood. The black booty mag and his chopped-off penis were right next to his head, and the desktop rebel flag was sticking out of his ass tall and proud.

Earl knelt down. "You okay, Sheriff?"

"The sumbitch cut off my goddamn dick, Earl. I'm not okay." He coughed. "There's a flag in my ass, man."

"You gotta make it, Sheriff. You just gotta."

"Sorry, Earl. Not this time."

"No."

Earl put his head down and began to sob, knowing that this was it for poor old Sheriff Wallace.

The sheriff looked up to Earl. "Earl. Do whatever you have to. Whatever it takes to catch this madman. He must be stopped by any means necessary, Earl, by any means necessary." Wallace's breathing slowed, and his lifeless eyes shut one last time. "Earl," he managed.

Earl leaned in. "Yeah, Sheriff?"

"... Avenge me."

And like that, Sheriff Wallace died, very reminiscent of the death of Yoda—but without disappearing into the Force.

_2:01 p.m._

As the cruiser putted along, Pistol Lee responded to a special request. "There's absolutely nothing in this world worse than losing someone who's been like a mentor to you. Pain in that loss is what this next song is all about. Here's Timmy Toot 'Two Barrels' Stevens with 'I Shot My Baby the Day She Died.' Right here on Ram-N AM. Your station and mine."

A whiny country song began to play.

Earl was beside himself. He stared down the long road ahead, a changed man.

Lester looked over. "So, whatcha think our next move gonna be?"

Earl remained silent.

"Earl?"

"Lester, I think I've taken just about all the shit that Imma take out of this sorry-ass sumbitch. Mabel didn't deserve that shit."

"Got that right. Shoot."

"*And* he shit on my desk."

"Sure did. Grodiest thing I ever seen."

"Un-fucking-believable." Earl shook his head.

"So, whatcha think our next move gonna be?"

"I might regret this, Lester, but the sheriff told me to take down this ass clown at all cost. You heard 'em yourself."

"Yep. Sure did."

"Said you wanna do something?"

"Anything, Earl. Just name it."

"Call your cousin Bud."

Minutes Later

Bud, a war-torn man of twenty-eight, sat on an old couch in the living room of his run-down trailer. An ashtray on the coffee table housed about a hundred cigarette butts, and various fighting knives were displayed next to a copy of *Heart of Napalm and Five Shots to the Face for Charlie: A Journal of War*. *Guns & Ammo*, *The Patriotic Soldier*, and kung fu magazines were scattered about. An old war movie played on a tiny black-and-white TV.

The phone on the end table began to ring. Seven rings later, Bud answered with a voice deeper than Rambo's. "Yeah?"

"Bud? How ya doing?"

"Who the hell is this?"

"Lester."

"Who?"

"Lester. Gilbert's boy. Lester Boone."

Bud paused to hit the fifth of whiskey from the table. It went down nice and easy. "Oh, yeah. Lester. How goes it? How you been?"

"Um. Not too great at the moment. Me and my senior partner Earl got us what one would call a dilemma of sorts, ya see? Some fella done fled that crazy place on the edge of town and went off on a gosh-dang killing spree. Been at it all day too. Even cut the sheriff's wiener off."

"Wait. His what?"

"His wiener."

"… His dick?"

"Yeah. His dick. He cut his dick off, Bud."

"That's some cold-ass shit."

"Yup. Even stuck a little flag up his butt."

"Wow. Now, *that's* some shit. But you wanna know what, Lester? I've seen worse. Much much worse. Did you know that I was in the Vietnam fucking War?"

"Yeah."

"The things I've seen, boy, would have turned your ass black."

There was an awkward silence.

"Well, like I said," Lester continued. "This fella's completely off his noggin and out for blood. You heard about it in town?"

"I don't socialize, Lester."

"Well, me and my partner are the only ones out looking for this fella. Only problem is there's two of us but only one gun. Ya follow?"

"Say no more."

2:45 p.m.

Switchblade's stomach growled. He cruised up to the drive-through burger joint, hit the button on the intercom, and began fixing his hair.

"Welcome to Wally's," a female voice said. "Home of the Double Jolly Wally. Can I help you?"

Switchblade leaned out the window and glanced at the selections on the board. "Uh. Yeah, bitch. Hmmm. Gimme yaaaa ... ahh ... ahh. Hold on." He reached in his pocket and pulled out a ball of lint. *Shit. I ain't got no money.* He ordered anyway. "Fuck it. Give me a ... ahhh ... ahhh ..."

2:55 p.m.
Switchblade sat parked in the middle of nowhere on lunch break. Next to him, the fast-food girl slouched forward with his knife sticking out of her mouth. A bloody puddle had formed in her lap. The killer began squirting ketchup onto a burger in his lap. "Done heard me all kinda good shit about a Wally burger from them assholes at the hospital. Been dying to try one."

He put the bun on top, smashed it down, and looked at his date. Holding out his burger, he gently nudged her cheek with an offering and smeared ketchup on her face.

"Wanna bite, bitch? No? Fine. More for me." He began eating like a pig. The burger toppings fell. "Lemme tell you a story, bitch. Happened a few days ago."

A Few Days Ago

Inside Rockwood's Home for the Criminally Insane, Terry, Shane, and Country Bob—three tough-as-nails rednecks—sat around a table in the day room on their assigned ward. With their feet planted firmly on the table like they were at home, they talked shop and gave shit to random patients that walked by. Many patients were soaked in urine and hadn't showered in days. Some hadn't in weeks. Many in months.

Ralph, the crazy lifer from the beginning of our story, approached the table with a tiny spaceship made with medicine cups, paper plates, and tape. He reluctantly stopped at the table and said, "T-t-t-Terry. C-c-c-can you o-o-open the cu-cu-cu ..."

Ralphie froze. His eyes locked on the ceiling.

The guards looked up to see what Ralph was looking at and waited.

Ralph snapped out of it with a shake of the head and, "C-c-commissary cabinet?"

Terry looked up with absolute disgust. "Ya know something, Ralph? If I had a baby that looked like you when it was born, I would have drowned his sorry ass in a five-gallon bucket of rat piss. Fucking retard."

Shane and Country Bob busted out laughing. Ralph started to fidget and blink rapidly.

"That was a good one, Terry." Country Bob said. "Real good."

Terry smiled with pride. "Bet your ass." He looked back to Ralph. "And who gave you the tape to make that stupid-ass spaceship? Some bleeding heart? That's contraband, you stank-ass little shit. Country Bob, get it."

Country Bob snatched it from Ralph's hand, threw it on the floor, and crushed it under his foot. The fellas laughed.

Country Bob stood proud. "That was real good what I did, huh, Terry?" he asked. "See what I did?"

Terry smiled with pride. "Bet your ass."

Separated from the others, Switchblade had a wing all to himself, in the deepest, most dank part of the ward. His cell revealed his obsessions. Taped along his walls were posters of muscle cars, chicks, and memorabilia from movies like *Rebel Without a Cause, The Lords of Flatbush, Grease 2,* and *Beat Street.* On his desk, five different Elvis shades were lined up next to his trusty boom box. An autographed picture of the Fonz in a hot-pink frame was signed: "To Frank. A killer-ass dude. Love, The Fonz."

Switchblade walked over to the boom box, slid in a tape, and hit play. The cassette's wheels turned. He casually walked to the center of the room, popped his collar, and stood in the hippest Elvis Presley pose ever.

The boom box exploded. "Din Daa Daa" from the *Breakin' 2: Electric Boogaloo* soundtrack roared, and he began tearing up the floor like a wannabe break-dancer. He continued to pop and lock all around his cell to the "def jam" as if he were actually good at it.

Down the hall, Country Bob shook his head. "I can't stand that fucking shit. How about you, Terry? Can you stand that fucking shit?"

Terry said, "I think the asshole has some kinda identity crises. A goddamn nigger-dancing greaser? Fuck's wrong with this guy?"

"Ah, hell," Shane said. "He ain't nothing special. Just some crazy-ass bug that likes to fuck with us like the rest of 'em. That boy ain't shit."

Terry looked down the hall towards Switchblade's cell. "He's a goddamn smartass. *That's* what he is."

Back in Switchblade's cell, the music, and him, continued to pump. Within moments, he was rocking mad skills like a member of the New York City Breakers crew. He was even starting to impress himself, which was rare. He broke into the King Tut, placed one foot on the wall, and began to boogie his way right up the side of it like a break-dancing Spider-Man.

He made his way to the ceiling and dropped into an upside-down, anti-gravity head spin.

Back in the dayroom, the telephone began to ring and interrupted the deep conversation the guards were having about welfare cases. Pissed he had to get up from his seat, Terry got up and answered it. "Unit B ... yeah ... again? Whatever. I'll get him ready." He slammed the phone down.

"Who was that?" Country Bob asked.

"That new doc wants to see Frank again."

"Again?" Shane asked. "What the fuck does he want with that stupid asshole now?"

"Beats the shit outta me." Terry walked toward the locked cabinet. "I'll grab the shackles."

Back in Switchblade's cell, he was dry humping the ceiling to the rhythm of the beat. His face beamed. He hopped to his feet and began gyrating like an upside-down Elvis. "I'm a bad motherfucker. Look at this shit."

Knowing the song was near its end, he Chuck Berry Duck Walked down the wall and steadily stepped it out to the fading rhythm. Halfway down, he jumped and landed in the middle of the room. No one had seen a thing. "Killer," he smiled.

The cell door flung open and slammed the wall.

"Frank," Country Bob hollered. "Doc wants to see your ass."

Terry, Shane, and Country Bob shackled Switchblade and led him down the corridor. His shackles clink-clanked along as he smiled his shit-eating grin.

The other patients ducked in and out of their rooms in an attempt to avoid the madman.

He reached into his jacket, pulled out his Elvis shades, and put them on. He looked back at Terry and curled his bottom lip like the King.

Terry shook his head. "I told you to leave them stupid-ass shades in your cell."

"Yeah," Switchblade smiled. "I know."

A six-foot-something, beefy, black chick approached. She sported red spandex and a championship wrestling belt made from a paper plate and tin foil. The rumor was Mighty Rhonda's DDT wrestling move could be lethal *if* she wanted. She put a DDT on Country Bob three months back for turning off *Gorgeous Ladies of Wrestling.* He was out for days, and his headaches would still not go away.

Switchblade nodded as they passed. "Rhonda."

"Switch," she replied, staring straight ahead.

Terry shoved Switchblade. "Just shut the fuck up and keep moving. You know, Frank? You been looking a little prettier lately. Almost younger. You been using some new kinda face cream with your cosmetics?"

"Nope. Just your wife's coot-coot juice."

The men entered an old freight elevator.

Nurse Betty, the first victim in our story, walked up and froze in her tracks when she saw Switchblade.

He just loved the ladies, especially nurses. It was a fetish for him. He gave her a childish giggle.

"Going up?" Shane asked.

Terry noticed the fear in her eyes. "Don't you worry your pretty little head over this jackass." He tugged on Switchblade's neck restraint. "I got this boy on a pretty tight leash. Ain't that right, boy."

Nurse Betty said, "No. I'll go up." She entered and turned her back to the men.

Country Bob slammed the elevator gate shut and flipped the lever. The elevator slowly creaked and stuttered along.

Switchblade continued to stare at the back of the nurse's head. The Dollar General perfume she wore filled his nostrils and began to give him a chubby that he was more than happy to get. He lunged for the nurse.

She screamed.

Terry yanked him to the ground. "Get 'em, boys!"

The guards pounded with a barrage of fists and stomps.

The nurse looked away, seeing nothing as usual.

Switchblade began laughing. "Oh! Stop it! Ha-ha! That tickles! Hey! Watch the balls!"

They continued to pounce.

Switchblade kept egging them on.

Out of frustration, Terry cocked back and delivered a bone-crushing blow to Switchblade's face, which broke his Elvis shades.

Switchblade gave in. "All right. Stop." He put his hands up. "I'm sorry. All right? Shit."

The guards pulled him back to his feet and hovered around him, huffing and puffing away.

Switchblade casually put his Elvis shades back on—half a lens missing. "Y'all done fucked up my shades. Now I look stupid. Like you." He spit a mouthful of blood at the nurse's back. She jumped and screamed like someone dropped ice down her scrubs.

The guards shoved him to the floor and started round two.

At his desk, Dr. Roberts was scribbling away on a yellow legal pad. His door flung open.

"Hey, Doc," Switchblade yelled, shuffle stepping to the desk. "These assholes just denied having clits, got mad, knocked me down, broke my goddamn Elvis shades, which I stole on my Memphis murder spree last year, hurt my feelings by saying they don't like me, *and* messed up my hair. You messed up my fucking hair, Terry!"

The guards shoved him into the empty chair.

Switchblade instinctively went for his comb and tried to fix his mop.

"Frank got tangled up in his shackles and tripped *again*." Terry looked down at him. "That's all."

"Yup," Shane said. "I seen it myself. That sorta shit happens all the time with this one. You want us to write a report?"

Dr. Roberts looked up to the guards. "Later. I need to see Frank alone. Just wait outside."

"Fine with us," Terry shrugged. "Against the rules and all. Fuck it. Come on, boys. Let's go."

"Yeah," Switchblade said. "Just wait your asses outside until I'm done. I'll let you know when I'm ready to go. I'll yell, 'Hey, dickhead!' That'll be your cue, Terry. You'll be dickhead. Okay, dickhead?"

The men left.

Switchblade blew Terry a kiss as the door closed. "He's so cute." He checked out the office and stopped when he saw a Daffy Duck figure on the shelf. "Huh-huh. A talking duck. I like him. Lots."

The Dr. looked Frank over with a slight smile and a fascinated gaze. Frank *was* his most interesting case. *Notorious* was hardly even the word to describe him. Delusional at best. Deadly at worst. Unstable? Always. The Dr. noticed a scuff on Frank's head. "You okay, Frank?"

"Yeah. I'll just rub a little dirt on it and get back in the game. By the way, I watched a nature show on TV last week—and they had turtles fucking. Huh-huh. Two of 'em. I liked it."

"Okay, I guess. Look, Frank. The reason I wanted to see you was because I got a look at your case study. Right before I arrived, some kind of outside agency came in to look you over and run tests. Something of that nature. Do you remember the group I'm referring to?"

"Well, fuck yeah, bro. It was only a week ago. What's the matter with you? Huh-huh. I think they was Dr.s. One was a chemist or biologist or some shit. No ... Scientist! That's it." He pointed. "*Scientist.*"

The Dr. began to scribble on his pad.

"On Tuesday, they had this sexy-ass, female bitch Dr. in pigtails come in that I tried to fuck, but she wasn't having it. She brought me in a week's worth of medication. Shots to be exact."

"Shots?"

"Yeah. Shots. Seven. Seven shots of some kinda green-glowing shit."

The Dr. stopped scribbling. "Green-glowing shit?"

"Yeah. Green-glowing shit. Green shit ... in a shot ... that glows. You know? Like a Halloween stick or some shit."

"A Halloween stick?"

"Yeah. Like the kind kids carry around at Halloween for protection. Helps keep 'em safe at night. Makes the little shits easier to hit with my car if you ask me. You know kids are worth forty-five points, right? Huh-huh."

"Did they happen to mention what was in these shots? What they were supposed to do?"

"Overheard one of the Dr.s in the next room saying some kinda bullshit about making a better man. Better than what I don't know. I'm already the sweetest, most badass, motherfucker this side of the Mississippi. Shit. Just look at my hair."

Dr. Roberts looked at it. It was still a mess. "I must admit, Frank, it is quite nice."

"I knew you'd dig it. I'll tell you something though, Doc. I've been feeling like a million fucking bucks lately. I'm able to do all sorts of cool-ass shit now."

"Really? Like what, Frank?"

"Oh. All kinda shit, Doc. All kinda shit. Check this out. I can now ... dance on the ceiling, just like Turbo did in *Electric Boogaloo*. No shit. Just don't tell anyone, okay? They'll all say I'm lying."

The Dr. smiled. "Frank, Frank, Frank. Where do you come up with some of this stuff?"

"Dunno." Switchblade shrugged. "All in my head, I guess."

The Dr. looked up from his notes and noticed the scuff on Switchblade's forehead had disappeared without a trace. Was he seeing this right?

"Oh shit," Switchblade said. "Check this out, Doc. I shot a load about ten feet the other day from my bed. It hit the fucking wall. You believe that shit? I thought to myself, damn, wonder what else I can do?"

The Dr. continued to not hear a word.

"Hey, Doc. We 'bout done here? Doc!"

"Yes, Frank?"

"We 'bout done here? *Happy Days* in twenty."

"Yes, Frank." The Dr. leaned back. "We're done. I wouldn't want you to miss your favorite show, now would I?"

"*All-time* favorite show. You know what, man? I like you. I'll let you know if I do any more cool-ass shit." Switchblade stood. "Hey, dickhead! Let's boogie!"

3:10 p.m.
Deep in the backwoods of Rockwood, things were getting spooky for the fellas. The patrol car crept slowly along the overgrown path that was leading them straight into no-man's land. No trespassing and warning signs were posted along the trail, making it look like something out of a hillbilly horror movie.

"I have a *baaaaad* feeling about this," Lester said.

Earl continued to ride the break and play it cool. "Lemme tell you something, Lester. Sometimes you have to travel through hell in order to take out that devil. True, using Bud might be dangerous, not to mention risky, but we *do* need the help, Lester. No question."

"I'm just a little nervous is all."

"Shit me some gravy and tell me about it, son. Bad enough I done heard things about Bud that downright worry me in the first place, but now I've been hearing some shit about him only living off the animals he kills in the woods behind his house."

"Lotta people hunt, Earl."

"But they use a gun, Lester! And they sure as shit ain't running around the fucking woods with their shirts off and a goddamn bandana tied around their fucking heads. Who the fuck does some shit like that? Cutty said he stumbled up on Bud in the woods once, and Bud was covered in squirrel's blood from head to toe, with nothing on but a knife strapped to his thigh, naked as shit. That very same knife had a compass on the end of its handle. Can you believe that shit? Cutty overheard Bud refer to it as a 'survivor's knife' or some kinda shit. For a survivalist type, I guess. Inside that very same knife handle was some waterproof matches and fishing string for catching bluegill. Said it's in case he got lost on his way home and needed to survive off the land for a few hours. Jesus Christ, Lester! Who in God's name would come up with or even need that kinda weaponry?"

"Perhaps just the man we need, Earl."

Back at the trailer, Bud watched the ceiling fan go around and around. Losing his grip on reality, his mouth hung wide open. The fan blades began to sound like a Huey helicopter in battle. With a heavy heart thumping in his chest, he began to pant and sweat profusely. The hellacious sounds of war filled his head and sent him deep into the madness of another full-on flashback. Soldiers from both sides screamed over gunfire and explosions.

"Get some, motherfuckers! Get some!"
Boom!
"Fuck you, yellow bitches! Come suck some of this!"
Rat-tat-tat-tat-tat. Boom!
"Somebody bring up the goddamn rear! Where the fuck is Bud?"
"I don't know, Sarge."
"Oh no. Rodriguez, to your right!"
Rat-tat-tat-tat!
"Ah!"

Earl and Lester made their way to Bud's front door. The yard was scattered with rusted crap, and a collection of about thirty trash bags on the side of the trailer made it smell extra nasty in the heat.

"I'm telling you, Earl, Bud's good people. Family. Stable as a table."

Back inside, Bud was going deeper into the madness.

"Guys, I think I'm losing him," a medic yelled over the gunfire.

"Goddamn you, Bud. Where the fuck were you? You didn't bring up the goddamn rear like you were supposed to."

The sounds of the gunfire began to slow.

"Guys, I'm losing him," the medic cried.

"If this man dies, Bud, it's on you. It will be on your conscience. Not mine. You careless asshole."

"I'm sorry men," the medic said. "I've done everything I can. I'm afraid I've lost him. He's gone."

"Nice going, Bud!"

Bud began to sob. "I'm s-s-so sorry, guys. I d-didn't mean to. Oh, no. Not you, Rodriguez. Not you too. We shared a bunk in boot camp, man."

"I got a new name for Bud, everyone: Private Dumb Ass."

The soldiers laughed.

Bud dropped to his knees by Rodriguez's corpse, held his arms up to the heavens, and screamed like Darth Vader in *Revenge of the Sith* with a, "Nooooooo!"

A knock at the door jerked Bud back to reality. Drenched with sweat, he made his way to the door and opened it.

Earl and Lester stood on the other side.

"Hey, Cousin," Lester smiled.

"Cousin," Bud replied, still half asleep. He hocked some phlegm, spit on the ground, and looked at Earl. "Don't think I know you."

"Me? I'm Earl Tubb. And you? You're Bud."

"Yes. I am Bud."

An ugly mutt with one eye and three legs came up.

"Say hi to Sissy," Bud said.

"Hi, Sissy," Lester and Earl replied.

Bud leaned down and patted ugly Sissy. "Been a long-ass time, Lester. How's my favorite aunt?"

"Fine. Fine. You know. Hanging in. Hanging in. How *you* been?"

Bud shook his head. "You don't want to know, Lester. You just don't want to know. I done seen some shit in my lifetime, boy." Bud leaned in and stared directly into Lester's eyes. "Did you know that I was in the Vietnam fucking War?"

"Yep. We already know about that. Look. The reason we're here is—"

"I know why you're here. Come on in, boys."

3:22 p.m.

Bud had an assortment of weaponry on the kitchen table, and it was quite an impressive sight. There were guns, knives, nunchucks, brass knuckles, dynamite, tons of ammunition, ninja stars, and the infamous Rambo-inspired survival knife that Earl had heard so much about. Pistol-gripped shotguns were perched on one of the chairs, and on the wall next to the fridge, a poster of a naked black chick with a huge Afro.

Bud, now full of pep, said, "What we have here is just a small fraction of my arsenal and everything one would need to take somebody out the picture. Plenty of firepower. Plenty of bang."

Earl had to ask. "Are these weapons registered?"

"No. Now, here we have an M-16 with a 203-grenade launcher. Ten grenades. One if you're any good. Got two pistol-gripped shotguns in the chair there with four boxes of shells. Them's all slugs by the way."

Lester picked up the nunchucks.

Bud pointed. "You supposed to spin those."

Lester tried to get a good spin going, but couldn't. He put them back in embarrassed defeat and looked at Earl. Earl shook his head in disappointment.

Bud continued. "Got a few bang sticks here. Bunch of bullets and shit. Throwing stars. Brass knuckles. You could be Aunty Em and knock the shit outta somebody with those motherfuckers."

"One question," Earl said.

"Shoot."

"Is there another pair of nunchucks or just the one?"

"Just the one. Why?"

"I get those, Lester. I called 'em first. Bud. What would you recommend here? What would be *your* weapon of choice?"

"Well, any of it, I guess—that's if you're proficient enough with the weapon." Bud pointed at the ninja stars. "Ninja stars have been used for years by the

Japanese ninja. I got those out of a magazine. I really like that one. It's got a picture of a ninja on it. Look at that." Bud looked at it, smiled, and continued. "You don't have to be proficient with the dynamite much. Just don't be there when it explodes."

"Got that right," Lester said.

Bud looked at the men. "You boys wanna test 'em out?"

3:45 p.m.

In the blazing sun, the three men blasted away at Bud's homemade targets on the firing range behind his trailer. On top of the bales of hay, pictures of "Hanoi" Jane Fonda, Ronald Reagan, and Richard Simmons were stuck to the targets. Richard Simmons had three ninja stars stuck to his crotch and was riddled with bullet holes.

Earl had the nunchucks dangling from his belt, and Lester was rocking an elongated gas mask that made him look like a human anteater. They continued their onslaught as two-liter bottles exploded, sending water ten feet high as glass shattered everywhere.

"Take 'em out," Bud screamed. "Blast that shit!"

They destroyed everything in a three-way attack.

Boom! Boom! Boom!

All was silent.

A dummy Vietcong soldier sprang up, complete with an AK-47 and an old drive-in speaker attached to its chest. "Go-da-donna-dahhhh!"

"It's Charlie!" Bud quickly pulled a grenade pin out with his teeth. "Get the fuck down!"

The men dove for the dirt as Bud hurled the grenade at the dummy and hit it square in the chest.

Boom!

There was nothing left of Target Charlie. When the smoke finally cleared, all three men were standing in their own Billy-Badass pose.

Earl spit. "Shit, yeah."

"Yep," Bud agreed. "I hate that motherfucker too."

Lester removed his gas mask and motioned behind the barn. "What's under the tarp?"

"That's my baby," Bud said. "Wanna see?"

Moments Later

Bud ripped a camouflaged tarp from an old wrecker that was tricked out—complete with a Gatling gun strapped to its frame and sheet metal welded to the sides. Up high in the back was a makeshift cage, made from an old lawn chair and some scrap chicken wire. The name Maura was proudly spray-painted on the sides in dripping-style graffiti. It was a redneck tow service from an apocalyptic hell: Mad Max style.

"Woo-wee," Lester shouted.

The officers looked over the beast in amazement. Bud smiled proudly.

Earl said, "Holy goddamn shit, Bud. What the fuck you been doing out here?"

"Getting ready, Earl. Getting ready."

"Getting ready for *what*, Bud?" Lester asked.

"Her name's Maura. Say hi to the boys, Maura." Bud leaned in and hit the horn. It howled louder than the blast of a train whistle.

Earl and Lester covered their ears.

Bud let off. "Got a turbocharged engine. Observation bubble. Nitrous tanks in the back. Cannon on the side, and she's coming complete with a set of my very own specialized, reinforced-rubber combat tires."

Lester stepped up, lightly kicked one of the tires, and thumbs-upped Earl.

"Got two Solar Bangster subwoofers with a 450-watt Rockstar Fuzzgut Punch amp. Running it bridge."

"Nice." Earl said.

"Also, got me a set of custom-cut-out component speakers in the front. Check *this* shit out." Bud flipped on the stereo.

Earl's favorite honky-tonk jam began to play, and the bass roared. Earl felt the banjo pump from his favorite tune like never before. He could no longer contain himself, and the music took hold. He began to shuffle dance in place—West Virginia-style. The banjo's speed picked up, and Earl had no problem keeping up.

Lester got excited and tried to join in. "Go, Earl! Go!"

They stomped and clapped along, completely out of sync. Bud stared in awe at the stupidity.

"Yee-haw," Earl shouted in a spin.

Bud reached in the cab to shut off the stereo, but Pistol Lee interrupted the festivities. "I'm sorry to interrupt the music, folks, but I just got a call to the station—and you gonna wanna hear this. I'm punching it through to you live. On the phone with me I have a Mr. Frank Butz—also known as Mr. Switchblade, the fella that got our whole town shook up. Are you there, Frank?"

"Yeah, Pistol Lee. I'm here. You called me *Mr.* Switchblade. Huh-huh."

Earl couldn't believe his ears. "I'll be a sumbitch, Lester. It's him."

Bud shushed him, and the three huddled around a subwoofer.

"Let me ask you a question, Frank."

"Sure thing, but first let me just say that I'm a fan of yours, Pistol Lee. Big fan. I listen to your show every damn night."

"Well, thanks. I guess."

"Well, like I said, I'm a fan."

"Okay."

"Big time, yo."

"Frank?"

"Call me Switchblade."

"Okay. Swit—"

"Wait. Call me Frank. Yeah. Call me that. You're allowed. Wanna know why?"

"Why?"

"Because I like you, Lee."

"Okay ... *Frank*?"

"Yeah?"

"Guess it's gonna be Frank then. Okay, Frank. Here we go. The good people of Rockwood, myself included, would like to know why you're doing the things you're doing. I mean, why, Frank? Why?"

"You don't like me rutting up your yards and shit?"

"No. Not that. The killing. You kill people, Frank."

"Oh, *that*? Fuck y'all. Next question."

"Will you ever stop?"

"Nope."

"Any regrets?"

"Shoulda banged that fast-food girl before I killed her. Next question."

"Can you be reasoned with?"

"Nope. Or bargained with. Just like a motherfucking Terminator."

"Shit."

"Oh yeah. Shit is that real over here. It's fun to do bad things, Pistol Lee. Don't you know that shit?"

"I'm not really one to judge a person till I get to know him first, but Imma guess by our little conversation we having that you just might enjoy being some kinda ruthless stone-cold killer, huh? Just having himself a hoot at our expense. Do unto others, Frank. And look atcha. Not a care in the world."

"Not really. Maybe my hair looking good—maybe—but since it always does, no."

"Come on, Frank. This stuff ain't right. It ain't right, and you darn well know it. Why don't you try turning over a new leaf? Just try and get to know us some first is all I'm saying. We's good people. I think so anyway. Shoot. You wanna know something, Frank? I know this one lady named Barbara, and she just so happens to make the best chicken and dumplings in town. And let me tell you, that ain't no kinda lie. Sounds real good, don't it? Making that mouth water I bet. Maybe if I sweet-talk her, she'll cook you up a batch. But here's the catch. I'll call and ask her as promised, but *only if you turn yourself in.* And, Frank, I give you my word as a Christian that I'll bring 'em in for you when you get back to that hospital. How about it? Should I call her? They real good now."

"Uh. No. I was really only calling in for that song request—and to throw out a challenge."

"A challenge?"

"Yeah, a challenge—to that stupid fathead on patrol that's trying to keep you shits safe and is failing miserably. You hear me out there, Tubb? Earl Tubb, that is. Get the dick outcha ear and listen when I'm talking to you, boy. Huh-huh."

Lester and Bud looked over to Earl and gave him a look as if he may be in deep shit for being singled out by this maniac.

"I know you're probably listening, Tubby, since this is the only radio station this shithole picks up. Check this out. I'm taking it back to grade school and picking me a fight with you—and recess is coming. But we all know you don't have the sack to meet me. Why? Because you're scared, and everyone knows it too. Nothing but a cold wet fart in the wind. You a disgrace to the uniform. Even heard the guards at the hospital talk about how much of a fuckstick you were, and they were right. You been letting off that pedal all day to keep from running into me. Holding back and letting so-called innocent people die. The bloodshed in this town is on your hands, you big, fat, tub of butt goop. Tell you what I'll do, since I'm such a nice guy. I'm gonna stick around for a while and help you out. How? Well, I'll tell you. You want to be the man? Your types usually do. Well, I'm giving you your chance. To be the man, you have to beat the man—and that's me. I'm the fucking man, and I'm giving you a shot at the title. Me and you, sweetie. Come get some—and consider it a gift, little bitch."

Bud and Lester looked sorry for Earl. The whole town heard him get called a little bitch on the radio. How embarrassing.

Earl fumed.

"Now, as for you, Pistol Lee. Play that fucking song I told you to play. I likes me a good soundtrack to kill to. Makes for a great movie. I'm the star of this show in case you didn't know. Hey. That rhymed! Huh-huh. That was completely by accident, by the way. I swear to God."

"Movie, huh? Who the hell would ever want to watch a movie about some stupid crap like this? How about I just quit playing music and call it a day then? Huh? How about that, Frank?"

"Call me Switchblade."

"Just shut the station down. I don't really think I want any part of this so-called movie of yours. Now whatcha got to say about that, Frank?"

"How 'bout I just kill your ass next, Lee? After I'm done, I think I'm going to pee in your fucking butt."

"And this next song comes from a little lady in Jackson. Been around for quite some time, and everybody loves it. Just loves it. And good reason too. Here's Melinda Childs with 'Put Up My Tailgate When You're Done with Her.' Right here on Ram-N AM."

Bud leaned in and killed the stereo. The men stood silent.

Bud broke the silence. "That fucking guy really hates you, bro. Shit."

"He sure did sound awfully sore atcha, Earl," Lester agreed. "Whatcha gonna do?"

Earl slowly looked up. Enough was enough. It was time to make a choice, and he made it. No more riding the break. He stepped up and declared war. "Let's pop this cocksucker's balloon."

4:01 p.m.

Back in Bud's kitchen, the fellas strapped what was left of the weapons on themselves.

Earl's gut let out a nasty grumble. He clutched at his belly and cringed. "Uh-oh. Better take me a nervous shit before we roll out. I feel it coming, y'all." On his way to the john, he spotted a kung fu magazine, picked it up, and read the cover. "How to nunchuck. Special l-l-lessons from the man who t-t-taught Bruce Lee. *Hymph.*"

Bud began applying camo paint to his face.

"I thank ya in advance for the help, Bud," Lester said. "We sure gonna need it."

Bud tied a bandana on his head—just like Daniel San's in *The Karate Kid*. "Not a problem, Lester. You're family. Besides, I know how to handle this stupid, communist faggot. Did you know that I was in the Vietnam fucking War?"

"Yep." Lester loaded a shotgun and racked a shell. "I sure did, Cousin."

Bud's face went blank.

"The *Nam.*" Bud's temple began to throb and a thousand-yard stare fell upon his face. He reached deep. Recognizing the warrior within, he latched on tight—never to let go again. It was time for Bud to do what he was born to do. A little no-holds-barred "get some." The needle on the record player mysteriously dropped. Sammy Hagar's "Winner Takes It All" began blasting through the trailer.

"*Over the Top*," Bud said.

"Ah, yeah!" Lester said.

The men began prepping for battle from both sides to Sammy Hagar's rocking tune.

- Lester put on some brass knuckles and punched a hole in the wall. Bud thumbs-upped him proudly.
- Earl wiped his ass on the toilet.

- Switchblade stomped on an old lady's head in the middle of a four-way stop.
- Bud pocketed some ninja stars.
- Earl flushed.
- Switchblade fixed his hair as he pissed on a corpse in the grass.
- Earl tried imitating the moves from the "how-to-karate" poster on the bathroom door.
- Switchblade centered himself with some Tai Chi on the hood of his car.
- Bud ripped the sleeves off his shirt, revealing a rebel flag tattoo with "Dixie Boy 4 Life" written under it.
- Earl posed with a shotgun in the living room and quickly cocked it, making it accidentally go off inside.
- Switchblade did backflips to his car, hopped in, and fired it up.
- Earl, Lester, and Bud assembled in the kitchen, strapped from head to toe.

The needle on the record lifted up and silenced the montage.

"I see you're in, Bud," Earl said.

"*All* in. I wouldn't miss this shit for the world."

Bud looked to the heavens. "Rodriguez, this is for you."

The men cocked their weapons.

4:13 p.m.

The three warriors came outside, ready to wreck shop, and made their way to the tricked-out wrecker. Bud had knives and ninja stars strapped to his suspenders but no shirt, which revealed the biggest farmer's tan ever.

Earl carried a pistol-gripped shotgun over his shoulder, and the nunchucks dangled from his belt loop.

Lester rocked an army helmet with the chin strap dangling, a bazooka, and an M-60 machine gun. "Ya know, Earl," he said. "When we nab this sucker, you just know somebody is gonna wanna make a movie about it."

Earl had that thought right from the beginning but played it cool. "You think?"

"Sure."

"You know something, Lester? I could see a young John Schneider playing you."

"Really? Wow. Thanks, Earl. I bet we could guest star on *The Dukes of Hazzard*."

"Shit. Not me. Replacing Bo and Luke Duke ruined that goddamn show. I want no part of that awful mess."

"Yeah, I still watch it, but it ain't the same. I don't get why when them TV people have something good going they have to go and mess with it. Remember *Hee-Haw*?"

"Oh, yeah. I remember *Hee-Haw*. Top-three material right there."

At the wrecker, Bud took full command. "Lester, you got the tower."

"On it." Lester tossed his weapons in back and climbed the wrecker.

"Put that headset on so we can communicate," Bud hollered.

"Sure thing, Bud. I mean, roger that."

Lester put on the headset and adjusted the mouthpiece. "What's my call sign gonna be?"

"Whatever you want it to be," Bud said. "Pick one."

Lester thought for a second and snapped his fingers. "I know! How about Spread Eagle? You know? Like an Indian name."

"Spread Eagle it is then. We're gonna be the Wrecker Boys. I'm Wrecker Boy One. Earl here is gonna be Wrecker Boy Two. Spread Eagle?"

"Yeah?"

"Let's do this!"

The men huddle clapped and shot into action. Bud and Earl jumped into the cab and slammed the doors.

Bud fired up the wrecker, hit the horn, and the wildlife in the area scattered. He dropped the hammer, hit the gas, and left behind a dust-coated trailer. Ten seconds later, they were bombing down the road at eighty-eight miles per hour.

The wind whipped Lester's face, stung his eyes, and they began to water. "Wrecker Boys from Spread Eagle," he managed. "Do you copy? I repeat. Do you copy?"

"We copy, Spread Eagle," Bud replied. "We copy. How's the situation up there?"

"Clear as a bell. How about some tunes?"

Bud flipped on the stereo, and Pistol Lee came through. "We done lost enough folks to this madman, and he flat-out needs to be stopped. Earl and Lester, if you're out there listening, fellas, then this next one's for you. Here's Billy Joe Jim Bob Kelley Jr. with 'This Town Needs Us a Boot-Scoot Hero' also known as 'Everyone Should Buy a Truck.' Right here on Ram-N AM. Go get 'em boys."

Earl bounced in his seat. "Hey, Lester! He just said our names on the radio!"

"I know. I heard. I heard. We're famous!"

The wrecker shot ten feet into the air from an unseen ramp like the *General Lee*.

The men yelled, "Yee-haw!"

4:20 p.m.

The hot rod crept along the town square. There wasn't a soul in sight. A blow-up doll was strapped safely in the back with a seat belt. Run-DMC's "It's Like That" blasted from the boom box. Switchblade rapped along and made hip-hop hand gestures.

"Unemployment at a record high. People coming, people going, people born to die. Don't ask me, because I don't know why. But it's like that. And that's the way it is."

He hit the break and looked around. "Fuck is everyone?"

4:22 p.m.

The wrecker continued bombing down the road. Earl checked his weapons and discovered some little silver balls in a side pouch. He held them up. "Hey, Bud. What the hell are these? You collect marbles or some shit?"

"Those are instant-no-fire-ninja smoke bombs."

"Instant-no-fire-ninja smoke bombs? For ninjas?"

"Yep. For ninjas. Open that glove box and give me that pouch in there marked 'special.' I need me a boost."

Earl opened the glove box, grabbed the camouflage tobacco pouch, and handed it to Bud. "Never smelled me a chew like that before. Interesting. What's in it?"

"This isn't for you." Bud shoved a chew in and tucked it firmly in his jaw. Within seconds, his eyes went blank. He stared off into the abyss and closed his eyes in ecstasy.

"Bud?" Earl said. "You okay?"

Bud's eyes jerked back to reality—full of awareness. He hit his headset. "How we doing up there, Spread Eagle?"

"Eyes are peeled, Wrecker Boys. Eyes are peeled. Whatcha say we hit town square? We might catch that sorry-ass bastard there."

Earl hit his headset. "Wow, Spread Eagle. Don't think I've ever heard you cuss in anger before. You must really be pumped."

Bud rolled down his window and screamed, "War changes a man, Lester. Just go with the shit."

Lester pumped his fist high in the air and shouted, "Whoo!"

4:25 p.m.
An old pickup truck with oversize mud tires pulled into Peggy's Diner. Terry, Shane, and Country Bob climbed out, slammed their doors with their bullish attitude, and strutted for the entrance.

"Yeah." Terry tugged his waistline. "Everyone's scared of this little shit on the loose, but Peggy said she was gonna stay open anyway. That broad ain't scared of shit."

"Hope so," Country Bob said. "I'm fucking starving."

"Well, no shit, Country Bob. When the goddamn hell ain't you hungry?"

The men entered the diner. None of them noticed the hot rod in the parking lot. Inside the empty diner, a jukebox filled the place with some old honky-tonk twang.

"Peggy," Terry yelled to the kitchen. "You back there?"

"Maybe she's in the shitter." Shane pulled out his Velcro-strap wallet. "Or out back fucking Cecil. Now, *that's* nasty. I hope she's the type to wash her goddamn hands before she cooks."

Terry and Shane sat down and grabbed menus.

"Think Imma take a piss." Country Bob headed to the restroom. "Order for me."

"Be sure to squat when you pee," Terry said. "What the fuck you want?"

"Usual, but with coffee."

Country Bob entered the dingy restroom, already unbuckling his belt on the way in. Inside were several rundown urinals next to a stall. The walls were littered with graffiti. He walked up to one of the urinals, unzipped his fly, and read the graffiti as he did his business. He giggled at the one with the cock reference, whipped out a pen from his pocket, and wrote some of his own: Terry loves the taste of my sweaty ... He stopped cold when a man in the stall began whistling the theme from *For a Few Dollars More*. He hadn't been aware that somebody was in there, but he knew very well who loved to whistle that little tune. Frank Switchblade Butz. He looked to the bottom of the stall for feet and found them. "Uh. Hello?"

"Country Bob? That you?"

The toilet flushed.

Back in the booth, Terry and Shane talked shop.

"Man, I wish we would run into that pussy," Terry said. "We outside the walls of that fucking funny farm now. Fair ground, motherfucker. Know what I mean? Wanna get some beer after we eat and go find 'em? Maybe kick his nuts in a little?"

"Nah," Shane said. "Worked a double. I'm tired."

"You know I used to take that greaseball to shock therapy?"

"Fuck that. Taxes. We pay for that shit. It cost too damn much for the electricity they use to shock these bugs. Bad enough my tax dollars gotta pay for a bunch of niggers and their kids to eat for free, but now I'm supposed to pay to have Frank zapped? Fuck that. One bullet. Cheap. Or how about I just push 'em into a big-ass bug zapper and call it a day. Save the good state of Mississippi some money. Bug zapper that size might cost though. What do you think?"

"Shoulda seen that boy shake when they shocked his ass. I used to love watching that shit. All twitching. Made my dick hard." Terry grabbed the table and shook as if he was being electrocuted. The salt and pepper shakers danced around. "It was a medical ass-whooping if I ever saw one. Shit himself on it once. Long ride back, man. Long ride back."

"I never did like that smartass from day one."

"Who the fuck did? Wannabe fifties queer, walking around like 'Look at me. I'm stuck in the fifties, and I'm a goddamn queer. Duh-duh-duh.' Dumb fucking Illinois Yankee asshole. His ass better hope I don't see him out and about. Put a size-eleven work boot straight up his ass. Just bought me a new pair too. Waterproof. I sure like 'em. One thing I gotta say, though. That boy sure can take a fucking punch."

"Think I'd look cool with a little mini handlebar mustache like Tom?"

"Maybe you, him, and that queer-looking Monopoly guy can fuck married bitches in the break room at work together." Terry looked back to the kitchen. "Goddamn it, Peggy! You back there or what? We're fucking starving out here!"

The bathroom door creaked open, and the two men picked up their menus.

"'Bout time, Country Bob," Terry said, not bothering to look. "You fall in again?"

Switchblade sat down.

"So," he said. "What we having?"

Menus came down, and eyes met.

4:33 p.m.
Maura continued to chew up the road.

Bud had yet to spit his chew juice since he loaded that bad boy up. Earl really admired a man who could swallow the juice. It meant he was tough. Earl wished he could do the same, but chew made his tummy feel all sick. "Hey, Bud. Stop by the station. I've got a great idea."

The wrecker hit the station's lot and slid to a stop.

Earl dove from the cab, rolled twice, popped up, then swiftly looked left to right for possible enemy.

"You're clear, Earl," Lester yelled. "Go for it."

Earl made a mad dash for the station.

Spread Eagle hit his headset. "What's the situation, Wrecker One?"

"Hell if I know. Your boy had some great idea. I didn't ask. Oh, here he comes."

Earl ran back out with a paper sack and a can of lighter fluid. He jumped in the wrecker, threw the bag on the floorboard, and slammed his door. "Now, I'm ready."

The wrecker hauled ass for town square.

4:39 p.m.

In the parking lot at Peggy's diner, Switchblade tied Terry's ankles to his bumper. Shane and Country Bob were already tied with forks sticking out of their heads. Switchblade gave a final tug at the rope, stepped back, and framed the bodies with his hands like a film director. He noticed something in the air didn't seem quite right. He spun in the direction of the disturbance and took a quick sniff of the atmosphere to examine its contents. He cocked his head and listened closely as *Bionic Man*-type sound effects began emitting from his hearing. *Bawn-bawn-bawn-bawn.* He picked up on the sound of an approaching truck.

Terry began to wake. "Ah. Oh."

Switchblade turned his attention to him, leaned down, and said, "Morning, Terry. Guess what? Imma 'bout to drag your ass, you fucking square prick."

He squatted and let loose a fart in Terry's face.

Terry's mouth was open, and the stench stung his throat and lungs. "Frank, you sick bastard. You farted."

Switchblade quickly delivered a stomp to Terry's balls.

Terry sat up and puked all over himself.

Switchblade skipped away like a happy child, hopped into his ride and slammed the door. He fired it up, and the car's hot exhaust shot into Terry's face.

Terry started pleading. "Frank! I thought we was friends!"

Switchblade adjusted the mirror, checked his hair, and dropped the hammer.

"Frank," Terry cried. "You sick bastard!"

Switchblade gunned it, and the strapped bodies shot off like a rocket, dragging behind by their ankles.

Terry screamed as the road chewed his ass to shreds.

Burning through town square like he was blind, Switchblade weaved back and forth. The strapped bodies smacked random curbs, posts, and parked cars.

He started singing Elvis Presley. "Like a one-eyed cat, peeping in the seafood store. Well, I can look at you till you ain't no child no more."

He cut quick. Terry and his dead pals slammed into a Ford Pinto and flung back into the road as a semi blasted by.

Terry managed to sit up just in time to see the semi face to face. "Oh shit!"

Smash!

Terry liquefied against the truck's grill. The driver slammed the brakes. The truck flipped on its side, smashed into parked cars, and began sending them one at a time through storefront windows.

Inside Maura the Wrecker, Bud hit his headset. "We're just about there, Wrecker Boys. Get ready for action. Earl. You climb out and hold on to that sidebar. Spread Eagle, you be my eyes in the sky."

"Roger that, Wrecker One," Spread Eagle said. "I'm looking now. I'm looking."

"Out there?" Earl asked.

Bud's look said it all.

Earl reluctantly opened his door, grabbed the sidebar, climbed out, and held on for dear life. The wind beat against his wide frame. "You ready, Spread Eagle?" he yelled.

"I'm ready, Earl!"

The sun blazed in the distance. Switchblade tore ass down the highway and dragged body parts like a set of morbid wedding cans. He checked his hair in the mirror. Looked good. He flipped on the stereo for a little showdown music.

"I guess I'm kinda obligated to keep playing these tunes out of fear for my life."

"Got that right." Switchblade looked at the radio. "Silly bitch."

"So, here's a little music. Something on the rough side. Nice and crunchy. Something that maniac ought to like. I hope so, anyway. Heh-heh-heh. *Ahem.* Here's

Dick Dale with 'Nitro.' Right here on Ram-N AM. Your station and mine. Set it and forget it."

Surf-rock blasted.

"Fuck yeah, bitch!" Switchblade cranked the tune and smashed the gas. The Duster charged like a bull. The speedometer climbed fast, and the car began to shake and vibrate.

"Huh-huh-huh."

He leaned forward and was able to make out a vehicle in the distance. *A truck maybe?* Out of nowhere, his eyesight zoomed straight into it. He began using his super-robotic cyborg vision, which he wasn't even aware he had, complete with a high-tech, self-targeting telescope. The crosshairs assessed all possible targets and displayed them in a digital readout. His bionic sight had finally kicked in. "Damn. That's some cool-ass shit! Looka dat! Huh-huh."

He zoomed to get a better look. It was one hellacious-looking beast indeed. The only problem was it had some scrawny guy sitting in a chicken coop, looking stupid with a military helmet that was way too big. Also, a heavyset guy hung from the passenger side like a garbage man, swinging nunchucks over his head and screaming some kind of hillbilly war cry.

"What the fuck?" Switchblade said. "Fuck outta here with that shit. Huh-huh. Ya'll straight stupid, yo."

It was a do-or-die situation. Both vehicles charged like pit bulls, and no one was backing off.

"A game of chicken is my shit," Switchblade screamed. "Bring it on!"

The speed and tension hit Spread Eagle, and he suddenly had to pee. He buckled his chinstrap for extra protection and crossed his legs tight to hold it in.

Earl continued to swing the nunchucks and scream his war cry.

Bud was in total control—with the help from his special blend. Steady, ready, and deadly—he smashed the gas harder, determined not to back off first. "Fuck this guy," he screamed.

Switchblade was rocking out, bobbing his head to the music, and pounding his fist on the steering wheel. "Damn, this song is badass!" He cranked it to the max and suddenly his speakers popped. "Motherfucker," he cried.

Bud gripped the wheel for impact. They were seconds away from collision. He hit his headset. "Now, Earl! Now!"

Earl lit the paper sack and heaved it at the hot rod. The flaming bag of shit from Earl's desk splattered against Switchblade's windshield.

Switchblade slammed the brakes and skidded. "Oh, shit!"

The vehicles blew past, scraped frames, and sparks shot between them as they barely missed collision. Switchblade came to a dizzying stop on the side of the road, and his engine choked on him and died.

"Shit bag, motherfucker!" Earl flipped Switchblade the finger.

"Woo-hoo," Lester hooted. "That got 'em!"

The wrecker made a hard right off the main road and made a beeline for the woods. They disappeared up a long, winding trail.

Switchblade sat in his vehicle dumbfounded. "Son of a bitch." He leaned forward and hit the wiper blades. Jimmy Lee hadn't filled the wiper fluid for some time. Shit smeared across the glass. "Son of a bitch."

The woods were deep and windy. Bud maneuvered with the skill of a racecar driver, never slowing as the wrecker barreled up the dirt path.

Earl climbed back into the cab and slammed the door.

"Just hang your ass on, Earl." Bud said. "I know these woods like the back of my hand. Oh shit. Lookie there. A deer!"

"Where are you going? He's back there."

"Don't you worry, Earl. After what you did, I guarantee he'll be coming after us. And when he does—"

"Ambush?"

"Damn straight."

Bud hit his headset. "Spread Eagle, do you copy?"

"I copy, Wrecker One. I copy."

"Man that gun, but be careful. It runs hot real fast."

4:55 p.m.
The hot rod left a dust trail in its wake. Switchblade drove with his shirt pulled over his nose to block the smell. He had tried to clear a space for better visibility, but shit still covered most of the windshield. He yanked his shirt down. "When I find you, Tubb, Imma slice me some jerky—right off from yo fat ass."

The road ahead was empty. He stopped to scan the area with his super vision. His eyesight viewfinder read out the assessments:

- No Enemy in Sight
- Proceed with Extreme Caution
- Power Levels at Maximum

He decided to use his bionic hearing. *Bawn-bawn-bawn-bawn.* Nothing. "Damn." He continued around the bend.

The wrecker was parked in the middle of a pile of brush, camouflaged, with broken branches duct taped to it.

Lester was on the lookout with binoculars, and Bud and Earl relaxed in the cab.

Bud looked over. "Good move on that shit-bag trick, Earl. I never saw no shit like that in Nam."

Earl nodded. "Thank you."

"Say." Bud leaned over. "You ever think about joining the Marines? They sure could use a man like you. They pay for college too!"

The CB came to life. "Is there an Earl Tubb out there? I repeat. Is there an Officer Earl Tubb out there?"

"Who the fuck is that?" Bud asked. "Some walkie-talkie boyfriend of yours?"

"Dunno. Let's see."

Earl grabbed the handle, did his left/right routine, and said, "This is Earl Tubb, but for right now, I'm Wrecker Boy Two. Call me that. Who the hell is this?"

"Dr. Roberts. Remember me?"

"Uh. Yeah. Just talked to you this morning. Do *you* remember?"

"Thank God I found you. Listen. I've been digging in this file on Frank Butz, and I've managed to come up with some pretty interesting things that you need to know about. Most are downright bizarre."

"Like?"

"Before I was transferred in, a group of scientists came down from Area 51 to run experiments on Frank."

"Area 51? You mean that UFO place out in the middle of the desert?"

"That's the one. He was used as some kind of experiment with DNA that was not of human origins. I don't really know why they chose him, but they did. He has been injected with an unknown substance called Serum 13B."

Sixteen Hours Earlier

The crickets chirped away in the peaceful moonlight at the Rockwood Home for the Criminally Insane. An unmarked, black car of indeterminate make and model pulled to the front of the facility and came to a stop. The engine shut off, and two strange-looking men exited the vehicle. They wore identical black suits with red and blue ties. Both had a look on their faces that was otherworldly. It was a two-man team from a rogue division of the Men in Black. They shut their doors and walked to the entrance. Blue Tie carried an antique medical bag. They opened the door and entered.

At the desk, a chunky lady with huge beehive hair and thick makeup filed away at her tacky nails. She looked up at them. "Think it's kinda late for a visit. Gotta good reason for being up in here this hour?"

Red Tie casually waved his hand. The woman passed out cold from a telekinesis hit to the brain. She fell over, took her cosmetics with her, and hit the floor.

He casually looked at his partner. "Ganipgonads should have came in with us on this bet. I mean, it's only fair."

Blue Tie shook his head. "Why? Because he had to come to this stupid planet and give a series of 13B injections? That's his job. I don't care if he had to spend the last two weeks on this shithole planet hiding out in his ship or not. Fuck that dude."

They ascended the stairs. Red Tie said, "You just don't like Ganipgonads is all. You're still pissed about the time he took that Draconian whore from you in that nasty titty bar out by sector three. Her stage name was Pig Pen, right? That name? She earned that shit."

"She wasn't no whore, man!"

"Sure."

"Can we just stick to the task at hand, please?" Blue Tie said. "Can we do that for once?"

"Yeah. You're probably right. I mean, I wouldn't want to be reminded of some rookie stealing my ugly bar bitch either."

"Dude!"

At the top of the stairs, they started down the corridor toward Switchblade's unit.

A janitor looked up from mopping the floor as they approached. "Evening, fellas. Got a pass to be up in here?"

Blue Tie casually waved his hand. The janitor passed out and fell onto his bucket. The water spilled, but the two men stepped over him and kept walking.

"Hey," Blue Tie said. "Been meaning to ask. What makes you so sure that this is gonna be the one? You've picked the wrong dog for this race before, you know?"

"I know, man. Fuck can you do? Happens. But this one here just has that certain *something*. It's a rare combination. Trust me. I've learned a few things in my line of work over the years."

"Rare combination, huh? Whatever you say. My money's with yours. All right. Let's do this."

They entered the unit, walked through the dayroom, and passed the sleeping guard. *The Benny Hill Show* played on the unit's TV.

"I love the theme song from that show," Red Tie said. "They used that shit in the big chase scene from that last Scott Michaels movie. Seen it?"

"Nah. Fuck his films. How's that new ship treating you? Gordagoo told me you got that new THX-5723B."

"No. Not the THX-5723B. Got the A. Fuck the B. That B is shit."

"The A, huh?"

"Yeah. In blue."

"Light or dark?"

"Midnight. Gabbadobba-Delly painted it for me just the other day. Special."

"Nice."

"Very. A straight-up pussy magnet."

They stopped at Switchblade's cell.

"Here we are," Red Tie said. "Room 237."

"Yep. This is his, all right. Why do you suppose he scratched off the original number and wrote 237 on his door?"

"How the fuck am I supposed to know? Dude's weird, man."

Inside the cell, Switchblade was cuddled in bed like a baby, sleeping the night away as he lovingly sucked his thumb. "Oh, Terry," he mumbled in his sleep. "Don't lick me there. He-he. It tickles. More than Tom's mustache."

One right after the other, the locks turned from the other side of the steel door. It slowly creaked open.

The men stepped in and cast long, creepy shadows on the wall.

Switchblade came to. He wiped the sleep from his eyes, looked up, and said, "Who the fuck you supposed to be?"

Blue Tie opened his medical bag, which began to shine a bright-green glow upon his sinister face. He pulled out an antique syringe with an eight-inch needle that was filled with a batch of the glowing serum.

Switchblade smiled at the green light.

"Last shot, huh?" he asked. "Let's rock 'n' roll."

Blue Tie held up the syringe. "Yes, Frank. Let's."

Switchblade jumped out of bed and yanked his pants down, exposing himself with no shame. On his right butt cheek, there was a tattoo of a heart ripped in two. In the heart's gap, it read: "And Life Taker."

Blue Tie stepped forward, plunged the syringe deep, and the tattooed butt jiggled. The plunger slowly pushed the green substance deep into him.

Switchblade felt the sudden rush and yelled like Rick Flair. "Woo! That's the shit, right there!"

The Next Day

Dr. Roberts continued to brief the Wrecker Boys at the ambush site. "It has apparently enhanced his healing factor by fifty."

"What the hell does that mean?" Earl asked. "We speak English around here, Doc."

"It means he's a goddamn super soldier," Bud said. "I've dealt with these in Nam. Very hard to take out."

Dr. Roberts said, "It means he heals fast. You could stab Frank in the chest, and he would heal fast. Shoot him in the leg, and he'd heal fast. You could run him over with a Mack truck, and he would still—"

"Lemme guess," Earl said. "Heal fast?"

"You guessed right."

"Wasn't a guess, Bob."

"The only way to take Frank out at this point would appear to be a head shot, but you didn't hear that from me. I'm telling you though—you better not miss."

"All this healing stuff makes him some kinda live wire. Well, tell me something, Doc. Does this asshole have some kinda kryptonite or carbonite or some shit?"

"I haven't found a weakness, and I've been through the whole file twice. Very bizarre stuff going on here."

"Well, find something, Doc, and get back to us. Anything else?"

"Just, good luck. May God be with you on your mission."

"Yeah yeah yeah. Thanks, Sphincter Rob." Earl put the CB back and giggled at his own little joke. "Huh-huh. Butthole Bobby."

Bud didn't get it.

Earl leaned back and shook his head. "Jesus H. Christ, Wrecker One. Can you believe this Mickey Mouse rat shit? Who the hell believes in UFOs, aliens, and shit like that? What the fuck's next? Goddamn tooth fairy gonna show up with a flamethrower? Good God Almighty."

Bud looked to the sky. "I believe Earl. I do."

Lester shouted, "Get ready, y'all! I see him coming!"

The three men cocked everything they had.

Bud held up the ninja star with the picture of the ninja on it, ready to throw.

And here we go.

Five Minutes Later

The wrecker was smashed to smithereens.

Bud had crashed through the windshield and was dead across the hood. Half his arm was missing. His stump bled down the truck's side and puddled in the dirt.

The hot rod was flipped over, riddled with bullet holes, and various patches of woods were on fire.

Earl and Lester were unconscious in a pile of brush. They began to come to, shook their heads, and looked at the remains of a smoking battlefield.

Switchblade was nowhere in sight.

"Uh. What happened?" Lester rubbed his noggin.

Earl sat up. The bottom of his shirt had a big hole that revealed his Lynyrd Skynyrd tattoo, which was arched over his belly button. (It was reminiscent of Tupac's "Thug Life" tattoo, which Earl would accuse the rapper of stealing in the years to come. Earl had it first. This is documentation of that.) Earl looked at Lester and smiled. "I distracted him with an instant-no-fire-ninja smoke bomb, and Bud boom-sticked his ass. I told ya I was gonna kick this guy's ass, didn't I?"

"Where's Bud?"

Earl knew the answer. He tapped Lester's shoulder and pointed.

Lester saw Bud's corpse and gasped. He struggled to hold back the tears. It was a sad moment for the Boone clan. Bud was a self-disowned member of the Boones, but that didn't matter to Lester.

Earl put a caring hand on his shoulder. "Sorry, buddy. He knew the risk, and he took it. He was a brave man, Lester. We needed him. Rockwood needed him. He was a man of high honor."

"He sure was. Thanks, Earl."

"Hey. No problem, buddy." Earl thumbs-upped him.

The two climbed out of the brush and made their way to the wrecker. They reached the bloody wreckage.

Lester put his head down in sorrow. This could very well have been his fault, and he knew it. Deep down, he also knew that men like Bud were meant to die on a battlefield—not of old age in a trailer. If he wanted to go out in a blaze of ass-kicking glory, then he definitely got his wish. Lester said, "Sorry, Bud."

"Uh-huh." Earl looked up from picking lint out of his belly button. "Me too."

Lester took Bud's bandana from his head. It would be an honor to wear his colors. He put them on his own dome and tied it in the back.

Earl smiled and nodded with approval. "That looks really cool on ya, buddy."

Lester popped a scrawny salute that was nowhere close to looking right by military standards. "Cousin Bud. We salute you."

"Yep." Earl cut a half-assed salute. "Me too. Let's go, Lester. I'm getting hungry." He reached in his torn breast pocket and pulled out a matchstick. "Shit. I did have a match this whole goddamn time. Damn it to hell. I could have used this shit."

"Just like *Cobra*?" Lester said.

"Nah, Lester. I don't copy the shit I see in movies like you. Don't be such a fucking geek."

Earl popped the matchstick in his mouth, and they walked toward the sunset. It was finally time to go home.

"Earl?"

"Yeah?"

"Why didn't we just call for outside help when this whole thing started?"

"We handle our own shit in Rockwood. Remember that shit, Lester P. Boone."

"Oh. Okay. Well, how far do ya think it is back into town? My foot kinda hurts."

"Damned if I know. I do know one thing though."

"What's that, partner?"

"Frank Butz is lucky."

"Lucky?"

"*Damn* lucky, son. That asshole's lucky I didn't—"

A loud scream startled them. Switchblade jumped from the highest of the trees and came down like a crazy, greased-out meteor, yelling the whole way down.

Lester screamed like a girl, and Earl shoved him out of the way.

Switchblade landed, moonwalking on impact to the drumbeat of "Billie Jean." "Boota-bah-tah. Boota-bah-tah. Who. Who. Whooo. Who. Hee-hee!"

Half his face was burnt to a crisp, and chunks of hair were missing, exposing burnt flesh and skull. Two ninja stars were stuck to the side of his head, and his coat was charred and smoking like he had jumped on a grenade. He continued moonwalking in a circle.

"What the shit?" Earl said.

Switchblade dropped into the splits, popped back up, and ditty-bopped towards them. "You dumb motherfuckers. You didn't think you was gonna get away with that shit, did you?"

Lester hid behind Earl and shook.

"Didn't I blow you up?" Earl shielded Lester.

"You did." Switchblade popped what was left of his collar. "Kinda hurt."

Earl tried his best to look tough.

Switchblade called him on it. "Huh-huh. Why you look so scared, Earl? I thought you said when you caught me you were going to … what was that? Kick my ass?"

Earl gulped.

"Talking shit like you some tough guy or some shit. You tough, Earl? You think you John Wayne with that shit?"

"Got a problem with John Wayne, you skinny little shit?"

"Nothing—except for the fact that he was a shitty-ass actor."

"Now you wait just a goddamn minute, Hoss," Earl said.

"Woo-wee! Look at 'em get mad. You boys don't like me talking shit about the Duke, do you? Fuck that pussy. I'd make him suck my blade while I ate me some fried chicken." Switchblade put his blade to his crotch, pushed the release button, and the blade popped out, making him fully erect. He grabbed an imaginary John Wayne's head and slowly began humping the air while he ate his invisible piece of chicken. "Mmmm-mm. Oh, Johnny. Easy now, girl. You're gonna make me come too fast. Slow down a little bit, baby. Lemme finish my chicken first."

Earl pushed out his chest and took a couple of fearless steps forward.

Lester remained glued to him, shaking like a cold, shitting dog.

"Now, looka here, you sorry-ass motherfucker," Earl said. "You better watch that shit. I'm telling you right now. Don't even go there. You don't want this."

"I find it cute how you rednecks love that guy. Like a little man crush. It's cute. A little gay but cute."

The accusations were not true. A crush? Earl flushed red.

"That make you mad, Earl? Huh? He plays the same character in every fucking movie he's in. Am I right? Well, am I?"

Earl stomped his foot like an angry child. "No, he doesn't!"

"No range. Not a lick."

Earl had heard enough of this mess. It was the straw that broke the camel's back. *Maybe* a few things in the past could have been forgiven—but not this. His voice remained steady and calm. "I think I'm done hearing just about all Imma gonna hear out of you about John Wayne. Come on, you greasy bitch." He drew a line in the dirt with his foot. "Let's get it on."

Switchblade snapped his fingers. The boom box came to life and blasted funk music that sounded like something out of a Blaxploitation movie. *Shaft* perhaps?

The boys began to circle and size each other up to the sputtering, electric funk guitar.

Woooonk-tikah-wonk-tih-wooooonk-wonk-tih-wonk!

Switchblade loved this kind of shit. He smiled.

Lester continued to shake.

Earl spit and wiped his mouth. He was ready to die for John Wayne's honor. Damn straight.

They continued to circle until the tension reached its peak. The boom box's batteries finally drained out, and the tape slowed to a crawl and died.

The men stopped. The scene was as silent as a spaghetti western—minus the tumbleweed—and both men were ready to draw. Tension filled the air. The wind whistled through the trees. A vulture screamed in the background.

... Draw!

Before Earl could make a move for his nunchucks, the switchblade found its way into the forehead of Lester. It pierced his brain, and he fell into Earl's arms, making them both fall to the ground.

"Lester?" Earl shook him. "Wake up, little buddy. It's time to go. I'll let *you* drive this time. How about that? Lester?" Earl looked up to the sky and cried, "Lester!" A single tear slid down his chubby cheek.

Earl began to reminisce about happier times with his little buddy. Memories played out in his head like a sappy movie montage—complete with soft, corny music, as they ran through a field of flowers toward each other in a romantic slow motion with their arms out. Earl remembered that day well. It was a Sunday, and it was the best. The image faded, and Earl came back to reality.

Switchblade was pissing on one of Maura's tires and looked over his shoulder. "Are you about done over there with that touching shit or what?" He zipped his fly with a hop and ditty-bopped back over to Earl. "What was you over here doing? Flashing back like you was in some shitty-ass movie montage or some shit?"

"Boy." Earl looked down at Lester. "You have no idea how bad you just butt-fucked yourself." He set Lester aside and stood. He gripped the nunchucks, leaned to the side like a gunslinger, and began to twirl them slow and sloppy.

Switchblade chuckled. "What a 'tard."

The chucks began to pick up speed. Within seconds, they were a full-on blur of motion. Earl quickly proved his worth and brought them up with lightning-fast speed, and began busting moves like Bruce Lee's little brother.

The chucks cut the air.

Shu-shu-shu-whomp-whomp-whomp-feshh!

Earl had owned kid-friendly, safety-foam nunchucks for some time. He won them at the Pascagoula Fair when he guessed his weight. He'd been practicing in the mirror every day since. Waste of time? I think not. He continued his onslaught of awesome skill.

Shu-shi-shi-whomp-whosh-whomp-feshh!

Switchblade shrugged, casually pulled out a ninja star from his head and threw it at Earl.

Earl swung and deflected the deadly star right back.

Switchblade jumped out of the way and dodged it just in time. "How'd you do that shit? Can you teach me?"

Earl continued to swing and made fight sounds with each move like a kung fu master. "Pit-ahh! Pit-ahh! He! Ha! Ho! Pit-ahh!" He finished with a backhand grab. "Wut-ahhh!"

"Oh. I fucking dig you." Switchblade said.

"Dig *this* you butt-coated, dick-lick sumbitch."

Ding!

The two charged. Fists began to fly in rapid displays of Switchblade's speed and Earl's power. The men wailed into each other without a shred of mercy. Knuckles broke on faces. Bloody snot flew.

Earl started to gain the upper hand—just like he knew he would. Going all out like the yellow belt karate student he knew he could be someday; he began delivering a series of vicious uppercuts to Switchblade's jaw that sent him completely airborne.

Switchblade landed on his feet each time like a character from *Street Fighter*. Earl decided to take it toe to toe. He could take it. With only inches between them, both warriors quickly saw an opening for an uppercut and went for it.

Earl thought about how cool it was that it resembled the end of *Rocky III* when they freeze-framed on Apollo and Rocky—and it turned into a painting. He'd love for that here, but this was reality. Since he wasted time thinking about *Rocky III*, and how he wanted a new painting, his concentration slipped. He caught a knuckle sandwich that cracked his nose. He grabbed his nose, kneeled, and held up his hand.

The fighting ceased.

Earl tasted his blood as it oozed out of his nostrils.

Switchblade laughed. "Huh-huh. Look atcha. How's it taste?" He grabbed the crotch of his war-torn jeans and began mimicking ghetto talk. "Whatcha gotta say now? Recognize, you weekend, volunteer wannabe cop."

"What the fuck did you just call me? A wanna what?" Earl went completely apeshit and attacked the maniac. He named John Wayne classics with each damage-inducing blow. "*McLintock!*" *Pow!*

Switchblade stepped back in pain. "Fuck," he rubbed his ear. "Fuck you do that for?"

"*Rio Bravo!*" Earl swung the nunchucks and cracked skull.

With his skull seeping fluids, Switchblade had to think fast. This was starting to look bad. *What if somebody is watching? I got it!* "What's that?" He pointed to the sky.

When Earl looked up, Switchblade delivered a kick to his balls.

Earl grabbed his empty sack and choked. "You dirty-fighting motherfucker. Okay. *True Grit!*" He released his empty sack and delivered a lightning-fast, Shaolin finger jab to Switchblade's throat and completely smashed his Adam's apple.

Switchblade stumbled back, gasped for air, and turned blue.

"And *The Cowboys.*" Earl jumped into a karate stance. "Fuck Bruce Dern—and mother fuck you." Earl charged and screamed his rebel yell.

He leaped into the air with crazy hang-time and delivered a Chuck Norris-style kick into Switchblade's chest, completely knocking the wind out of him and sending him back twenty feet.

Switchblade finally had it. He exhaled, collapsed, and hit the ground.

Earl stared down at his mortal enemy. His very own Joker to his Batman, so to speak, was unconscious on the ground, hopefully dead and done with. *I did it. Hot damn. I did it. Maybe I'll get me that special VFW celebration in honor of me after all. If only I had some friends to invite. Oh, well.* Earl turned and began to walk away.

Unbeknownst to Earl, Switchblade's face began to heal, mushing and squishing around as if he were a T-1000 Terminator. New strands of hair sprouted from the missing chunks. Within moments, he was completely healed and looked better than ever. He looked to the sky.

"Earl," he called mockingly.

Earl stopped dead in his tracks and turned just in time to see Switchblade leap to his feet in one swift motion.

"We're not done yet," Switchblade said. "One more round, Tubb."

Earl's jaw dropped. *How in the hell is this man still standing? His face looked like pounded ground meat not ten seconds ago. This man can't be real. He's tougher than that Russian guy from* Rocky IV *for Christ's sake. Probably on the steroids. Must be why his face healed so fast.* Earl was ready as ever to die for a cause *and* John Wayne's honor. "Let's do this," he said.

The two got on their starting blocks.

Earl dug into the dirt like a man at bat and smiled. He put his hand out and rang an invisible bell. "Ding-ding ... sumbitch."

They rushed one another with everything they had.

Twenty Minutes Later

The temperature finally began to drop. The two warriors looked like a train had blasted into them at high speed.

Switchblade came to and sat up. Dazed and confused, he looked around and reached up to rub his broken nose. "Ow! Shit." His face was banged up even worse than before. He stood and began to dust himself off. He popped what was left of his collar and looked at Earl. "Maybe next time, Fat Chops."

He walked over to Lester, looked down, and smiled. His face began to heal itself even more rapidly than before. Within seconds, he was as striking as ever. That's what *he* thought, anyway. He kneeled down, pulled his blade out of Lester's forehead, and wiped the blood on the leg of his battered jeans. "You too, little fella."

He walked over to the hot rod and inspected its damage. It looked bad. He shrugged, reached underneath, and then flipped the car over with ease. It slammed to the ground. He jumped in, fired it up, and drove off to his next adventure.

Left for dead, one of Earl's fingers began to twitch and wiggle back to life—and then it stopped.

The Next Morning
Earl began to regain consciousness in some sort of weird scientific lab. He looked around the room as lab assistants in white coats worked on Serum 13B and filled test tubes with the glowing green stuff. All around the room, cheesy 1980s computer boards blinked off and on.

Earl looked down at a government-style emblem in the center of the tile floor: Section 8 Universal Division. Its mascot was a yellow jacket, poised and ready to sting.

A man in a suit appeared, walked up to Earl, and said, "Now that you've come to, I need to brief you on our current situation. Things are about to get worse. Much worse."

"Where is he? Where is Frank Butz?"

"Escaped. Earl, I'm afraid I have some bad news for you. You've lost your left arm."

"Shit no. Imma goddamn lefty."

"Not to worry. Your arm has been replaced with one of our new Hydraulic 3000 Grip Plus models. I think you will be quite pleased with it."

"*Hymph.*"

"Earl Tubb, you have been recruited into Section 8. We work under—and for—a secret society that does not exist. The governments of the world are even unaware of our existence. We've come here because it is our job to stop these *outsiders* and their sick ways. I won't go into why they do what they do because it's not important. What *is* important is that this needs to stop."

A lab assistant in safety goggles walked up behind the man and held up a syringe of the green substance with an extra-long needle.

"Are you ready for your mission, *Agent* Earl Tubb?"

"A new hydraulic 3000 Grip Plus model?" Earl asked. "For squeezing?"

"Yes. For squeezing."

Everyone in the room stopped what they were doing and turned to Earl. He slowly raised his robotic hand for close inspection. The sounds of the robotics in it filled the room as Earl closed it into a slow, vengeful fist.

"I will crush this man's nuts and eat 'em for lunch. You can gauran-goddamn-tee that shit."

THE END

RAZORBACK BILL

BOOK TWO

THIS IS A TRUE STORY

The events in this book took place in Rockwood, Mississippi in 1984. At the request of those still living, the names have been changed for confidentiality.

This is how it all went down...

Chapter One
THE RECRUITMENT OF A MADMAN

"I gots me this problem, you see? I hate when some stupid-ass sumbitch gets in my way, and that is *exactly* what you did, boy." The paneled office was dark, and the man's name was Razorback Bill Nedick, the most feared man in town. He sat behind his desk with his cowboy boots propped high and sported a slimy smile across his fat, pinkish face. On the wall behind him hung a stuffed razorback pig's head with large smoke-stained tusks—ready to gouge anyone that dared to back into them.

He took his boots down, leaned into the light, then interlocked his fingers on the desktop like a redneck Godfather. "You shoulda just told me what I wanted to know, you dumb sumbitch. First dumb sumbitch I ever had to deal with here, I shoved his sorry ass into an oven. I know you probably done heard about the shit. Cooked his sorry ass at four hundred degrees Fahrenheit for about two hours. Sat there and watched that bullshit too, boy. *All* of it."

Razorback stood, pulled out a vial of cocaine from his pocket, and took a big hit up the nose. "Guess I'll just go ahead and wrap this shit up by saying the biggest regret Imma have with you, boy, is not putting down some plastic before this here pop."

Pow!

The man's brains sprayed all over the desk as the sound of a .45 Automatic reverberated through the tiny office. The victim hit the desk and tumbled to the shag carpet with a thud.

Billy Ray, black as midnight with a dripping Jheri curl, purple Chuck Taylor sneakers, one eye stuck on crooked, and stone-washed jeans (tight-rolled extra-tight), stepped from the darkness with a smoking .45 in hand. His gold tooth matched the chain around his neck that would have made Mr. T envious. "Bitch-ass motherfucker," he shouted before popping off two more shots. *Pop! Pop!* "Punk-ass, bitch! Eat a fat baby's dick, you trick-ass nigga!"

Razorback picked up the blood-spattered cowboy hat from the desk, placed it on his head, smiled big and proud at Billy Ray, and said, "Feed his stupid ass to the hogs."

*

Sheriff Jack Bigelow sat behind his desk with a look of stress and worry all over his tired, middle-aged face. The Mississippi summer heat was in full-swing, and his portable fan conked out on him hours ago making the office even more miserable than one could imagine. He began rocking in his chair in dismay when there came a knock at the door. "Go the fuck away!"

Another knock.

"What, goddamn it?"

The door opened and in walked Deputy Alan Wayne, the Sheriff's clean-cut deputy. "Morning, Sheriff," he said with his ever-present, optimistic, Boy Scout smile. "Brought you in some coffee just the way you like it. Two creams, right?" He carefully put the steamy cup of joe on the desk.

Sheriff Bigelow looked up with tired eyes. "Coffee, huh? You wouldn't happen to have a solution to our little problem in that cup of joe, would you?"

"I don't think so, Sheriff. I saw Peggy pour it herself, and she didn't put anything like that in it. She sure does make great coffee, huh?"

Sheriff Bigelow opened his drawer, whipped out a metal flask, unscrewed the cap, and began to top off his cup with added whiskey. "When we get done here," he said as the whiskey splashed in, "I want you to go out there and snatch me up a fucking fan that works."

"Sure thing, Sheriff. Shoot, you can have mine!"

The sheriff leaned back in his chair, exhaled hard, then took a swig of his special blend of joe.

"Something wrong, Sheriff? What's gotcha so creased this morning?"

The sheriff exhaled with whiskey-hot breath. "Bill Nedick and that little band of butt-buddy bastards. That's *what*. Where the fuck you been, Alan Wayne? Out fucking sheep?"

"I don't know about that one, Sheriff. Everybody in town been scared of that fella since the day he arrived. Billy Ray been getting pretty bad too. If I see *him* coming, I'll cross the street just to avoid him."

"Yeah. You and everyone else. That Billy Ray sure is one mean-ass, unstable motherfucker, boy. Shit."

"Shoot, heard just last week that he made Karl down at the pool hall poop his pants in front of some girls."

The sheriff nodded. "... See what I mean? I never shoulda taken this job after Sheriff Wallace up and got killed by that lunatic greaser last summer. Been nothing but bloodshed and mayhem ever since. Not a goddamn lick of order can be had in this shithole."

"Not with all the corruption going on. Shoot. Ain't an honest cop left standing but a few of us. Last night I was watching this movie about a small-town Sheriff that—"

"I ain't talking corruption here," the sheriff interrupted. He poured in more whiskey, sipped, then changed the subject. "I'm more concerned with the crazy rumors floating around all the goddamn time about strange happenings. Got me a little spooked, to be honest. This town is like some kinda southern *Twilight Zone* episode gone to shit. It's to the point, all I care about is me and my own. Fuck the rest. I should just take my daughter, and my happy ass, back to Sparta and be done with it all."

With a finger to the chin, Deputy Alan Wayne dwelled for a moment. He wanted to help. He was a fixer-upper-type individual and a lawman through and through. Seeing the sheriff start to lose sight of their oath to uphold law and order, he dug deep and raised a finger. "I have a suggestion, Sheriff. And it's a good one *this* time. May I?"

The sheriff grunted with, "What is it?"

"What the people of Rockwood needs now—more than ever—is someone to look up to. We need a *real* hero. Maybe we can put in a request for one of them Super Cops."

"Fuck is a goddamn Super Cop?"

"You know," Alan Wayne beamed. "Like on television! Like our very own Dirty Harry. Someone who plays by their own set of rules and won't turn on his fellow man just for a little protection. Someone fearless. It'd be great if we could hire Chuck Norris for a week. Bet he wouldn't take any of Bill's crap. Uh-uh, no way. Maybe we can hire the Cobra! You see the new *Cobra* movie, Sheriff?"

"Nah," the sheriff said, not really listening. "I don't watch movies about fucking snakes, Alan Wayne." The sheriff stood, finished his coffee off with a gulp, unscrewed the flask, then poured a double. "I'll tell you what, Deputy. You do me a favor. I want you to take your ever-so-eager-to-please-me ass out there and get me this *Cobra* cop you speak of. Salary? Sky's the limit! You see him, hire his snake ass on the spot. Hell, he can have my fucking salary while we're at it. You do this for me. Go grab me one cobra, two turtles, John Wayne, Dirty Harry's little brother, and a fucking fan that works. Oh! And while you're at it, get me a realistic solution to our goddamn problem!"

With his head down, Alan Wayne exited.

"And shut my fucking door!"

Almost teary-eyed, Alan Wayne shut the door.

Sheriff Bigelow took a hit straight from the flask and belched. "Super cops. *Pfft.* Who the hell ever heard of such stupid-ass horseshit?"

*

He was a man on a mission and had a mullet built for rocking. His name was Chuck Thunders.

Sporting his best *Top Gun* aviator shades, Chuck Thunders bombed down the desolate highway in a black 1974 Plymouth Duster—which looked as if it had seen a few battles but somehow survived. Dusty, dented, and bent, the hot rod burned up the road as "Feel the Heat" from the *Cobra* soundtrack blasted from the massive boombox in the back seat, filling the highway with the sounds of one mean-ass engine and hero music maxed out. Down in the passenger seat was a badge, a pile of cassettes, and a plastic *A-Team* lunch box a grade-school kid would use.

With eyes dead-ahead, he dug around inside his black fanny pack (with the hot pink trim), removed a matchstick, placed it in his mouth, and using his tongue, began tossing it back and forth with much attitude. He looked into the rear-view mirror and nodded at his awesome reflection. It nodded right back in approval.

He hit the on-coming exit hard, skidding the whole way through and showing the world this driver was either insane or had mad-driving skills. The car finally grabbed the hot pavement and hauled ass straight for Rockwood, Mississippi, population: ninety-five. He passed by a sign that read

WELCOME TO
ROCKWOOD MISSISSIPPI
WE DON'T WANT YOU HERE

Unafraid of course, Chuck pressed on.

Suddenly and without fair warning, "No Easy Way Out" from the *Rocky IV* soundtrack exploded from the boom box, and Chuck got amped. The car accelerated with ease.

The tape's chorus hit, Chuck gripped the wheel and sang with total conviction, "There's no easy way out! There's no short-cut home!" He settled back in his seat and nodded in agreement to the lyrics.

Up ahead, a sexy southern belle walked the side of the road with an empty gas can in hand. Her name was Bobby Beggs. She spelled it like a man, but she was all woman to Chuck Thunders. The red cowboy boots and cut-off jean shorts she wore to help rock that strut of hers were just what the doctor ordered; it drove Chuck wild with all her small-town sexiness. As he slowed down on the approach, he just flat-out couldn't wait to bang her, and he knew there wasn't any way she could deny some Chuck love. He was the man. How could she resist? He pulled alongside her with the engine in rumble mode and stopped.

The sweaty southern belle paused to get a look at the greatness. She walked up and leaned in the passenger window. "Hey, baby," she smiled. "Are those Bugle Boy jeans that you're wearing?"

"Why, yes." Chuck admitted in his low and gravely tough-guy tone. "Yes, they are Bugle Boy jeans."

Struck down by the bad-boy with a badge, the sweaty southern belle threw the empty gas can to the ground, opened the door, hopped in with a sexy slide across the hot seat, and slammed the door.

Chuck hit the gas and sent them into a lover's spin as The New Kids on the Block's "Hangin' Tough" roared from the boombox. Was she impressed? Yes! This just so happened to be her new favorite song. They came out of the spin and shot off like a rocket.

"I really like your car," she yelled over the music. "Rocking tunes too!"

Chuck didn't respond. The strong, silent types drove the bitches crazy, so that's what he gave her. She asked if she could take her boots off and get comfortable and before he could answer they were off, and Chuck immediately noticed the smell of her sweaty feet. As soon as the scent hit his nostrils, it pierced his brain and soul and a little pre-cum came out the tip of his penis. He tried his best to shake it off.

"Name's Chuck Thunders, baby," he said, adjusting his crotch like a kid in class hoping she wouldn't notice. "Imma badass that doesn't exist on a secret mission of epic proportions, and I have yet to lose."

"Wow," Bobby beamed. "That is so neat! I'm starting to get a little wet in my panties from your testosterone levels. I can't help it. I hope that doesn't embarrass you or make your car smell funny."

"Of course, you're getting wet. I didn't wake up today to be average, baby."

"Can I help? What can I do?"

"You? You don't do shit but look hot so everybody can see that I got it like that. Know your role."

"There's more to me than just being hot ... but I thought you'd never ask." She leaned over and began to playfully tug his ear. "Chuck, baby. I have something I want to confess to you about me. Are you listening?"

"Not really."

"I have finally decided to do something about my life and my virginity ... and it's you. You are the shit, and I only want to be with you. I'm not good for anyone else in this crazy town. C'mon, baby. Come with me and let's ignore this world *together*."

*

After dropping Bobby off at the salon to get her toes done for him, Chuck Thunders entered Rockwood's town square fast, hit the sheriff station's lot hard, then skidded with precision into the nearest parking space.

He tapped the gas. *VRooOOOM!*

Old people walked by and shook their heads at the idiot who kept revving his engine. He hit the gas one last time just for them. *VRooOOOM!*

He exited the car, slammed the door, then adjusted his fanny pack to the front.

The locals eyeballed the stranger.

Chuck made a right-face and strutted for the station. He reached the station's doors, roundhouse kicked them open, and strutted inside. He passed the lobby of cops, compared himself to all of them, and continued towards the Sheriff's door, ignoring the shouts of the secretary. "You can't just go in there. Hey!"

He kicked in the door like he owned it and scared the hell out of Sheriff Bigelow on the other side, causing him to drop his flask onto his desk and spill whiskey.

Chuck slammed the door and announced with pride, "Chuck Thunders reporting for goddamn duty!"

"Goddamn it, boy," the sheriff said holding his near heart-attack chest. "You scared the living shit outta me."

"I tend to do that to people."

"Well, now that *that's* established, I don't recall putting in any requests for an Italian Stallion such as yourself, so, just who the fuck you supposed to be and why you kicking doors in my station?"

"I'm here on special assignment. I hear you have some garbage needs taken out. That's where Chuck Thunders comes in. I take out the garbage. You like my mullet?"

"Who sent you? Couldn't have been the mayor. Mayor Bradley ain't good for shit but helping Mayor Bradley."

"I can't say. I'm in renegade, top-secret, undercover mode. Besides, none of my superiors even know about me *or* my existence. I'm *that* legit." Chuck stepped to the desk with determination. "Now, what I need from you, Sheriff Jack Bigelow, is cooperation. I got this shit from here on out. Understand? Now, if you can somehow muster up enough energy to lift that lazy-ass, drunk finger of yours to help, then use that booger-picking son of a bitch to point me in the right direction."

"Well, I need to know where you wanna go first. I can't just guess. You said something about taking out the garbage. Applications for trash pick-up are at city hall, son."

"Bill, you dumb fucking hick! Goddamn Razorback Bill Nedick. You know? The man you're too much of a pussy to arrest with all his flagrant bullshit and wrong doings. What the fuck is wrong with you? The entire town knows this man. You retarded?" Chuck calmly put his hands on the desk, got uncomfortably close, and stared dead into Sheriff Bigelow's eyes. "North?" he said scary and low. "I bet he's hiding up north, ain't he?"

"What smells like feet?"

"That sneaky-ass motherfucker." Chuck slammed his fist on the desk and stepped back. "Or south, perhaps? Just point me to where this cocksucker's at. That's all I need out of your ass. Point ... now!"

And against his better judgement, the half-drunk Sheriff Bigelow assisted the crazy man before him, and he had no idea why. It just came out. "East end of town. Couple miles past Cutty's Garage. Find Cutty's and just keep heading east on Brokeback road."

Chuck quickly about-faced. "I can't wait to punch this faggot right in the face." He strutted out and slammed the door so hard its glass shattered to the floor.

"You broke my goddamn door!" Sheriff Bigelow yelled.

Surrounded by broken glass, Chuck ignored his own awesomeness and scanned the crowd for a partner to roll with. Standing around was a small group of officers, cutting up and wasting taxpayer money.

Rodney Tibbs, the only black man in the station, stood in the center of attention and entertained his fellow officers with a tale from last night's sexcapade. He carried on loudly with, "So, then I told that stupid-ass bitch another thing. I said, 'Bitch, you gotta be shitting me. You think Imma be kissing you after I just blew my load all up in your mouth?' Fuck that shit. I mean, it was still dripping off her lips, man! I likes to kiss on me a white girl and shit, but I gots limits, man."

The fellas burst out laughing *hard*. "Oh, Rodney," one managed. "You and your pussy stories. You slay the shit outta me."

"I know, right?" Rodney smiled. "So, anyway. So, then I told that bitch. I said, 'Bitch, you best go gargle with some motherfucking hot lava.'"

The officers burst out laughing even harder, slapping each other on the back and pointing as tears streamed down their faces. This was the funniest shit they've heard all week.

Rodney continued. "I'm right, right? Lava. Hot ... motherfucking ... molten-ass ... lava. *Shiiieet*."

Chuck Thunders had found his man! He walked up and stared at the back of Rodney's afro to get better acquainted.

The group settled down to get a look at this Chuck Thunders character.

Rodney turned from his fellow officers to see for himself the Super Cop in the building. He looked Chuck over head to toe. "'Sup, man?" he smiled. "Like that fanny pack you got."

"Just heard the tail end of your story. You're funny as shit, bro, and I like your style. You down to go kick some ass today?"

Rodney cocked his head with that smile of his, but Chuck remained stone. He was obviously crazy as shit, but damn it if Rodney didn't get a kick out of him already. He looked over Chuck's shoulder and hollered, "Sheriff B!"

"What?" Sheriff Bigelow shouted through the hole in his door.

"You mind if I roll with this dude?"

"Sure! Just get the fuck out of here and leave me alone! And the rest of you assholes get to work! You're not getting paid to stand around and listen to stories about Rodney's goddamn cock all morning! Now move!"

With a few snickers aside, the men dispersed.

Left alone, Rodney continued to stare at the stone-faced man. He decided to take the odd moment to peep his reflection in Chuck's mirror shades and gently patted his afro to make it look all nice and round, and said, "Alright, let's do this."

The two men turned to leave.

"Wait," Rodney halted him. "What is it we's about to do *exactly*?"

Chuck turned to Rodney, and for the first time in months allowed a slight grin, and said, "Our fucking jobs."

*

The Pig Pen was this nasty, little, shit-hole strip club secluded on the swampy outskirts of town. It was just one of Razorback Bill's many hang outs but definitely his favorite. A bright neon sign read

THE PIG PEN
CUM MAKE SOME BACON
OPEN ON SUNDAYS

In the dirt/gravel lot sat a boat-sized, purple Cadillac with a pig hood ornament, a kick-ass, yellow Trans Am with blood splatter across its hood, and a blue van with flames going down its sides hot-rod style.

Inside The Pen, Poison's "Nothin' But a Good Time" blasted as a trailer-trashed woman in her early twenties stripped on stage in a pill-induced slumber. In the audience, and with Billy Ray standing by his side, Razorback sat alone and feasted on a large order of baby back ribs with one of every side imaginable—two of the beans. The bib around his neck had a cartoon depiction of two pigs fucking, and he had yet to wipe his mouth, which was smeared in his very own brand of spiked barbecue sauce that he would sell to the Rockwood elite, made straight from the blood of his enemies.

The girl on stage continued her dance, smiling her missing-tooth grin but not getting Razorback's attention in the least.

Billy Ray glanced over and noticed the Kael Boys standing by the entrance. Meryl and Gay-Bob Kael: a large and small father/son version of the same man, in their so-called nice suits, large cowboy hats and matching from head to toe except for little Gay-Bob's Colonel Sanders mustache. Rumor was the two were used as inspiration for the Enos Boys in *Smokey and the Bandit,* but they have denied this.

Next to the Kael Boys and ready to smash at a moment's notice was the flannel wearing, six-foot something, beard-rocking bouncer, Rough House—who did just that, he bounced people. And he loved it. Anything for Razorback Bill. With his arms crossed across his chest, he hatefully eyeballed the Kaels who wouldn't even look his way, but with Rough House's reputation, who could blame them? Little Gay-Bob gulped instead.

"Hey, Boss," Billy Ray leaned over. "Motherfucking Kael Boys at the door."

Razorback didn't even bother to look. Instead, he shoveled beans into his mouth and gobbled. "Send 'em over."

Billy Ray motioned at Rough House.

Rough House tapped little Gay-Bob's shoulder and startled him. "You can go over now, you scared little bitch."

Despite the rude comment, the Kaels made their way over to Razorback's table as the music continued blasting about Bret Michaels need his good times.

Razorback slammed his hand on the table. "Turn that shit off!"

The stripper, with her feelings hurt, wobbled over to the jukebox, jerked the plug from the socket, and killed the tune instantly.

"Goddamn pussy-rock," Razorback shouted. "Who the fuck keeps putting this Agua Net, heart-break, faggot bullshit in my box? Chuck Berry'd be rolling over in his goddamn grave, and the fucking spook ain't even dead yet."

Side by side, the Kaels stepped in front of Razorback's table, and, in unison, adjusted their larger-than-life belt buckles.

"Ain't that right, Kael Boys?" Razorback looked up with a smile that wasn't returned. He snapped his fingers, and Billy Ray immediately took a parade rest in the shadows behind the Kaels, which made both of them *very* uncomfortable.

Meryl cleared his throat. "Sorry to interrupt your meal and all, Bill, but me and my boy got a few things I think we needs to discuss witcha immediately."

The Kaels had a seat.

Meryl took off his cowboy hat, revealing a horrible comb-over swirled on top of his head. He licked his hand and fixed his fake bangs with care.

Razorback showed impatience. "Well, make this shit quick, Meryl with a swirl. As you can see, you interrupting my shit."

Meryl flexed but with caution. "Okay, Bill. You want me to get right to the point? Fine. You been cutting into our bait and tackle business. *That's* what this bullshit's about. Plus, our homemade pocket pussies and dildo sales over at the Gas-N-Grab been taking a dive ever since you opened up that floating barge of pussy down on Belmont Creek. This goes directly against what was agreed upon with The Council when you came here to set up shop, and we never betray our own, Bill. Not on a money deal. I know that don't mean much to you, but it has always been our motto and our way of life. You should know that. It's what separates us from *them.* It's also how our kind have remained in power positions for so cotton-picking long. We live by a code, and you been shitting all over that goddamn shit lately." Meryl leaned back, stared daggers of disbelief and continued.

"Now the latest we been hearing around the campfire is you planning on sponsoring Stroker 'Poke Her Twice' Johnson in the monster truck rally ... and you know how much we hate that goddamn sumbitch! He ain't even one of us, for Christ's sakes. Now, I ain't one for starting no shit with my own kind, but you seem to be forcing me into a—"

"Don't be threatening me, Meryl." Razorback sat back and picked his teeth with his pinky finger that had an oversized, Mason ring squeezed onto it. "We ain't the same as you put it, despite blood, affiliations or species. So, do yourself a favor and stop waiting on me to act like it. Haven't you two dicks learned that about me yet? Blood don't mean shit to me, boy, even when it spills all over my fucking floor. It might be yours next if you don't start checking that false bravado of yours at the door, which *I will fucking smash.* I ain't nothing like you, or that little shit-clone you shoulda flushed twenty-five years ago."

"You low-life scum sumbitch!" Gay-Bob fumed out of his chair, his little-man complex taking over.

"Now look at whatcha done did, Bill," Meryl said holding Gay-Bob back with one hand. "Easy now, Gay-Bob. Easy."

"I can kick 'em low and climb high, Daddy!" Gay-Bob fumed. "Lemme show you! I'll wreck your goddamn ass, Bill!"

Razorback chuckled. "Look at 'em go. Adorable."

Billy Ray stepped in front of Meryl, and just inches from his face, stared with his one good eye, and said, "You best tell that little, Oompa Loompa-ass clone to back the fuck up before y'all mess around and I fuck both y'all niggas up."

Obliging the crooked-eyed gangster, Gay-Bob came to his senses and stopped his hissy fit. He popped his jacket straight, fixed his cowboy hat, proceeded to fix his mustache, and said, "Goddamn disloyal sumbitch," under his breath.

Meryl shook his head in disbelief. "I think The Council just might like to hear about all this defiant bullshit, if one were inclined to tell 'em."

Razorback, wiped his mouth with his bib. "Go ahead and tell 'em. Look, fellas. Imma just level witcha. Shit's changed. Me and The Council ... well ... we pretty goddamn tight, as in I done took the shit over, and quite frankly, I just can't stand y'all. You're never gonna make it to level thirteen with me around, so color yourselves fucked. And if you must know, *I'm* the reason you two don't get invited to our cookouts and washer tournaments anymore."

"That's bullshit!" Meryl said with his feelings hurt. "I'm the goddamn Rockwood washer champion of eighty-two. Why can't we play anymore?"

"Because. Y'all just a couple of side characters now, and this is *my* goddamn story. Just a couple chicken-shit minnows in *my* pond ... and I gots bigger fish to fry."

"*Your* pond?" Meryl asked insulted. "*Your* pond? You can't just come into Rockwood and knock us outta our own goddamn boats!"

"Yup. That's *exactly* what's happening. Hope you don't mind the change. Learn to swim, bitches."

Gay-Bob was in shock. "This goddamn sumbitch done lost his mind, Daddy."

Razorback's grin disappeared. He ripped off his bib, placed both hands on the table, and took command. "Now, you two are gonna take your sorry asses out to The Village, and you're gonna tell them stank-ass niggers that they can no longer buy jack shit without my say so. Not one pill, joint, or ounce of juice will be sold up in there, or to there, unless by me. I'm cutting you the fuck out."

"I knew it, Daddy!" Gay-Bob stomped. "Told you he was gonna try and ruin our bait and tackle shop! Where else we gonna operate out of? And we need that extra money from them rude nigger people who always laugh at me! We'll be ruined for sure! Shit on me!"

"Maybe later," Razorback said. "But that stupid-ass bait shop won't be standing much longer anyway. Not after what the fuck I'm about to do. And what I'm about to do ain't got shit to do with you two pecker-head sumbitches *or* any of your supplemental income issues. Not anymore. Your moonshine tastes like piss, your beer smells like someone farted in the shit, and the sex toys you sell are complete shit and break after one use. *I* know. Rockwood deserves better. That's us. What's going on here is *my* thing ... and *Billy Ray's* thing. We coming together like two chicks doing the scissors and ain't no pair of dicks like you gonna stop the grind. So, just shut the fuck up, sit your stupid *Smokey and the Bandit*-looking asses in the back seat, and let me drive. Before you fuck around and get slapped." Razorback picked up a rib, ripped the meat from its bone with his teeth, and chewed. "Damn it feels good to be a gangster."

*

Twisted Sister's "We're Not Gonna Take It" pumped from the boombox in the backseat as Chuck Thunders bobbed his head and pounded his fist on the steering wheel to the beat.

Oblivious to Chuck's reckless abandon for public safety, Rodney Tibbs sat in the passenger seat and casually sifted through cassettes. "What? You ain't got no Al Green tapes? Whatcha fuck to?" Rodney snatched a tape and held it up in disgust. "Debbie Gibson? Duh fuck is this bullshit?"

Rodney's look of disapproval stung. Chuck knew how important music was to black people. This could have very well put a dent in their relationship. He learned from his mistake, brushed it off, and said, "I think my little brother left that in here. I'm glad you came by the way. I knew it'd be cool as shit to have a black partner like in *Lethal Weapon* or *Samurai Cop*, and so far, it has been." He looked over sincerely. "Thank you for this."

Rodney nodded with a grin.

"The scales of justice are gonna tip the fuck over today, Rodney. *Way* the fuck over! For the longest time I chose to hide the pain inside, but Chuck Thunders can no longer live like that. Razorback Bill will fall, and he must know it was me who did it. I'm just glad you're gonna be here to see it when Bill Nedick goes down like the little, shit-talking bitch he is."

"You sure about that shit? I'm not sure what dude been doing lately, but what I *can* say about Bill Nedick is he's one mean cat. He that dude that'll straight wipe boogers on your couch and just not give a fuck. Maybe you should ease into this thing some. He's the biggest dick in town."

"I eat dicks for breakfast." Chuck slowly looked over. "And right now, I'm *very* hungry."

Rodney chuckled. "You know what?"

Chuck focused back on the road. "What's that, partner?"

I really dig you, man. You over the top and shit."

"*Over the Top*. Great fucking movie! Lincoln Hawks, man. All day. Won a brand-new rig *and* the love of his son, all with one magnificent slam of the hand. I cried when I saw that shit, but don't tell anyone. I have the soundtrack if you wanna hear it!" Chuck began to excitedly rummage through tapes.

"No, I meant *you* yourself. *You* be over the top."

Chuck quit sifting, looked back to the road and played it off with, "I knew what you meant. What? You couldn't tell? I was just dropping one of my badass movie references on you. We're you impressed?"

"Sure." Rodney shrugged. "Why not?"

"Cool. You ready to get some?"

Rodney smiled. "When you get up here, make a right. Few miles down that dirt road. I can't wait to see what the fuck you're gonna do to this dude. You scared, man? Me? I'd be scared."

"Chuck Thunders, scared? Fuck no! Lock and motherfucking load, partner."

Rodney whipped out his nickel-plated pistol and cocked the hammer for show, never intending to use it against anyone in Bill's crew *ever*. He knew better. He was just along to watch.

Unaware of this betrayal, Chuck raised a proud fist to his partner. Someone who was like a brother to him. Someone who he'd lay his own life down for like a true Super Cop should. And he would. They fist bumped as the muscle car tore through a long row of mailboxes.

"Damn!" Rodney shouted as mailbox wood flew. "Chuck don't give a fuck!"

*

Around the back of The Pen, by an actual pig pen filled with large, hungry hogs, Billy Ray was hacksawing the limbs off of a deputy and tossing them into the pen one at a time for the hogs to feast. The hogs tore feveriously into their bloody-fresh meal with violent squeals and snorts.

Razorback and the Kaels came bursting out the back door and made their way over.

Billy Ray held up the cop's bloody badge. "Here that motherfucker's badge that I hit with my car. You want it, Boss?"

"Yeah," Razorback said. "Gimmie that." He pinned it to the front of his cowboy hat then slammed the hat back on his head. "Shame about the deputy here. I fucked his momma last week. Y'all know her? Ugly bitch, but she sure could suck a mean dick. And one hell of a good cook."

Billy Ray continued sawing into the deputy.

Razorback whipped out his cocaine vial and took a hit. That's when Harold Nedick, Razorback's seventeen-year-old, chunky, lazy, spoiled-rotten dummy son came outside carrying a fudge sickle that had begun to melt all over his chubby hand. With a candy bar in each pocket, he walked up to the men, and said, "I clogged the toilet in your office again, Daddy."

"Thanks, dumbass." Razorback said.

"Grody!" Harold pointed at the corpse. "Who was *that* guy?"

"Him? Needed some feed for the hogs. Hey, Meryl. Whatcha say I wrap up a doggie bag of this cop's ass for you and your little gay-ass son?"

Meryl stared at the dismemberment. "Killing cops now, Bill? What'd he do?"

Razorback smiled. "He fucking died."

Moments later, Razorback, the Kaels, Harold, and a blood-soaked shirt wearing Billy Ray walked from around the back of The Pen to the front lot.

Harold looked nervous. "Shit, Daddy. This might mean some serious trouble when that deputy comes up missing. They might come looking."

Razorback smiled. "I don't sweat the small shit boys. I practically own this fucking town, and I'm just getting started."

That comment stung the Kaels.

Billy Ray kneeled down to tighten his tight-rolled jeans and chimed in. "If they do come down in this motherfucker, I ain't gonna sweat it. I bust caps for you all day, Boss. Know what the fuck I'm saying? I gets high off violence and shit."

"You do that for me, Billy Ray?" Razorback asked with pupils indescribable from all the coke intake. He quickly hit some more.

"For you?" Billy Ray said. "All day, every day."

Harold, feeling left out, quickly spoke up. "Me too, Daddy. I can bust caps too!"

Razorback sniffed backed hard, pocketed his vial, and attempted to wipe the coke from his nose but failed. "Billy Ray."

"Wussup?"

"I want you and Harold to take Harold's van and swing by The Village. The shit belongs to me now. Get me ten black bitches that'll do anything I want *sexually*. Darker the better. Think I might have one take a piss on my chest while I watch me some porn and do a crossword."

"Consider *that* shit done," Billy Ray said strutting towards Harold's van. He pulled a bottle of activator from his back pocket and gave his hair a quick spritz. "And I know just the ten."

With a childish stomp of the foot, Harold protested. "Do I have to take *him*, Daddy? He wets up my headrest with grease!"

In the distance, a muscle car could be heard bombing towards The Pen's lot like a heat-seeking missile.

The crew turned to the incoming wall of sound.

Inside the speeding vehicle, Chuck was more amped than ever. "I'm ready, partner! Are you?"

"I'm ready, Chuck!"

"Then let's get some!"

"Can I get a what-what?"

"What?"

"Never mind."

They skidded to a stop in the middle of the road. Chuck revved the engine to get everyone's attention that not only has he arrived, but it was time to wreck shop and whoop some serious ass.

"Friends of yours?" Meryl asked.

"I got no friends here." Razorback looked to The Pen. "Rough House!"

Rough House abruptly came out the front door with his fists already balled up and walked over. "What's up, Bill? There a problem?"

Razorback pointed.

Chuck saw this rude finger point and double tapped his gas back for extreme intimidation.

VRooOOOM! VRooOOOM!

Through Chuck's dusty windshield, the two men watched Razorback's crew line up side by side in the dirt lot like an Old West showdown, ready for a brawl.

Chuck looked over to Rodney. "You, my friend, are about to see some serious shit."

"Think Imma just watch from the car," Rodney said. "I ain't no Super Cop like you. Like you said, you got this, right?"

Chuck opened the door and hopped out. "Yep. I got this." He slammed his door shut, jumped onto the hood of the car and began taunting the man he came to destroy. "Well, well, well. If it isn't Bill Nedick and his little crew of ass heads. I'm *so* scared! You know what, Bill? I think I'd love a B.L.T right about now. Mm-mm! Think I'm gonna have to come over there and cut me off a slab of bacon from your fat ass. After that, I'll feed your momma by letting that bitch drain the milk from my very own between-the-legs cow tit I got waiting." Chuck grabbed his crotch. "It's right here, man!"

Razorback looked left to right at his crew. They were all dumbfounded. "What the hell?" he said. "Fucking circus in town?"

They crew began to laugh.

Chuck got pissed. Nobody laughs at Chuck Thunders!

"Oh, you think that shit's funny? Come over here and say that shit! Bet you don't! You know better! Why? Because I'll straight get in your ass like a fucking gerbil! Come here, Richard Gear! I know you want my gerbil!" Chuck yanked his jeans down to reveal *Rambo: First Blood part II* boxers then raised his arms out by his sides. "There you go! The hard part's already done, Razorbutt Bitch!"

Razorback cocked his head. "Fuck he just call me?"

"Razorbutt Bitch, Daddy," Harold said.

Inside the car, Rodney was frozen stiff. Maybe he shouldn't have come after all. No story to tell the fellas back at the station was worth *this* risk. He looked to the floorboard and spotted a *How to Do Karate in Three Short Weeks* book next to Chuck's badge. He picked up the badge and quickly realized that it was made of plastic and had obviously come from the toy department.

He picked up the book, flipped it over, and read the back cover aloud.

> Complete with illustrations and an in-depth interview with Ralph Macchio, the *real* Karate Kid. He too will teach you how to fight like a man.

Rodney looked back to the man on the hood still taunting Razorback with his pants down.

"You don't have a clue who the fuck you're dealing with," Chuck yelled. "You wanna know who the fuck I am?"

"... Sure," Razorback yelled.

"Fine! I'll tell you who the fuck I am! I'm—"

*

Meanwhile, it was routine as usual at the Rockwood Home for the Criminally Insane. Dr. Roberts, the head psych in charge of the needier cases of the asylum, made his rounds on the hospital's lower levels with Donna DeWitt, a young intern who was obviously scared to death to be around so many strange and violent characters. The beer-bellied security officer (who spit tobacco into every trash can they passed) didn't make her feel any safer. He walked behind a little too close for comfort and constantly undressed Donna with his eyes. He began jiggling the keys hanging from his belt as if they were his balls, took a sniff at her perfume in the air, and smiled with a hungry, "Mm-mm."

"Is it true you were Frank Butz's last Dr. before he escaped?" Donna asked, staying extra close.

"That's true," the Dr. said with a reminiscent smile. "Switchblade Butz was a patient of mine."

"And what was *that* like? Can you describe him in a word?"

"Unstable."

Donna nodded with a scribble to her clipboard.

"Yeah, everything was a joke to Frank," the Dr. added. "Even cold-blooded murder. It was hard to hold any kind of meaningful conversations with him to get at the root of his problems."

"I can imagine. I was actually there in the audience the day Jessie Lake tried to interview him on her show."

"I've seen the tape. Killed her on live TV. Tragedy. They should have known better. Him and that weekend volunteer Earl Tubb are still missing since Frank's escape last summer. No one really knows for sure what's happened to the two of them. It's almost as if they fell off the face of the earth and vanished."

They approached the room on the far end with the extra locks and thicker, steel door.

"This was Frank's room down here. I didn't think we'd ever need this room again to be honest with you, but then we received a patient that turned out to be our most delusional yet. He's pretty unstable. Deep obsessions too. He's the one I'll be assigning you to."

"Obsessions?"

"You'll see. The room speaks for itself. I found out though, his main issue really isn't his delusions, but rather the fact that he's impressionable—and in the worst way imaginable. It's gotten him into all sorts of trouble. That's why I keep him secluded from the rest. Less influence on the monster inside. But the seclusion isn't all bad. It gives us all a much-needed breather and gives him time to work on his comic books. He loves to draw. Unfortunately, I think I'm going to have to cut off his paper privileges. His comics have become a bit off a problem lately."

"How so?"

"He keeps imitating the hero in them, even going so far as to use a deep, tough-guy voice. It's really starting to annoy everyone here. And as soon as someone laughs at him, the fight is on. He can't fight, but it never stops him from throwing the first punch. The man has no fear. At the rate he's going on assaults, he may never see the light of day. But there's always hope."

Donna nodded with a smile. "I'd like to think so."

The guard following rolled his eyes at the bleeding hearts.

Dr. Roberts grabbed the cell's door handle. "Ms. DeWitt, allow me to introduce to you our newest special-needs patient, Larry Pimpleton, and please try not to laugh. This one is *very* sensitive."

He swung open the door to reveal the room of an action-movie junkie of the highest degree. The film posters for *Deadly Prey, Ninja 3: The Domination, The Beastmaster,* and *Missing in Action II: The Beginning* hung with band aides and medical tape. A life-size, cardboard cut-out of Kurt Thomas from the film *Gymkata* stood in the corner with Kurt smiling in his deadly, aerobics fighting stance. On the room's only shelf, an entire cache of martial arts toys was proudly displayed, and the bed had *Spiderman and his Amazing Friends* sheets covering up an apparent sleeping body. Scattered across the sheets, an assortment of G.I. Joes, *Chuck Thunders: Super Cop* comics drawn with crayons, and two copies of Teen Beat, one with Kirk Cameron wearing a crucifix necklace and a smile so bright that no airbrushing was needed.

Dr. Roberts approached the lump under the blanket. "Hey, Larry. I have the new intern here that'll be working with us on your case. Wake up so I can introduce the two of you."

No response.

The Dr. got firm with the lump under the blanket. "Listen, Larry. You can't stay up all night practicing your karate, drawing your Chuck Thunders comics, and then expect to sleep all day without attending any of your scheduled therapy sessions. If this continues, I shall be forced to confiscate every single one of your toys. That was the deal, remember? Now, wake up. I'd like you to say hi to Donna and try and make her feel more welcomed like we discussed yesterday."

Still no response.

Dr. Roberts grabbed the blanket and yanked it back to reveal a blow-up doll wearing a camouflage bra and panties. A paper machete military helmet (which was colored with crayons) rested on its head. On the side of the helmet: Born to Thrill. Next to the doll was a note.

Dr. Roberts picked up the note and read it to himself with a look of confusion.

"What is it, Dr. Roberts?" Donna asked. "What's wrong?"

Dr. Roberts handed her the note.

She read it aloud.

Heading into town. Be back before the street lights come on. The guards told me last night that Razorback Bill said my comics looked like shit, that I write like a child, talked like an idiot, and called me a punk-ass bitch. Chuck Thunders don't play that. Razorback Bill must pay. It was him that started the war and now it is me who will end it. Sincerely, Chuck Thunders. P.S. Tell Ralph I'll pick him up a copy of *Mad* magazine.

The intern was baffled. "What's all this mean?"

"Guard!" the Dr. yelled.

The security officer, who was off flirting with one of the house keepers, walked in like he was being bothered and responded with a rude, "Yeah? What is it?"

"Anything out of the ordinary happen this morning?"

"Oh, you know, Doc. Same old Unit B bullshit. Caught Stephens drinking out of the toilet earlier and had to tie his stupid monkey-ass down. Then Ralphie shit himself at breakfast *again.* Maybe that has something to do with all the prune juice you have the nurses shove down these goddamn bugs' throats. Oh! And that car Brad bought to try and shoot that stupid-ass movie about Frank Butz got stolen from the parking lot."

"Today?"

"Yup. Just this morning."

"Call a code red. Find Larry now!"

The guard looked around the room confused. He spotted the blow-up doll looking back at him. It took a second, but his eyes finally went wide, and he bolted down the hall with his large ring of keys bouncing off his leg.

Donna could see the worry in Dr. Robert's eyes.

"Good God, Larry," Dr. Roberts said. "What have you gotten yourself into this time?"

Minutes Ago

"You wanna know who the fuck I am?" Chuck yelled from the hood of his car.

"Sure," Razorback yelled.

"Fine! I'll tell you who the fuck I am! I'm Chuck Thunders, and I came to shove a little vengeance up your ass and make it hurt! Wait! Hold on a sec!" Chuck pulled his pants up, hopped off the hood, and, in an attempt to size up the crew, began strutting back and forth.

In the distance, a siren began wailing from the Rockwood Home for the Criminally Insane.

Ignoring the wails, Chuck put his fist up Fighting Irish style and began bouncing like an idiot. "Put 'em up! Come on, Bill! Been talking shit about my shit? Think you can do any better? Put up your dukes, boy! What? You scared of me? Smarter than you look!" Chuck began to hum the theme from *Rocky* and threw air jabs.

Razorback whipped out his vial to hit what little coke was left inside.

Chuck stopped cold. His jaw dropped, and he came completely unglued. "Oh! Oh! Oh! And what the fuck is this? Cocaine use? You gotta be shitting me! That's drug charges right there, mister! I have so had it with you and your shit! Come on, you shit-talking bitch!" He jumped back into his *Rocky* dance, throwing jabs and humming.

Razorback watched for a few ridiculous moments, spit on the ground, and said, "Rough House."

"Yeah, Boss?"

"Fetch his ass."

Without hesitation, Rough House made a b-line for the bouncing idiot.

"But don't kill him just yet!"

Rough House came to a dead-stop in front of Chuck and looked left to right along with Chuck's dance.

Chuck finally stopped dancing and put his arms down. "What? Pig Butt send you over here to get your ass kicked? I'll tell you what, you big, burly-ass motherfucker. Why don't you just take your—"

Pow! Rough House silenced Chuck with a fist to the face that sent him down with a crushed nose, hard and fast. Next thing he knew, he was being dragged across the dirt lot by his ankle. His demeanor went from Super Cop to pussy in distress instantly. "Rodney! You're supposed to be my friend! My partner! I'm in trouble! Help me!"

Rodney remained frozen stiff in the car. Rodney wasn't helping shit.

Rough House lifted Chuck by the ankle and dangled him helplessly in front of the crew like a rag doll. "Here you go, Bill," he said. "I fetched his ass for you."

"Good boy," Razorback said with a pat to Rough House's shoulder. He kneeled down to get a good look at the terrified stranger. "Good God almighty. You a crazy fuck, you know that? Guess you thinking I'm supposed to be the expediter of your dreams or some shit, huh? Come to take me down? Be a big hero? That's cute. And I also bet that siren blasting from that nut house on the edge of town was because of you. Well, you being crazy and all don't mean shit to me. Sorry about that. I just never sympathize with you people. But I must say, I do admire your zeal. That's why I'm not gonna have my boys kill you ... *much*. Billy Ray?"

"Wussup?"

"Do me a favor and go fetch the nigger," he pointed, "in *that* car."

Billy Ray cocked his .45 Automatic and began strutting towards the idling muscle car.

The car went into gear and shot off like lightning.

Billy Ray began popping off shots and shattered the car's windows and filled its body full of holes.

With shattered glass in his afro, and the pedal to the metal, Rodney hauled ass screaming, "Oh shit! Oh shit! Oh shit!"

"Rodney!" Chuck screamed from his upside-down point of view. "Don't leave me here, man! That's Brad's car!"

It was too late. Rodney was gone.

Billy Ray spit and released the empty clip onto the street. He popped in a fresh one and walked back to the crew where Chuck was still dangling upside down by Rough House who had no trouble holding onto the weird, little man.

"So, what we gonna do about this faggot?" Billy Ray asked before delivering a kick to Chuck's head with a massive *Pow!*

"Ow, man!" Chuck screamed as he swayed back and forth. "What I ever do to you?" he whimpered.

"Shut up, bitch!" Billy Ray shouted, placing his gun's barrel to Chuck's temple and causing his swaying to cease. "Lemme cap 'em, Boss. Blow this cracker's brains all over The Pen's dirty-ass lot, then we can feed this little bitch to the hogs. They'll straight gobble yo nigga-ass up." Billy Ray threw his arms up, and shouted, "What do you say, Bill? Can I pop?"

Razorback casually stepped forward with a pat to Billy Ray's back. "Calm down, Billy Ray. You're too violent, man."

Billy Ray gave Chuck his angriest crooked-eye look. "You're lucky, bitch." He kicked him in the head again. *Pow!* "So motherfucking lucky."

Swinging back and forth from that last kick, Chuck began crying like a baby.

Razorback looked to the pathetic man and decided to have mercy on him, sort of. "I got just one question."

"What?" Chuck managed.

"... You ready to feel pain, boy?"

The crew began to laugh.

Razorback laughed. Harold laughed. Rough House laughed. Meryl and Gay-Bob Kael adjusted their belt buckles in unison and laughed. Even Billy Ray laughed. All of them laughed.

AND NOBODY LAUGHS AT CHUCK THUNDERS!

The giggles were the last thing he heard before everything faded to black.

*

Chuck Thunders slowly began to awaken in extreme butt pain, only to realize he was dangling with his ass in the air by some weird contraption, dead-center in the middle of a futuristic, high-tech hospital lab, complete with an 80-inch television sunk into the wall above a blinking, computer-board terminal. On the floor was a governmental-style logo; a yellow jacket was its mascot. Section Eight: Rockwood Division, Here to Save Us All was printed on the emblem. Off to the side, a cryogenic chamber of sorts? Inside it was the notorious Frank Switchblade Butz, frozen in an Elvis Presley prose and incarcerated.

"Ah!" Chuck yelled as the pain in his ass kicked in full-gear. "Fuck me, Jesus!" There wasn't a soul around to explain how he ended up there, just hanging mid-air with two black eyes and a crushed nose, so his mental voice-over kicked in to keep him company. *As I laid up in this strange, futuristic room, or should I say dangled by stirrups, straps, and shit like that with my ass up in the air hurting like holy hell, I remember the faces of the men who did this. The laughs. The chuckles. The sneers. The snickers. The name calling. The embarrassment of it all that I will now have to deal with for the rest of my life. I'm Chuck Thunders, you see? Things like this don't happen to Chuck Thunders. I kick ass. It's what I do. Not get my ass kicked. Not really sure what happened back there, but it sure did suck balls.*

Chuck held up what was once his hand, now just a bloody nub.

They took my hand, they took my dignity, but they didn't take my life. Big mistake. They beat me. They peed on me. They covered my hand in that gross-ass, Heinz 57 shit they try and pass off as a sauce, and then they let one of them fucking hogs eat my hand off—right down to the wrist. Even lost my Pac Man watch because of it. Cruel bastards. And what was up with that thing they kept shoving up my ass? That was rude. Real rude. It had splinters and hurt my butt, and Chuck don't get down like that. And what's the deal with Rodney? He just drove off. I thought blacks were supposed to be cool. Well, we all know that's a goddamn lie now. Fuck that dude. Goddamn my ass hurts.

A nurse walked in holding a tray with pain killers in a cup. She made her way over and leaned down to give Chuck a welcoming smile. "How we doing up in here? You hanging in there, sweetie pie?"

"Nurse," Chuck managed. "You have no idea the kind of shit I've been through today. Where the fuck am I? The shit looks like a bad, science-fiction B-movie."

The nurse smiled.

"What the fuck are you smiling at? Find something funny? Is it my ass in the air? Whatcha got in that cup?"

"These here," she shook the cup. "Are pain killers."

"Oh, shit! Pain killers! Fuck, yeah! Give 'em to me."

The nurse knelt down and placed them in Chuck's mouth. "Yeah," she said as the pills poured in. "This ought to help get rid of that pain in your bum."

"Thank you." Chuck chewed like they were candy. "My ass hurts so fucking bad. You just don't know."

The nurse got sympathetic. "I bet there, sweetie. Bless your heart. It took three orderlies just to help lift that thang and pull it up outcha. What was that by the way?"

"Nurse," a voice from outside the room shouted. "I need you!"

"Hang on just a minute," she said. "I'll be right back." She exited.

Left dangling, Chuck began to think long and hard about his current situation and shook his head in total disgust. "Them ... punk-ass ... motherfuckers."

That's when two mysterious men in fedora hats and 1950's-style business suits entered the room, one of them puffing heavily on a non-filtered cigarette.

"Larry Pimpleton?" the smoke-free one said before shutting the door.

"Who's there?" Chuck replied with a jerk of the head. "I can't see."

"Your eyesight will return in time."

"No, Princess Leia. I can *see* just fine. I just can't see you. I can't turn my head. I have limited mobility here, bro. Not carbonite freezing in my eyes. Don't you see my ass all up in the air. What are you? Fucking retarded?"

"It's not important that you see us," the agent replied. "Just listen. We have a proposition that we feel you will find very interesting."

The agent began to walk the room and checked out its high-tech equipment. "Truth is we've been watching you for quite some time. Allow me to introduce myself. My name is Agent Orange, and my associate here is Agent Black. We work for an organization on behalf of Lambda Moo Omega the Third: a being very feared by the ones we are up against. He has sent us to specifically seek you out for recruitment into Section Eight: a secret organization of the highest intergalactic order."

"Like a space version of *Remo Williams*?" Chuck asked all excited. "I love that idea!"

"We go back further than him. Did you know the earth has been destroyed, reduced to rubble, and started over from scratch five times, Larry?"

"Who's Larry?"

"It's true. On its third destruction, a group of intergalactic guardians known as Section Eight were sent in to help man protect what is his."

"My action figures?"

"No. Planet earth. Your home."

Agent Orange walked over to the window and looked out to the backwater town of Rockwood with great concern. "There is trouble brewing on the horizon for your people." He turned back to Chuck. "And that is where *we* come into play. When needed, we recruit, train, and assist the special ones who walk the earth in this time—but *only* if their time has come, and yours has. You can help us put a stop to the criminal behavior that's been going on amongst interplanetary species. This includes crimes against—"

As I dangled helplessly, being forced to listen to this governmental, Nick Fury-wannabe-type asshole babble on about fighting aliens or whatever, all I could think about was Razorback Bill and the pain in my ass. Boy, it sure hurt. Good God almighty. It almost feels as if a midget drove a go-cart up my ass, did a doughnut, and crashed...

The agent continued. "And we will supply you with the best in weaponry. The best tactics in hand-to-hand combat will be instantly loaded into your brain as well as the latest in the anatomy and take-down of the serpent beast known as William Nedick. He has infiltrated seats of power in Rockwood's inner-circles and now controls everything. But this is just the first step in his master plan. We believe—"

Boy, my ass sure does hurt. I hope them pills kick in soon. Just think about when I have to go number two. That shit is going to suck soooooo bad. Jesus H. Christ.

"These are the stipulations of membership into Section Eight. As far as the rest of the world knows, Larry Pimpleton has escaped. On the run. Never to be seen again. It's almost like he's dead. Like we killed you. *Now*, you will be supplied with a new face, a new name, and a top-secret identity. And you will only exist when needed for planetary safety. In the end, the odds are against us, but you have something deep inside you that most men do not. An *extreme* belief in yourself. It's up to you how deep you are willing to pull from it. To *become* what you've always wanted. The hero in your very own comic-book version of life. To actually become ... Chuck Thunders. Are you in?"

"I have a question for your secret, governmental ass."

"Yes?"

"Can I get a hook for a hand over my bloody nub? If I can, I'll go *Rolling Thunder* on his fat, alien ass. Ever seen that movie?"

"How about a Sure Grip 4000?" Agent Orange asked.

"That robotic?"

"It's robotic."

Chuck signed up. "Then count me right the fuck in."

Genesis 5:2 He created them.
New Living Translation

Chapter Two
ORIGINS OF THE ROCKWOOD RAZORBACK

One Week Ago
In the deepest part of the Rockwood swamps, a paint-chipped stilt house sat amongst the alligators and various vile swamp creatures. A hand-painted sign above the doorway read

      THE HALL OF INJUSTICE
      Level 13 Members <u>Only</u>

Inside, Razorback sat with nine of the area's local crime bosses (known in Rockwood's Draconian underworld as The Council). The overweight, out-of-style, misfit mobsters sat around a large folding table and feasted from various trays stacked with both raw and cooked human limbs.

    Unimpressed with what he heard so far, Garth Dennis leaned back in his seat, took a puff from his cigar, and exhaled with, "I don't know, Bill. All of us are pretty comfy and shit right where we at. Just like it's supposed to be. Sure, we don't roll like the big dogs with tax money and such, but we *do* get union dues from the local asylum *and* the prison, not to mention, we run the bingo hall, *both* car washes, pool hall, laundromat, and, as of last week, the second-hand shop across town. Because of *that* little business maneuver, I get to sift through all the garbage bags of clothes first *and* get all my suits and shit for free. Heh-heh. Our kind, sure, we're lazy-asses. Everybody in the galaxy knows that. But we're also thinkers, and we are continually expanding. Growing and shit. We take over in the dark because it's the easiest way, and most of these human, loser-ass sumbitches don't even know it." Garth snapped a finger from a hand on his plate as if it were a crab leg, dipped it in some bloody, barbecue sauce, and took a bite. "And that's what the secrecy is about," he said chewing. "Makes the shit easy, you know?"

"Yeah," Billy Joe Jim Bob said sweating profusely and loosening his Salvation Army tie. "Me too. What he said. I'm with him. Shit just sounds like more work. Start doing shit different, fucks up my schedule. Need my Tuesdays free for horseshoes. Is it hot in here?"

"That go for the rest of you?" Razorback asked.

The mobsters nodded with responses of,

"Sure."

"Yeah."

"I can play horseshoes.

"What were we talking about?"

"Can we order a pizza too?"

Razorback shook his head in disbelief. "Well ... I guess me and ole' Billy Ray just gonna have to go it alone."

"You can't, Bill," Garth spoke heatedly. "We discussed it already, and none of us agree. That means it's final. We are The Council. And *that* means it's a group decision. And if you don't start getting that through your fat—"

"Um." Billy Joe Jim Bob raised a timid finger. "Can I interrupt for just a sec?"

"By all means." Garth exhaled. "Speak, Billy Joe Jim Bob."

Billy Joe Jim Bob wiped his mouth with his bib, looked at Razorback, and cleared his throat. "Well, Bill, it's about you picking a human for your lieutenant. Now, I don't wanna step on your toes and all, because hey, we all have a human or two in our lives we respect. Right, guys?"

"Right."

"Most definitely!"

"I got several I like to fuck," Jimmy Haggard beamed, "I don't give a fuck about race when it comes to pussy. I fuck anything. How about you, Barnett?"

Barnett smiled. "Oh, shit. I love humans. I eat at least two a week. Barbecued, oven roasted. I really dig the wood grilled. Just something about that smoke flavor, you know?"

"You use hickory?"

"Well, I use several kinds of wood. Depends on the species. For instance, Asians are already sweet tasting. But if you get one at the right age, he or she can—"

"Shut the fuck up, Barnett," Razorback shouted. "We're not here to discuss your goddamn bullshit-ass recipes on humans. I'm talking about some serious shit here. Pay the fuck attention for once."

"Sorry, Bill. Got side-tracked talking about food again."

"That's okay. I guess it's not your fault you're so goddamn stupid. I'll just blame your daddy for all his cousin fucking."

Barnett looked to the men, offended.

Several shrugged.

Razorback continued. "Look, goddamn it. Our people been waiting for someone to come run shit right ... *and that's me*. Don't y'all see that? I got ideas, boys, and they best not go to waste."

"Your ideas are dangerous, Bill." Garth said.

Razorback shrugged. "Regardless how *you* see things is not my problem, Garth."

Garth fumed. "Look, we said no. End of story! You can't go monopolize the town's beer supply and put that anti-hallucinogenic shit in your Pig Sticker beer and let these man apes see us for what we really are."

Razorback smiled. "Already done put the shit in the next shipment. *And* I plan on running a TV ad for Pig Sticker before the next episode of *The Dukes of Hazzard*. So, how about that shit? Shit'll fly off shelves faster than a dick to the mouth of a Kael."

Jimmy Haggard gave a confident chuckle. "Guess you don't wanna sell no beer then, Bill. Don't you know? Nobody watches that shit show anymore."

The gangsters laughed.

Razorback smiled. "Guess y'all ain't been checking your local listings. Soon marks the second coming of Bo and Luke Duke. They returning to the show. Shit's about to get real in Hazzard."

Eyes went wide.

"Everyone in town'll be tuning in for that goddamn shit, and we all know it. All I gotta do is bounce a microwave off a satellite to redirect the signal back to the station. That'll override their jizzawatt thing so I can plug my commercial, and then my plan will be in motion."

Billy Joe Jim Bob nodded. "Hmmm. Satellite bouncing and such. Inventive."

"Yeah, I got the idea from watching *Used Cars* last week."

Garth, the only one seeing the implications here, finally interrupted. "Look, everyone. Let us not forget. The elite, we *don't* piss off. If they were to get wind of this little plan of yours, Bill, god help you. And if you *do* piss off the top brass, they won't send your ass to live back on Osiris like before. Or the caves below us. No. They will kill you! Plain and simple. You can't go fucking up their good thing. Or ours! Don't forget, Bill. There was a deal made long ago with our ancestors. Because of that deal, we were able to use stupid-ass humans to our advantage. And now *we* the ones that get to benefit from all that shit. Why would you ever want to change that? We were born into the sweet spot of the matrix, boy. Breaking the illusion will change *everything*. No more free living for our kind in Rockwood. All these humans might flip the goddamn fuck out, start a revolution, quit working and get the bright idea to fend for themselves. Bye union dues. Bye local taxes. C'ya local pussy. You have any idea how pissed off we're all gonna be with you about this? You pissing in our pools and taking away our freebies from the bottom feeders in effect. These bottom feeders start a goddamn war with us and that's the end of everything! And what about Section Eight? Let's not even get into how them silly bastards be recruiting all them crazy fucking weirdos all the time. They *always* ruining my schemes! They will come after you, Bill! Trust me. Why in the fuck would you even consider this shit? Are you fucking crazy?"

The room went silent.

A little steamed from Garth speaking like he had a pair, Razorback stood, stared at the silent room, and said, "Because, Garth. It's quite simple. Only a pussy like you lives in fear. Hides who you really are. That don't make you shit but a piddly-squat, chicken-shit sumbitch in my book. You ain't worth two dicks in a chick. Last time I checked, I don't fear or hide from shit, and I for one didn't make any kinda goddamn deal with some monkey-men assholes, nor would I ever. And I sure as shit don't give a flying fuck about some stupid-ass, intergalactic watchers who are nothing but a bunch of third-rate, G.I. Joe retards. We all wanna stand for something? Have a purpose? *Be* something? Imma be a ruthless sumbitch that does what the fuck he wants in the open. Why? Because I get off on it." Razorback adjusted his crotch. This excited him. "Taking from the man apes in secret? Not my thing. Humans? Fuck 'em. They so goddamn stupid as a species, they kill their own kind over affiliations. But they ripe for the ruling because they full of fear, and that's where *I* come in. I'm leaving my goddamn mark on this planet, and it's gonna be deeper than the ones I left on that black bitch's booty I had for lunch. They gonna carve my goddamn face into that concrete wall out by the Rockwood dump like some kinda Mount Everest up in this sumbitch by the time I'm done. Imma be known. Imma be feared. Imma be a *baaaaaad* man."

"What you are," Garth finally spoke, "is done for." He whipped out his brick-sized cell phone and began punching numbers with his fat finger. "And your short stay here is over."

In a flash, Razorback whipped out an antique pistol, fired, and blew Garth's brains all over the place. Garth slowly slumped over then hit the floor. The gangsters watched, frozen in shock.

"You just killed one of our own in cold blood," Billy Joe Jim Bob finally said, dumbfounded. "That hasn't happened in two hundred and thirty-seven years."

Razorback slowly walked up and pointed the pistol at the terrified Billy Joe Jim Bob, and said, "Who the fuck put you, or anyone else for that matter, in charge of *me*? I don't know what the fuck I am, why I was born like this, who made me, or where the fuck I'm going when I die ... and neither do you. But until I figure this shit out, which I probably never will," he cocked the pistol, "keep your fucking hands off my life."

"Bill! You fat, individualistic fuck!"

Pow! Billy Joe Jim Bob was no more.

Razorback casually went back to his spot at the table, put the smoking pistol down, and smiled at the remaining gangsters' blank faces. "Thousands of years ago, dragons decided to take human form and hide in secret. I wasn't one of them sneaky, little, flying shits. Face it, fellas. This is *my* time. And I don't need your goddamn help *or* permission. This pussy way of living inside secret groups is coming to an end. Imma rule Rockwood in The Great Wide Open like a *real* motherfucking boss. Any objections?"

Not a one.

"And there ain't a prick alive that's gonna stop me."

I have come here to chew bubble gum and kick ass. And I'm all out of bubble gum. —Nada

Chapter Three
THE RETURN OF CHUCK THUNDERS

Present Day
Equipped with a robotic hand, new identity, and a face that resembled Corey Haim (which he asked for specifically), Chuck Thunders drove his Section Eight hot rod down the very same road we first met him just a few short hours ago. As usual, he lit up the road, but this time with the Beastie Boys "No Sleep til Brooklyn" thumping from a modified sound system. He rapped along with the fellas. "Foot on the pedal never ever false metal! Engine running hotter than a boiling kettle! My job ain't a job, it's a damn good time! City to city, I'm running my rhymes!"

Chuck decreased the volume and filled us in. *I love the shit out of this new car. Got six sub woofers in the trunk, a talking dashboard named Katz, and a full tank of gas for the mission that I didn't even have to pitch in on.*

He passed the Rockwood sign. *And this time, shit's gonna be different. Why? Because I got me one of them flat-top haircuts like Ice Man, with a touch of Van Damme from* Cyborg *in the back. Frosted tips too. Holy shit! That's Rodney Tibbs!*

Chuck was right. It was Rodney, and he was pulling into the Gas-N-Grab in his 1975, Ford Gran Torino with the mighty Al Green playing from the stereo. Rodney parked, hopped out, then strutted inside the shop with much swagger.

Chuck pulled in and parked next to him.

Inside the store, Rodney rapped to the white girl behind the counter who smacked away at her chewing gum. "Yeah, baby," he said. "I'll take me a pack of Kools, some of this peppermint gum for my breath and shit and two missiles of this here Colt 45 for tonight, so I can get to them drawers faster, you know what I'm saying?" He placed the two cans of beer on the counter and smiled. "Works every time," he said imitating Billy Dee Williams.

The clerk smiled back. "*What* works every time?"

Chuck entered the shop with his hands on his hips like an angry parent looking for their child. He spotted Rodney and approached.

Not noticing, Rodney continued digging through his condom-ringed wallet for a food stamp to pay for the gum, still smiling at the clerk with his sly grin.

Chuck stopped behind him, and yelled, "What the fuck, Rodney?"

Rodney spun around to see the man with the Danger Zone haircut. "I know you, homeboy?"

Chuck leaned in. "I'll give you a hint. *Ahem-hem.* 'You over the top, man. You ain't got no Al Green? Wow, Chuck don't give a fuck.' Any of *that* shit ring a bell?"

Rodney cocked his head. "Chuck? That you?"

"Yes, Rodney. It's me."

"Sure in the fuck don't look like you." Rodney pocketed his change. "How the fuck you grow a new face in like an hour and shit? Seems like something of that magnitude would have taken longer."

"I know it's hard to believe, but it's me. You'll just have to go with it in order for this to work. Just don't tell the sheriff it's really me, okay?"

"No problem, Chuck. I can do that for you." He pocketed his Kools with a smile. "You my boy."

The clerk smiled. They finally buried the hatchet.

Chuck smiled too. They were back in business.

Moments later, Chuck and Rodney exited the store. Chuck sucked on Slurpee through a crazy straw. In his fanny pack was a handful of Slim Jims hanging half out and in his back pocket was a *Mad* magazine rolled up next to a brand-new paddle ball.

Rodney looked down at Chuck's hand, which held a fistful of Twizzlers, and noticed for the first time that it looked abnormal and metallic. "Damn, Chuck. What the fuck is up with your hand? You part robot now and shit?"

"Got a new one," Chuck bragged. "The Hydraulic 4000 Grip Plus model. Just released."

"I'll be damned. You get that at the flea market?"

Chuck took a hard sip and held up his Slurpee. "Now, that's some good-ass shit."

"Looks like it. So, how you been, Chuck? I been wondering what happened to you. The whole department, all six of us, went looking for you when we found out it was you that escaped from that nuthouse this morning. They even got your picture up back at the station. Good thing you got that new face, huh? So, what's new?"

"One thing at a time. Just wait until I show you my bag of tricks. My fanny pack can double as a parachute, *and* I even have a healing factor now." Chuck quickly grabbed his survival knife from its sheath and held it up. "Check out my *Rambo: First Blood part II* knife! Want to see me cut myself and heal really fast?"

"Nah. So, whatcha want me to call you in front of the sheriff?"

"I don't know. I'll think of something cool?"

*

Back at the station, Sheriff Bigelow was teetering on the brink of a heart attack. Chuck and Rodney stood side by side in front of his desk.

Sheriff Bigelow ripped into Chuck's ass with, "Me and Mayor Bradley got one thing in common, Agent Rambone Brick Fists! One thing! And that's neither one of us want your help, nor do we need it! I got enough fucking problems as it is! You haven't been on the job five minutes and you've shown nothing but insubordination, a refusal to work well with others, *and* you have an appearance that doesn't jive with our regulations! Why don't you just take your flat-top hair, your little fly-boy shades, get back in your fancy-looking agent mobile, and putt-putt your ass the fuck outta my goddamn jurisdiction!"

"Come on, Sheriff B," Rodney smiled. "Give old Brick Fists a chance. You never know. Maybe he'll get some things shook up around here for once. Besides, he's hellafied cool and knows this cop shit better than anyone on the force."

Chuck said, "That's true. I know my shit."

Sheriff Bigelow looked at Rodney with fire. "But that's just the thing, Tibbs. I want things to quiet the fuck down for once. Not all shook up and shit like some kinda goddamn martini by some tough-guy cop. Just don't be provoking Bill is all I'm saying. That pig bites every goddamn time, and I'm sick of cleaning up Rockwood bodies from the streets. We don't need Rambone Brick Fists coming in stirring the fucking pot, making more goddamn trouble. All we have to do is let Monty handle this. He gave me his word that—"

Just then, Monty Hughes, the internal affairs investigator sent in from Jackson, entered the room and everyone got quiet and nervous except for Chuck. Monty slowly walked up, stopped, scanned Chuck head to toe, and with a finger point to the face asked, "Is this the one?"

"Yep," Sheriff Bigelow said. "He's the one. Agent Rambone Brick Fists, a real smartass. Got a listening problem too. Maybe needs his ears checked."

Monty looked at Chuck. "Look here, *friend*. I've already heard all about how you think you're some kind of loose-cannon tough guy, but on my watch, you better watch that insubordinate shit. Fuck around during any of my investigations on Razorback Nedick, and I swear to God I'll fuck you raw, friend."

Chuck whipped out his badge. His badge number 237 emitted an aqua, blue glow. "See this shit?"

Monty leaned in. "Yeah? And? So, what? You have a glowing badge. Big deal. What's it supposed to be saying? That I'm supposed to be impressed? Give a shit? What, Brick Fist?"

"It doesn't say shit because it's a badge, dumb ass. But I *can* say shit. And you better listen and listen good when I tell you that I come backed with more diplomatic immunity than that evil dude from *Lethal Weapon II* and Roger Moore combined. I'm also equipped with more gadgets than that little bitch from *Small Wonder*. So, why don't you take two steps back and go fuck yourself."

Monty was appalled.

Rodney smiled. He was really starting to dig this Chuck Thunders.

Standing firm, Monty continued his slime-ball look.

Chuck didn't like it *or* him. He slowly stepped to Monty and balled his robot fist. The sounds of its robotics filled the room.

"What?" Monty smirked. "You wanna hit me with that thing? Well, go ahead. I'll have you locked under the fucking jail to rot, Rambone. You have any idea who my dad is? Take your best shot … I dare you."

And with that, Chuck punched him right in the face with his Sure Grip 4000 hand, which smashed Monty's nose and sent him to the hardwood floor. Monty immediately began snoring away.

Chuck looked down. "I'm not waiting till the end of the story to do that. We all knew the shit was coming anyway. Come on, Rodney. Let's roll!" He strutted out.

Sheriff Bigelow and Rodney looked down at Monty.

The sheriff shook his head in disbelief. "Jesus H. Christ. Look, Rodney. Do me a favor and babysit this fucking guy. He's *your* responsibility. Take 'em out and show him the town. Go bust some jay walkers or some shit."

Rodney was happy to oblige. "Not a problem, Sheriff B. We go bust all they jay-walking asses."

"Just keep an eye on him and keep him busy is all I ask. Give him some crayons to play with or some shit. And do your best to keep him far away from Bill and his crew. Do me this favor."

"*Shieet*, Sheriff. He just some crazy-ass dude with a robot hand is all. To be honest, he's actually kind of funny to me. But don't you worry, I'll watch 'em. He ain't gonna do no harm."

Monty sat up. "W-w-what happened?"

"Well," Rodney added. "He ain't gonna do *no more* harm."

*

Back in the tiny confines of Razorback's office, Razorback kicked back and spoke with his main soldier, Billy Ray, who sat across the desk from him and nibbled away on a batch of steamy chicken wings.

Razorback smiled big. "You ready to hear my master plan, Billy Ray?"

Billy Ray paused to wipe the hot-wing sweat from his forehead and looked at his boss. "Speak on it."

Razorback reached in his pocket, removed a test tube filled with a thin, yellow-colored substance and gently placed it on the desk. "It's this."

"Fuck's that shit, boss? You gotta piss test coming?"

"This sure as shit ain't piss, boy."

"Mello Yello?"

"Nope."

"I'm out."

"Called Valaxium 10, and it's designed to counter act all the shit they been putting in the water all these years to make people all dumb and docile and shit. Its effects are instantaneous. Anyone who drinks *this* shit," he tapped the tube, "will see me for what I truly am."

"So, tell me, Boss. Just what the fuck *is* you, besides one ruthless-ass motherfucker?"

Razorback leaned in. "Hope you ready for this one, Billy Ray. You ready, boy?"

"Always."

"Alien, Billy Ray," Razorback smiled. "Imma goddamn alien." He put his finger to his lips. "*Shhh*. It's supposed to be a secret. They be listening in through the TVs and shit, and I ain't supposed to be telling any of y'all."

Billy Ray dipped a wing into some ranch dressing. "Shit! So, you like one of them motherfuckers in that crazy-ass movie with Roddy Piper. *They Live*, yo!" He took a swig from his forty ounce of malt liquor and put the bottle down with a *thunk*. "Bubble gum, bitch."

"Exactly." Razorback pointed. "I guess. Tell you the truth, never seen the shit. But *that's* why I'm so goddamn ornery and shit. Heh-heh. Yeah. Imma goddamn alien. A Draconian lizard underneath all this exterior, Boss Hogg-looking bullshit."

"It's like you right out of a made-for-TV, Sci-fi flick and shit."

"Yup. Like you said. And I'm sick of hiding the shit. How the fuck would you feel if you were made to look like a man ape all the goddamn time—no offense. But that's *exactly* why I'm about to lift the illusion in Rockwood." He hit a line of coke. "Now, Billy Ray."

Billy Ray dove into a new wing. "Yo."

"In order for me to pull this off, Imma need you to be with me to the very end. I'm all alone from both ends on this here thing."

"One thing you ain't, Boss, is alone. Not while the fuck I'm still standing."

Razorback nodded with a smile. "Well, to show my appreciation for so much loyalty, after this is all over, name it, it's yours. How's that sound? My gift to you."

Billy Ray stopped eating and smiled. "You know what I want."

"What?"

"The Village."

"Whatcha gonna do with that monkey cage?"

"Imma straight sell my rap group's three-cut demo all over that motherfucker for ninety-nine cents apiece. I had Mike BMC do the beats; the bass on that shit sounds like a motherfucking guerilla's fighting to get outcha trunk."

Razorback smiled, high as a kite off its string. "The Village is yours, do with it as you please."

"Boss," Billy Ray said with hot sauce lips. "I swear before you, God, and ten white honkies, that I'm with you to the motherfucking end. I love you, man. Alien or not, we the same. All this shit may be illusion like they say, but *that* shit is real. Besides. You about to make me the motherfucking Willie Dee of Rockwood."

"Don't think I know that dude, but shit, why not?" Razorback hit some coke and sniffed back. "So, I take it you get the picture."

"Big-screen."

"Great!" Razorback celebrated. "Now I no longer have to hide doing this." He pulled a mouse from the desk drawer, dipped its head into the ranch dressing, and shoved it into his mouth with a squealing crunch.

Billy Ray lost his appetite, stood, and walked out of the room.

"What?" Razorback munched. "Too soon?"

*

Chuck and Rodney were on the job. Chuck was trying his best to impress Rodney with *Star Wars* references. "But my robot hand is different than Luke's," he said holding up his robot fist. "Jedi Knights wouldn't rate this shit anyway. And plus, I'm not ashamed of my deformity. I don't try and cover it up with a black glove like Luke does. I'm not ashamed of our people, and as far as I'm concerned, it only makes me look cooler. What are your thoughts on the subject?"

"You think that metal hand of yours is gonna take out Bill Nedick and that crew of his? Probably gonna take a little bit more than that. Dude's got the whole town in his back pocket, *and* they say he's in cahoots with the mayor. So, there's *that* shit."

Chuck unwrapped a Blow Pop from his fanny pack and quickly crunched into it to get at the gum inside. He threw the stick out the window. "There's a reason these assholes stick together," he chewed. "They hate our race."

"Whatcha mean *our* race? We ain't the same. You white. I'm all black and shit. Regardless, this man doesn't care what race you is. He will fuck your shit up with no repair. You got lucky last time since he was just toying with you. Next time you might not be so lucky."

Chuck jerked the wheel and hit Brokeback road.

"Where we going?"

"Gotta check in."

"We just did that. Bigelow told me to babysit your ass, remember?"

"Not with Bigelow. Have to check in with *my* people." Chuck looked to the dash. "Katz, make sure all systems are up and running before we head back out."

The dashboard replied back with an English accent and blinking lights from the stereo's equalizer as it spoke. "I will sir," it said. "Shall I phone ahead and let them know we are coming?"

Rodney freaked. "Holy shit! You like *Knight Rider* up in this piece. Car's all talking and shit."

"Fuck David Hasselhoff." Chuck made a hard right off the road, skidded into the lot of Cutty's run-down garage, then pulled into the only bay.

The bay door closed as if on cue, and Chuck killed the engine.

Cutty, the sixty-year-old, grease-covered mechanic, came out of his office with an oversized wrench in hand and walked up to the vehicle.

Chuck and Rodney hopped out in unison.

"Agent Thunders," Cutty said with a spit and splat of tobacco on the bay's floor. "They're waiting inside."

"Cutty?" Rodney questioned. "You in on this shit too?"

Cutty smiled. "Follow me, gentlemen."

They headed in with Rodney trailing behind, dumbfounded by the madness.

Inside stood Agent Orange and Agent Black, waiting impatiently.

"You were supposed to be here thirty minutes ago, Agent Thunders," Agent Orange yelled.

"Listen up, everyone." Chuck said. "This is my black partner. We done been through hell and back. He's like a brother to me even though I'm white. Ain't that right, partner?"

"Sure," Rodney replied, being polite. "I guess so."

Chuck gave a proud nod.

The agent was not pleased. "You were instructed *not* to tell anyone regarding us *or* your mission. You can't just waltz into a local police station and take on a civilian partner. We are a secret organization! What in the hell is the matter with you, Thunders?"

"He's entitled to a ride along like the rest."

"Yeah," Rodney said. "I'm supposed to babysit and shit. It's cool."

Chuck attempted to ease the agent's minds. "Fuck all this noise. He's the coolest dude I know. Besides, I need a partner to roll with while I'm fighting bad guys. That car Katz sounds like some queer-ass, British, C3PO fag that don't know shit about anything cool. The car's a geek, man. Who programmed that bullshit?"

The agent shook his head in disbelief. He picked up a brief case from the floor, placed it on Cutty's desk, and opened it. Inside were several pair of aviator shades next to a futuristic blaster that had intensity, adjuster knobs and a self-targeting telescope—just in case the shooter sucked.

Chuck was unimpressed. "Steal that off a Stormtrooper?"

The agent ran his finger along the weapon and spoke proud. "*This*, Agent Thunders, is our very own P-34. It's a self-powered, Draconian, protoblasting alien stopper."

"Cute name."

Cutty chimed in. "I just finished the final touches. Regular bullets won't cut it with them Alphas unless we talking direct head shots. You'll probably need this bad mamba-jamba right here. Shit shoots blaster bullets and shit and when it's hooked up to a tank can double as a flamethrower of sorts."

"I only use my fists on Drakes," Chuck said. "Makes the kills nasty and personal—just the way I like it."

Rodney leaned over to Chuck. "Hey, bro. Um. What the fuck exactly is a Drake? Some new gang up in The Village?"

"Alpha Draconians." Chuck schooled him. "I call 'em Drakes for short. Just sounds cooler. They're the reptilian race that walk among us posing as humans. Bill Nedick is one of them evil bastards. I don't really give a fuck about *what* he is. All I wanna know is *where* he is."

Rodney started laughing. "This is a joke, right? Y'all fucking with me? That's it. We on *Candid Camera*? Where's Alan Funt? Hiding in the closet? And what's the shades for? Wait, wait. Lemme guess. You put those on so you can see who's human and who's not, right?" Rodney laughed.

The agent handed him the shades.

"What? You want me to put these ugly-ass things on so you can try and make me look stupid for the camera, huh?"

No response.

Rodney humored them. He placed the shades on his face and looked through the tinted lenses at the agents whose faces remained the same. He looked to Chuck who also stayed the same. He then looked to Cutty who was not only reptilian but had a lizard tongue that shot out with a *hisssss!*

"Oh, shit!" Rodney jumped back and ripped off the shades. "Fuck's going on up in here with this crazy-ass shit? Cutty looking like Cobra Commander and shit?"

"Don't sweat it, partner," Chuck assured. "Cutty's on our side. He's a double agent. He's not Cobra Commander by any stretch, but they all look this way under the illusion. *Even* Cobra Commander, which I'm sure is a Drake level thirteen member. G.I. Joe is my shit, bro."

The room was silent.

Rodney took it all in. He placed the shades back on, glanced at Cutty, and, once again, Cutty hissed.

Rodney tossed the shades on the desk and headed out with his hands up. "Y'all motherfuckers straight-up crazy with all this *V: The Final Battle* bullshit. I'll be in the car, Chuck."

"I'll be right out, partner," Chuck said as Rodney exited. "And don't mess with my radio!" Chuck looked at the agents. "Hate when people do that."

Agent Orange was not pleased in the slightest. "Have you told anyone else who you are or what you're doing here?"

"Nah," Chuck replied. "I wouldn't do that. Jesus, you're paranoid."

"You told that friend of yours out there?"

Chuck thought for a moment. "Yeah. But that's different. He's black. They're not into aliens and shit like white people, so I don't think he'll say anything to his friends and family about all this stuff. They'd probably make fun of him. So, it's cool. I've thought this out way in advance."

Agent Orange shook his head then looked to Agent Black who just kept puffing away at his cigarette.

"What?" Chuck said. "Y'all mad at me now? It's because Rodney's black, right? Just go ahead and say it."

Agent Black put his cigarette out on the floor under his shoe, reached in his pocket for a small metal baton, and headed directly for the garage bay.

"Whoa!" Chuck said. "Where's the mute dude going? He ain't gonna kill Rodney with that metal dildo, is he? You guys are sick!"

"No," Agent Orange said. "He's simply going to erase the last few hours of his memory. Now, Agent Thunders."

"That's me."

"Your main objective right now is to get this Rodney character back to the station. He'll be dazed for about twenty minutes before he snaps out of it. Just leave him in his car. After that, you are to retrieve a video cassette."

"You want me to rent a movie? Can I pick it?"

"We have word that Bill Nedick will be illegally running a commercial to the citizens of Rockwood tonight, and you must stop him at all costs. We *must* get that tape. You will more than likely have to go through his entire crew to retrieve it. If he activates his plan and runs that commercial, Rockwood is doomed. This will ruin *everything*. Wherever it is, find it. Then you are instructed to bring it back here so we can box it up and put it in a secret warehouse like they did in your earth film *Raiders of the Lost Ark*. Are we clear?"

Chuck smiled. "I fucking love that movie!"

"I knew you'd like that." Agent Orange smiled proud.

"And I guess it's safe to say that Bill's crew just got fucked."

Moments later, Chuck hopped back in his ride. He looked over at the drooling, brain-drained Rodney and sadly began to mourn what could have been the greatest partnership since Dirty Harry and any one of his many partners that always ended up getting killed. What a shame. His all-time best friend was going to miss all the fun. *Shit.*

Chuck fired up the car.

Agent Orange poked his head into the bay. "Take him straight back! You now have fifteen minutes!"

"Yes, Mom!" Chuck pulled out with a skid and slid to a stop at the main road.

Through the dashboard speaker, a beep began to emit, which steadily got faster and faster. Chuck quickly looked around for the blip's target. In the distance, the sound of a Harley Davidson came roaring in. Chuck looked up and could see it was the mighty Rough House with the wind in his hair and being Bad to the Bone. Chuck fumed. Rough House was the man that embarrassed the hell out of him earlier with that sucker punch when he wasn't looking. Chuck hated sucker-punch pussies. He turned to the drooling Rodney and decided his current plans had suddenly changed.

The motorcycle blew past.

Chuck hit the gas, steadily kept his distance, and followed the biker like a hungry shark.

Chapter Four
THE NINJA TAINT-BLAST TECHNIQUE

Elsewhere, a raggedy van was parked on the side of the road. Inside it, Meryl and Gay-Bob Kael snacked away from a rusty, tin pail that was filled with chunks of raw meat. The radio played "The Bandit Express" from *Smokey and the Bandit 3* (their favorite soundtrack) at low volume.

Gay-Bob licked the blood from his fingers. "Look, Daddy. We're still in a pretty nice place. I mean, we can basically do whatever we want. We got access to some of the hottest poontang Rockwood has to offer, got a nice little nest egg at the trailer park and can basically live like kings out there for the rest of our goddamn lives. I'm not really sure fucking with Bill is worth all this risk. I mean, why bother?"

"Gay-Bob," Meryl exhaled. "You about as idget as they come. I already explained the shit once. If Bill drops the goddamn illusion like we done heard he been planning, all the shit you done grown accustom to will be dead and gone. *And* after all the change that's gonna happen, he's gonna be putting that Billy Ray in charge of all kinda shit. A human of all things. You want that? That human nigger hates our asses. *You* especially. We already hurting bad enough as is. What's the matter with you?"

Gay-Bob popped the top on his Coors Light. "Whatever, Daddy." He took a sip. "All I know is if we get caught trying any shady shit outside The Council's approval, we're gonna be in some serious trouble. Just because we can live four times longer than these man-apes doesn't mean we can't be put to death. You willing to risk that? Bill's a made-man now, and we can't touch 'em. You need to just learn to accept the shit. I have."

"Never." Meryl wiped his bloody lips with his tie to get presentable. "Bill's too big for his goddamn britches for our kind anyway, and I'm sick of getting fucked by one of my own. The Council assigned here ain't nothing but a bunch of retard bosses letting this shit happen. No idea why they always dump 'em here. But don't you worry, Gay-Bob. We in the right, and I'm sure when it's all said and done, the Lizard/Earth Coalition of Reptiles That Can Walk and Talk will agree one-hundred percent with me on this and pardon both of us for going at a made man. Besides. Won't be much risk. Not if I planned this right. If I planned this right, then the stupid ass that'll take the fall," Harold's van suddenly appeared and slowly pulled in, "is that one right there."

Both *men* began to laugh.

Minutes later, in the back of the van, the Kaels sat with Harold around a small card table that was bolted to the middle of the floor.

"Okay, Harold." Meryl said leaning into the light. "Here's the deal. You do this for our people and we can make *all* your dreams come true. You can be held in high regard as a true Draconian patriot. Think about that, Harold. Respect! And seen as an upholder of tradition amongst our kind, which is important to me. Just like I know how much it's important to you. Loyalty *is* important, Harold. To sacrifice to something bigger than yourself."

Harold nodded, not really following.

Meryl continued. "And I hate to bring this up, Harold, but I best go ahead and tell you anyway. It's rapidly becoming well known around The Council that that goddamn daddy of yours is planning on cutting off your allowance starting next week."

Harold was shocked. "What?!"

"Yup. And from the look on your face, I can tell this is news to you. Uh-huh. Gonna give it to Billy Ray instead. He's not even one of us. A goddamn good-for-nothing, human sumbitch. That's the kicker." Meryl leaned back, disgusted. "Your daddy thinks he can just do whatever the hell he wants. Doesn't seem fair, does it? Giving your allowance to Billy Ray. If we don't stop this, our people will end up with nothing in the end—unless *you* take a stand like the true Draconian warrior we know you can be."

"You really think he'd take my allowance away, and I'd have to get a job at the Piggly Wiggly or something?" Harold asked with great concern.

Meryl removed his cowboy hat. His comb-over fell and touched his shoulder. "Believe so, Harold," he said trying to fix his mop. "Just gonna leave your ass behind to rot. He doesn't take you all that serious, anyway. Our kind don't really accept half-breeds. They always come out slow and stupid and shit ... no offense."

None was taken.

Meryl held up the pail of meat to offer Harold a piece, which he gladly accepted, popped into his mouth, and chewed away on.

Meryl put the pail down. "That's not your fault though. We can't help the way we're born, right? Or the way people see us. But things can be different for you, Harold. Regardless. Things can change. If you make 'em, that is. And that's where *we* come in. To help you make that happen. Anyway, it's high time you quit living under your daddy's shadow for once. He'll leave you, Harold. Trust me on this. At least with us, you can getcha self a piece, before it's all gone and vanished and you're up shit creek without a paddle. Shit. Never know. Maybe with us you could even run a titty bar someday. Be a gangster. Maybe even run your own town. Could you imagine that?" Meryl tapped Gay-Bob's arm. "How about you, Gay-Bob? Can you imagine that shit?"

"Nope." Gay-Bob replied with a quick, uninterested sip of beer. "I can't imagine that shit, Daddy."

"I can't either," Meryl said. "How about that shit? It's like we all connected. Heh-heh. But seriously, Harold. Just think of it." Meryl, hands up, framed an imaginary poster and pitched, "Harold Nedick! The scariest crime boss *of all time!*"

The van fell completely silent.

Harold began to think. The promise of a lieutenant's position in Uncle Meryl's gang *was* pretty sweet. He wouldn't even need daddy's weekly allowance with the Kaels by his side. He could have whatever he wanted. All the Twinkie cakes in Rockwood could be his for the taking. *Mm-mm.* But could he pull it off? Doubt began to creep into his expression.

Meryl could see this and proceeded with caution. "We believe in you, Harold. Don't we Gay-Bob?"

Gay-Bob sipped. "Yup."

"I don't know, uncle Meryl. If my daddy finds out what I'm up to, I could be grounded for a really long time. He might even take my van away for this."

"And a damn fine van it is!" Meryl celebrated. "Royal blue with flames going down the sides and an observation bubble to boot? Are you kidding me? How cool is that shit?"

Gay-Bob chuckled but cut himself off quick.

Meryl looked at him stone-faced, then ever so slowly back to Harold with a cheap grin, and said, "You probably even got one of them eight-track players in it, I'd bet."

"It does!" Harold said. "And a CB radio too, so I can talk to the truckers."

"You hear that, Gay-Bob? The boy's got a goddamn CB radio!"

Gay-Bob said, "Wow, Daddy."

Meryl leaned in. "So, what's your call sign, Harold? Bet it's something cool."

Harold smiled. "... Ham Solo."

"Hey. I like that! Heh-heh-heh-heh. So, what's it gonna be, Harold? Are you in ... or are you out?"

Harold's stomach began to growl. If he could pull this off, he'd never have to worry about that sound again. And there was no way he was getting a job. Screw that. Convinced he was right, he looked at his uncle, and nodded. "Ok, Uncle Meryl. I'm in. What do you need me to do?"

The Kael Boys smiled.

*

Outside the No Monkey Business Club, Rough House came roaring in on his Harley. He parked next to a row of bikes, got off with much attitude, then entered the bar built for the rough-and-tough customers only.

Moments later, Chuck and Rodney pulled in and idled back as far as the gravel lot would allow for a good stakeout, then parked facing the redneck establishment. Rodney was still zapped out and drooling down the front of his shirt.

After a moment of Chuck checking out the scene with a pair of high-tech binoculars, Rodney snapped out of his trance in shock. "Where the fuck am I?" he asked. "Who the fuck is you?"

That's when Rough House exited the bar with a rough-looking biker babe by his side.

"Shit," Chuck said. "I'll explain everything in a minute. There's our target. Just sit tight and remain calm, partner."

Rodney was in a world of confusion. He looked around the car and wondered just what the hell he was doing in it.

Katz spoke up. "Sir," the car said. "I have scanned his bike and have found no traces of the Valaxium 10 drug or the video cassette. This is not the best course of action at this juncture."

"Shut up, Katz," Chuck said.

"I shall report this."

"Yeah? And I'll punch your ass right in the fucking equalizer. Just butt out. Do something useful. Play 'One Way Street' from *Rock IV* at low volume."

The track began to play.

Rodney's eyes went wide. "Motherfucker what? What the fuck is going on up in here? And why is your car talking? You *Knight Rider* or some shit?"

"We already did that joke. Just hang loose, partner. You see that big dude *right* there?"

"Who?" Rodney asked. "Him? That's Rough House."

Rough House was now leaning against the building with the biker babe kneeling before him. She quickly yanked his pants down and went to work.

Rodney continued. "You don't wanna be fucking around with that dude, whoever the fuck you are. Me neither. We best just leave. They don't like black folks here and in case you haven't noticed, I'm blacker than a motherfucker."

No response.

"Hey!" Rodney shout whispered. "Did you hear what I said? We need to leave, like, right now. They see me here, and it could very well be my black ass last day on earth."

"Look, Rodney. Here's what's going down. I'm a top-secret Super Cop that specializes in taking down sick fucks like that *right there*. He rolls with a very bad crowd and needs to be taken out. That's where you and I come in, partner."

"Say what? Partner who? Partner me? Are you fucking crazy? I don't even know you, dude. Take me home, right now before he—"

"Hold up. He's about to bust that nut."

And he did. Rough House busted that nut all in the biker babe's mouth with a grunt of ecstasy.

Chuck looked to Rodney, and said, "Hope he enjoyed that nut. It's going to be his fucking last." He exited the car and strutted straight towards his target.

Rough House was still leaning against the wall with his pants down, smoking a cigarette. "Get me a beer, bitch."

The biker babe wiped her mouth, got up, and wobbled her way back into the bar.

Chuck suddenly appeared before Rough House and the odd stare-down began.

Rough House hesitated a moment, rudely blew smoke in Chuck's face, then proceeded to warn him nicely with a finger poke to the chest. "I highly advise you to get that black dude in that car over there the fuck outta here, before me and my boys inside string 'em up by that big, black dick of his and make you watch as we murder his nigger ass."

"Know who I am?" Chuck asked.

Rough House took a slow drag. "Nope."

"No?"

"That's what I said, fucking punk. And why should I? And do like I told you and get that fucking nigger the fuck out of here. Know where the fuck you're standing? This Klan country, boy. Flavel Division."

Chuck pointed back. "Where Chuck Thunders goes, Rodney Tibbs goes, and I go here. We're joined at the hip, and I won't take any disrespectful shit from you, or anyone else for that matter, towards the fact that he was born all brown, which, by the way, ain't his fault." Chuck turned to Rodney and gave him an approving thumbs up and a smile.

Rodney was still blank.

Chuck looked back to Rough House. "You got that? You big, stupid, burly-ass bastard."

"Fuck Rodney Tibbs, his porch-monkey momma, *and* the rest of the niggers in Rockwood. Hang 'em all."

In a flash, Chuck dropped to the splits and did a robotic-hand uppercut to Rough House's taint (that space between the ass and balls) so bad that it rocked his world. Rough House clutched at his empty sack, gasped, then dropped dead on the spot.

Rodney sat in shock; his mouth wide open. He could not believe what he'd just witnessed.

"*Bloodsport*, you racist bitch," Chuck said from the splits position. He popped back up to his feet, adjusted his aviator shades, then strutted back to the car. He hopped in and shut the door.

The biker babe came back outside with Rough House's beer. She spotted his corpse on the gravel lot, dropped the bottle on the ground with a crash, then ran back inside screaming.

Chuck threw a fresh matchstick in his mouth, checked his hair in the rear-view mirror, fired up the car, then punched the red button on the dash labeled Thunder Cracker. The trunk abruptly opened and out sprang a self-targeting M-60 machine gun attached to a swivel turret.

Rodney gulped.

Men began to pour from the bar, a horde of leather-clad, tattooed bikers and rednecks, all hooting and hollering at the top of their lungs with various chains, knives and beers in hand.

Chuck reached forward. He pushed play on the stereo and Vince Dicola's "Training Montage" from *Rocky IV* began playing at high volume. The M-60 came alive and started blasting random men to smithereens to the music. What started as a bum rush quickly turned into a beach invasion gone wrong, and not one man could turn back as the bullets and blood flew. Rodney sat in total shock as bodies, one right after the other, hit the parking lot, some intact, most in pieces.

Chuck casually reached in the backseat, grabbed the P34 Draconian Protoblasting Alien gun and stepped out. He leveled the weapon at the crowd and joined in with a thousand-round burst of laser bullets that went *phew!* with every bright, blue blast. Men began catching fire left and right and ran in agonizing circles around one another before finally dropping like burnt flies.

Once the last man fell, the machine gun stopped firing; its barrel was smoking. It quickly retracted back into the trunk.

Chuck hopped back in Katz, tossed the weapon in the back seat, casually put the car in gear, and pulled out.

Rodney sat speechless as they headed down the road. After a few moments, he finally spoke. "Who the fuck is you, and what the fuck just happened?"

"Ninja, taint-blast technique. Popped him so hard in the taint that it caused a chain reaction of blood vessels to pop straight to the bastard's heart, causing it to explode on site."

"... Say what?"

"I learned that shit from the ninja upload. I guess I should have at least tried to get some info out of him first. Fuck it."

"Okay. I'll ask again. Who the fuck is you, and why the fuck did I wake up in your talking car?"

"Who am I?" Chuck unzipped his fanny back and pulled out his badge. "Chuck Thunders. Intergalactic Patrol. Section Eight. It's how *we* roll."

Rodney was speechless.

*

Back at The Pen, the entrance door flew open and in ran one of the locals in a panic. "Bill!" He stepped to the bar panting. "We got trouble!"

Razorback didn't even bother looking. "Can't get a moments rest. Fuck is it, Cooter?"

"Shirley came out the No Monkey Business Club and saw some feller in aviator shades kill Rough House. Then he shot the shit outta half the gang at the bar before taking off with that nigger cop Tibbs, and we ain't seen neither since." Cooter looked down in shame. "Sorry, Bill. They got away."

Razorback immediately boiled from the loss of one of his main soldiers. He stood from his bar stool, slowly turned to the messenger, then gave him a vicious head butt which sent him to the floor. Razorback then proceeded to viciously stomp Cooter in the chest and stomach until finally tiring himself out. From the looks of the bloody Cooter, he may be dead.

Razorback looked down at his custom, human-skin boots. "Look what the fuck you did to my boots, you prick!" He stomped Cooter directly in the face and dislocated his jaw to one side. Motionless, Cooter let out a gurgle and then nothing. If he wasn't dead before, he was now.

Razorback calmly reached over the bar, grabbed the phone, punched in numbers, and took a shot of whiskey.

The person on the other end answered. "No Monkey Business Club. Where white is right, day or night. Huh-huh."

"Cletus."

"That you, Bill? You hear what the fuck happened?"

"Spread the word to The Flock. I want this aviator-shade-wearing man dead. Free trash pickup and Playboy Channel for a month if anyone can bring him in alive. You hear me? Spread that shit!"

"Free titties? For a whole month? Woo-hoo! I'm on it!"

Minutes later, robed Ku Klux Klan members exited the No Monkey Business Club in a screaming frenzy. They jumped over the barbecued bikers' corpses in the parking lot and quickly mounted their pick-up trucks with shotguns, pitch forks, and torches blazing. All the vehicles fired up and hauled ass out.

Razorback began pouring himself a double shot when the phone rang. He wiped his sweaty brow with his handkerchief and answered with a frustrated, "What, goddamn it?"

"I have some news for you, William. There is a man coming your way that spells trouble."

"So, I've heard. Just who the fuck is this guy? What's his deal?"

"He's the man you beat down in the parking lot of The Pen earlier. He's been recruited into Section Eight, and as you know, they make some of the best self-proclaimed heroes in the game."

"I don't make heroes, I make victims."

"Not this time."

"Well, every hero needs a villain. And that's me." He slammed the phone down and threw back the shot. "Bring him on."

He reached into his pocket and pulled out a Star Trek-inspired, flip-phone communicator. And with a flick of the wrist, the screen opened up a glowing red, and Razorback pushed the communicator's only button.

A beep later, a voice came through the other end. "What's up, Bill?"

Razorback looked down at the glow. "Getcha asses over to The Pen. I need a favor."

"Dude. Are you out of coke already?"

Without responding, Razorback flipped his futuristic phone closed, pocketed it, then looked at his image in the bar's mirror. After a moment of reflection, his shot glass found its way through the air and shattered the image into a thousand pieces.

Chapter Five
THE COREY FELDMAN IN BLACK

Chuck and Rodney were headed back to Cutty's Garage. Chuck was letting Rodney in on his past and all of Section Eight's secrets.

"What?" Rodney asked sifting through cassettes. "You ain't got no Al Green?"

"Shit yeah."

Rodney excitedly grabbed a brand-new tape and held it up. "Holy shit. You do!"

Chucked smiled on the inside.

"I swear I ain't never met me no cool-ass, white dude like you before. You like Al Green. *And*, you white! I can't believe this shit. From now on, Imma have to tell everyone I meet on the street that Chuck Thunders got tunes."

"It's true, Rodney. I like Al Green. *And* I'm white. Been a fan for years. Want me to tell you something about Al Green that others might not realize?"

"Lay it on me, Chuck."

"He's much better than that Debbie Gibson."

"Yo," Rodney beamed. "I say the *exact* same shit all the time. Fuck that bitch."

Chuck actually smiled. He couldn't have been happier. They were bonding all over again and on even better musical terms than before.

They entered Cutty's bay, parked, and got out.

"Cutty know about this shit too?" Rodney asked. "You sure this cool? Thought you said they wanted me gone."

"Don't sweat it. I got pull."

They entered the office.

The two agents were dumbfounded when Rodney came walking in. "What is that man doing here?" Agent Orange asked. "Were you not instructed to take him back?"

Chuck remained calm. "Just hear me out. I was getting ready to, and all of the sudden this big guy on a Harley came blasting by, right?"

"Yeah," Rodney helped. "Rough House."

"Yeah!" Chuck said. "That's right! That's him. Rough House. I hate that fucking dude. Anyway. I just assumed that if—"

"You deviated from a mission priority to go pick a fight with a civilian on board?" Agent Orange asked. "Did Rough House even have possession of the tape?"

"No."

"Did you find out from him where it was or where they were planning on broadcasting the signal from?"

"No."

Agent Orange pointed at Rodney. "And when this man woke back up, did you happen to tell him everything about us all over again?"

"... *Maybe.*"

"Please tell me what significance this man could possibly have in all this."

"He's Rodney," Chuck said matter of fact. "Duh."

Agent Orange looked at his partner. "Just do it."

Agent Black walked up to Rodney, pulled out his brain-drain rod and smiled.

Not knowing what was up, Rodney smiled back. "How you doing, sir?"

The agent pushed the baton's button, zapped Rodney, and he hit the floor.

"Shit!" Chuck said. "At least let him sit down first. Jesus."

Moments later, Rodney was gently placed in Chuck's front seat, where he continued to sleep like a baby until...

...he woke to a pickup truck smashing into the side of them at high speed, the Ku Klux Klan on both sides with pitch forks and torches in hand screaming,

"Kill that goddamn nigger!"

"Yee-haw!"

"Ah shit! My torch went out!"

Rodney freaked. "Ahhh!"

"Grab the wheel!" Chuck yelled, already climbing out the window. Rodney grabbed the wheel, and with screams of panic, slid over and took control. Chuck leaped to the roof of the car, took a stern fighting stance, then quickly began blocking random pitchforks jabs from all angles with ease.

Suddenly a circular-shaped flying saucer came flying by their vehicles.

Rodney completely lost it. "What the fuck? We're being invaded!"

A few Klansmen took shots at the flying saucer, but it was no use. It had protection shields and was gone in a flash.

"Hold the wheel steady, partner!" Chuck yelled before jumping into a series of helicopter split-kicks and kicking Klansmen in the face from both sides. The last kick knocked off one's hood, revealing a little old lady underneath with a bloody nose. Chuck kicked her again and sent her flying into on-coming traffic.

*

"What?" Razorback shouted slapping Sheriff Bigelow across the face with a wad of cash. Hundred-dollar bills filled the air as the sheriff's new fan swayed back and forth. "Guess I'm not paying your ass enough, huh?"

"I'm sorry, Bill," Sheriff Wallace managed.

Razorback stepped in. "Don't flinch! What, you goddamn pussy? You gonna cry now, you little bitch?"

"I'm sorry, Bill."

"You already said that!" Razorback brushed off his ugly, leisure suit, threw his cowboy hat on the desk, and had a seat in the sheriff's chair. "Sit," he ordered.

"May I?" the sheriff pointed at the guest chair.

"Sit!"

Sheriff Bigelow sat.

Razorback stared at the pathetic lawman, whipped out his vial, then took a hit right in front of him. "I gotta quit doing so much cocaine," he confessed before pocketing the vial. "So, what exactly are we gonna do about your inability to keep these Section Eight fucks off my ass? Gotta earn your keep."

"I have been! I even told Officer Tibbs to babysit this fucking guy. I have no idea where he even came from or why Officer Tibbs would ever dare go against a—"

"How old is that daughter of yours?"

The sheriff tensed.

Razorback chuckled. "What's her name again?"

"... Dawn."

"That's right! And how old is Dawn now?"

"She's thirteen, Bill, and she's all I have."

Razorback smiled. "Hmmm."

"Look, Bill. I don't have a clue what the hell a Section Eight even is. I'm just a small town—"

The sound of a strange beep emitted from Razorback's golden wristwatch. He punched the watch's face and a six-inch hologram sprouted from the time piece. It was a call from Princess Adrianna, Razorback's sister (or as he would call her, the biggest bitch in the galaxy). She was sexy enough to be front and center in a Ratt video and used plenty of hairspray to hold her eighties hair in place, but unfortunately suffered from permanent bitch face.

Razorback leaned back in his swivel chair and smiled at the hologram. "Adrianna! So, how the hell's my favorite sister in the entire galaxy doing? Haven't heard from you, say, oh, I don't know, hundred and twenty years or so. You still a bitch? How's aunt Tessa?"

Princess Adrianna, all about business, spoke. "Hello, brother. I have a message to deliver to you from back home. We need to talk immediately. I'm coming in for a landing now."

Just then, the conversation was interrupted by the sound of something massive, and the ground beneath the station began to rumble.

Sheriff Bigelow ran to the window.

Razorback remained glued to his seat.

"What the goddamn fuck?" Sheriff Bigelow shouted as the flying saucer approached. It hovered over the station's lot and slowly landed, kicking up a massive dust storm in the process.

The officers in the station remained glued to their seats, afraid of what was happening outside.

"Fuck is that?" an officer asked.

"Russians, maybe," another answered.

Outside, the ship's door slowly lowered with a *hummmmm* and stopped with a puff of dust when it hit the dirt lot. Princess Adrianna and her two escorts exited the ship, all three dressed in maroon, one-piece, flight suits with glossy, knee-high, black boots. Both guards carried blaster rifles at the ready and wore helmets with goggles so thick they seemed almost impossible to see out of—for a human anyway. The three Draconians in human disguises walked in unison to the front of the station and entered.

The officers turned at the guests.

Staring dead-ahead with her piercing blue eyes, Princess Adrianna and her escorts proceeded straight for Sheriff Bigelow's office.

"You have an appointment?" the secretary asked.

Without hesitation, one of the guards shot and zapped her into disintegration, leaving nothing behind but a small pile of red dust.

An officer spit coffee. "Holy shit!"

Princess Adrianna, without missing a step or raising her voice in the slightest, gave the order. "Leave."

The officers jumped from their seats and the office emptied in no time.

"Look at that," the first one out of the door shouted. "A goddamn flying saucer!"

Princess Adrianna entered Sheriff Bigelow's office with escorts in tow. You could hear a pin drop as Sheriff Bigelow stood next to the desk with his mouth wide open.

Razorback spun around in his swivel chair to reveal a gleeful smile. "How you doing, sis?"

Princess Adrianna stepped forward. "William, ... let's talk."

*

As Chuck piloted his vehicle for town, he filled Rodney in on everything all over again. His partner was attempting to make sense of it all.

"So, let me get this straight," Rodney said. "You mean to tell me that the UFO we just saw *was* real, there were some lizard-aliens flying the shit, *and* the KKK is after us because you're an intergalactic soldier who punched Rough House in the balls with your metal hand? And on top of all this, you're supposed to try and stop a beer commercial Bill Nedick is running before the *Dukes of Hazzard* tonight? Am I missing anything?"

"Just that I'm an Al Green fan."

"Yeah, he's alright. And I'll be sure and tell everyone I meet that Chuck Thunders is one cool, white dude for liking Al Green. Because I know that's what you want so you can look all cool and diverse and shit; I get that. But you really smashed Rough House's taint, man?"

"Not only smashed it. Killed his ass."

"I see. Guess that means I'll be dead by tomorrow."

"Not with me around."

"Uh, okay," Rodney said sarcastically, "Being with you is safe alright. You drag me into anything else I should know about just because you think it's cool to hang out with a black dude, whatever that means?"

"That's about it. Pretty simple, huh?"

"Yeah. I guess. A little racist, I'll admit. But think about this shit, Chuck. Bill Nedick can't be touched, and I sure in the fuck don't want to die in the middle of some madness that has absolutely nothing to do with me. You got me feeling like some token black, throwaway character in a bad revenge flick over here. Like I could die any minute. You need a serious plot change, and I'm not your fucking monkey, bro."

"What the hell are you talking about? I don't even like pets."

"And besides, I don't give a fuck if Bill Nedick is a human, lizard, or whatever, he's a goddamn redneck monster—period. Why don't you just forget about this crazy shit and go fuck that Bobby bitch you were babbling about. Raise a kid or something. She seems like a helluva lot better time than tangling ass with Bill Nedick. Besides, I got a date tonight. And she's white!" Rodney licked his lips. "It's a done deal. Got that shit *all* set. I may have forgotten a lot of shit today, but I ain't forget that coochie. Never happen."

"An intergalactic battle like Rockwood has never seen is about to go down and all you can think about is pussy?"

"No-no-no. *White* pussy."

"Are you kidding me? Have you not heard a word I said?"

"Yeah. Aliens and shit. Kinda stupid if you ask me. Look, Chuck, Larry, whoever you are, I think I better go back to the station. Imma ask the sheriff for the rest of the day off. I'm tired as a hell and need some rest for my date tonight—if I'm still alive by then. Thanks for that by the way, *partner*."

Chuck slammed the breaks to a stop in the middle of the road. He looked at Rodney in shock. "I can't believe you're gonna bail on me. It can't end like this."

"Oh, yeah. Ending. Roll credits. Fuck this crazy shit."

"We're supposed to be a team. *The* team. And after all we've been through? After all I've let you in on? I'm giving you a chance to be somebody, Rodney. You could be more than the token, black guy in all this cool shit if you really wanted. Your role in this challenge is really up to you. And you're saying no?"

"Yeah. Imma say no. We don't all have the same dreams. You want to be some kinda action star to impress people who don't really give a shit about you in the first place, I want to be left alone, knee-deep in pussy and have a few laughs. I don't really care about the rest. The only reason I'm a cop is because it was the only job in town available after my aunt kicked me the fuck out. I'm just in this shit for the rent, you know, and to keep the tank in my Torino filled so I can drive around and tap ass. My ambitions don't *really* exceed much past that. Mexican food is a close second. Cajun is good."

Chuck took it all in. He couldn't believe what he was hearing. "So, you're saying you're out?"

"I'm out, Chuck. Drop me off."

Moments later, Chuck and Rodney pulled into the station and parked right next to the spaceship.

"Look," Chuck said. "You mean to tell me the intergalactic safety of this town doesn't mean anything to you? This shit is just beginning. You got to help me locate that tape. What if Bill Nedick broadcasts that stupid commercial of his?"

"Nah. Seems like you ain't in this shit for results. You just want some payback for what they did to your booty. Understandable, I suppose. Still not sure why you even admitted that happened to me. Ever hear of *too much information*? But that's why you went after Rough House first without thinking. You're reckless. Look, Chuck, I'll just be honest, I kind of agree with Bill on some of this shit."

"Say what?"

"Yeah. Fuck all this living-a-lie bullshit. This organization you work for, Section Eight, well, they seem to suppress truth. I don't care what their motives are, but they do. I might be a lot of things, Chuck, but one thing I can't do is lie to everyone. But anyway, space politics aside, this shit really sounds like nothing more than a good way to get my black ass killed if I keep hanging out with you. Just because you can kick this guy's ass now, don't mean you should. Think about what's important, my man. Look, Chuck. You be cool. Take care. And, Katz."

"Yes, sir?" the dashboard replied.

"Keep an eye on this fool. And don't you go fucking any Ford Pintos. Them shits explode when you hit 'em from the back."

"I'll take it under advisement. Please, take care, sir."

Rodney opened the door, hopped out, and with his trademark swag, walked towards the station without a backwards glance.

Chuck dwelled as he watched Rodney walk away from the cool Section Eight mobile and out of his life. Maybe Rodney was right. Maybe he put Rodney in danger after all. But in Chuck's defense, he was left unsupervised as a child and raised himself on action movies and cereal. He didn't know any better when it came to real life. Still, it hurt. He put the car into gear and drove off.

Rodney entered the station and looked around at the empty lobby. He walked pass the secretary's desk, glanced down at the red dust in her chair, then entered the sheriff's office. The first thing he noticed, Sheriff Bigelow in his chair with a gaping, artery wound, slowly dying with a look of frozen shock. The second thing, a sexy, white woman in maroon with blood all over her mouth and chin, chewing on what Rodney figured was a piece of Sheriff Bigelow's neck. Then he heard the sound of a stun-gun blaster, and Rodney, for the third time that day, hit the floor.

Princess Adrianna looked at her brother. "Take this man. Find out what you can from him on where this secret agent Chuck Thunders could be hiding. Then finish both of them off, so we can get down to business without distractions. I'll meet you back at The Pen."

"Don't you worry, sis," Razorback assured. "Don't you worry. Once I find out something, and I always do, I'll personally put my right-hand man Billy Ray on the shit. He got that special cheese I need to catch rats."

Princess Adrianna stared daggers. "No mistakes." She exited with her escorts.

Razorback whipped out his handkerchief and wiped the sweat from his double chin, and said, "God, I hate that bitch."

*

The black car of indeterminate make and model drove the backroads of Rockwood as Devo's "Planet Earth" pumped from the stereo. Inside, two rogue agents from the Men in Black casually cruised, both in matching black suits but with different ties, one solid red and the other solid blue. Blue Tie was obsessing over his hair in the mirror, a new habit he picked up. "What do you think?" he asked. "You ever see such a good-looking head of hair? I look like Johnny Depp or what?"

"Why the fuck do you watch that stupid-ass cop show? Them dudes, and the black chick on there for that matter, are like thirty-years old still trying to act like they're in high school, only *they can't act*. And I don't buy a single one of them as a cop. And this

Johnny Deep dork you been man crushing over lately—that I've turned a blind eye to—will never last as an actor. Him *and* the shows on this planet are total shit, man."

"Then why do you watch *Benny Hill* reruns every night?"

"The chicks. These Rockwood chicks look like Super Fly Snuka head-butted their asses from the top rope twice then took a jackhammer to their frigging teeth, man."

Blue Tie ran his fingers through his hair and paused when he saw his reflection in the mirror. "You know, if I make my hair blond, I could look like River Phoenix. A little shape shift of the face and boom."

"Getting pretty sick of you changing your goddamn face all the time. This ain't *Critters*, man."

"I dug *Critters*. Dee Wallace, bro." Blue Tie readjusted the rear-view mirror.

Red Tie shook his head. "She's just okay."

"Uh-huh. So, what the fuck do you think that fat head wants now? Must be important. We already had the sheriff killed for him last year."

"Who knows? All I know is I can't wait to get the fuck out of this shit town and away from him. He can have the shit. One fucking gas station, no movie theater, and the food is bunk."

"I like Cletus and Clarence's Barbecue myself."

"I've had better. But back to the subject at hand. You know how I tend to stay away from those who abuse their power? It's why I talked you into leaving outer space with me in the first place. But now look. Look at us. Look at this *shit*. Two steps back. Being pulled away at a moment's notice to go meet with this greasy asshole. Sort of defeats the purpose of us being rogue agents, *but* here we are. Time to move on after this."

"Couldn't agree more." Blue Tie adjusted the mirror and fixed his mop again. "You like Corey Feldman?"

Red Tie looked over. "Don't even think about it, dude."

*

Back at The Pen, Razorback sat behind his desk and questioned the man standing before him: Rodney Tibbs. As cool as Rodney could be, the office steadily got hotter. The unstable Billy Ray stood behind in the shadows.

Razorback continued. "I know your kind, boy. Lazy and all about yourself, but loyal to a few. And this Chuck Thunders might be one of your few. And *that's* what's gonna get you killed."

Rodney tried to talk his way out. "Wait just a minute, Mr. Nedick. I was *never* that man's partner. I just met that dude this morning. It's not like I conspired to get Rough House killed with him. This crazy dude kept draining my brain all day. I didn't know what the fuck was happening from one minute to the next. Last thing I know, I wake up and some Klan rednecks and spaceships are attacking us. All I knew then—and all I know now—is I want no part of this crazy shit. Any of it. I just want some pussy, man."

"Give me his location."

"Look, man. He ain't got no location. He's probably done up and left anyway with that Bobby bitch like I suggest he do."

Razorback took this in. "Bobby? Bobby Beggs? Only person in town named Bobby I know has one of them things called a vagina, and she sure as shit ain't never give me any of it. Must be saving it for one of them special occasions."

Billy Ray chuckled in the shadows. "Guess Chuck Thunders was it."

Rodney, realizing he just gave up Chuck's groupie, slowly closed his eyes and gulped.

Razorback smiled. "Guess this means we're done with *you*, boy. Thanks for the help. Happy trails."

Pow!

The bullet went through the back of Rodney's head and out the front. His brains sprayed, and he hit the shag carpet.

Billy Ray stepped from the darkness, .45 in hand.

Razorback said, "Feed his ass to the hogs."

"Then what?"

"Go fetch me that Bobby bitch. Think I might have that little whore for dinner." Razorback looked down at the bleeding Rodney. "There sure is a lotta blood in people, huh?"

Harold walked into the office holding a box of Milk Duds in one hand, a half-eaten rib in the other and had barbecue sauce smeared ear to ear. "Those two guys in black suits are waiting by the stage, Daddy."

"Thanks, dipshit." Razorback shrugged.

Harold asked, "Is it true that aunt Adrianna is here for a visit from Osiris? Did she bring me anything?"

Razorback responded by snorting back a loogie and spitting it on Rodney's corpse. Him and Billy Ray walked out, leaving Harold standing by the doorway. Harold noticed it on the desk immediately. It was the tape. The one uncle Meryl spoke about. It was time for Harold to step up and be a man. He proceeded to the desk with his sticky fingers out and snatched it up.

By the stage, the two Men in Black were seated front and center as a stripper slow danced to some old Hank Williams in hopes of tips from the two. That, of course, wasn't going to happen. Blue Tie, now looking like Corey Feldman with long, black, *Dream a Little Dream,* wet-head hair was disgusted by the stripper's music selection. He looked to Red Tie, and said, "What the fuck kind of stripper-joint music is this?"

"Fuck if I know. Dude almost sounds like he's about to cry into the microphone though."

"Maybe he's sad because he only sold one album, and it was Bill who bought it."

Razorback stepped behind them. "Let's mosey over to my table, fellas."

Over at Razorback's booth, the Men in Black sat across from him and watched him cut up six over-sized lines of cocaine on the table. He quickly sniffed half it up his nose and looked up with powder all over his face, and said, "I need something."

"More blow?" Red Tie asked.

"Yeah. But something else. Something special."

Blue Tie asked, "Alright, Bill. What's up?"

"Well, it's—" Razorback suddenly noticed Blue Tie's new face and did a double take. "Who the fuck are you supposed to be this time? Some honky-ass version of Michael Jackson?"

Blue Tie smiled. "... Perhaps."

"Anyway," Razorback continued. "I need something."

"Naturally," Red Tie said. "That's why we're here."

Blue Tie shrugged his head to get the greasy hair from his eyes, and said, "Absolutely. We supply the best for the best with our *License to Drive* all *The Lost Boys*. And you're our favorite lost boy from here all the way to the Goon Docks. One of the best, Bill. You know how *we* do it."

Razorback paused. "What the goddamn fuck are you talking about, stupid?"

Red Tie stepped in. "Tell us what you need, Bill."

"Some of that Serum 13B you boys stuck that greaser with last summer."

"Some 13B?" Red Tie asked. "You do know it doesn't always work on Draconians, right? We have yet to perfect Section Eight's serum without—"

"It's not for me," Razorback interrupted.

"Ok. Well, do you mind if we ask who's it for?"

"Yes, I do, fellas. I do mind."

"Well," Blue Tie said. "What if we don't have any? What if we live by a set of rules and standards for our business? What if—"

"What if," Razorback interrupted. "Hear me out. What if I don't give a shit? Now, give me the goddamn shit, take your cash, and get the fuck out of my sight." Razorback dropped a leather satchel on the table, partially open exposing a lot of cash. "I'm sure this is more than plenty. Now, take the cash and take your black-suit wearing asses the fuck outta here. And you, you nameless blue tie wearing prick. You can moonwalk the fuck out."

Insulted, Blue Tie leaped from his seat in an attempt to speak in defense on Corey Feldman, but Red Tie quickly halted him, and said, "I'll tell you what, Bill. We'll make a deal with you. If you can somehow pull some strings in any way possible and do us a serious solid, the serum is yours."

"Fuck is it you want?"

"Switchblade Butz released. Deal?"

Moments later, Razorback was in his office staring down at the empty spot where the VHS tape used to be. In its place, a few smears of barbecue sauce streaked the desktop.

*

In their rusted van, Meryl and Gay-Bob cruised, both of them half drunk and looking extremely nervous. Gay-Bob fidgeted with his mustache non-stop from the passenger seat and rambled. "We got sent for, Daddy. I told you we couldn't trust that Harold. We shoulda just been grateful for what we have and went back home and got shit-faced, but no. You and your greedy plans had to take a shit on my night, huh?"

Meryl reached down and grabbed his beer. "Just calm down, Son. Damn." He took a drink and belched.

"We ain't for sure why we got sent for yet. Maybe Bill done come to his senses and realized just how great we *really* are at designing pocket pussies and dildos. Maybe he wants to form a partnership and branch off into butt ticklers or something and wants our insight. Ever think of *that*?"

Gay-Bob gave his daddy a look of disbelief.

"Of course, you never thought of that." Meryl took a drink. "But I have. And that's why you're just the son, and *I'm* the daddy."

"I'm more than just someone's son, Daddy. And all this shit's coming from a man trying to bribe Bill's son to double cross him? Shit doesn't make you a thinker. It doesn't make you a schemer. It makes you an asshole, Daddy. A fly-by-the-seat-of-your-pants asshole, dragging me along for the flush like I'm just some turd done come outcha ass."

"Don't you be talking to your daddy like that. What's the matter with you, boy? We need to make a beer stop?"

"What's the matter with me? What the matter with you? Just because I'm your son, I'm supposed to go along with every goddamn scheme you come up with? I should be at home watching mud wrestling or some shit, but since I came out your goddamn nut sack a few years back, that, by default, means I'm supposed to go along with you on every goddamn thing comes outcha mouth? So, here I am. Possibly a dead man riding in a shitty van."

"Settle down, son. I ain't ever heard you talk like this before. Someone upset you earlier?"

Silence.

"Look, Gay-Bob. I give you my word, everything is gonna be just fine. I'm sure all this worry won't amount to much anyway. Trust your daddy." Meryl took a swig. "He knows best."

*

At the Tastee Freeze, Chuck and Bobby were enjoying their lunch date. Both had on matching pink, Buddy Band bracelets that Bobby made for them. Katz played *Over the Top's* "All I Need is You" from an open window.

With paper and crayons scattered across the table, Chuck colored in the bloody areas for the next issue of *Chuck Thunders: Super Cop* comics, issue #237. Scribbling away, he brought his woman up to speed. "Then that big bastard Rough House sucker punched me when I wasn't looking."

Bobby was in disbelief. "Oh, no he didn't. Now, who on earth would wanna hurt my man?"

Chuck looked up. "... Bad guys?"

"And then your best friend took off in your car?"

"Yeah. Well, I actually stole *that* car from the parking lot at that mental hospital this morning."

Bobby giggled. "You sure lead an exciting life, baby."

"No other way."

Bobby continued, amazed. "And then some anti-alien agent changed your face to look like an older Corey Haim, and then drained Rodney's memory?" She sucked some cherry Coke through a straw, swallowed, thought for a moment, and smiled. "You are *action packed*."

"I know. I saw him whip out this shiny-ass dildo-looking thing and head straight for Rodney. I almost felt sorry for him until he left me hanging high and dry without a partner. And after all we been through."

"I wouldn't be so hard on him, baby. He's just trying to find some happiness in Rockwood and not get killed like the rest of us. But we have nothing to worry about anymore, huh? Not with my man being some kind of Super Cop with a license to kill. Is that right?"

"*Unofficial* license to kill, which I fully intend to use. If I see Bill and his crew out, I kill 'em. One by one, I'll take 'em, Bobby. What Bill did was *not* cool. Worst experience since high school. Want to hear my back story?"

Bobby's eyes widened. "God, yes."

"I grew up in this town and got zero respect. Not one girl would touch it. Ever. Not once! And I begged *a lot*. All the guys would laugh at me and make fun of my rat tail, and one day in class when I wasn't looking one of those evil bastards cut it off. I was devastated! It took me eight months to grow that bad boy out. It had this cool little swirl on the end that I'd like to pull on and play with when I got nervous. And they cut it! But that didn't change who I was, and it sure as hell won't stop me from saving this town."

Bobby picked up the cherry from her sundae and sucked off the ice cream coating. "No room for a simple life? New roles? Me, you, a little Lincoln Marianne Thunders?" She gently placed the cherry in Chuck's mouth.

Chuck spit it on the ground. "What the hell? That shit was just in your mouth."

Bobby persisted. "So, no room in life for any role reversals, baby?"

"Like putting me in a dress and fucking me with a strap on? Well, maybe if—"

"Uh, no. Change your role *in life*. You can do whatever you want. *We* can do whatever we want. But no matter what you decide for the both of us, I'll always love you no matter what."

"I call bullshit. You don't want that. You want a Mr. Excitement badass, and that's what I am. It's what makes you so attracted to me. Without that, I'm nothing. *We* are nothing."

Bobby shrugged. "Maybe. I was never really that bright on such things. For instance, I don't have a clue what you just said, but it sounds to me like you are way deeper than I could have possibly imagined, and you are obviously way smarter than me about life and stuff."

"They loaded books on warrior philosophy into my brain."

"But can I ask you a question? Why should we even risk putting our happy lives on the line for these people? I mean, they cut off my man's rat tail."

Chuck hesitated. "Because it's the right thing to do, Bobby."

She smiled. "You know what's also the right thing to do? Taking me in the back of that talking car of yours and fucking the ever-loving shit out of me."

The virgin Chuck Thunders gulped.

Bobby leaned forward. "And please choke me hard as you pound, secret agent Chuck Thunders."

Chuck blushed beneath his aviator shades then quickly flashed her his glowing badge.

Bobby squirmed with sexual tension.

One minute later they were in the back of Katz, already finished.

"How'd you like that?" Chuck asked cocky.

"It was fine, sir," Katz said.

"Not you, Katz." Chuck looked through his shades at Bobby. "I meant you. How was it?"

Bobby assured him, "That was the single greatest thirty-five seconds of my life."

*

After dropping Bobby off to get her hair done for him, Chuck Thunders slowly cruised and mourned the death of his partnership with Rodney Tibbs, a man who he thought was the coolest black guy on the planet. The radio played "I Will Be Strong" from *Over the Top*.

Chuck pulled into Cutty's garage, and the bay door closed on cue. Chuck got out, but there was no Cutty to greet him this time. Chuck leaned in the car's door, and said, "Katz, check for any life readings."

"I found one, sir."

"Oh, yeah?" Chuck pulled out his pistol and cocked it. "Where?"

"Next to the car. It's you, sir."

"Fuck, you're stupid. Is there anyone *else* here?"

"No, sir."

"Thanks, asshole."

Chuck entered the office and found Cutty and Agent Orange on the floor dead with their throats cut wide open. Agent Black was nowhere to be found.

Chuck kneeled down to get a better look when all of the sudden a panel on the wall opened up and revealed a tube television sunk into the wall. The television came to life and the image of Billy Ray stared down at Chuck.

"What's up, bitch? We gotcha bitch, you fucking bitch. Bobby Beggs in the motherfucking house! Fuck you gonna do, huh? Fuck you gonna do, white boy? Fucking geek, motherfucker. What?!"

The sound of Bobby cried out on the television's audio. "Help me, baby. They're h-hu-hurting me."

Chuck's stomach sank.

Billy Ray continued. "Meet me at the Village Projects. You don't? Well, let's just say that me and my posse gonna do a murder rap on this dingbat bitch's ass she won't recover from. Don't delay, motherfucker. Much longer—" Billy Ray whipped out a pistol, pointed it at the screen, pulled the trigger, and killed the image feed, giving Chuck nothing but static on his end.

Chuck slowly stood and decided that the Pig Sticker beer commercial was the least of his concerns. Bobby was in danger. And that meant Billy Ray was next to be crossed off the list.

Chapter Six
FOLLOW THE DRIP

The Village Projects
Deep inside Rockwood's only ghetto, Billy Ray's yellow Trans Am sat guarded by several teens. One of them was washing the blood off its hood with a bucket of soapy water and a sponge. To the side, surrounded by dirty hypodermic needles and used, scratch-off tickets, a boombox blasted J.K. McCoy and the Homicide Squad's "Pussy Ain't Sellin' No Mo" at high volume.

Up on the second floor, inside Scooby Doobie's project home, apartment 13B, Bobby Beggs sat tied to a metal chair in the middle of the smoke-filled room. Her face was already beat to hell, and she was barely conscious. Several of Billy Ray's posse sat around and talked shop as a horribly, cheap-sounding, rap beat played in the background.

Scooby Doobie put a freshly-rolled blunt to his lips, took a hit, and exhaled heavily with, "So you saying that if we help this redneck motherfucker out with his alien bullshit, then he gonna make us rap stars up in Rockwood? I don't trust it. What planet this nigga grow up on? Who he repping?"

Billy Ray hit the joint. "Shit, I don't know. Repping his motherfucking self. Outer space. Ain't that some shit? Always knew that nigga was cold blooded, but I didn't know his ass was motherfucking full-fledged lizard."

You-Can-Get-the-Gat-For-That Jackson chimed in. "I got me a chameleon at the crib that likes to get high and shit. I blow smoke in the tank for him."

Bobby began to whimper. "Chuck is gonna turn that fat, lizard, gangster boss of yours into a belt for me to wear, you sorry bastards."

Billy Ray slowly stood and casually walked over to Bobby. She could barely look up. When she finally did, she caught a crushing blow to her nose from Billy Ray's fist.

Billy Ray smiled. "Fuck you, you cum-dump bitch."

*

Chuck Thunders, ready to die to save his beloved groupie, proceeded for the west end of town; a place where no whites were allowed. Despite hating gangster rap, he made the musical sacrifice for the mission and blasted Eazy E's "Boyz N the Hood" in hopes of getting into character and blending in when he reached The Village.

The volume on the stereo decreased and Katz spoke. "Sir, once again, this is not the best course of action. Billy Ray is not a mission priority and is surrounded by his gang. We should either retrieve the video cassette or find and neutralize the source from where the main feed will run. Time is running short."

"Fuck you and your programmed loyalties, you stupid-ass car. Shut up."

"I shall report this."

Chuck began applying shoe polish to his face, working the areas around his sunglasses.

Katz continued. "Sir, applying shoe polish to your face to look like a black person is quite possibly the most racist thing you can do. I seriously doubt that you will blend in well. You still have a white man's hair style that looks odd with a black face. I have researched all possibilities and found a much easier solution to retrieve the tape. Perhaps you should simply try and—"

Chuck silenced the car with a fist to the dash, crushing Katz, and the stereo, in the process. He passed the entrance to The Village, found a spot next to some break-dancers and parked. Leaving the P34 alien blaster in the back seat, Chuck went to the trunk instead and removed a double-barrel shotgun and a

Conan: The Destroyer replica sword; it was time to go old school. He shut the trunk, walked past the breakdancing kids who called him a stupid honky for his black face, and proceeded to Bobby's rescue.

Back inside Scooby Doobie's apartment, with his chair turned backwards, Billy Ray sat facing Bobby and kept blowing weed smoke in her face. "You know," he exhaled. "You been strutting your shit around this motherfucker for quite some time, little girl. Just begging for a nigga to jump out the bushes at you. Fuck the shit out of you, huh? Huh, bitch?" He flicked his ash on the floor.

Bobby was unable to respond—or maybe chose not to. Either way, she was motionless.

"This bitch pretty hot." Curtis Jones said entering the room in his Adidas jump suit and EPMD-inspired bucket hat. "I say we put a quarter in this bitch's slot and gallop her face like one of them kiddie rides outside the Piggly Wiggly." He walked by, flipped a quarter in her lap, and said, "You wanna be my horsy, bitch?" He entered the homemade recording booth made from cardboard boxes and duct tape. Inside, a microphone hung like a shower head with the cord disappearing into the wall to God knows where. Curtis put on a pair of Fisher Price head phones, and shouted, "Y'all niggas hold off beating that bitch for a second. Gotta lay down my vocals for this dope Mike BMC beat and shit. And kill that music out there!"

The music outside the booth stopped.

Business in the room continued.

Curtis went for it in the background, spitting horrible lyrics about his penis size, gun supply, and hoes, providing the scene with a horrible, acapella soundtrack.

Bobby managed to look up at the horrible sound and grimaced.

Billy Ray smiled at her. Because she was still alive. And there was a lot more damage he wanted to do before her death.

In the dark corner, Skittle Bug was getting a little too stoned on the space chronic Billy Ray scored from Razorback; it was not for amateurs (or humans for that matter). He was completely zoned out, paranoid, and beyond high—even slipping into dangerous schizophrenic territory. On the TV played *V: The Original Miniseries*, and the blond, white girl on screen was holding a male, space dignitary hostage at gun point, and screamed, "They are not who they appear to be!"

Skittle Bug brushed off the two hoes by his sides and leaned forward. The white girl on the tube grabbed the cheek of the space dignitary and peeled back his skin, revealing a terrifying alien underneath with green scales and reptilian eyes. That was enough for Skittle Bug. He shut off the TV. He leaned back on the couch to ponder, took another irresponsible drag, then twitched.

Girlfriend Number One asked. "What's wrong, Skittle? You not looking so hot, sugar."

"Yeah, baby." Girlfriend Number Two grabbed his crotch. "And why ain't yo dick hard? What? You don't *love* me no more?"

Skittle Bug shouted, "Billy Ray, my nigga! Gotta question for your black ass."

Still facing the battered Bobby, Billy Ray kept his crooked eye on his victim, and said, "Fuck you want, Skittle?"

Skittle Bug stood and wobbled his way into the hostage area. "Um, I'm over here watching some scary-ass bullshit on the tube and all this alien shit ain't looking too cool for my tastes."

Billy Ray looked to Skittle Bug. "Fuck you on now? Ain't you supposed to be trying to impress me or some shit? Don't you know I'm about to run these projects? You best proceed with caution, cuz. Really ain't feeling that tone. And you smoke too damn much. You know that?"

Skittle Bug twitched and took another drag. "Yo, man. Why you got to take it there? You know I only smoke to calm my nerves and shit. I'm under a lot of stress. It's hard out here for a pimp. Plus, it helps me write stronger lyrics about my dick going up in pussies and shit. But that's not the issue. I got a legit concern. You see? This white bitch on the TV just—"

"How much of that joint you smoke, Skittles?"

Skittle Bug hit it one last time to finish it off, coughed, and said, "All of it." He giggled once, dropped it to the stained indoor/outdoor carpet, and stomped it out. "But that's beside the point. There's something I just realized watching this flick on the tube with a couple of my bitches. Got me thinking. These alien motherfuckers ain't like us. We can't coexist and shit. That's what I'm getting at. Blacks and whites and reds and yellows have all had beefs and shit, but we *can* coexist if we really wanted to because we semi on the same page. Now, you wanna act like you all loyal and shit to this alien cat, but he ain't loyal to us as a species. From what I understand, *his* kind eat *our* kind. Gobble up our gerbils and shit too. And quite frankly, cuz, I happen to love my two gerbils back at the crib."

Still being the fly on the wall, You-Can-Get-the-Gat-For-That Jackson chimed in, and repeated. "I got me a chameleon at the crib that likes to get high and shit."

Billy Ray stood up, a little amazed at Skittle Bug for even bringing this ridiculous stuff up.

The two gangsters faced one another from across the smoke-filled room. With the exception of Randy in the booth still spitting horrible lyrics, there was a silent tension.

If Skittle Bug wasn't so high, he would have had every reason to be scared. Instead, he proceeded to dig deeper. "I'm loyal and shit, Billy Ray. That's all I'm saying. We all loyal. Loyal to you! Who you loyal to besides this shapeshifting crime boss, who quite frankly cannot stand black folks?"

"Not true. He hates *all* people."

"Well, I'm people! And that just proves my point. And if this motherfucker would eat my gerbils Blunt and Mary Jane like they some kind of hairy-ass burritos, and you are in fact rolling deep with this dude, then that means you have no loyalty to me or our kind either. I paid ten bucks a piece for them Gerbils, you insensitive nigga!"

"Fuck you talking about, *our* kind? Just last week you shot B-Ball in the face for stepping on your Jordans."

"But that was different!" Skittle Bug protested. "Them shits was brand new."

Billy Ray stepped to Skittle Bug and got face to face.

Skittle Bug didn't budge.

Billy Ray placed his chrome .45 automatic to Skittle Bug's temple, and said, "Say one more goddamn word about stupid gerbils and shit, yo. Watch what happens."

"Oh, yeah? Fuck you gonna—"

Whap! Skittle Bug got backhanded, and the sting took over the entire right side of his face. Second nature and ego kicked in, and he foolishly pulled his pistol.

Billy Ray pointed his .45.

Scooby Doobie grabbed the AK-47 off the floor and cocked it.

Curtis came out of the booth, asked "You fools hear them lyrics?" and then quickly realized the situation. He pulled two nine-millimeters. "What the fuck?"

Still looking down, You-Can-Get-the-Gat-For-That Jackson chimed in. "Y'all niggas hear about that spaceship earlier?" He looked up and seen gun barrels pointing left and right. He jumped from his beanbag chair and exhaled smoke with, "Fuck y'all fighting over this time? The tracks are fine, man!" He had no gun to pull, so he stepped back away from the scene. He leaned against the wall next to the Hoes with Attitudes poster and proceeded to watch the show unfold. If the bullets were gonna fly like last time, he'd be safest here.

Billy Ray was losing his patience. "Listen, man. You thinking too hard on shit, Skittles! That intergalactic weed got you all kinds of fucked up, and you starting to spiral down a rabbit hole of hypocritical questions. Don't question things. Don't question me. Understand! I got all this shit covered. All you need to do is follow my lead. Fuck, yo?"

Skittle Bug, arms out by his sides, threw his head back and rambled, "Well, ain't that a bitch? What? What? You think just because Razorback Bill's all cool and shit, and you wanna be all loyal to him based on some superficial, opposites-attract bullshit reasons, then that's somehow okay for him to eat my gerbils? And as your man, I'm supposed to be cool with you being cool with all this? Tell me something, Billy Ray. If all this gerbil eating shit ain't the case, then why you tripping when I bring it up? Why you tripping? Getting all defensive? I'll tell you why you tripping, okay. I'll tell you. You hate my gerbils, don't you? You think just because I'm some big, hood nigga with lyrics for days and has bitches—who half the time I can't remember their names—that I'm supposed to just buy a bulldog or some shit. Well, fuck you *and* your stereotype views on my life, nigga. Blunt and Mary Jane my peoples, fam. Just like you. Just like my thirteen kids are. And another thing. Gerbils don't exist just so you can hurt their feelings by saying some bullshit that—"

That's when the *Conan: The Destroyer* replica blade came through the wall and went through You-Can-Get-the-Gat-for-That Jackson's body and impaled him.

The gangster rappers froze.

The two hoes screamed.

Skittle Bug pointed his gun at the impaled rapper and panicked. "It's a gerbil eater! Kill it!" He started shooting at the wall and filled You-Can-Get-the-Gat-for-That Jackson full of holes. The joint finally fell from Jackson's grasp. His neck went limp, his head hunkered down, and with a final exhale, smoke exited from the various holes in his body.

Skittle Bug's hoes ran for the door, and with the exception of having some new Ghetto trauma, left unharmed.

Then without explanation, the room's only lightbulb popped to pieces, the room went dark, and the apartment's door slammed shut by an unseen force.

Billy Ray's gang emptied their entire clips into the door and within seconds turned it into wooden, Swiss cheese.

Curtis high-tailed to the bathroom and slammed the door. "The fuck is going on up in here?"

Suddenly a voice came from outside the bathroom window, that said, "Yo, Buckwheat," followed by a blast of a double-barrel shotgun, and Curtis' head was gone. His headless body flopped aimlessly around, smacked the wall once, then dropped to the tile twitching with the headphones still around what was left of the neck.

Chuck looked at the mess. The bathroom will need redecorated. *Not my problem* he thought. He jumped in, hugged the bloody wall, then tossed a specialized, canopy-inducing, smoke grenade across the floor.

Skittle Bug kicked in the door, fired rapidly into the smoky bathroom without regard for Curtis' safety, then stepped back. The smoke got thicker by the second and quickly coated the apartment's floor with a three-foot sea of perfect canopy. (Chuck could slink around undetected like the garbage-disposal worm in *Star Wars* with this. Anyway, that was his plan.)

Waist deep in smoke, Skittle Bug ran back into the living room/music-studio lounge, and shouted, "Shit, Billy Ray. I can't see him anywhere." He threw his arms up and took a quick step back. "Whoa! Fuck was that?"

"What?" Billy Ray asked.

"Something just slapped my ass and flicked me in the dick at the same time. What the fuck? I'm starting to get really scared here. What do we do? What do we do?"

"Just calm your black ass down before you shoot me and shit. Relax. We got this."

Behind the two men, Chuck's head slowly raised above the smoke screen like a special forces soldier emerging from enemy waters. He adjusted his aviator shades, then disappeared.

The tension was too much and Skittle Bug lost it. He began to scream and fire into the sea of smoke.

Billy Ray jumped out of the way of the maniac's misplaced shots.

Skittle Bug looked around in a panic. He tried to make a run for the kitchen counter—safe above the smoke—and then it happened. He got pulled under the smoke screen as if a shark attacked him. All Billy Ray could hear were the sounds of the agonizing, girl-like screams coming from Skittle Bug. Then silence.

Billy Ray leveled his weapon at the smoky floor, ready to fire at the first signs of life. Skittle Bug suddenly popped up from across the room, missing an ear and screaming bloody murder. Billy Ray didn't hesitate. He filled his hype man full of bullet holes until Skittle Bug finally expired and fell back into the cloud dead.

Billy Ray ran over to Bobby who was still tied to her chair passed out, her head slightly above the smoke. He aggressively put his gun to her head. "Show yourself, you *Jaws* motherfucker! Do it! Do it or else I'll straight-up shoot this hoe bitch!"

Chuck started to low crawl the room undetected. "Dunn-dun! Dunn-dun! Dun-dun-Dun-dun-Dun-dun!"

Billy Ray pointed the pistol at the smoke screen. "You think you funny? Okay. Laugh at this shit, you crazy-ass motherfucker!" He put the gun to Bobby's temple, but before he could pull the trigger, Chuck raised up from behind and sent his robotic hand straight through Billy Ray's body and out his chest, revealing a bloody, mechanical fist with two fingers out.

Chuck whispered in Billy Ray's dying ear, "That's called the Shaolin Finger Jab, you human-sell-out prick. Fuck you, Billy Ray."

Billy Ray fell dead.

Bobby began to awaken. The smoke finally started to dissipate the room. Her eyesight cleared and standing before her like a badass in half-done blackface was her hero. She managed a smile, and said, "My man."

Chuck ripped Bobby's metal shackles off with ease and helped her to stand. They began to leave when he saw the bump. It was Bobby's baby bump, and it wasn't there earlier. Only Draconians can birth that fast Chuck learned from his input programs earlier.

"Bobby," he stopped. "You have something you want to tell me?"

That's when the apartment's entrance broke down as if the Hulk smashed through. Bobby and Chuck were caught in the wrecking ball-like explosion, got tossed clear across the room, and slammed against the wall.

Through the smoke, dust, and dry-wall rubble stepped Razorback's son, Harold, who was now twice his original size in every way, shape and form—fists big enough to hold fifty twinkies. In his ripped-to-shreds, purple sweatpants and green shirt, he slowly stomped forward, and in a horrible Hulk impersonation, said, "Daddy gave me a shot of glowing stuff and now Harold big and strong." He took another step. "Stronger than Rough House was." Another step. "Stronger than everybody!" He grabbed Chuck by his head, lifted him off the ground, held him helplessly in front of his face and pointed. "And Harold is for sure more strong than little Chuck Thunders." He launched him through the air.

Chuck flew helplessly into the refrigerator and smashed its door. Styrofoam containers of hot wings and 40-ounce bottles poured from the fridge onto his back.

Harold chuckled his fake, evil laugh. "*Bahahaha*! I guess you want some din-din in the kitchen? Harold help." He walked over, grabbed Chuck by his frosted-tipped hair, and said, "Hungry? Eat fist," and socked his face.

Blood spewed, and Chuck's eyes quickly filled with blinding water.

Harold put his fists on his hips, leaned back, and evil laughed again. "What? Healing factor slow? Maybe Chuck just needs fresh air? Harold help!" Harold grabbed him by the arm and leg, hoisted him up over his head, and made for the window.

Chuck began to fight and squirm, but it was no use. The massive grips held with ease.

Harold stopped at the window, and asked, "Can Super Cops fly?" then threw Chuck out of the second-story window down to the ghetto streets.

Chuck landed on top of a moving ice cream truck and smashed its roof.

The driver stopped and leaned out to inspect the damage.

All Chuck could do was lay there and moan in agony.

Harold leaped from the apartment window with an idiotic, monster growl and landed with a mini-quake when his bare feet hit the street. He walked towards the ice cream truck, grabbed Chuck's ankle, and said, "And if Harold brings you back in one piece, all will be forgiven about uncle Meryl and cousin Gay-Bob, then daddy won't take away my allowance anymore." He ripped Chuck off the truck's roof and onto the pavement.

Chuck couldn't heal fast enough from blows of this magnitude.

And Harold knew that. He grabbed Chuck, lifted him, and with ten Ding Dongs on his breath, said, "And more important, daddy will finally love Harold and give me all the snacks I want." He threw Chuck through the air and into some power lines. The electricity shot through his body like sizzling hellfire. The street lights began to flicker. The shocking finally stopped, and he fell to the pavement, finished and done for.

Harold stepped forward. He pulled from his pocket a syringe filled with a glowing red substance, and stopped at Chuck's lifeless body. "Daddy also gave me something to give you. It takes away your powers, Harold thinks." Harold grabbed Chuck's pants, yanked them down, and flipped him over.

Chuck's scream could be heard for miles.

*

Back at The Pen, Razorback sat behind his desk as Princess Adrianna slowly walked the dim-lit room and spoke on the reasons for her arrival. Off to the side, her two guards stood, weapons at the ready. On the wall behind them a fluorescent, Pig Sticker, bar-room sign glowed beautifully.

"The federation knows what you been up to, William," Princess Adrianna said. "It's why they sent me. To try and talk some sense into you. Believe it or not, what you do on this planet affects us up there too."

"Not much my concern," Razorback said.

Princess Adrianna ignored the comment. "Now, it's true you and I are not that fond of one another. But you *are* my only brother, and because of that, I have spoken with our head office, and as a personal favor to me, they said I can finally bring you back home, but only under double-secret, Delta probation at which time you will be closely supervised by me. If you behave, you'll get freedoms rewarded over time. If you don't, well, you know the outcome. No second chances after this, William. You break our laws again, it's vaporization. And there won't be a thing I can do about it."

"Sounds charming. Almost as charming as being supervised by you all goddamn day up on some cold-ass spaceship." Razorback looked at the two guards. "How about it, fellas? She a pain-in-the-ass bitch to work for or what?"

Princess Adrianna looked at the guards.

One nervously shook his head, and said, "No. Uh-uh."

Razorback looked back at his sister. "But, you see, sis? Your sales pitch, no matter how good it comes outcha mouth, don't matter much. I really like it here, I do. It's, well, it's ... *me*. I done grown accustomed to this redneck lifestyle. Even started to talk all redneck and shit and can't seem to turn it off."

Princess Adrianna finally smiled. "You can't be serious?"

"As a heart attack. You heard me. The boots are fucking cool, and I happen to think cowboy hats are the shit. Not to mention this leisure suit makes me look like I'm all ruthless and powerful *but* cheap—which is a nice touch if you ask me."

Princess Adrianna sat. She reached forward, grabbed the copy of Draconian Life magazine from the desk, and thumbed pages.

Razorback continued. "And besides, there's always plenty of humans for me to eat and slap around down here without permission. *Plus*, the music selection on this planet is a damn fine one—if you ask me. Best in the entire galaxy. You ever listen to Charlie Feathers? If you did, you'd wanna stay in a heartbeat."

"You *are* serious. Don't you know where you live, Bill? There is a housing project not five miles away. I can smell their bananas from here."

"And I can tell you're still a complete bitch, Adrianna. Now, I appreciate you flying your royal snatch my direction to try and save me and shit, but who asked you to? Ain't nobody ever pulled for me once back home. So, come clean. What gives?"

"I admit, I have personal reasons to bring you back. This plan of yours will hurt my human, meat supply I need for my gatherings. I heavily depend on earth's supply for all my catering needs with royalty, as does my closest friends—whom I also speak for on their behalf."

"Once again, sis, not my concern. I don't care who you sling your slop and shit with. Take your sorry ass to the grocery store like everybody else."

"Not your concern? It soon will be. Look, I tried to reason with you. I tried to give you a chance. But if this is how you want it, fine." Princess Adrianna stood and motioned to the two guards.

The guards popped to attention, did a right face, and walked out.

Princess Adrianna stopped at the door. "I will be reporting you to Emperor Serpent-Orr immediately, and you will surely be arrested and tried for treason against our people." She walked out.

"All good to me, sis," Razorback said. "And while you're at it, take your loyalty to them control-freak sumbitches and go fuck yourself. This is Rockwood!" Razorback jumped out of his seat and kept screaming at the empty room. "Rockwood, bitch! This my goddamn town! Nobody tells me what the fuck Imma do in my goddamn town! And wipe your feet the next time you enter my establishment! Show some respect for once! You hear me, sis? Sis? Adrianna!"

They were gone.

Razorback sat down, leaned back, and said, "Fuck all y'all."

He picked up the phone and dialed.

Back in Scooby Doobie's apartment, Bobby slowly woke amongst the rubble to the sound of a phone ringing. She crawled over to the source of the sound, flipped over Billy Ray's corpse, pulled the brick phone from his belt clip, and answered with silence.

Razorback's voice came through. "Billy Ray? You kill that bitch yet? I need you back at The Pen ASAP. We got a serious change of plans."

Bobby responded, "I'm sorry. Billy Ray can't come to the phone right now. He's dead."

"Say what?"

"What."

"No, bitch. Repeat what you just said."

"I said what."

"No, right before that!"

"Oh. You heard me the first time."

"Who the fuck is this?"

"Bobby Beggs, the future Mrs. Thunders, and if you hurt my man and take that away from me, I swear to God that I'll avenge him with every inch of my dying, red boots-wearing, sexy-strut-having breath. You will have *nowhere* to hide from me."

Furious, Razorback threw his receiver against the wall that housed human-head trophies, and the phone busted to pieces. He slammed his fist on the desk, and screamed, "Fuck!"

*

Outside Cletus and Clarence's Barbecue Shack, Princess Adrianna's spaceship sat parked in the dirt lot. Cletus and Clarence stood next to it, excitedly taking pictures with random poses and hand gestures.

Inside the ship, Princess Adrianna's two guards stood off to the side of the ship's bridge and munched from take-out filled with barbecued chicken, ribs, sausage and drank Barq's Root Beers. The food was delicious. One of them even had on a fluorescent, Cletus and Clarence Barbecue Shack, souvenir shirt over his uniform.

At the ship's controls, Princess Adrianna ordered her ship's communicator to make the call. "Punch it through, Goba Gooty."

Goba Gooty said, "Right away, Princess," and punched in a quick series of numbers. The large screen above the ship's windshield came to life. An image appeared of a full-fledged Draconian in its natural form looking like a man in a bad, rubber suit instead of something to fear. The Draconian spoke an alien language that read out as English subtitles on the ship's screen.

"Report," it said in its dialect.

"I have made contact, and it's a wash. He has no intentions of backing down or staying loyal to our people."

"I see," the reptile hissed. "Have you spoken with The Council there?"

"No, Emperor Serpent-Orr, I haven't. And from the intel I've gathered, The Council we assigned here is of no use. They may even be frightened to the point they went into hiding."

"Perhaps William Nedick has begun to eliminate all traces of authority in Rockwood?"

"Perhaps. As long as I've known my brother, he has always had trouble dealing with authority."

"*Your* brother? I hope any relation you have to immediate bloodlines doesn't interfere with your loyalty to us all."

Princess Adrianna was taken back for a second. "You know very well where my loyalties lie. Satan and our people."

"Yes. Yes. That's how it works." Serpent-Orr reached off camera, grabbed a baby's severed leg, and took a bite. "But it seems William Nedick didn't take to our system of operating too well. He worships no one but self. He is a rebel against the ultimate rebel: our beloved Lucifer." Serpent-Orr laughed maniacally. "Perhaps William Nedick thinks he is going to take some of Satan's real estate and rule Rockwood like his very own private hell on earth?"

"Not today he's not."

"We will no longer risk bad negotiations." The emperor leaned into the screen. "We must move quickly into position ... and strike."

Above earth, a small fleet of flying saucers hovered in a triangular formation. The lead ship located Rockwood, Mississippi on its radar, and the ships, one after another, formed a line and slowly began to ascend down to the beautiful blue planet.

Chapter Seven
SECTION EIGHT

Ten Miles East of Rockwood

With the maximum body weight allowed for service, Captain Earl Tubb stepped before the Section Eight squad and everyone came to attention. The shine on the top of his head wasn't from a bald spot, but rather from a battle-damaged, metal plate that took up the right side of his head.

He adjusted his cool-looking Han Solo vest, placed his hand on the blaster attached to his hip, and spoke to the squad like one of the Drill Instructors from the movie he watched earlier for inspiration. "Now! My name is Tubb. *Captain* Earl Tubb, and I will be your Section Eight squad leader." He spit his fake jerky-tobacco on the ground with a *splat* and readjusted the wad with his tongue.

He packed the can, added more jerky, and continued. "It was told to me by my superiors that I was to put together a crack-commando squad of badasses ... and here you are before me. I hand-picked each and every one of y'all sumbitches from the files deep within Section Eight's high-tech, Commodore 64, computer system, database disc thingy. With a fine-tooth comb, I think I made me the right choices." Captain Tubb smiled at the squad. "Fine selections—if I may say so myself." He began to pace back and forth.

"It'll be our jobs to infiltrate and take out the Rockwood fairgrounds. Our target, one Razorback Bill Nedick, a low-life, alien sack of shit if I ever met one. The bastard has kidnapped one of our own and is now trying to take over my home town like some kind of goddamn one-man *Red Dawn* gone wrong ... and that ain't right. He done made his move with a little backing from them two Men in Black sumbitches that's been running around stirring up their bullshit again. You see them two pricks, kill 'em on sight!" He spit, wiped his mouth with the back of his hand, smeared jerky spit all over it, and continued.

"These are the very same two assholes responsible for making Frank Switchblade Butz the man he is today, and they sure as shit are the ones who started all this mess. Y'all may have read about them two jokers in that one book *Switchblade: A Killer Comedy*. Some little pussy named Brad McCormick wrote that bullshit. Tried to make me look stupid in it too." Captain Tubb took a step forward. "Let's get one thing straight. I in no way have a goddamn crush on John Wayne! I never admitted that shit once in my entire life. That part of the book was made the fuck up by a smartass writer. But I digress." He spit.

"Bill Nedick's the man of the hour. Not my reputation for being gay. Razorback-Bill-Nedick. The dude is on some intergalactic, security-level, problematic bullshit, and he needs to g-o pronto."

Captain Tubb looked over to the girl in her late teens, standing in formation in aerobics attire, casually looking around and chewing gum. He quickly stepped to her. "Fuck you looking at, Sam Dickey? Quit eyeball fucking the area! I'm over here!"

Startled, Sam Dickey swallowed her gum and quickly saluted Captain Tubb.

Captain Tubb leaned in. "I read your file. *Well*, I had someone read it to me. So, you some kinda aerobics instructor, huh? Possessed by a ninja or some shit? Guess that's what you get for fucking around with them dark forces. Think you can just play around with Ouija boards witcha goddamn friends at slumber parties and there'd be no consequences? Huh? You need Jesus, bitch?"

Sam Dickey responded like a valley girl. "Yeah, like, we didn't believe in it, for sure, but, yeah. We, like, totally conjured up a dead, ninja demon or something. He, like, totally takes me over from time to time and kills people for revenge. Totally. For sure." She giggled like an airhead.

Captain Tubb, with his plated head, screamed, "From time to time my ass! We don't need aerobic instructions on this mission! I looks like I needs me some aerobics?!"

"Yeah."

The squad giggled.

Captain Tubb shook off the comment. "Bullshit! We need an evil-ass ninja on our side! I highly suggested you break outcha Linda Blair bullshit and get possessed real goddamn quick and shit me a goddamn ninja. Not a bimbo. A ninja! Why? Because it's gonna be your job to take out the power grid, Sam Dickey. We *need* that power grid shut down! You understand me, you goddamn crazy ninja bitch?"

"Like, for sure. I'll make it happen. I'll just squint my eyes like I'm Japanese. Like, that might make it kick in at the right time. Totally." She giggled again.

Captain Tubb shook his head, looked down at Sam Dickey's workout sneakers and noticed the gym bag by her feet. He looked back up. "Like that shiny, purple-ass bag you got there. Well, guess what? This ain't the gym, and it sure as shit ain't the goddamn mall! What's in that purple piece-of-shit anyway?"

"Like, you know. My Walkman, a towel for after aerobics, my purple water bottle, my Debbie Gibson Electric Youth perfume. Oh! And the *Valley Girl* soundtrack with the song "Girls Like Me," which is like the greatest theme song for me *ever*."

Captain Tubb grimaced. "Anything else in that stupid bag of no fucking use to our mission?"

"I have my ninja supplies in there. A sword too! A ninja mask, ninja boots, ninja this, ninja that. And a letter for Billy. I'm breaking up with him because his back is too hairy." She pointed at her open mouth with a fake gag reflex. "Like, gag me."

Captain Tubb smiled. "Well then, ninja bitch. I think there just may be some room for you on this squad after all. But I'll be keeping a sharp eye on your chop-socky ass, Sam Dickey."

They both nodded. The camaraderie was growing thicker by the second.

Captain Tubb looked to Sam Dickey's left at the Draconian soldier holding the big-as-shit, blaster gun that had to weigh at least a hundred pounds easy—and that's without ammo. His eyes were yellow and snake-like and the scale patterns on his skin were a dark green, almost appearing brown in some areas. The tattoo on his neck said "I Kill My Own" and on his chest was a Rage Against the Machine t-shirt. Dog tags dangled from his neck to complete his one-man-army image, and on his feet, brand-new Jordan Five sneakers.

"Hugo!" Captain Tubb said stepping in front of the Draconian soldier. "I had somebody read me your file too. Said you some kinda time-traveling, Draconian, snake-alien soldier that hates Draconian, snake-alien sumbitches. I like that. I like that a lot, *boy*. It also said that you the son of that rookie Chuck Thunders and his side chick Bobby Beggs, sent from the future like some kinda cold-blooded Kyle Reese to try and save your momma and daddy from certain death." Captain Tubb thought for a moment. "Well, I guess just your daddy. Otherwise, how would you have been born if your momma ain't survive all this shit, right? This is called a motivator, boy, and it works well in certain situations. And that's why I'm putting you in charge of rescuing Chuck Thunders, lizard boy. You gotcha Draconian ass about one hundred confirmed kills—or as I like to call 'em, snake bites. And that's why you the man for the job. You ready to rescue your daddy, Private Hugo? You ready to get some for the human race?"

Hugo smiled his snake smile, cocked his weapon, and hissed.

Captain Tubb smiled. "I like you already, boy. Now, you run along and go get your daddy out faster than an Ex-Lax shit."

Hugo slung his weapon over his shoulder and walked away.

A convertible Volkswagen bug pulled up with three giggly teenage girls, the radio blasting eighties pop full blast.

The driver yelled, "Hey, Sammy! Ricky finally asked me out!"

Sam Dickey yelled with a jump for joy, and said, "Excellent!" She looked at Captain Tubb. "Well, that's my ride." She kissed him on the cheek like a father and daughter, and said, "Gotta go." She grabbed her gym bag, skipped over to the convertible, jumped into the air with a triple ninja-flip into the backseat, and high-fives were given all around by the girls.

"I got a new tape!" the driver said.

She popped it in and Tiffany's "I Think Were Alone Now" began to play. The girls sped away, giggling and singing along.

Captain Tubb shook his head in disbelief at teenagers these days. He focused his attention on the last few squad members remaining, all alien fighter pilots from different galaxies dressed in matching Section Eight flight suits. "The rest of y'all follow me," he said strutting away. "Radar picked up some movement above. We got us an invasion coming."

*

Back at The Village, Bobby Beggs exited the apartment building, hurt, limping, and cradling her almost full-term baby bump. She walked the sidewalk in pain with every step and had to stop to gain some motivation. Glancing down the block, she spotted the Section Eight mobile. It was missing its hub caps and had spray-painted graffiti all over it. Across the hood, The Zoo

Gang was written in neon bubble letters. She made her way over, opened the door, and carefully sat inside.

She looked at the stereo and seen the damaged screen, its wires hanging out. Being a small-town girl, Bobby knew how to install and repair stereos. She reached forward, twisted a few wires, and the car started with ease.

Katz tried to speak but an electronic stutter came through instead.

Bobby twisted and jiggled a few more wires. The dashboard lit up, and Katz spoke clear. "Hello, Ms. Beggs. Thank you for fixing me."

"Can you locate my, baby?"

"Of course. It's in your uterus."

"No. My *other* baby. Chuck. He's in trouble."

"I will do my best, Ms. Beggs."

"And I need a weapon."

"Might I suggest the P34 in the backseat? You will need a tank for the flamethrower though. Agent Thunders used every round issued to him earlier on a single group of humans for no reason."

Bobby smiled. "That's my man."

"Being that the local Section Eight branch has been completely taken out, I would like to offer my services to you, Ms. Beggs."

"You'd help *me* like that? You're so sweet. But you know I have a boyfriend, right? Let's just make that clear."

"Yes, Ms. Beggs. In extreme situations of no hope such as this, my programming allows me to become self-aware enough to make certain decisions on my own. And I chose to help you."

"That is *so* neat."

She put the car into gear and took off. Michelle Pfeiffer's "Cool Rider" from *Grease 2* blasted from the windows out into the ghetto streets.

*

At the local fair grounds, the stands quickly filled with residents and heavy anticipation as monster trucks lined up on the oversized, dirt track, revving their engines, each one ready to smash the junk cars before them.

Mayor Bradley stood front and center on a flat-bed truck and faced the crowded stands. Many spectators donned camouflage head to toe. Regardless of the smell of wild game on the crowd, the love was felt.

The mayor tapped the microphone twice, and asked, "This thing on?" He heard his voice through the megaphone speaker, threw up his arms, and yelled, "How's everybody feeling out there tonight?"

The crowd hooted, hollered, and applauded with shotguns and stadium food held high. One local took a bite of his hotdog, raised it high, and yelled, "Mustard hotdogs are the shit!"

The mayor pointed to the beat-up movie screen on the side that was running a slide-show of John Schneider and Tom Wopat images. "Tonight! Tonight! Tonight! The return of Bo and Luke Duke! And we gonna get to see the shit on this big-ass screen here! Look at the size of that canvas!"

The crowd went wild. Someone blew an air horn that played "Dixie" and several hunters fired shotguns in the air.

The mayor attempted to settle the crowd. "All right now, y'all. It's a coming. It's a coming. Patience is a virtue. And you know what else is coming? Have you heard? Free beer provided by one of our favorite locals, Bill Nedick. All you can drink!"

Air horns and shotguns blasted again. Several men hooted to the sky.

"But before we get to the return of the magic that made Rockwood's favorite show so dang good in the first place, I think we should—"

"Babba dubba bubba, maber!" the local mush-mouth Murdock interrupted.

"What's that you said, Murdock?" the mayor asked.

"I said, 'Babba dubba bubba, maber.' Budded tuh Wanced and Coo!"

"That's correct! As Murdock Dangle has so kindly pointed out for us, Coy and Vance Duke are absolute crap!"

Murdock smiled.

A few locals patted his back.

Murdock yelled, "Durbba burrba turbba!"

"You betcha, Murdock!"

Murdock smiled again.

The mayor continued. "But before we celebrate the rectification of one of the greatest missteps in casting ever on one of the greatest shows on planet earth ... let's smash some cars!"

Monster trucks roared from their idling positions, and the crowd erupted as if it was raining gold. The mayor yelled over the crowd, "Up first, Stroker 'Poke Her Twice' Johnson in his monster truck "The Condom Breaker!"

Stroker approached the row of cars slowly, stopped, hit the gas, and flames shot from the truck's exhaust.

The crowd went wild.

Inside the trunk of the last car in line was Meryl and Gay-Bob Kael, hog tied and sweating bullets. Gay-Bob pulled hard at the tape, but it was no use. He yelled at his daddy in the dark. "We done for now, Daddy! Just because we can live four times longer than these man-apes don't mean that—"

"I know! I know! We can't die!"

"What we gonna do?"

"Now, lemme just think for a minute, Son. You worry too much. I can handle this."

The sound of the truck roared as it took off. It hit the first car, leaped into the air and came down with a smash.

The Kaels screamed.

Stroker "Poke Her Twice" Johnson stepped on it, and the monster truck ran across the top of the heap like a charging ram.

Behind the movie screen out of view, Razorback stared at the battered Chuck Thunders who was strapped with barbed wire to a metal box spring against the movie screen's frame, his arms out like Christ. On his head, a red bandana dangling by the side of his face. On his chest and testicles, jumper cables clamped like bulldogs that wouldn't let go which slowly bled the life from his body.

Razorback snapped his fingers.

Off to the side, Agent Black rotated the knob on the black box and electricity shot through Chuck's body like a lightning blast, convulsing him into tight-muscled agony with a scream that was drowned out by the next monster truck taking its turn smashing cars.

The sound of the crowd roared.

Razorback snapped his fingers, and Agent Black shut off the juice.

Chuck went limp, his sweaty and exhausted body still hanging on by the barbed-wire wrapped around his bleeding wrists.

Razorback pushed back the cowboy hat on his sweaty head, leaned towards the half-dead man, and said, "Crazy fucking day, huh? Son, lemme tell you. Gotta minute?" He hit some cocaine and kept the vial in his palm, randomly hitting it as he continued. "I rolled outta bed, pinched a loaf the size of an aborted fetus, had me some fried, Japanese guts with my eggs, had my morning dose of adrenalized blood, then came to work to do some gangster shit ... and here you come. Everything went to shit. I had my day all set. Was gonna slap the Kaels around a little, take over some shit, and then free Rockwood from the lies once and for all. All I had to do was run my commercial from the VCR back at The Pen. Press play and walk away, but no. And now my sister from back home done found out about my shit, showed up, and will surely enough, with all her high, technological-ass bullshit, be jamming my frequency. So, fuck it. We going live in front of the whole town."

Behind the movie screen, the next monster truck moved into position. The Kaels were still alive but running out of time, and room, fast.

Gay-Bob screamed, "Daddy! I don't want to die because of you!"

Meryl shouted back, "Trust your daddy for once! There's always a way out!"

The truck took off.

The Kaels screamed.

Razorback snapped his fingers, Agent Black hit the juice, and the electric torture continued.

*

Bobby pulled into town with Katz in rumble mode. She scanned the town's square, spotted the pawn shop, and parked. She walked over to the shop, looked in, and with her dusty, red boot, kicked the shop's window and smashed it. She crawled through and immediately began to scan inventory.

A patrol car drove by, double-backed around the square, and parked. The door opened and Deputy Alan Wayne got out. He walked up to the shop, looked through the forced-entry opening, and spotted his long-time crush Bobby Beggs behind the counter rummaging. "*Ahem-ahem.* Ms. Beggs? That you in there?"

Bobby turned around.

"You know you ain't supposed to be in there after hours. Willie know you're in his store?"

"Hey there," Bobby smiled innocently. "How you doing tonight, Alan Wayne? You know I always thought you were a cutie."

Alan Wayne blushed. The cutie comment worked every time.

Bobby continued. "Where you been all my life?"

"Me? Well, uh, I been at the station. Someone killed the sheriff and maybe even ate part of his neck. Then there's this spaceship I keep seeing flying overhead that's really strange. *And* all the cops hightailed it out of town. Are you pregnant?"

"They didn't? They left you here all alone, Alan Wayne?"

Alan Wayne put his head down. "Uh-huh. And I don't know what to do."

"You don't need them, Alan Wayne. We don't need them. And you *are not* alone."

"Well, thanks, I guess. I think the sheriff was corrupt. There was bloody money all over his floor. And I remained so loyal all these years. I feel like an inept, judgement dummy, Ms. Beggs. In a way, I helped a bad man because of my blind loyalty to the force. I feel terrible."

Bobby looked to the sad and lonely man and tried her best. "Look, cutie pie. We all get fooled. But your heart was in the right place. It's not your fault the evil assholes of the world are usually in charge."

Alan Wayne looked up solemnly. "A movie I watched on the late show about a cop on the edge said, 'You can sit back and let the bad guys win, or you can step up and be a man and earn that shield.' Every penny, Ms. Beggs."

"Wow! That sounds really cool. You must have really great tastes for inspirational movies, Alan Wayne."

Alan Wayne blushed again.

"Maybe we can get together and watch it sometime. Just as friends."

Alan Wayne became thrilled. "Okay!"

"But for now, first and foremost, what we need is a tank for that alien gun in that talking car over there."

"Gee, Ms. Beggs. I been chasing that spaceship all day and can't seem to catch it. I don't think we have the capabilities to handle something like this." Alan Wayne cocked his head. "Really? A talking car? Like *Knight Rider* or a Transformer?"

"Where can we get some fuel for that flamethrower?"

"Oh, Bud Boone's old trailer. We dug a hole in his yard to try and locate a stench after he died and discovered a big, old pile of weapons. I think there was a flamethrower tank in there somewhere. It's all locked in evidence in the shed behind the station."

Bobby looked down at her pink Buddy Band bracelet, and said, "I'm coming, baby."

*

Back at the fairgrounds, the next monster truck moved into position. The crowd was rowdy as ever.

On the field, Meryl was crushed in the trunk and couldn't move an inch but was still alive. "Gay-Bob?" he yelled. "Gay-Bob? Look, I think I know how we can get out of this. Do you still have that promotional, dick-shaped, beer-bottle opener that doubles as a refrigerator magnet?"

Behind the screen, Razorback stood in Chuck's face. He held up a green-scaled, alien hand with an extra-long, fat index finger, and smiled. "Hold up. I love this part."

The monster truck shot off.

The knob was flipped to maximum. Chuck felt the volts travel through his body and out of every orifice he had. The monster truck finished its run in the distance, and Agent Black shut off the juice. Chuck's nipples were smoking. Behind his aviator shades, one of his eyeballs had popped out. Bloody slobber dangled from his chin.

Razorback grabbed a folding chair, popped it open, and had a seat next to Chuck. He took off his cowboy hat, wiped the back of his sweaty neck, and looked up. "Let's have a serious talk. You and me. Hero to villain. Before I go and sacrifice you for the whole town to see. And the kicker about this, I'll get 'em to go along with it. That'll be a damn fine way to pop off my shit and send a message to anyone wanting to challenge me, huh? Can't wait to show 'em my true self. They gonna shit when they swig that beer. They'll never look at their favorite celebrities the same again." He looked up and saw Chuck was passed out. *Whap!* He slapped him awake. Chuck's dangling eye detached from the slap and splatted on the ground. "Wake up! I'm talking here, don't be rude!"

Chuck's good eye found Razorback.

"I was just curious," Razorback continued. "Is being good as lonely as being evil? Had nobody in my corner for a partner but Billy Ray, and you killed him. Now I'm all alone except for that dumb-ass son of mine. You must think I'm some kinda monster, huh, but the reality here is I'm for the truth, boy. I don't lie. Lying is for cowards. I'll say to your goddamn face what the fuck is up, and we can take it from there. Like this here illusion they got everybody under. It's all a lie. I want to lift that shit. And *I'm* the bad one? All these fuckers I been killing off have been secretly involved with screwing you humans over from the word go. And on a scale, most of y'all ain't ready to comprehend. My kind creates division amongst your kind. We sit back and watch your asses fight over your misplaced sense of loyalties outside yourselves. It's almost too easy. I want to blow the lid off that shit. I'm a liberator." He leaned forward with his reptilian hand and slowly scratched Chuck's cheek.

Chuck released a painful moan.

Razorback said, "Hurts, huh? Not so easy being a hero without some convenient powers to help your common ass out, huh? You're common, Larry Pimpleton."

"You're an asshole, Razorback Bill, who killed the coolest black dude I ever met."

"Yep. Rockwood's first black cop ended up as a stain on my floor right after he slipped up and gave me your stupid tramp, Bobby. All because of you, people like him die. You useless asshole."

"All this slanted crap coming out of your fat-ass mouth means nothing. This whole day started because of that mouth of yours. Cut me loose, and I'll show you what's up."

Razorback gave a look of confusion.

Chuck said, "Don't act like you don't know what I'm talking about. Think you can do better? Can you even draw, bro?"

"No idea where you're coming from," Razorback said. "Fascinating. Always assumed I'd wanna know the full backstory of the man that almost went the distance with me. But I don't. Motives don't mean shit in Rockwood. And that's the beauty of this fucking town. I love it! Agent Black the Traitor?"

Agent Black looked.

"Wheel his ass out. The show is about to start."

*

Above Rockwood, Captain Tubb led his squad of four in an attack formation through the clouds in what Captain Tubb considered their "cool-looking" space fighters. He looked to his monitor and saw multiple blips coming across the screen. "Retar-D-Four," he yelled to the mechanical droid stationed behind the cockpit with its head hanging out. "I see some bogeys coming. Looks like it might be them. Or ducks! Wish I had my shotgun. Scan it to be sure."

The droid let out a series of beeps.

Captain Tubb got mad. "What the fuck did you say?"

The droid beeped again.

"How the hell am I supposed to understand goddamn bleeps and shit? We speak English in this country."

Retar-D-Four let out a long, swirling, beaten bleep.

"Damn foreigners." Captain Tubb hit his helmet's microphone. "We have multiples coming up our rear! I mean ... they might try and take us from behind. I mean ... they just coming, alright. If they alien, they ass is ours. Check in and stand by for orders."

Ship one responded with alien grunts.

Ship two responded with an electronic, Chinese voice.

Ship three screamed twice, whistled, then clicked his jaw three times.

Captain Tubb said, "Goddamn. Doesn't anybody on this mission speak American? How the hell we supposed to talk?"

*

Back at the fairgrounds, Chuck was center stage on display for the whole town to see. Harold, still mighty, stood to the side in his purple sweatpants and had green, body paint all over his face, chest, and feet. The stage underneath him creaked and buckled from his weight, and a horrible new bowl-cut sat on his head to complete his Hulk image. Next to him, Agent Black loosened his tie with a look of worry that the stage would be collapsing soon.

Razorback, microphone in hand, paced the stage back and forth and preached. "And this man behind me. He's not even one of us! An outsider! Don't let his looks fool you either. This man is *not* the real Rambo with a new haircut, despite appearances. Only *thinks* he is! He is a phony. He's not a real man. Y'all might look up at him and maybe wanna feel sorry for him, huh? Understandable. But just wait until you hear what this man did. I didn't wanna take it there, but I'll just go ahead tell you what he did. Truth shall set you free. You ready? Kids in the audience, cover your ears."

The crowd went silent.

Razorback looked left to right and brought the microphone up. "This cocksucker, excuse my language, was just backstage talking shit ... about Bo and Luke Duke."

The crowd gasped.

"And I caught him red-handed! He even went so far as to say Coy and Vance Duke are better looking than Bo and Luke, and fuck anyone in Rockwood who disagrees!"

You could hear a pin drop.

A lady yelled, "Bullshit?"

Razorback pointed. "Truth! I'm all about the truth, nice lady. And tonight, I plan on showing each and every one of y'all a big dose of some *real* truth. How's them free hot dogs working out?"

The crowd applauded.

"Best meat supplier I know." Razorback smiled. "Kind of meat that would make you wanna eat your own, huh?"

The crowd applauded.

Razorback paced the stage. "Well, tonight, I have a special treat for you fine folks. Not only did you get to see some cars get smashed to shit on my dime, but now we gonna celebrate tonight's special *Dukes of Hazzard* episode by watching this Bo and Luke Duke traitor behind me suffer first!"

The crowd roared.

Razorback shouted, "This man has no loyalty! No pride in what we hold dear. He is nothing but a sorry-ass Duke Boys resister and that makes him enemy number one in my book! How about y'all? And don't forget, free food, *and* I got beer on the way!"

The crowd roared.

A lonely man in back, Razorback promised free lap dances to, yelled on cue, "Hang that sumbitch high!"

Another wanting to feel included joined in, "I agree! He don't belong around us!"

A lady yelled, "I'm with them!"

Another yelled, "Luke Duke is sexy! And I'll be damned if I go against the current opinion of *my* people!"

And another, "I even have his poster on my wall and show people in hopes they give me a thumbs up so I can feel good about my tastes! Kill all naysayers!"

The crowd roared.

Razorback smiled. This was too easy.

*

Inside Katz, Bobby and Alan Wayne flew down the road as Alan Wayne prepped for war by tearing the sleeves off his uniform. In his hand was a hatchet, sharp as a razor. Bobby reached forward and hit the stereo's monitor. A live feed of Chuck on stage appeared. Razorback was still getting the crowd hyped on the promise the Hazzard Resister would suffer, and it made her heart sink down into her Calvin Klein cut-offs.

Above, Captain Tubb's squad blew passed in a futuristic dogfight of epic proportions. Laser blasts lit up the sky and caught random trees and barn rooftops on fire.

Captain Tubb hit the headset, and shouted, "Echo Station Two-Three-Seven. I got enemy on my ass and not in a good way. Take the sumbitch!"

The wing-man alien flew in for the attack and blasted the enemy ship to smithereens.

Captain Tubb grabbed the stick, pulled back hard with a grunt, and sent his ship up into a throttle roll for no reason other than it looked cool. He shot through the clouds, paused in front of the moon like Michael Keaton's *Batman*, and then dive-bombed straight for earth. "I got the fairgrounds locked in my radar," he said. "Several of them tainted beer trucks approaching from the east. Squad, go after them trucks. I'm gonna head to the fairgrounds and end this bullshit at the source."

Back at the fairgrounds, Razorback was standing to the side of the stage talking on his *Star Trek*-inspired flip phone growing impatient. "Where are them goddamn beer trucks? I don't give a shit if some stupid, *Battlestar Galactica* pussies are chasing you or not! Get your fucking asses over here now! The show is starting in a few minutes!"

Up on the screen, the commercial for Pig Sticker beer began. The crowd hushed one another and watched the local businessman's ad. In it, Razorback sat in a backyard pool on a flotation device, wearing polka-dotted shorts and his trademark cowboy hat, surrounded by black women in bikinis caressing his body. Several massaged his feet. "Howdy, you loyal Rockwood natives!" the ad said. "You like beer and shit? Well, guess what? I do too, strong and dark—just like my bitches. Ain't that right, bitches?"

Two of the ladies smiled at the camera, and said, "Love that Pig Sticker."

On the side of the stage, Razorback continued his phone conversation. "Just do it! The shit supposed to been here already! My commercial running and everything!"

The sounds of Captain Tubb's ship suddenly came to the party like a screaming kamikaze.

The crowd looked up.

Razorback dropped his communicator and screamed to the heavens.

Inside the ship, Captain Tubb smiled. He spotted Chuck Thunders center stage, nodded in approval at the Rambo bandana he had on, then flipped a switch on the dash. A targeting system retracted from behind him and an electronic viewfinder flipped around and covered his eyes. He immediately zoomed into Razorback's chest. He took a breath, then imagined the sound of his former partner Lester Boone speaking from beyond the grave.

"Hey, Earl." Lester's pretend spirit said. "How you been, buddy? Look at you. A Captain!"

"Lester?" Captain Tubb asked in phony shock. "Is that really you?"

"Yep. Sure is. Use that force stuff, Earl. You know you can do it."

Captain Tubb nodded with confidence. He retracted the view finder, grabbed the jet's blaster controls, and took his shot.

The laser blast missed by a mile and hit Harold right in the face, decapitating him on the spot.

The crowd screamed.

Harold's body began dancing around like a headless chicken, spewing green blood everywhere as he smashed the stage to smithereens. The structure finally collapsed, and everyone fell through with Chuck still attached to his box spring.

"Oops." Captain Tubb said. "Quit rocking the damn ship, Retar-D-Four. You made me miss!"

Retar-D-Four beeped back.

Captain Tubb's ship made a flyby, buzzed the event, and the crowd scattered in panic.

Razorback screamed, "Fuck this shit! I gotta quit doing so much cocaine," and ran for his purple Cadillac with Agent Black trailing close behind.

Captain Tubb hit the headset on his helmet, and shouted, "Hit it, Sam Dickey!"

The stadium's lights zapped out and darkness fell over the fairgrounds.

Razorback kept for his vehicle but was quickly kicked in the face by an unseen foot that made him stop dead in his tracks. "Who kicked me? I can't see a thing!" He spun around and received another kick. "Ouch!" And another. He screamed, "Quit kicking me, goddamn it! The shit hurts!"

Sam Dickey's voice cut through the darkness. "Like, only a ninja can destroy a ninja." She kicked him in the ass. *Whap!*

Razorback grabbed his butt cheek. "Damn you, bitch! You kicked me right in the ass!"

Sam Dickey giggled. "And *you* are no ninja."

Razorback took off running in the dark but received a ninja star to the ass every step of the way before finally reaching his Cadillac. He grabbed the car's door handle and began pulling ninja stars from his butt like cactus needles.

The stadium lights flicked back on. Razorback looked to the rubble and neither Chuck Thunders or the ninja were anywhere to be found. He swung his car door open, looked at Agent Black, gave him a happy salute, said, "Sorry, boy. Your ass is on your own," then hopped in the front seat.

Captain Tubb's squad finally showed up in attack formation, ready to destroy.

Agent Black saw this and ran.

Razorback pushed the car's cigarette lighter and a protective, glass bubble quickly covered the convertible like a cockpit. "Fuck this shit!" He hit the gas. Chuck Berry's "You Can't Catch Me" blasted from the stereo, and the car took off into the air like a rocket, a stream of jet fire shooting from the rear.

That's when Bobby ramped onto the scene with Katz and Deputy Alan Wayne. They soared high through the air and accidentally clipped Razorback's Cadillac which sent him into a tailspin over some fields. Katz crashed through the movie screen and disappeared on the other side.

Spinning out of control, Razorback kicked the emergency break, and the car's canopy flew off. The front seat ejected from the vehicle with him safely strapped in. Two miniature parachutes opened from the headrests, and he sailed safely to the ground. He unbuckled his seat belt, jumped to his feet, and ran for cover in some nearby woods. He leaned against a tree and listened for a moment as the ships hovered above. "I gotta stop doing so much cocaine. Shit." He bailed on foot into the darkness.

High above, Captain Tubb and his squad continued to search and scan the area for the gangster.

Back on the ground, Bobby and Alan Wayne exited the vehicle.

They looked at the front of the smashed car and saw Agent Black crushed dead in the grill.

Bobby reached deep, and said, "Wow."

Ten feet before them, a rip in time opened up, and out stepped Chuck Thunders with his son, the Draconian soldier Hugo. Chuck was wearing a World's Greatest Dad shirt, Bermuda shorts, a Disneyland hat, and an eye patch.

Bobby beamed, "Baby, it's really you!" She ran up to her man standing next to the lizard soldier, hugged him, and said, "Did you go to Disneyland without me?"

Chuck said, "Yeah. It's overrated."

Bobby said, "I really like your eye patch. Who's your green friend?"

Chuck smiled, "Bobby, I'd like you to meet our son, Hugo. He's a Draconian soldier for Section Eight that was sent back in time to rescue me like a Terminator movie."

Bobby said, "Hmmm."

Hugo smiled at his mom.

Chuck continued. "While the lights were out, our brave little son here snuck in and cut me loose and took me to the year 2037 where he came from. We went shopping, grilled, hung out, just all-around bonded."

Bobby said, "Wow."

"I've decided something about my life, Bobby. Are you listening?"

"Not really."

"Good. Because I've realized that my tale is not one of revenge, but of realization. The realization that real men put food on the table, bang their side-chicks on the regular, and raise kick-ass kids that grow up to be half-breed Draconians that'll save us later. My job isn't to *be* a hero. My job is to *raise* a hero." He looked at Hugo. "Right, Son?"

Hugo hissed, "To me, Dad, you *are* the hero."

Chuck teared up. "You hear that? He called me dad." A mosquito flew by and Chuck smashed it with a hand clap. He held out his hand to Hugo.

Hugo's tongue shot out and snatched the dead bug from his father's hand, and he chewed away.

Bobby looked at her man, and said, "Baby, you are *action packed.*"

*

Outside of town, Razorback walked the shoulder of the road and tried to wave down random motorists but with little luck.

Down the road a piece, Frank Switchblade Butz piloted his freshly, stolen 1974 Plymouth Duster with a hostage in the passenger seat. Under the circumstances, the hostage seemed calmer than he should have been.

Switchblade looked over to the man, and said, "So you're Brad McCormick, huh? Heard you wrote a book about me and were gonna make it into a movie. When's it coming out?"

"It's not. Shit happened."

"Oh, man. I fucking love movies. Especially ones they make about me. You see *They Called Him Switchblade* yet?"

"Last week. It's not bad. Mine was gonna be twice as good though. More true-to-life."

"Sounds boss. What's the worst thing that happened while you were trying to film it?"

"I don't know. Maybe that time the guy I was making the movie about stole my car with me in it, right after I finally got it back from that Larry Pimpleton idiot who already fucking stole it once this morning."

"Yeah. Sorry about that. I needed a new set of wheels."

"I figured."

"This is kind of neat talking to you like this. How many characters get to shoot-the-shit with their creator? But now that you're here in *my* new car, I have to ask. Why the fuck you write these weird stories anyway? Serial killers and rednecks and aliens. The continuity with the dates on some of the references don't even add up, man. If I was as stupid as Earl Tubb, I'd fail to realize that you smoke way too much shit."

"I've had my share."

"I'd say so, Daddy-o. Especially considering the way you're just plopping your own ass right into the fucking story like this. So how you gonna end this one?"

"I'm glad you asked. You see that guy up ahead?"

Switchblade's super vision zoomed into the tired and stumbling, obese target ahead. "That fat one begging for a ride?" he asked.

"That's the one."

"What about him?"

"Do what you do best."

Down the road, Razorback stopped for a breather. He heard the muscle car steadily gaining speed. He quickly turned, saw the headlights, and that was it.

Inside the hot rod, the thump was loud. Blood coated the windshield.

Switchblade yelled, "Woo! Fifty points!"

THE END

THE GHETTO BLASTER

BOOK THREE

Chapter One
Initiation in the Land of the Lou

The Year: 2037
The Place: East St. Louis

Run-down apartment buildings, drug houses and graffiti lined the dangerous, nighttime city streets. Decked-out in breakdance gear, jheri curls and box-top-fade haircuts, a group of teens were having a friendly breakdance battle on the corner next to a tall boombox—all dressed in the freshest, red sweat suits money could buy. The young kid on the cardboard, Boogaloo Jones: the crew's number one breaker, was busting his craziest moves as his crew cheered him on. "Keep that shit poppin, yo!" Breaker One yelled.

"Hell yeah, son," Breaker Two agreed. "Show 'em how you can spin on your head and shit, Boog!"

Down the block, four gangsters cruised in a rusty low-rider of indeterminate make and model. All but one sported a yellow bullet tattooed on their foreheads.

The one without a tattoo, Randy Watson, sat in the backseat and took a hit from an over-sized joint. Ten seconds later, he exhaled with more smoke than a chimney and said, "Check this out. The best shit was his earlier stuff. That *real* shit. That 'Bitches Can Get the Slap Fah Dat' was a classic album. Wore my shit out, yo. Let my tape rock until the tape popped."

From the passenger seat, the twenty-eight-year-old Hammer Jones reached in the backseat, grabbed the joint from Randy, took his turn with a hit and said, "Got that old-school shit in the glovebox right now, lil' nigga." He hit the joint again. "Who ain't got that shit? Unless you just stupid and ain't got no kinda taste in music and shit." Hammer dug into the glovebox, pulled out the tape and held it up. On the cassette cover were three women with black eyes, lined up, ready to get slapped by a pimp with gold teeth, his pimp hand cocked back, ready to strike a hoe.

Randy beamed at the album cover. "Ah, shit! That's the one! That's that shit, yo!"

Hammer nodded in approval at Randy's enthusiastic taste in tunes. He popped the tape in the car's head unit, and the sounds of an Ice T wannabe began pumping through the speaker system.

The fellas bobbed their heads in unison and sang along,

> *"Rolling down the block with my hand on my cock.*
> *Hoe licked it from the bottom to the tippy tippy top.*
> *Crack rocks for ya pops while I'm popping shots at cops.*
> *Rim job from ya momma and she pulls no stops!"*

All four men celebrated the dope lyrics with a simultaneous, "*Ahhh* shit!" along with high fives slapped all around.

Once the celebration settled, Hammer looked at Randy. "Now what's up, Randy? You got some good-ass weed in you, some straight-up nigga, theme music and," Hammer held up an AK-47 assault rifle and cocked it, "Mr. AK-47. You ready to elevate your status or what, my nigga?"

Randy took a hit, held it in, contemplated a second and nodded. "Gimme that shit."

Hammer handed him the assault rifle.

"Turn that shit up!" Randy exhaled.

The driver increased the volume and the bass rattled the trunk's seams. The vehicle's license plate—which read GANGSTA—vibrated uncontrollably, fell off and hit the pavement.

Down the block, a small crowd of happy spectators had formed around the breakdancers and were enjoying the show.

But from around the corner, a group of Puerto Ricans dressed in blue suddenly stepped on the scene and killed the vibe; it was the notorious B-Box and his crew from the two-three-seven projects: the enemy crew with nothing to lose.

One of the boys in red moonwalked over to the radio, stopped the tape and yelled, "Raise up!"

Both gangs immediately lined up for a face off.

Everyone on the block froze.

B-Box looked left to right at his crew then stared dead into the eyes of the enemy leader and said, "Yo, you bitch-ass motherfucker. I heard about what you done did to Rat-a-Tat-Tat back on the two-three-seven. That be on some bullshit, yo! Don't be sending one of your boys into *my* neighborhood busting no weak shit like that on *my* cousin. I'll take any one of you Electric Boogaloo bitches on any day of the week, *sucka!*"

The crowd gasped.

Being called a sucka on your own turf was the ultimate diss, and the so-called Electric Boogaloo bitches didn't play that shit. *Not one bit.* You could hear a pin drop.

The red leader, T-Ron, pointed to the old lady sitting next to the boombox.

The old lady nodded, hit play, and began bobbing her head to the scratching tune that immediately filled the air.

The gangs began to size each other up in a staredown of epic proportions; the tension was thick as each member stood firm in his own B-boy stance. This was it.

The old lady yelled, "Battle!" and the breakers came to life, busting moves back and forth as if their lives depended on it. Sneakers filled the air as breakers spun on their heads and flipped every way imaginable.

The crowd reacted in awe.

The old lady smiled. These old-school, non-violent break battles made her heart proud to be an East St. Louisan.

Back in the low rider, Hammer could see the breakdance battle happening through the vehicle's cracked windshield. He shook his head at the cheesy sight. "Real niggas don't dance. Yo, Randy!"

"Wassup, Hammer?"

"Kill all they asses."

The car spun to a one-eighty halt.

Randy quickly leaned out the window, yelled, "Fuck *Beat Street*," and fired rapidly into the crowd.

*

With his large frame and duffle bag slung over his shoulder, the unshaven one-man-army in the fatigue military jacket walked the dangerous streets without fear. Looking around, Charlie Jones began to wonder just where his city went wrong. He had been away a long time and everything he looked forward to seeing upon his return from military service had changed. Combat had also taken its toll on him mentally, so he wasn't necessarily looking for a utopia when he got home—maybe a little peace. Not a chance in the new Lou. He continued down the block to the apartment complex on the corner.

A young man wearing a half-cut neon shirt, trench coat, and roller skates, rolled up, skidded to a halt and said, "Fuck you doing up in here, white boy? You looking to buy some shit or what?"

Ignoring him, Charlie continued walking.

"I'm talking to you, bitch!"

"It's a school night," Charlie said without a second thought. "Take your punk-ass home, boy."

The roller skater bit his lip, turned and jetted off down a dark alley. *Was that who I think it was?* he thought as he hopped over a dead junkie and disappeared into the darkness.

Charlie approached the final section of the housing project and entered. He walked through the corridor that was littered with drug needles and empty assault rifle shells and headed straight for apartment 237 and knocked.

From the other side of the door, a voice screamed, "I'll get you the rent tomorrow, motherfucker!"

With a fist, Charlie knocked once more, hard.

The door flung open. "What?" the large man screamed. "Fuck your cracker ass want?"

Looking down, Charlie could see the man was wearing nothing but an open robe and worn-out briefs that were stained with little dots of urine on the front. Probably stained in the back too. But Charlie wasn't there to inspect underwear; he was there to pick up LaQueefa.

"LaQueefa here?" he asked, trying to hold his breath. The smell was awful.

"Who the fuck is you?"

"I'm Charles, man. LaQueefa knows me. I just got back from the war, so don't push me. I've seen too much, my thoughts are as dangerous as my hands are in a street brawl, plus I'm damaged on the inside."

"I can tell from the contrived military jacket you wearing and the duffle bag and shit. Plus, you unshaven, which is kinda cliché, but whatever."

"Well, like I said, LaQueefa knows me. Get her for me, will ya?"

"You musta been gone for one long-ass motherfucking time, war boy. Ain't you heard the news? LaQueefa doesn't know shit about anything anymore."

*

Deep in the abandoned bear cave at the old City Zoo, The Zoo Gang held a meeting by way of torch light. Stacks of drugs, weapons and cheap imitation purses were scattered about. Graffiti littered the walls. In the corner, on a stolen bench, sat a dead man in an expensive business suit. A politician perhaps? The boombox sitting in his lap played something from the X-Raided "Psycho Active" album, Hammer's favorite, at low volume.

The gang listened along as Hammer held the floor wearing his trademark, spiked shoulder pads and knee-high wrestling boots. A custom Zoo Gang graffiti-style shirt donned his chest and in his hand was a large rusted hammer the size of Thor's. "The official meeting of Hammer's Zoo Gang will now come to order," he said. He raised his Hammer high. "Can I get a muthafuckin 'what-what?'"

The crew threw their fists in the air and shouted, "Muthafuckin what-what?!"

"As all you muthafuckas be knowing, we have officially banned together and are about to shut this bitch down for good. Everybody inside *and* outside of The Lou is scared as fuck to even come challenge us. And who can blame them? That has been my plan all along. To gather the nastiest in gangster-ass muthafuckas like yourselves and take over. I have recruited the best bangers from all the crews ... and here you are. Here *we* are! We've come a long-ass way, my niggas. And we're about to go even further and get our gangster fucks on like this city has never seen before. I look around, and I don't see criminals. I see liberators! Like you, Dookie."

Everyone looked at Dookie who was sitting on a cinder block chilling and drinking a forty-ounce of Gorilla Stomp malt liquor.

Hammer continued, "You know why I recruited Dookie? Because, check this shit out, Dookie here kills cops ...*for kicks*!"

Dookie smiled. "We all need a muthafuckin hobby."

The gang clapped.

Dookie stood, took a bow, poured some brew on the ground and said, "For all the dead homies we be missing and shit."

Several men joined in and poured their beer in honor of fallen soldiers. "Yup-yup," they said as the gravel foamed around their feet.

Hammer continued. "And what about Ginsu? Can't forget about Ginsu. He's one of the most offensive stereotypes we got, *and* a gang favorite! Where you at, Ginsu?"

Everyone looked for Ginsu.

The five-foot Asian man slowly stepped from the shadows wearing his usual red, Michael Jackson jacket that had about fifty zippers—each one housing a different style blade. On his head was a Wu-Tang hat cocked to the side that covered his braided, cornrow hairstyle. One of his eyebrows even had several lines shaved into it, Vanilla Ice style.

"There he is!" Hammer pointed.

Everyone spun in Ginsu's direction.

Bangers responded with,

"Where did he come from?"

"I didn't know he was even here, yo!"

"Dude came out of stealth mode and shit again."

Hammer said, "Go ahead, G-su. Show 'em that thing you do."

In a flash, Ginsu produced two butterfly knives and began flipping them with a fury like nunchucks. The men stood in awe as the blades swished and swooshed the air in a constant blur of razored death. And like that, Ginsu closed the blades with a quickness, pocketed them, humped the air once like Michael Jackson, then stepped slowly back into the shadows out of sight, his expression blank.

The crew clapped.

"That boy good at that shit," a member said.

"I fucking love that dude," another agreed. "On that ninja shit."

In the shadows, Ginsu smiled proudly.

Hammer continued. "Tomorrow marks the day that will forever change this city. We shall move forward with the takeover as planned, starting with a new development in our plot with a little help from Kimbo, our gang's new tech nerd. Introduce yourself, Kimbo."

Kimbo, a skinny, computer nerd with no fashion sense, glasses, and a grin that showed braces across his teeth, stood from his computer set-up in the corner and with a timid wave said, "Hi-yah, fellas. Kimbo here. That's me." Next to Kimbo's set-up was what appeared to be a giant metal box the size of an elevator. The electrical wiring coming from behind it plugged into various extension cords and looked like an electrical fire just waiting to happen.

Hammer continued. "Kimbo, our little, nerdy computer guy here, has just invented a dope-ass time machine made from the elevator we stole from that mall we looted last week. Ain't that right, Kimbo?"

Kimbo pushed his double-taped glasses up the bridge of his nose, shyly put his hands back in the pockets of his butt-tight jeans and said, "Uh, yeah. That's affirmative, boss. If my calculations are correct, and they always are, I should have it up and running by tomorrow. Just need a few more extension cords and some time travel juice."

Hammer said, "What the fuck? Time travel juice? Is that even a real thing? You got some of that shit, man?"

Kimbo said with a push of his glasses, "Yeah. But we could use some more. It's a complex situation. I can break it down for you, if you'd like."

Hammer held up a hand and said, "No-no-no. Leave all that technical stuff out of it for me. I just do the gangster side of this shit and fund it through my various frowned-upon criminal activities."

Kimbo nodded, had a seat and got back to work.

Hammer looked at his gang and continued. "Our plan? We are sending someone back in time in order to get some super-human serum bullshit that I heard about from an inside source. With this serum, nothing will be able to stop us. And I mean *nothing*." Hammer hopped up on a stack of dead bodies to appear even taller over the crowd. He raised his rusty hammer and yelled, "He who controls the super-human serum, controls the future of The Lou! Hail Hammer!"

"Hammer time!" the crowd yelled back.

Hammer's eyes burned like riot fire. "Nothing, and I mean *nothing*, will stop us."

Interrupting them, the roller-skating drug pusher came rolling in at high speed with his trench coat flapping behind like a superhero in flight. He flew into the center of the crowd, spun in circles like a figure skater, dropped into the splits, then came up with a fist in the air. "Hail Hammer!"

"Hammer time," the members shouted back.

"What is it, Reggie?" Hammer asked the man on wheels.

"Yo, Charlie's back! I just seen that muthafucka outside. At first, I didn't recognize him, but it *was* him. He's back, Hammer."

The gang looked to Hammer in silence.

Hammer gulped.

Chapter Two
Turkey in the Wagon

"I can't believe this shit happened to you, LaQueefa," Charlie said as he looked down at his former ghetto queen who was lying in bed with her arms and legs cut off. Her afro—which was once sexy as hell—was a chunky mess of extensions, burnt bald spots and ringworm infestation.

"Yeah," the robed man scratched his balls behind Charlie. "That Zoo Gang really did a number on her. Cut her shit off, peed on her, burned her the fuck up, raped her. In that order too. I think they were mad."

"You think?"

"I guess so, *war boy*. Did you *not* just hear what I said they did?"

Unconscious, LaQueefa began twitching, stopped, then farted.

Charlie was totally distraught.

"She farts all the time now," the robed man said. "It must come from that mushy diet that's full-a broccoli and cheese the state sends over that I tube feed her through the nose. I try and drown it out with the tube; the farts. Hard sometimes. You should smell the room when I open up her Diaper Genie."

Charlie fumed. "We were supposed to get married after I returned home from the war. That was a promise I made to her."

"Yeah. It's a real bitch. I'm guessing you can just wheel LaQueefa around in a wagon if you want. She won't mind much. She's usually doped to the gills from the pain medication anyway. Tried some of her shit myself and it fucked me the fuck up, and I'm a pro. Listen, I'm not into all this sentimental-type shit. I just get paid to tube feed her and maybe wipe her ass every now and then. Anyway, *Christians in Compton* is on the tube. Think I'll go have a look. There's a wagon in the kid's room if you wanna take her for a pull around the block." The robed man exited the room. "Need anything just holler," he shouted.

Charlie began to lightly stroke LaQueefa's head. One of her extensions fell off and hit the floor. He reached down, grabbed it and slowly looked back up. LaQueefa's eyes were wide open and lovingly locked on his. A moment passed and a sad tear ran down LaQueefa's cheek in an epic display of reuniting between souls. You could almost hear the sad piano music.

"Charlie?!" she cried in disbelief. "It's you. It's really really you."

"Yes, LaQueefa. It's me."

"You look so built in the chest area now. The military was good to you. And your guns are massive. Even more so than before."

Charlie took one look at his biceps and said, "One fifteen, three sets of ten, baby."

"But do I still look pretty to you though, Charlie? Am I still your ghetto queen with the big booty?" She farted again.

Charlie looked at LaQueefa's legless, thanksgiving turkey-looking body and tried to reassure her with, "You bet, baby."

"Oh, Charlie. I've really missed the shit outta you. I know I can't roller boogie, cook, or fuck like I use to, but we can still have a meaningful life together."

Charlie looked away and shook his head in disbelief. "You think so, huh?"

"What does *that* supposed to mean, Charlie?" LaQueefa asked. "What's the matter? You don't like my hair this way?"

Charlie jumped from his seat. "This is unbelievable. What kinda life can a human potato sack and a fucked-up vet have? I feel like I'm losing my mind."

LaQueefa thought for a moment then gave a bright-eyed smile. "You can prop me up in the window, and I can let you know when the mailman comes."

"I can't deal with this ridiculous shit on top of my PTSD too!"

"No!" LaQueefa cried. "Don't go crazy like last time and get locked up again, Charlie! I know that look in your eyes! Just think of our son, Boogaloo! He needs a father in his life for once!"

"We'll get to *that* issue soon enough! Now, tell me who did this?"

"Who did what?"

"This!"

"Can you be more specific?"

"Who Butterballed you the fuck up like a goddamn Thanksgiving turkey and ruined our future?"

LaQueefa exhaled. "So, it's true. You don't like my hair now." She teared up.

"*Who*, LaQueefa?"

LaQueefa gave in. "It was your brother's gang." She farted.

Charlie turned, slowly walked over to the window, and looked down at the busy ghetto streets. "Hammer's boys did this bullshit?"

No response.

"I won't lie, LaQueefa. You look bad. *Real* bad. But I'm supposed to keep my nose clean and stay outta trouble; it was part of the deal with the judge before they gave me the option to either serve my country or serve time in jail for my Punisher-like style of vigilantism. Still, it only makes sense that I avenge you. That I avenge *us*. Despite the costs. Guess it's all part of being born a one-man-army. There always seems to be a fresh face for me to smash wherever I go. And Hammer's will just be one of the many faces I smash. But don't worry, me being his white, adopted brother just adds an extra layer of dramatic tension to it all. But that sibling shit doesn't faze me one bit. Rest assured, the men who did this will pay, one right after the other. Because I'm back and armed with a new set of serious, military-style fighting skills. Plus, Imma copy all the shit in the vigilante movies from the seventies and eighties when I take 'em out too. I'll stick one in a meat grinder like in *The Exterminator*. I'll even shoot one in the face through a boombox like in *Death Wish II*. That was really cool. Remember the first time we watched that shit, LaQueefa?"

No response.

"LaQueefa?" Charlie turned from the window, looked down, and LaQueefa was no more. Her lifeless, turkey-shaped body could no longer hold her beautiful soul hostage to a soiled bed, and Charlie knew it was for the best. He turned and walked out, more damaged than ever. He exited the apartment complex and forever walked away from his hopes of a beautiful future with the love of his life.

Down the street, four Zoo Gang members sat parked in a rusted, busted Cadillac and watched Charlie walk away. In the backseat, taking up all the room due to his spiked, football shoulder pads, Hammer blazed on a blunt. He passed the blunt to the driver whose head was covered in pink hair curlers.

Reggie roller skated up slow and low to the side of the vehicle and leaned in the window. "There go dat muthafucka right there," he whispered. "I told you, Hammer. He's back. I told you."

With a fresh bullet tattooed on his forehead that was slightly bleeding, the gang's newest full-fledged member, Randy Watson, sat in the passenger seat. "Just give a nigga the word," he said. "Whatcha want me to do?"

No response.

He asked again. "Whatcha want me to do, Hammer?"

"Yo," Hammer said. "Just calm the fuck down and lemme think for a muthafuckin minute."

Being too eager to please, Randy turned around to face Hammer and spoke again. "I'll go pop that nigga in the face right now if you—"

Pow! Hammer's fist shot forward and slammed Randy's face and silenced him.

Blood shot down Randy's throat and gagged him as he clutched at his smashed nose.

Hammer bit his lip. "I said shut the fuck up and lemme think, you stupid-ass nigga. You being too eager."

The banger in pink curls behind the wheel handed Randy his own personal gang colors to use as a rag and said, "Not a drop on the seats, baby boy."

Randy took the handkerchief to catch the blood, snot, and tears that ran down his face and said, "Goddamn. Fucking hit me?"

The driver looked at Randy and shook his head no: a silent warning.

Randy got the message and zipped it.

"We still move forward tomorrow," Hammer said. "Nothing's gonna stop our dope-ass muthafuckin time-traveling scheme. Once we get that serum from the eighties, not even my own brother will stand a chance in hell against us." He looked at Charlie walking away. "And this stupid nigga, I'm gonna deal with my muthafuckin self. Give me the brick."

The pink-curled banger handed Hammer an early-days cell phone from the front seat. Hammer dialed and said, "Ginsu? Konichiwa, yo. Yeah. Follow his ass. Call me back when you have something useful and shit."

On a rooftop above, low and out of sight, Ginsu left his post and began to follow Charlie down the block, trailing along like a silent ninja.

Hammer hung up the phone with a push of a button and looked at the driver. "Let's go get some muthafuckin chicken and waffles and some sweet black pussy."

The driver fired up the lowrider, hit the hydraulic switches, and the car rose with a jiggle and a bounce. They pulled off with DJ Quik's "Sweet Black Pussy" bumping full volume from the stolen stereo system.

Chapter Three
The Secret Life of a Junkyard Dog

The fifty-eight-year-old Rudy Ray Jones, uncle to Hammer and Charlie Jones, sat in his favorite chair and watched boxing on the living room's TV. He jumped from his seat with cane in hand, wearing nothing but a pair of boxers, and with his gravelly voice screamed as Sugar "Smack" Robbins started to pound on the white boy that dared to enter the ring with him.

"Beat the shit out that honky-ass muthafucka! Hit 'em! Hit 'em! Boo-yah! That's it! That's it!" The sounds from the crowd on the television went wild, as did Rudy Ray. He danced in circles. "He ain't getting up! He ain't getting up! Woo-wee! That was a knock out *like a muthafucka*. They should know better than to fuck with my boy Sugar Smack."

Lamar Jones, with his out-of-date clothes, large mustache and uneven afro (in desperate need of a cut), walked into the room covering his ears. "Shoot, Pop. What's with all the ruckus? You know I'm trying to study in the kitchen for my class."

"Shit, you big, stupid-ass, cock sucking dummy. You call that writing workshop you take at night something? You call that a class? Growth? I call it a waste of time. Just like that white boy that got in the ring and wasted *his* time. Shit. Sugar smacked the white off that nigga. Won me five hundred smackers off the shit too."

"Good," Lamar pointed. "Now you can pay back Father Strickland at the church all the money you owe him."

"*Shieet*! You musta done lost your goddamn mind. Imma buy me a new record player ... and some beer. Chicken wings too! Maybe even a new TV. Color! That way when Sugar 'Smack' smacks the shit outta the next fool who comes along, we're gonna see some goddamn red on the screen, not this black and white *Raging Bull* bullshit."

There was a knock at the door.

With the aid of his cane, Rudy Ray limped over to answer it. "If there's any money left over, maybe we can get you some pussy from the east end of town followed by a penicillin chaser. My treat, Son."

"Come on, Pop. You know I'm saving myself for marriage."

Rudy Ray shook his head in disbelief. He opened the door to reveal Charlie Jones on the other side.

"Charlie," he shouted, giving him a quick hug. "You made it back from the war in one piece! Just like we knew you would. What brings you over to my junkyard? Are you looking to repair an old fridge or some shit?"

Charlie looked over to cousin Lamar and greeted him with a nod and a forced smile.

Ever the pacifist, Lamar walked back into the kitchen without saying a word to the war veteran.

Rudy Ray continued. "Don't worry about that dumb-shit son of mine. He's still a virgin. Maybe if he finally got his pecker wet, he wouldn't act so goddamn ornery all the time."

"We all have our problems," Charlie agreed.

"Yep. And that's just *one* of his. Come on in, Charlie. Grab yourself a 40 ounce from the fridge. In fact, make it two."

"What are we drinking?"

"Does it matter when it's free?"

Moments later, Charlie and Rudy Ray were sitting in separate chairs watching *Christians in Compton* on the tube.

"And when there's no more room in muthafuckin hell," the TV said. "I will stand by the gates of Heaven *myself* with a flamethrower! Can I get an amen? And I'll burn every democrat homosexual that comes prancing my way with Jesus on my side egging me on as he refills my holy-water-powered flamethrower tanks. Woo-wee! Holy shit! I will light sinner's asses up!"

The crowd reacted with a joyous, "Amen!"

Rudy Ray grabbed the remote and turned down the tube. He looked at Charlie—who was doing his best to drink the nasty beverage offered to him—and said, "Sorry 'bout the warm beer and shit. Fridge conked out on me last week. Lost a shitload of bologna and cheese too, goddamn it."

"Not a problem."

"So, whatcha gonna do now that you're back in the Lou? Want a job washing peep-show windows? Because I know a guy hiring. Even has dental!"

"I came back for LaQueefa."

Rudy Ray went tight-lipped and looked down. "I heard about what happened to her, Charlie. I'm sorry. How's she doing?"

"She looked like a fucked-up honey ham with a head, fresh out the oven and with a serious fart condition. It stunk so bad that I'm surprised you can't smell it on me."

"*That's* what that is? I just thought you had a bad case of the silent but deadlies."

"It's all her. Trust me. She died right while I was in the middle of talking to her about my revenge plot."

"You don't say. Guess you all sad now, huh?"

"Later when I regain my sanity, I'll grieve." Charlie leaned back and took a harsh swig. "But this tale of revenge might be tough because of all my mental problems. I have a ... *condition.*"

"One of them *conditions*, huh?"

"Yeah. A *condition*. The war-torn vet kind like in vigilante movies. That's why the Dr. they assigned me to has me on four different pills, to keep me from going apeshit. But the side effects are too much to handle at times. The red ones make my dick go limp, the blue ones make my pee burn, the pink ones make me shit green liquid that smells like black licorice, and the black ones cause me to have hallucinations. On the way over, I swear to God I saw a midget in a clown suit peeing on a sleeping bum. I'm one seriously fucked up vet."

"Actually, that clown could have been real. Lil' Pookie from the two-three-seven, he's a breakdancing clown. That's his schtick. Bit of a drunk though. Hates bums. So, she looked like a honey ham, huh?"

"With a head."

"Mm-mm," Rudy Ray smiled. "You know, Charlie. I fucking *love* ham. Fuck all that Muslim shit." Rudy Ray took a drink. "So, you were saying?"

"I know who did all that shit to her."

"Lemme guess. Hammer and his boys?"

"How'd you know?"

"Hey, your Uncle knows shit."

"So, do I."

"That right? You know shit, Charlie? Well, tell me, *little nephew*, just what is it you *think* you know."

There was a pause.

Charlie looked over and said two simple words. "*Section Eight.*"

The mood in the room changed immediately.

Moments later, Rudy Ray and Charlie made their way to the back of the junkyard towards a little tin shed that sat amongst the rubble. No longer with a limp and completely breaking his Fred Sanford routine, Rudy Ray carried his cane and spoke with a professional touch. "So, how did you find out about us, Charlie?"

"A lieutenant in my outfit was related to Earl Tubb."

"Ah, the Rockwood legend they recruited back in eighty-three. Bit of a slob. He was our most dedicated member."

"Until *you* came along. The lieutenant told me all about it as he died right in my arms during a raid gone bad."

"One of them tragic scenes, huh?"

"Right outta *Casualties of War*. We used to talk a lot during down time. Got close. He trusted me. Once we even got drunk together—maybe *too* drunk—and I talked about how much I loved the *Death Wish*, *Breakin'*, and ninja movies growing up. But the moment I mentioned that I prefer Chuck Norris over John Wayne, that's when the L.T. spilled it all and told me that I'd make a perfect soldier for Section Eight. I *had* heard of Section Eight before, but I thought it was just some made-up fantasy. Fairy-tales about one-man armies, vigilantes, and aerobic-instructor ninjas for movie geeks to spank their shit to. Imagine my surprise when I found out it was true."

"It's true, Charlie. *All* of it."

"But you? You *were* The Ghetto Blaster. I checked into it."

The men stopped at the shed.

Rudy Ray went silent, looked away to the junkyard horizon and said, "The batteries in my boom box drained out years ago."

"The fall of Section Eight forced you into retirement, so you came to the Midwest to escape death? Something like that?"

"Nah, we were still kicking much ass until that Zoo Gang in The Village Projects took over the night one of our arch enemies, Razorback Bill, fell. Bill wanted to unmask his entire alien race just so the humans in his town could see his true colors. He absolutely hated living a lie. Found him smashed to bloody pieces on the side of the road. Still no idea how that even happened."

"The Zoo Gang goes back that far?"

"Oh, yeah. Shit went downhill fast once they cropped up. The godfather of The Village Projects, Mr. Brown, funded their entire operation. I might have had a better shot at defeating them cocksuckers if I had better gadgets at that time, but it was no use. That gang grew like a wildfire that I couldn't extinguish alone. The Village labeled me The Darkie Knight. Guess it was some kinda racist, black Batman reference. Only it was mostly black dudes calling me that, so maybe not."

Rudy Ray opened the shed door. "Nephew or not, you tell anyone what I'm about to show you, I'll kick you right in the dick. Got it?"

"Got it."

They entered the dark shed, shut the door, and Rudy Ray flipped a switch. The shed lit up and revealed tons of ebony center-folds on the wall. Rudy Ray reached up, tugged a dangling extension cord, and the floor began to drop slowly into the earth like an elevator.

Rudy Ray leaned on the workbench. "Thing about Section Eight was this, our threat was alien; the ones demonic in nature. That's why we had the best in weaponry at the time. Including the P34 Protoblasting Draconian Popper Stopper. Nuke pellets. Even ninja stars that were heat seeking so that our operatives could use them without the proper, ninja-training upload. A couple of our guys even had robot hands."

"Sounds cool."

"Yeah, they looked pretty cool. Section Eight even masqueraded as a film company at one point to test out their latest weapons."

"Cannon Films?"

Rudy Ray nodded proudly. "All the props in those films *were* actual weapons designed by Section Eight. Not only did we get to test our weapons out in the open, but we also got to see them featured in some cool movies. Remember that motorcycle that Chuck Norris rode in *The Delta Force* that shot little rockets out the ass?"

"Fuck yeah, I do."

"That was my design. Unfortunately, I don't have any of that technology on hand. Not anymore. I have to make my own. Dabbling, I guess you could say. Keeping busy. Experimenting with stuff using junk from the scrap pile above. Until, shall we say, the *right man* came along."

The elevator shed reached the lowest level and stopped with a *ding!*

Rudy Ray pushed the door open to reveal a large chunk of hollowed-out earth. A computer terminal with an extra-large screen was built into the cave's wall. A mini-gym, a dojo, some junkyard weapons, and a black van with killer red rims and a short-range missile attached to its roof were also on the scene.

Charlie stepped out in awe. Rudy Ray had his very own bat cave! *This* was getting good.

"Follow me," Rudy Ray smiled. They walked the short, cavernous hallway as Rudy Ray continued. "Been working on a prototype suit, too. Sort of like the one in that shitty-ass *G.I. Joe* movie back in the day. Shit's got everything, and I mean *everything*."

"Everything?"

"*Everything*. Even has an adapter in the helmet so you can hook yourself up some tunes and listen to your own choice of theme music as you fight against the injustices of your choice."

"I like what I'm hearing."

"Well, you're about to like it a helluva lot more."

They reached a metal door and Rudy Ray punched in a three-digit code on the keypad. The door slowly opened on its own to reveal a wannabe Iron Man suit pieced together by rusted, discolored crap from the junkyard. Charlie was in even more awe.

Rudy Ray went into a sales pitch. "Flames can be shot from the wrist, but just so you know, you have to go limp wrist when you fire the shit; burnt the hair off the back of my hands more than once." He rubbed the back of his scarred hand with a somber nod. "Metal is all bulletproof. If you pull the lever here on the hip," Rudy Ray pulled the lever and roller blades shot out of the bottom of the feet, "you can skate around. I can't skate, but I put 'em on anyway."

"I'd never use 'em."

"Never say never. Been working on getting it into full-flight mode, but the only problem is I can't get the fuel to quit burning off so damn quick. Couple minutes in the air and you drop straight to the ground. But if that does happen, I lined the suit with a poly-fill. That's that same shit they put in subwoofer boxes to slow down the frequencies to make the sub have a tighter punch. Makes the suit hot, but it does help you take blows, punches, kicks, all that stuff."

"Good with the bad."

"Also, inside the helmet is a hypo, double-linked sqizzawatt 23-7B. It allows you to link up to my central intelligence computer, which is tapped directly into every camera in the city. Got the idea for that when I spliced my shit for some free cable and picked up the *Playboy Channel* for free. The central computer will even talk to you directly through its artificial intelligence. Had different voices I could download for it. British butler, Southern Belle, even celebrities." Rudy Ray leaned forward to push a button on the suit's neck. "Me? I chose Mr. T." He pushed the button.

The suit came alive, and its eyes lit up. "Whatcha want, fool?" it said.

"At ease," Rudy Ray said to it.

"Shut up, Murdock!" the suit replied.

Charlie looked at the suit, leaned in and said, "This shit is off-the-hook. How do you shoot the proton blasts from the hands and make it fly?"

"What do you mean?"

"Well, it's not operated by a joystick obviously."

"Obviously."

"So, I'm assuming it works by voice command."

"No. You don't tell it to shoot. Just point your palm and shoot the motherfuckers. Wanna fly, then fly, man."

"But when does it know when to fire or when I'm just waving hi to someone? I can't go around shooting old ladies just for waving hello."

"It doesn't shoot little, old ladies for waving hello. But it'll shoot when there's a bad guy there. Don't ask so many fucking questions. Just go with it." Rudy Ray powered the suit off with a double clap, and the door slowly closed on its own. "Installed the Clapper on it last week. So, when do we begin?"

"Begin?"

"Kicking Zoo Gang ass for what they did to your woman. You're gonna need some serious help though."

"What do you call this?" Charlie motioned around the room. "You, the computers, the flight suit."

"I call it a helping hand. From someone you can trust, Charlie."

"Yeah, and it's considered help. And it'll be all the help I need."

"You have something against help, Charlie?"

"Let's just say I'm done with the team dynamic thing."

"Even if that team dynamic has something to do with, say, oh, I don't know, working with the original Section Eight squad from Rockwood?"

"What are you getting at, Uncle Rudy Ray?"

"Well, shit is a little more serious than you might think, Charlie. Remember how I said I was linked up to every computer in the city? This includes cell phones and plus I follow the ZooGang4Life hashtag on Twitter. If anything by them goes out, it gets picked up here by me."

"Jesus, talk about an invasion of privacy."

"Fuck 'em. Anyway, I got word just this morning that they plan on going back in time in order to steal some Serum 13B from the eighties. Rockwood, Mississippi eighties to be exact."

"Holy shit. The human enhancement serum that turned Earl Tubb into an intergalactic guardian of Rockwood?"

"Uh-huh. And much like them Zoo Gang assholes, I *too* have a time machine, always one step ahead—except I'm all low on time juice at the moment."

"Time juice? Is that even a thing?"

"Yep. In fact, I'm gonna be picking some up on my trash route tomorrow. As it stands, I only have enough for two jumps at the moment. I can get you from point A to point B and that's about it for now. Used up most of my last batch chasing down some decent copies of the uncensored *Sanford and Son* VHS set. But how about this? After I score me some more time juice tomorrow, we can have you jump time, snatch up that serum first before the Zoo Gang gets their diabolical hands on it, grab some random Section Eight members along the way, then hop your ass back here just in time for the final battle like in *Avengers: End Game.* All these cool characters all lined up on the battlefield against Hammer's Zoo Gang. Good versus evil. How exciting would that shit be?"

Charlie said, "Sounds like some pretty far-fetched shit. Rushed. Maybe even outlandish. I'm thinking I can easily just hop back in time once and grab LaQueefa before her *accident* and then the two of us can leave for greener pastures. I think I deserve it." Charlie pulled LaQueefa's hair extension from his fatigue jacket pocket and gently rubbed it with his thumb. "We both deserve it."

Rudy Ray sympathized, but threw in two more cents. "But what about the city, Charlie? How many innocent lives will be lost once you decide to sit on your hands and retire from being a badass? Sure, you'll be knee-deep in some LaQueefa pussy, but once that nut gets busted, will you be able to wipe up the cum stain in peace knowing the innocent people here in our time-line will be suffering?"

"She swallows."

"You know what I mean. Look, the city needs us. If the Zoo Gang gets that serum, possibly even the world will need our help then. But we can't do something of that magnitude alone. We might have to go for the whole enchilada. We might have to ... *assemble*."

"Only if I fail at getting that serum."

"So, you're at least going after the serum?"

"... I don't know."

"Look, Section Eight is dead," Rudy Ray continued. "We can reboot the shit *and* save LaQueefa! Fuck the military, man. We can form our own squad of superheroes and shit! Besides, I need to pass this torch of knowledge on to someone worthy of it, and your Lieutenant was right; you'd make a perfect soldier for Section Eight. I've seen every Cannon Films production Chuck Norris and Charles Bronson has ever been in. More than once. Trust me on this. I'll be the man in the chair ... behind the computers because my ass has gotten too old for the physical side of the shit. Hell, I can't even fit into any of the cool-ass superhero suits I have in storage down here. Been collecting them suits and shit for years too."

"How about we just call all this crazy shit Plan B just in case I fail?"

Rudy Ray gave up his dream of reforming Section Eight and smiled with a pat to Charlie's shoulder. "Your vendetta is a personal one. I understand, Charlie. I do. And I'll respect it. Your revenge story, your plan. We keep it simple. Whatever choice you make come tomorrow; I'll be there for you all the way. Just remember, this gang won't stop. Wherever you go with LaQueefa, the Zoo Gang will still be doing their thing. And their time of domination will still come, and it will eventually catch up to you wherever you land with her. There might not be any escaping this life mission, Charlie. Acquiring this serum first might be your only chance for a happily-ever-after ending, with or without LaQueefa."

Charlie agreed. "The serum it is."

"We start tomorrow, high noon."

Minutes later, they reached the back door of Rudy Ray's home and stopped.

"Don't mention any of this shit to Lamar, okay," Rudy Ray said. "He has no idea about my past. He's adopted anyway, sort of. Somebody left him in the backseat of a Cadillac that was brought in for me to smash one day. I took him in and decided to use him for my cover. Had himself a quarter pile doo-doo in his drawers too. I hosed 'em down, named him Lamar and here we are."

They entered the home.

Lamar was sitting at the coffee table typing out a short story for class.

Rudy Ray immediately went back into his Fred Sanford routine with, "Would you look at this big, shit-stained-looking dummy right here? Look at him. Pecker drier than dust. Me and my dust-dick son. Sounds like a TV show! *Rudy Ray and Dust Dick.* Make it a western. I'd watch that. How 'bout you, Charlie?"

Lamar looked up from his typewriter annoyed and said, "Please, Pop. I'm trying to concentrate. I turn in a crappy story for class, I'm blaming you. That's right. 'All pop's fault, Mr. Readmore' is exactly what I'll tell 'em too."

Rudy Ray put his fists up. "I'll straight knock yo ass out if you give me that smart mouth again." He drew his cane back like a batter and bit his bottom lip. "Come on, boy! Try me!"

Lamar tried to brush off his pop's comments and began typing away.

Rudy Ray looked at Charlie and smiled with a wink.

*

At the No-Tell Motel, Charlie slapped the bell on the desk with a *ding!* The clerk looked up from his stiff-paged, nudie magazine with a look of disgust and said,

"Goddamn it. Not another one of you vigilante looking bastards."

"Just give me a fucking room, man."

The clerk began getting the paperwork and keys in order and mumbled to himself. "Third goddamn vigilante-looking bastard this week. Why can't these dudes just get a room somewhere else with all their shoot-em up shit in my halls? Don't need it, man."

"What's that you said?"

"Nothing. Look, the room is two hundred thirty-seven dollars a night. No loud music after eight and no prostitutes before nine. And *no* weapons. I can just take a fucking guess at what's in that duffle bag of yours. Bazooka?"

"Clothes and shit."

"*Hymph.* Heard that one before. Boy last week said the same shit, right before he drove a tank through my fucking lobby trying to save some prostitute he didn't even know from a life of debauchery. The bitch of it all, the prostitute was staying across the street. Crazy world. Anyway, condom machine in back," he slid the key across the desk with a gross smile. "Please, *enjoy* your stay."

Moments later, Charlie walked the disgusting second-floor hallway to the sounds of music, loud TVs, random arguments, and sex coming from the surrounding rooms. A junkie laid next to his door, passed out cold, needle in arm. Using his key, Charlie opened the door to his room, stepped over the junkie, and entered. Inside, a sex swing hung over a hot pink, heart-shaped bed, and the shag carpet was crusted with cum. On the wall was scribbled "Save Iris" next to a Charles Palentine for President bumper sticker that had cross-hairs drawn over the candidate's image. On the bedside table was a bowl of campaign buttons with "We <u>Are</u> the People" written on them.

Charlie placed his duffle bag on the floor and walked over to the window. Sliding the smoke-stained curtains aside, he glanced down at the dangerous streets. The crime filled the air with the sounds of gunshots, screams, sirens and booming subwoofers. He pulled out one of his prescription bottles, took a red and swallowed it. Taking some deep, concentrated breaths, the pill quickly began to take effect and everything around Charlie began to slowly fade to black.

*

The next morning, Charlie woke, grabbed his duffle bag from the sex swing, pulled some c-rations from it, ate on the commode with a plastic spoon, showered, then swallowed three pills—not really knowing if any were even red or not (The black pills had been playing with his perception of color lately). Regardless, he threw on his army fatigue jacket and left for the funeral to say his final goodbyes to LaQueefa.

*

Only four attended the LaQueefa funeral. Charlie walked up and made it five as the preacher preached on. "LaQueefa was loved by many. I guess most of them were too busy to attend since the numbers are so low. Actually, it's the lowest I've ever seen. And I've been doing this for a long time. Oh, well. Jesus is the way and may God rest her soul. Drop her, kid."

The young kid standing by kicked the lever, and LaQueefa's child-sized coffin began to drop into the earth.

A grief-stricken old woman in back bawled her eyes out in an embarrassing fashion. Everyone looked as she continued to wail and slide out of her chair onto the ground with her Jesus handkerchief catching the nonexistent tears.

Charlie continued to watch the casket drop.

The kid began shoveling in dirt.

The grief-stricken lady was finally dragged away by several ushers.

Charlie looked at the attention seeker and shook his head. That's when a fifteen-year-old around-the-way girl, wearing oversized hoop earrings, slut-wear, and carrying a fake Gucci purse, walked up next to Charlie. For a moment, with the exception of the bawling lady being escorted away, the two stood side-by-side in silence.

"Did you know LaQueefa?" the gum chewing girl finally asked.

"Wouldn't be here if I didn't."

"Hear what they did to her?"

"Yeah. Why the small coffin? Looks child size."

The kid shoveling dirt stopped to chime in. "Cost issue, Mister. The city doesn't wanna have to pay full price on a coffin for just half a chick. You know what they did? Did you hear? They cut her legs off, man."

"I know."

The kid shoveled more dirt. "Yeah. Peed on her too."

And with that, Charlie abruptly walked away.

The girl quickly followed. "Excuse me, but are you Charlie Jones," she asked.

Charlie kept moving.

"*Excuse me.* I'm talking to you. I said, 'Are you Charlie Jones?'"

Nothing.

The girl looked harder. "You *are* him. It's me, Iesha!"

Charlie stopped dead in his tracks. "Iesha?" He turned and looked her up and down in disbelief. "Is that really you? What are you doing dressed like a skit-scat tramp? What are you now? Fourteen?"

"Fuck you talking about? I'm fifteen, thank you very much. You wanna catch me outside and talk that shit?"

"We *are* outside. Why aren't you in school?"

"My sister's funeral."

"Oh, yeah. Right. Well, it's good to see you," he looked her over again, "... I guess."

"Look," Iesha chewed her gum. "We need to talk about LaQueefa for a second; I wanna clear some shit up. Just so you know, LaQueefa wanted to keep poking her nose in my business. Telling me to stay off the streets. Stay in school. Well, fuck that! I told her to just catch me outside and we can handle the shit like real bitches."

"Trying to save you from these streets is what got her killed? She always did love you, Iesha. Why the hell are you talking like this? I have never heard such stupid-sounding vulgarity in all my life."

"Shit. Fuck yo ass talking about up in this bitch and shit? I ain't muthafuckin Vulcan."

Charlie exhaled. "*Vulgar.* Look, Iesha. What do you know about Boogaloo? You know where he's staying now?"

"Oh, your son, Boog? He got shot in a drive-by yesterday and is all crippled now and shit. This new nigga named Randy needed to be initiated, so Hammer had him open fire on a bunch of breakdancers. Hammer can't stand male dancers. He just all jealous and shit though. He got no rhythm on the floor *or* in the sack. And please don't repeat this, but he has a small dick too. Looks like a Tootsie Roll."

"Boogaloo has been shot?"

"Yeah."

"My son?"

"Yep."

"Shot?"

"Uh-huh, but back to Hammer's dick. One time, I—"

"Can't you think about anything outside of goddamn dick? Shut the fuck up for a second and focus! Where is Boogaloo staying?"

"Oh!" Iesha threw back attitude. "Oh, okay. My bad. Guess everything is all about *you*, huh, Charlie? Fine with me. Boog been staying at the rec center lately. Ya happy? They right in the middle of trying to save it from an evil, rich, white, real estate developer who wants to tear it down and put up a nice string of shopping centers."

"What a bastard."

"I know, right? Can't stand when people with money be buying dilapidated buildings and improve the area. They always be pulling that bullshit."

"Is Boogaloo there now?"

"More than likely. The hospitals will kick you the fuck out now after twenty-four hours if you ain't got no money, and Boog broke as they come. So, where else could he be?"

*

Over at the local graffiti-ridden, recreational center Miracles N Shit, Boogaloo Jones sat in a wheelchair, immobile—except from the neck up, and talked to his fellow neon-clad dancers about his current situation. Next to him was his sexy-as-hell Latino girlfriend with her hand on his shoulder, hanging on every word but understanding zilch English.

"And on top of not being able to try and dance on the ceiling anymore or magically levitate brooms," an almost tearful Boogaloo cried, "I can't even learn the latest dance moves on the street. All of you will surely surpass me as time goes by, and all I can do is sit here in my jumpsuit, which my girlfriend here gave me," he looked at her through watery eyes. "Thank you, baby. It was a great get-out-of-the-hospital gift. Matches my Adidas."

She looked down and responded in a sweet and lovely Spanish accent that he didn't understand. It didn't matter. She was hot.

Boogaloo continued. "And by next week, if we don't raise enough money to pay for the repairs on the building, then that evil, real estate sucka gonna wrecking-ball our hopes and dreams of supplying these poor kids with a place to breakdance at after school. It just ain't right, man," he shook his head. "It ain't."

The surrounding breakers nodded in sympathy.

Boogaloo added. "And I know this is out of left field, but my relationship with my father has been strained for the longest time. We don't see eye-to-eye at all. Never have. Maybe by some weird circumstance, or miracle 'n shit, he will come back into my life unexpectedly so we can reconnect."

A man from outside the room stuck his head in and shouted, "Boogaloo, man out here says he's your dad! Wants to reconnect!"

All the breakers looked at Boogaloo and smiled.

Boogaloo slowly looked up with tearful eyes that quickly turned to joy as if he had just seen Jesus. "Guys, did you hear that? My father is here! My father is here! Oh, my God! Oh, my God! Dad! My dad!"

The breakers began to celebrate with thunderous applause, random dance moves, high fives and acrobatic flips. Several hoisted Boogaloo up on their shoulders and Boogaloo's crippled arms and legs dangled helplessly like wet noodles. But it was a beautiful moment and you couldn't wipe the smile from his tearful face.

"My dad is here, guys!" Boogaloo's head wobbled. "He's really really here! Oh, my God!"

The head of the moonwalking department looked up at Boogaloo.

They locked eyes and shared a moment.

Boogaloo almost started to cry again.

The moonwalking teacher gave him a thumbs up, turned around, and walked out, off to make a connection in Miami and was as proud as he could ever be of Boogaloo. He was never seen again.

Moments later, Charlie and Boogaloo, father and son, sat on the front steps of Miracles N Shit and talked. Boogaloo hung on his father's every word.

"And that's the truth, Boogaloo. That's why we haven't gotten along all this time or connected like a father and son should. Can you ever forgive me?"

"I forgive you, Dad. But I couldn't fight back now even if I wanted to. I'm a crippled breakdancer from the neck down. Uncle Hammer's gang really jacked me up."

"They did the same to your mother, Boogaloo. Not only did they hurt you, but they hurt her ... and worse. She's gone and buried now. Never to roller boogie again."

Boogaloo saddened even more. "She was so proud of me when I'd learn the latest dance moves. She'd clap every time."

Charlie switched gears to a hopeful tone. "Once we get done clearing the streets of these pricks, I promise you, we will finally start working on being a family for once. And that's something I think we *both* need."

"A family needs a mother."

"And when the job is done, and if all goes right, you'll have one. All we need is a little time jump juice."

Boogaloo's head lifted. "Time jump juice? Is that even a thing?"

"Apparently so. Hammer needs to fall first though."

Boogaloo put his head back down and began to cry *again*. "But there's absolutely no hope for my revenge story in all this. I can't even moonwalk now, Dad."

"Trust me, Son. There's *always* a way to wreck shop and fuck shit up."

Chapter Four
The Story of Tuck Pendelton

Two hours later, Charlie sat in The Wet Spot, a germ-infested, one-stripper-pole bar, and had a drink with his war buddy, Tuck Pendelton; a man who was never without his black bandana, black tank top, camouflage pants, jungle boots, and permed mullet. A sign "We Are Not Responsible for Any Diseases Caught on Grounds" hung above the liquor display. The jukebox blasted "Slave" by The Rolling Stones, and the stripper on stage entertained the other two patrons sitting front-and-center by making her butt cheeks clap to the rhythm of the snare with precision.

Charlie slammed his empty glass on the bar. "Reload," he demanded from the bartender.

"Shit, dude. That's your eighth shot in ten minutes. I'm trying to watch *Coffy* over here." On a tiny TV behind the bar, the sexy actress, Pam Grier, was blowing a man's head off with a shotgun. The bartender continued. "What do you say you just give me a fifty and keep the Jack?"

Charlie slapped a fifty on the counter. "Keep the change, lazy asshole. And move the fuck out of the way so we can watch too."

The bartender put the bottle down on the counter with a *thunk,* swiped up the money, then repositioned his casual lean for TV viewing courtesy.

Charlie raised his glass to Tuck and said, "Here's to Fox Company 2/7, second platoon. May they rest in peace."

"Rest in peace, my ass. Chesty Puller probably got them motherfuckers attacking commies in hell as we speak."

Charlie smiled at that. "A devil dog's work is never done."

Both shots were thrown back with ease into their cast-iron stomachs.

Charlie poured another and looked at the screen. "You ever seen this movie before, Tuck?"

"I don't watch movies. Never have. They influence too much. Creates copycats. You know how much I like to be original, Charlie."

"True that, Tuck. True that. So, whatcha been up to, man?"

"Me? I got spit on and fired from a car wash after I returned home from the war. Then I went walking and got picked up by this asshole sheriff who accused me of smelling like an animal and demanded that I eat elsewhere. All I wanted was something to eat. But he had to push it and ended up drawing blood first. In the end, I fucked the entire police department the fuck up and shot that sheriff in the legs. Heard him creeping on a roof and lit his ass up. Remember Colonel Carpman?"

"Yeah. Always wore a beret?"

"That's the one! He showed up and finally talked me down in the end. I was crying, spitting and mumbling about this and that. Chances are, you couldn't make out what I was saying. Hell, I didn't even know myself. Anyway, I ended up in jail, then in a serious twist of events that are highly unlikely, I was released to go take photos of POWs. But do you think I could just sit by and watch as our fellow soldiers sat all sweaty and sick behind bamboo cages? Hell no! It was Tuck Time!"

"Shit, man." Charlie poured for them both and threw his back as Tuck continued.

"Oh, yeah," Tuck grabbed his glass and held it up. "I rescued the POWs, blew motherfucking Vietnam up all by myself, came home, shot some computers straight to technological hell, scared the shit outta this dude named Murdick, gave a speech about wanting what they wanted, the POWs that is, and then I simply walked off. No wallet, no shirt, nothing. That was about forty-five minutes ago or so. And that's how I ended up here. Maybe I'll come in handy or something later on. Until then, I'm staying right here and getting shitfaced."

"Maybe you can go into some violent stick fighting for cash, give the money away to some monks who are peaceful but have no problem taking the violent, blood money anyway?"

"Fuck, that. Shit sounds stupid."

"Never say never."

The bartender's phone began to ring. He answered. "Wet Spot ... Yeah ... Fatigue jacket? Unshaven? Yeah, he's here." He handed Charlie the phone. "For you."

Charlie popped a black pill in his mouth, threw it back with another shot and took the receiver. "Go for Charlie."

"Ch-ch-Charlie," came the sounds of an injured Rudy Ray. "They hit us. They got us bad. Lamar ... he's dead."

"Christ, Uncle Rudy Ray. What the fuck happened?"

What the Fuck Happened

Earlier that morning, Rudy Ray and Lamar rose with the sun, grabbed a couple of microwaveable, fried chicken biscuits from the kitchen and hopped in the garbage truck around back. Rudy Ray looked over to his son and said, "Goddammit. Why you gotta bring a book with you? We on the job. The trash can't pick itself up with you reading. Best quit reading them stupid books and get your mind on some garbage, dummy." Rudy Ray fired up the truck and hit the horn—which hurt poor Lamar's ears every time. Rudy Ray smiled at Lamar's discomfort, kicked the truck into gear, then pulled out with the vehicle jerking along from the bad clutch. Once Rudy Ray got the large vehicle smoothed out, he looked over and said, "Pour me some coffee."

"Sure thing, Pop." Lamar poured and handed his father the steaming thermos cup.

Rudy Ray sniffed the aroma and took a sip. He decided it was time to get sentimental. "You know I just be fucking with you all the time, right? *Even* though you just a great big, shit-stained dummy, I still love you."

"Yeah. I know, Pop. I know."

Rudy Ray sipped more coffee.

Lamar looked over. "But you need to back up off me and let me be a man for once. No matter what I do, there you are poking at me. Harassing me. Insulting me in front of people, my friends, family, even customers. That stuff's not right, Pop. You're going to cause me to have a complex. I mean, what's your problem with me?"

"Just part of the routine, Son. Just part of the routine."

"What are you talking about now? What routine?"

"Well, guess you're old enough to know the truth."

"What *truth*?"

"You ever watched *Sanford and Son*?"

"No."

"Used to be my favorite show. Better than the shit you watch, lemme tell ya. Well, anyway, I have the entire series in my closet next to the nudie mag stacks. Go grab it and watch it sometime with the—"

Boom! Another garbage truck slammed into their side and sent them flying off the overpass. They dropped twenty feet into an alleyway, crashed on top of a sleeping bum and his dog, rolled several times, then slid to a stop.

Rudy Ray quickly regained consciousness to see Lamar dangling upside down from his seatbelt, knocked out cold and bloody. Broken glass was everywhere. Rudy Ray dropped his Fred Sanford routine and yelled, "Damage report!"

The dashboard speaker replied back with, "Structural damage at eighty-two percent. There is a small fire forming under the hood. Evacuate at once."

Rudy Ray quickly unbuckled Lamar's seat belt. He grabbed him by the overalls and began to pull him from the smoking wreck.

That's when a large group of neon-clad gangbangers appeared, hungry for blood with knives, bats, and torches in hand. They began to surround the vehicle.

Rudy Ray looked out at the colorful characters and screamed, "Give me the Solo!"

A hidden compartment on the dashboard opened up. He reached in and grabbed the blaster he had made just a week prior, inspired by Han Solo's. He flipped the switch on the barrel, and the homemade pistol began to warm with a *Bzzzzz*.

The gang slowly closed in on the vehicle like a pack of cheesy-dressed zombies. A banger yelled, "Come out and *play*, Rudy *Ray*. Come out and *play*!"

A punk-rock banger, with a pink mohawk and nose-ring chain attached all the way to his wallet, kneeled to see inside the truck's cab. He smacked his spiked bat on the ground for intimidation and asked, "Sup, punk muthafuckas? Ready to die?"

Rudy Ray reached out and quickly grabbed the punk's nose chain and yanked.

Blood shot from the thug's face, and he began to scream like a wailing goat.

Rudy Ray leveled the Solo and shot a laser blast directly into the punk's throat.

The banger jumped up, grasped at his neck in an attempt to stop the blood spray, stumbled a few steps back, then dropped, kicking and gurgling to death on the concrete.

Someone yelled, "Bum rush that muthafucka!"

The entire crew rushed with weapons held high.

Rudy Ray looked over to Lamar. "Well, Lamar. I'll miss you. It's been real." He held up a homemade grenade and pulled the pin. Seconds later, the explosion destroyed the entire city block.

Back at the Wet Spot, Charlie continued listening on the phone to Rudy Ray's tale. "It was a bunch of them Zoo Gang sissies. I blew every one of them pussies up with a mini-nuke grenade I made last night watching *MacGyver* reruns. Only reason I survived is because of my overalls, which are made from the best flame-retardant stuff on the market. NASA even uses the shit to get through the Van Allen layer. Saved my life."

"I'm coming over."

"Do. And bring chicken."

Charlie hung up the phone and looked at Tuck.

Tuck looked back through red eyes and slurred, "Hey, Charlie. I was just sitting here thinking about the time we took out that battalion using just two rolls of toilet paper and a stick of dynamite. Remember that shit?"

"Good times. Look, I'm about to take out the local Zoo Gang with some futuristic gadgets made from inside a mock Batcave that also has an *A Team* rip-off van with a missile attached to its roof. They are the ones who killed my LaQueefa, fucked up my boy, and they just killed my cousin. I have to put a stop to this nonsense once and for all. You down for another mission, Sergeant Pendelton?"

Tuck took it all in. "An *A Team* rip-off van with a missile attached to its roof?" he asked, amazed.

"Uh-huh. A missile. On the goddamn roof."

*

Twenty minutes later, Charlie and Tuck showed up at Rudy Ray's junkyard with a box of Popeye's chicken in hand and a forty ounce of Nine-Milli malt liquor. They entered and immediately noticed Rudy Ray sitting on the couch, his hand down the front of his boxers, looking dead as the chicken in the take-out box. On the TV, an old episode of *Sanford and Son* played. Charlie walked over, slowly reached down and checked for a pulse.

Rudy Ray suddenly came to life with a gasp.

Startled, Charlie took a few steps back. "Jesus, Uncle Rudy Ray. I thought you were dead. Fuck you doing scaring me like that?"

Rudy Ray took a deep breath and smiled at the aroma in the air. "Mmmm. You got the spicy."

Minutes later, Charlie and Tuck helped the injured and limping Rudy Ray through the junkyard and headed for the shed. Charlie opened the door and they entered. Charlie pulled the extension cord, and the shed began to drop into the earth the same as before.

Tuck was amazed at the coolness of riding in a shed elevator. "This is kinda fucking cool, man." He took a swig from the canteen on his hip. "So, tell me more about this van. Will I get to drive the shit?"

The shed reached its destination and stopped.

Charlie opened the door, and the men got out.

They proceeded forward to the main computer and Rudy Ray, because of his injured leg, stumbled into his computer chair. He pulled a chicken wing from the box and began to nibble away as he typed one handed on his keyboard. "Just need to eat and regain some strength here. Are you sure you're ready for this mission, Charlie?"

Charlie looked at Tuck then back to Rudy Ray. "As I've ever been in my life."

"Give me just a second here." Rudy Ray continued to type. "Imma calculate our mission's odds really quick." Rudy Ray took the travel napkin from the box and tore it loose from its plastic wrapping with his teeth. "They call this spicey?" he asked, wiping his mouth. "Here we go. My system is starting."

The sounds of nineties dial-up internet came through the computer speakers.

Charlie and Tuck waited. And waited. And waited some more.

Tuck decided to hydrate during the wait. He pulled the canteen from his hip and swigged water for the upcoming battle. When the canteen was finally empty, he held it upside down over his head, shouted, "All done, Sir!" then slammed the canteen back onto his belt.

The computer's dial-up noise finally ceased.

Rudy Ray looked up at the large screen and updated the situation. "The odds are that if we move quickly, we can pull this off. Your mission, get your hands on that Serum 13B before the Zoo Gang does and report back immediately so we can get down to the business of kicking every last one of them big dummies in the dick. But we only have enough time juice for two jumps since them Zoo Gang dickheads ruined my route today. Probably killed my time juice connection too. So, don't go sightseeing or your ass might get stuck some place, unless it's in the eighties—which wouldn't really be a bad thing. A lot of good music back then. The 1970s were pretty good too. But fuck disco."

Tuck said, "What the fuck is time juice?"

Rudy Ray continued. "For our time-travel plan, man."

Tuck said, "Holy shit. We're gonna do some time traveling on this particular mission?"

Rudy Ray nodded. "Uh-huh. Time travel. And the Zoo Gang are sending one of their very own back to Rockwood eighties within the hour. It's a chase between us and them for that serum. The healing properties inside this serum they are wanting, not to mention the muscle as senses enhancements that come along with it, should be more than plenty for you and your war buddy there to kick the Zoo Gang's asses left and right when you get back. I love your buddy's badass mullet by the way."

Tuck said, "Thank you. Name's Tuck."

"You're welcome, Tuck. You look like a white Lionel Ritchie and shit with that hair but without the Soul Glow shimmer."

Tuck pointed. "That's *exactly* what I was going for."

"Nailed it, dude." Rudy Ray looked at Charlie. "So, what do you say, Charlie? You ready to pull some *Back to the Future* shit?"

"Suit me the fuck up."

"Um, yeah, sorry, but the junkyard suit won't go through the time warp. It'll flat-out disappear during the jump. It's flimsy on the stable molecule side of things. Until then, only certain weapons and gadgets will do. Maybe even a cool outfit at least, something to help take your presence to the next level for extreme intimidation?"

"I'm not wearing any of the superhero suits that you collect. Don't want sued for copyright. So, how about we mix and match?"

"Whatever you'd like." Rudy Ray turned in his chair and put both hands on his keyboard. "Ready when you are."

"Give me a Punisher-style trench coat and boots."

Rudy Ray began to tap the order on the keyboard.

Charlie continued. "Plain black shirt. Black pants. Thrown in Cable's big fucking blaster gun. He's that old dude from X-Force."

Rudy Ray stopped typing and turned around. "Well, are we talking comic book Cable, X-Men nineties cartoon Cable, or Josh Brolin in *Deadpool II* Cable? Each gun looked a little different."

"Give me the Brolin."

Rudy Ray spun back around and typed. "And?"

"Give it the capabilities to magnetically strap to my back in an instant like his did. Not a fan of slinging my weapon."

Rudy Ray typed. "Anything else?"

Charlie thought. "Throw in that hologram wristband like in the movie version. One that will have the digital read-outs full of convenient information on my Zoo Gang bounty."

Rudy Ray nodded with a furious type. "*Damn* good idea. Makes tracking people down much easier. Any headgear? He had a glowing red eye. How about we try something different with the eye?"

"Like?"

"How about a cool pair of eighties shades with a single eye slit all the way across. We can make it glow red! You'll look like a new wave Cyclops from the X Men and shit. Might look cool."

"Sounds more like one of the mutant army members from *The Dark Knight Returns* to me."

"Yeah, well, whatever."

"Fuck it. Better give me them too. Shit might look all badass together."

"Never hurts to try." Rudy Ray typed and hit send.

The computer terminal lights danced in and out of unison. Seconds later, the light show was over. A large rock door built into the cave's wall next to the mother computer opened and inside the small closet, already pieced together and laid out on display, was the superhero inspired gear, ready-made to order and still steaming from the rapid sewing involved.

Charlie stepped forward and looked at the awesome outfit. He had never been so impressed in his entire life.

Chapter Five
The Density of Charlie Jones

Rockwood, Mississippi
The Early Eighties

On the desolate backroads of Rockwood, Mississippi, the storm beat the heavy rain against the windshield. Agent Earl Tubb, Section Eight's chosen intergalactic guardian of Rockwood, Mississippi, cruised the night shift in his high-tech Section Eight mobile that was cleverly disguised as a friendly, fifties police cruiser. But under the dashboard, hidden out of civilian view, was the activation knobs for the vehicle's various secret gadgets—ones which would make James Bond cream his shorts. In the passenger seat, a large bag of extra-hot pork rinds sat, and in Earl's hand—the cool robotic one—Earl clutched the cruiser's CB and spoke out into the void. "This is Earl Tubb. *Agent* Earl Tubb to be exact, and I'm coming atcha once again on one of them dark, spooky, rainy-ass nights, keeping a sharp eye out as usual for any big trouble in little Rockwood. Why? Because *that's my job, people.*"

He reached down, grabbed a pork rind, threw it in his mouth and crunched, crumbs fell with every syllable. "Now, don't get me wrong. I'm not trying to scare you. I'm here to *reassure* you. Reassure you of *what*, you might ask. Well, I'll tell you like I told the dude at Jiffy Lube. When the rubber hits the road and Earl Tubb is the one doing the laying, you best believe there will be some major skid marks, boy." He grabbed another pork rind but waited. His thought process took over and he had to speak on it.

"You know that dude, Captain America? Imagine *him* guarding this town and you'd get the general idea of what I'm getting at." He threw the pork rind in his mouth and continued. "Now, I know exactly what you're thinking. You're thinking just what in the hell could the kid who farted but shit his pants instead while standing in the lunchroom cafeteria line back in the fourth grade possibly have in common with the amazing Captain America. Am I right? Well, I'll just go ahead and tell you good people."

Earl lifted the two-liter of root beer from between his legs and took a long, hard swig of the warm soda. He belched, put the two-liter back between his legs, pushed the CB radio handle's button and continued. "They say that everything special about Captain America came in a bottle. Much like they may say that about *me*. I don't really know; I haven't heard anyone say this about me yet. But if they ever did, and it started an argument between two Section Eight fanboys over which character is the best, I'd just like to remind everyone that Captain America earned every goddamn drop in that bottle because of who he was as a person, who he was on the *inside ... just like me.*"

An old voice screamed over Earl's CB radio. "Get off this station and quit playing on the CB before I call your goddamn parents, boy!"

Earl quickly turned off his radio, slightly embarrassed. He shrugged it off, pulled a toothpick from his shirt pocket, tossed it in his mouth and leaned back.

The storm and rain began to subside.

A female voice with a professional touch came through the dashboard speaker. "Agent Tubb," it said. "The vehicle's radar has picked up an object. There appears to be something meteor-like falling on our left."

Earl looked right.

"No. The other way."

"Well, what in the hell did you tell me the wrong way for then?" Earl looked the other way and spotted the glowing object falling fast and watched it hit the ground in the distance. Earl thought for a moment. With his robotic hand, he rubbed his chin and said, "Wonder if that's one of them Imperial probe droids."

"A probe droid?" the car asked.

"Yeah. A probe droid. They're the ones that abduct people and go probing up the butts for their own sinister amusements. *Just* to get your location."

"Oh, my. That's no good."

"You'd think so, huh? I wonder what it's doing here."

"It landed just outside the Rockwood Home for the Criminally Insane. Whatever was inside the craft is now moving East on foot."

Earl groaned, "I have a *bad* feeling about this."

Minutes later, Earl pulled up to the town's only telephone booth located at the old, abandoned drive-in and parked his cruiser. He got out, entered the phone booth and closed the door. He looked around to see if anyone was watching. Not a soul was in sight. He picked up the receiver, threw in a dime, dialed 237, and the phone rang.

Someone on the other end answered with, "Can I take your order?"

Earl spoke the command. "I'll take a Pepsi," and hung up.

The voice recognition was accepted. The floor beneath Earl dropped at roller coaster speeds. Within seconds, Earl was transported hundreds of feet below the surface and arrived at the hidden, sub-level headquarters of Section Eight, far away from the prying eyes of the unsuspecting citizens of Rockwood above. He stepped out of the elevator and greeted the Section Eight commander in charge of the Rockwood Division, Agent Smith, who was never without his fifties-inspired business suit and professional demeanor.

Earl abruptly walked by the emotionless agent and through the random War Room staff, who relentlessly tapped away on their computers and watched various monitors. High above them all on the wall, three large screens showed maps of the local area. Off in the not-so-private corner, Section Eight's gadget maker, known around the office as Tinker, was working on his latest creations.

Earl and Agent Smith entered Tinker's set up and looked on the metallic table that was full of the latest gadgets.

Earl gave a quick yank of his sagging pants and said, "All right, Tinker! Show me what you got."

"You're just in time, Agent Tubb." Tinker reached into his lab coat's pocket. "I just finished putting the special touches on your Pac Man watch. I arranged it like you asked so the ghost can't eat you. This way, you'll finish the entire game with just one man. But that's not all. Observe!" Tinker slapped the watch on his wrist, raised the watch eye level, and with a push of a button on its side, shot a laser blast from the watch that blew the head off a nearby reptilian alien statue.

Covering his ears from the sound of the blast, Earl was impressed. "Goddamn, that's cool." He gave a quick tug at his pants and asked, "Anything else it can do?"

"That's about it." Tinker removed the watch.

Earl grabbed it. "Good enough for me. Finally, gonna beat this damn game!"

Agent Smith looked at Tinker and finally spoke. "Anything along the lines of time travel yet, Tinker?"

"Absolutely," Tinker assured him as he reached into his lab coat's pocket again and took out a digital watch with an extra-large face. "This is our time-jumping wristband. Type in the date and time here on its face, hit send, *poof*, you're gone. Just a few more touches, and it will be ready to go. With it, unlimited jumps. Batteries are rechargeable; just pop out the hidden sockets on the back of the device and you can plug it into your nearest wall outlet. Takes about eight hours to charge and will last for an astonishing four hours *max*. We have three prototypes on standby if any more are needed."

Earl was amazed. "Damn, that's cool. Rechargeable batteries? What'll y'all think of next?"

Tinker walked over to a curtain, grabbed it and said, "How about this?" He yanked the curtain back. "It's my latest invention."

Earl about shit. "Is that a goddamn jet pack with a gatling gun attached to the shoulder?"

Moments later, Earl and Agent Smith stood before the large radar screen on the wall above them all and spoke.

"Switchblade talking yet?" Earl asked without looking.

"He hasn't shut up since you caught him earlier."

-Earlier That Day

Earl stepped into the dark interrogation room. He walked up to the table, tugged his trousers, put his hands on his hips and stared down the shackled, wannabe greaser the local media had named The Switchblade Killer. The hot lamp above the suspect shined hard, but even in his leather jacket, Switchblade didn't break a sweat. Earl smirked, "I see the animal is finally on a leash, right where *it* belongs. I told you I'd get your ass, son. You goddamn sick, degenerate, smart-ass sumbitch."

"Tubby!" the killer shouted with a reunion. "Thought I killed you once already. How you been? You look good, by the way. Parting your hair different? You use moose? I use gel, myself. Helps keep the hair wet looking. But you have to use hairspray too. That helps give it that all-day wet look. Hey! Remember that time I shit on your desk and killed your squirmy little partner?"

Earl slammed his robot fist and dented the table's surface.

Instead of jumping, Switchblade beamed. "Still got that robot hand, huh? Boss as ever! You wanna use it to jack off my R2-Dick to? I know you want to." Switchblade leaned in and whispered. "I won't tell if you won't."

Earl leaned in also. "Nobody believed I'd catch your ass again, boy. None of them. But here you are. Before me and looking as stupid as ever."

"Third time's charm. But let's face it, Tubb. If I wasn't so distracted this time by showing them black dudes in The Village my moonwalking skills, you wouldn't have gotten me. But it's the never-ending game we play, huh? But much like last time, I won't be here long. I ain't sweating this shit. I *never* sweat you Section Eight bitches and shit. Huh-huh."

"You in The Hole, son. And not one you wanna be in. This holding facility, The Hole, is knee-deep in the earth and guarded by some of the most highly trained guards the Galactic Space Union will allow Section Eight to hire. And in case you are unaware, Frank, we house *all* of Section Eight's most dangerous rogue gallery of supervillains at this here facility." Earl tapped the dented table with his robotic finger. "*And not a single one has escaped yet.* We house The Skanky Slit, The Dick Rider along with his evil sidekick Cock Blocker. The bitch with the tentacles, Octopuss E. Even that weird freak-show sumbitch with the lizard tail and raccoon head that shoots poison needles from his spiked, metal nipples named Jerry. All of 'em, son. And remember, ain't a one of 'em escaped from here yet. This facility, including the shackles that are keeping your punk ass chained to the floor, are made from adamantiumous metal, collected from Uranus."

Switchblade chuckled.

Earl continued. "So, don't get *too* cocky on me there, *Frank*."

"Call me Switchblade."

Earl turned and walked away. "Get comfy, *Frank*. This is your new home. Your stupid, greaser ass ain't going anywhere any time soon." He reached the interrogation room door and opened it.

"Never forget, Tubb," Switchblade spoke for the first time without humor. "I'm the one that made you. Without me, Agent Tubb wouldn't even exist. It's almost like I'm your daddy, fat boy. I came into your town, blew my nut, birthed you, and here you are. Remember that shit."

Earl turned and looked. "I'll come visit you on Father's Day then, Frank. Bring you a snack. Might rub my dick on the shit." He exited and slammed the door. From the hallway he yelled, "Get comfy! You ain't going *nowhere* this time, *Frank*!"

Switchblade, without a plan and shackled to the floor, shrugged and said to himself, "Never say never, *Tubbster*."

Back in the War Room, Agent Smith and Earl looked up at the large radar screens above. Agent Smith briefed Earl on the situation. "The reason you were called in," Agent Smith said without emotion, "is because we have just received word from our Section Eight's intergalactic computers and a priority mission has come through. You were chosen as the only one suited for this particular mission."

"Because I'm the best, right?"

"Well, not exactly. All of our other agents are busy at the moment with other missions."

"Picked last again? Just like gym class all over again around here. Will I be going in solo?"

"Yes."

"Again? What in the hell could the other team members possibly be up to right now? Being lazy? Having another party and forgetting to invite me again? I am always working solo, man. Haven't had a partner since Lester got killed. How about Lightning Bug? The dude with the jumper cables rigged up the sleeves and shoots lightning from the battery connectors which are powered by the riding lawn mower battery inside his backpack?"

"He's busy."

"Damn. How about that giddy, ninja-warrior bitch, Sam Dickey?"

"At the mall, maybe. Her shift starts soon though."

"Lizard boy Hugo Thunders? Now that boy's badass!"

"Off-world mission."

"Oh. Molecular Man? I know his little, shrunken, action figure-sized ass is available. Gotta be!"

"Unavailable."

"Shit. Summer Soldier with the metal leg?"

Agent Smith shook his head.

"Not even that cheerleader chick with the Uzi, Sammy Comet?"

"Off tonight. Squad practice for the upcoming game tomorrow against their rival team, the Red Dust Zombies."

"Well, shit. Guess it's just me *again*; like you said. Unless Machina Man decides to show up at the last minute and steal everyone's thunder like some asshole Superman again. Dude is a bit of a glory hog. Anyway, what's the latest threat?"

"This latest threat should be your number one priority for the evening. So, please pay close attention this time." Agent Smith held up a remote control, clicked it, and the screens above them zoomed in. "The latest intel from the Commodore 64.5 computer tells us that this is currently our main priority."

"I hate that damn computer, man. Always stopping my hot pursuits and shit to tell *you* to tell *me* what to do. Robots don't tell *me* what to do. I should have told you that before I signed on. And I don't know if you know this or not, but the games on that computer over there are lame as shit. Word Wizard? Who in the hell thinks that shit is fun except that nerdy, intern, professor dude over there with the mullet, tube socks and K-Mart flip-flops?"

"That's actually my brother."

"Oh. ... My bad. Really like that guy. Smart fella. Tell 'em I said that for me! What's his name again?"

"Are you done?"

"I'm done."

"Good. Because as I was *saying*, it appears that there are various individuals coming here from the future. They plan on landing here in Rockwood at various places in our timeline. From what we gather, their goal is to retrieve some Serum 13B ... but not from us."

Earl got serious. "The Men in Black?"

"Yes, we believe so. We still don't know who is manufacturing this bootleg substance for the ever-elusive Men in Black in town. We assume it's being cooked up somewhere local though. All we *really* know for sure is there are people coming from the future, and we don't know which ones to trust—if any. Until we figure out exactly what is happening from our end, every last time-traveling outsider is a suspect. Are you following so far?"

With his robot hand, Earl rubbed his chin and thought. And then thought some more.

Agent Smith waited long enough. "Are you going to say anything, Agent Tubb?"

"What year?"

"Excuse me?"

"*Year*? What *year* are they coming from?"

"2037 to be exact."

"2037, huh?" Earl stepped forward, puffed out his chest at the monitors above and proudly proclaimed, "Earl Tubb: Intergalactic Time Guardian of Rockwood. I like the sound of that shit right there, boy." Earl turned to face Agent Smith. "Don't you? You like the sound of that shit?"

Instead of responding, Agent Smith checked the time on his watch.

Earl turned back around, pointed at the screens above and said, "Okay, you John Conner sumbitches. We all have a story to tell, unfortunately yours sure as shit ain't going down in *my* town and in *my* timeline."

*

A few miles from where Charlie landed, inside The Village Projects (Rockwood's only ghetto and was considered by many in the future to be the Zoo Gang's motherland), Tyrone and Road Dog leaned against a large, pimped-out Cadillac and shared a forty ounce of Pig Sticker brand beer that was wrapped in a paper sack. The car's stereo pumped Schooly D's "Saturday Night" loud enough for everyone on the block to hear. "I don't know, Tyrone," Road Dog said over the music. "These white muthafuckas around here be tripping something fierce. All kinda crazy shit been popping off the last few years. Serial killers taking out rednecks, titty bar owners that are really aliens underneath; that was the rumor anyway. Spaceship battles and shit. Why they gotta act like this?"

Road Dog tilted the forty ounce back and took a swig.

Tyrone continued. "Hey, you remember when that big, fat muthafucka fucked up Billy Ray's apartment last year?"

Road Dog looked at the demolished building down the block. "How could I not? When that boy hit the pavement, it cracked the concrete like the Hulk done come to town. Knocked over my fucking grill."

Tyrone lit a joint and said, "Damn, bro. Were you grilling?"

"Ribs."

"*That's* some bullshit."

"I know, right?" Road Dog took the joint. "Like you said, white people, man."

Tyrone took a swig of Pig Sticker. "Fuck can we do?"

"I think they here to stay, bro."

"Good for nothing, really. I'd give up a month of food stamps just to get rid of half of them."

"But if you do that, your food stamps might stop, bro."

"How so?"

"They the ones who pay taxes and shit just so we can get that monthly check. We kinda need 'em." Road Dog hit the joint and exhaled with, "They are a necessary evil and shit."

"... Damn. Well, that sucks."

Charlie appeared out of nowhere. "Sorry, but is this your car?"

Tyrone laughed at the sight of the man dressed like it's a superhero Halloween party. "Look at this muthafucka right here! Yo, Road Dog, you got some candy for this trick or treat-ass muthafucka with the glowing red shades and the big toy gun?" He imitated shooting laser blasts at Charlie and mocked him. "*Phew-phew-phew*!"

Both men started roaring with laughter and pointed.

"How do you even see out of them shits?" Tyrone laughed. "Look-look-look! It's Han Homo! Han Solo's dick sucking cousin and shit."

Charlie continued to stare through the glowing red slit in his shades as the two men slapped fives and roared with more laughter.

Once the exaggerated laughter show was over, Charlie simply asked. "Are the two of you Zoo Gang affiliated?"

Taken back by the question, Tyrone giggled once, got dead serious, took a step forward and said, "Fuck you say? Buckaroo Banzai-ass nigga?"

"Buck Rogers wants to know if we Zoo." Road Dog said. He threw the joint to the ground and took a step forward next to Tyrone.

The face-off with the stranger began.

Tyrone looked at the time traveler. "Yep, we sure in the fuck are Zoo," he produced a switchblade knife, flipped out the blade with click and said, "for muthafuckin life, boy."

Without hesitation, Charlie unslung the magnetic gun from his back to the ready position, fired two blaster shots, and the car that the bangers were leaning against was instantly repainted blood red before their bodies even hit the pavement.

With a shove of his futuristic military boots, Charlie scooted both headless corpses aside, walked to the car and threw his blaster rifle in the passenger seat. He raised his forearm, slid the digital slider across his cool electronic wristband, and a holographic image of a toothless hillbilly in overalls without a shirt projected before him, road map sized.

The profile's description read:

MISSION TARGET
Past History of Benjamin Ash aka Buzz Benny
-Rockwood Native
-Shine Runner
-Aided and Abetted the Rogue Men in Black
-Annual Rockwood Pickled Pig's Feet Competition (Blue Ribbon Award)
-Residential Coordinates Locked In
-Proceed to Route

Charlie hopped in the pimp wagon, tossed his red slit shades out the window, put the car in gear and left the scene.

*

Back in 2037, deep inside Hammer's lion's den lair, Hammer chilled from behind his solid stone desk and custom chair—which was wrapped in animal hides and had elephant tusks going up its sides like it belonged to the *Flintstones* prehistoric president. Hammer tightened the left side of his spiked shoulder pads with a quick tug of the strap, stood from his prehistoric seat, walked around the desk and put a proud hand on the shoulder of Ginsu's Billie Jean jacket and said, "You did good, Ginsu. As usual, there was never any doubt when it comes to you and your abilities. It was a tough mission. That's why you were chosen."

Ginsu gave a warrior's nod.

Hammer turned and walked over to the drug table and started to casually sift through it. "So, Rudy Ray, my blood uncle, was a member of some intergalactic group of secret agents known as Section Eight, huh? And he's gonna help that adopted, honky-ass brother of mine try and stop me from getting my gangster, time-travel fuck on, huh? I suppose my brother having the ability to travel through time might throw a wrench up in my shit. Especially if they get the jump on us with that serum first." Hammer found an untouched blunt on the table, grabbed it and took a whiff of its cigar leaf wrapping. He walked back to his animalistic chair and had a seat. He opened the desk drawer, pulled out a mini blow torch, used it to light his blunt and exhaled smoke.

"I'll tell you what, G-su," Hammer leaned back. "I got this shit covered. Go ahead and take that muthafuckin elevator time machine back and do your thing, baby. No more waiting. Once that serum is in your possession, I want you to slaughter the shit outta every Section Eight member you can find, ninja style and shit. Once the blood has spilled and that galactic organization of punk-ass bitches in Rockwood is over, come on back home. But I'll be sending in some reinforcements now to aid you in your mission."

Ginsu's expression showed that he did not approve.

Hammer continued. "Now, I know you like to work alone. And you will. But Imma let the muthafuckin Dogs loose on Charlie. Get him off your tail, so you can do your thing in peace. Just in case and shit. Now go. Make me proud. In the meantime, I'm gonna do some muthafuckin research on this so-called Section Eight group of soon-to-be-dead men."

Ginsu bowed, turned and walked out.

Hammer reached forward, grabbed his brick-sized cell phone and dialed.

A deep voice from the other end answered. "Who dis?"

"It's your latest paycheck, Chestbro, with your bald, metal-plated ass. The Mad Dogs available?"

"If the price is right."

"Good. Because I gotta special job for their asses."

Chapter Six
Benny and the Wack Men in Black

The Men in Black cruised the desolate Rockwood night in their usual ride, a black four-door car of unrecognizable make and model. In the backseat, L.L. Cool J's "I Can't Live Without My Radio" blasted from a boombox. In his new gear, a Def Jam shirt, bucket hat, shades, gold chain, and fresh Adidas sneakers, Blue Tie annoyingly rapped along. *"My radio, believe me, I like it loud. I'm the man with the box that can rock the crowd. Walking down the street to the hard-core beat, while my JVC vibrates the concrete. I'm sorry, if you can't understand, but I need a radio inside my hand. Don't mean to offend other citizens, but I kick my volume way past ten!"*

Red Tie, who still respected the dress code by wearing his black suit, red tie, and dark shades, reached in the back, stopped the music on the boombox cold and pointed at Blue Tie.

But before Red Tie could even speak, Blue Tie halted him with both fists up to show off the four-finger rings across his knuckles. One read "Love" and the other "Hate," both covered with the finest 18 karat gold-plating the Pascagoula Flea Market had to offer. "Before you say anything," he said with wisdom in his voice. "Let me tell you the story of Right Hand, Left Hand. It's a tale of good and evil."

Obviously beyond annoyed hanging out with this guy any further, Red Tie shouted, "If you start to recite that goddamn movie again, I swear to the Bukkadump God of Nippleton, that I will pull the fuck over right now and throw that goddamn boombox you just bought into the nearest woods!"

"Stop acting straight-up booty, brother. I'm just trying to *Do the Right Thing* over here."

"Here we go. Sonofabitch."

"You see, hate," Blue Tie threw up his hate ring, "it was with this hand that Cain iced his brother." He threw up the other hand. "Love—"

"Every time you come across something new on this planet that you like, you can't just like it and be yourself. No, you have to go all out. Last year it was Corey 'Fuckface' Feldman, last month it was that crybaby group The Cure. You looked like an asshole in that eyeliner, by the way. Now, you're supposed to be some kind of homeboy-from-the-hood rapper. I just can't keep up, and I have to say, I don't think I want to anymore."

"You won't be thinking all that when I start rocking coliseums and get my own sneaker line. The honeys gonna be all on my jock for the way I hold my piece of steel. And *that's* what's up. Why you gotta hate? You know that's a sign of jealousy up in my hood?"

"You do realize we are supposed to be incognito, right? Are you purposely trying to ruin everything we've worked for? You stick out like a sore thumb around this redneck shit hole. More than ever before."

"More like I stand out from the rest of the pack of wack MCs, and you damn well know it. I ain't sweating you, homie. I know the deal because the streets are talking to me now—on the daily."

"Excuse me?"

"You wanna break up the group, fine. I'll go solo after this next deal. I write all our lyrics anyway. You suck at the shit."

"What the fuck are you even talking about?"

"You know what? You're right, yo. After this last batch from Benny, we go our separate ways. I have found my calling. Forget this rogue Men in Black shit. It's for the suckas with nothing better to do. All looking the same, dressing the same, zapping people's memories the same. Imma be an original dope MC from here on out. Get all the pussy Rockwood has to offer."

"You can have it."

"Gonna have a fly ride, rims, the dopest chains to rock around my neck, finally move my moms up out the projects."

"Your mom lived on another planet, dude. And she's been dead for over two hundred years."

"You can't talk me out of this! I can make it." Blue Tie looked to the future horizon with hope. "I *gotta* make it. For my people, not yours. Besides, you can't even work a fucking drum machine, nigga."

"What the fuck?"

*

Twenty minutes later, deep in the backwoods, the Men in Black both sat on logs by a small campfire and watched as the toothless Buzz Benny stirred a thick, glowing green substance that simmered and bubbled deep inside a cast iron pot that dangled over the flames.

"This new batch," Buzz said stirring, "this shit is a little on the experimental side. I added a few extra touches to the recipe. Threw in a little gamma radiation in liquid form. It's why it's glowing so bright now. With this liquid gamma sample, I received from an undisclosed source of mine, I think this batch here will enhance more of an animalistic type of power inside the user this go round. Almost like their true spirit takes form. If they are like a snake sumbitch with the shingles, they might look like a snake man or some shit. If they are good people and their spirits wanna soar like an angel, they might sprout wings like a pigeon or some kinda shit."

Red Tie said, "Are you trying to tell us that this serum *here* will change the DNA of a person on a molecular level and reveal who they are deep down in spirit through some ...*physical* manifestation?"

Buzz stopped stirring the glowing substance, looked up from it and said, "Yup. Something like that. Mutant, super villainous type-a shit. Or you could give it to the kinda man that would jump on a grenade to save his fellow man; give it to him, and he might become some kinda Captain U.S.A. that shoots stars and stripes from his dick hole and shits apple pie. Who knows?" Buzz went back to stirring. "Like I said, experimental, fellas."

Red Tie was floored. "This is amazing. They don't even have anything like this in middle earth." He looked at Blue Tie. "Are you hearing this?"

Blue Tie was busy writing lyrics in his notepad. On the notepad's cover was a lenticular Fat Boys sticker that he got from the quarter machine by the entrance of the local Piggly Wiggly earlier that day.

Red Tie said, "Dude, are you even listening?"

Blue Tie looked up and said, "Give me a word that rhymes with M.C. Niggy-Niggy Nuts."

Red Tie didn't even respond. He couldn't.

Seconds later, M.C. Niggy-Niggy Nuts snapped his fingers and said, "Got it! Never mind," and then went right back to writing.

Red Tie shook his head. He couldn't wait to get away from this guy. He looked back to Buzz who was stirring the glowing substance and said, "So, Mr. Benny. Buzz. You are basically talking about some super mutation here, not just human enhancement?"

"Who knows? Like I said, it's experimental. Just get back to me if the shit doesn't work, and I'll refund your money. I'm pretty sure the damn shit works though. I gave some to my prized pig, and the sumbitch tripled in size, grew tusks out of nowhere, sprouted horns all down his back, then ate the fucking mailman. Didn't even have to bury any remains either. I think Charlotte may have shit some of him out behind the barn though before she ran off. You see a pig that matches that description, don't go trying to pet it. Just run."

Red Tie rubbed his chin. "Very interesting results indeed. One could build an army of nameless, faceless beasts for battle with this version."

With a padded glove, Buzz pulled the cast iron pot from the flame and poured the glowing substance into a five-gallon, metal container for shipping. He capped the lid, spit a loogie in the fire that stunk and sizzled against a burning log, then put the container down at Red Tie's feet. With a greasy hand, he held out his palm, and with a grin only showing two teeth said, "Payment please."

Chapter Seven
Fishin' with Earl Tubb

From the comforts of his Section Eight mobile, Earl Tubb sat on the side of the road, semi hiding in the bushes, and did his thing on the CB, as usual, while also keeping a sharp eye out for any time travelers in the area. "And that's what I'm getting at, good people of Rockwood," he told his listeners. "In order to accomplish a mission, sometimes you just have to drop your personal beliefs, try another way, and the problem can fix itself. You have to quit thinking you're always right. Be a *team* player. Take another man's advice. Drop that ego. It's one of the first things I learned working as an Intergalactic Guardian for the good people of Rockwood, Mississippi; even way back when I first got my robot hand. Just remember, wipe front to back. Then you won't get shit on your balls and go around for years, like I did, wondering just why the hell your goddamn dick region smells like poop so bad all the damn time. Our janitor, T'boo Teddy, he was the one that finally pointed that out to me when we were—"

The vehicle's dash interrupted Earl's tale of exemplified wisdom. "I sense a vehicle approaching," the female voice said. "A scan of the interior from the Section Eight satellites above confirm that the driver of the vehicle is *not* from our timeline. Shall I lock on with radar?"

"Yep, lock on his ass!" Earl threw the CB down and fired up the engine. He hit a button on the control panel and a seven-inch screen extracted from the dashboard then rotated upright for driver viewing. A map of the area popped up on the screen and showed two red dots, one sitting and the other fast approaching. "Here he comes," Earl said calmly. "When I give the signal, hit whatever gadgets we got to shut off his engine."

"We have no such gadgets."

"Well, what the hell am I supposed to do?"

"Perhaps try pulling him over, and if he refuses, you can chase him down until apprehension. Like your job description entails."

"Piss on that shit." Earl reached in the backseat and grabbed the Section Eight proton blasting bazooka.

"He's almost here."

Earl stepped out and stood in the middle of the road to face the oncoming suspect.

Inside the fast-approaching vehicle, Charlie Jones braced for impact as he witnessed a heavy-set man aiming a rather large weapon right at him.

Earl pulled the trigger.

The proton blast hit the bottom of the pimp mobile and sent it airborne. Charlie's vehicle flipped high over Earl's head. It landed in the middle of the road with a crash and tumbled down the pavement into a smashed ball of smoking metal and busted parts before finally sliding to a stop.

Waiting for the dramatic pause to be over, Earl finally turned to face the wreckage down the road. He threw the bazooka to the ground by his cruiser, drew out his pistol and proceeded slowly with caution. "You are trespassing in this timeline *and* in my jurisdiction," he shouted. "Step on out the hunka shit pimp wagon with your goddamn hands up where I can see 'em, time traveler!"

Two hands came into view from the wreckage, along with a voice. "I'm coming out! Don't shoot! I'm a fucking good guy here, man!"

"Okay, then, good guy here, *man*. Bring your time traveling do-gooder ass up out of that busted hunka shit, and when you do it, you do it slowly. You make any sudden moves, you die. Fart, and you'll die comfortable, boy. I shit you not. I'll shoot first and Greedo your goddamn ass outta my town, timeline *and* life. Try me."

The stranger yelled from inside the metal mess, "I'm not here to cause you trouble. I'm only here to take some serum from The Men in Black and then leave. So, just relax! I'm zero threat to you."

"How the hell do you even know about them two Men in Black dickheads in the first place?"

No response. Charlie tried to climb from the metal heap instead. He finally got out, stood and brushed the busted glass from his chest, shoulders, and hair. Considering the accident, he was just involved in, he was lucky he wasn't more banged up aside from a few scrapes and bruises.

Earl took another step. "I asked you a question! You better talk fast, future boy—because I'm Earl Tubb: The Intergalactic Time Guardian of Rockwood for the night. And I'm the welcoming committee around these here parts. And when it comes to the intergalactic safety of Rockwood, Mississippi, you *don't* have a right to remain silent; not on *my* patrol. So, don't make me beat the shit outcha, son. Now, who *are* you and state 'cha business for being here."

"I told you why I'm here," Charlie said with hands held high. "For the Men in Black. And I already know *exactly* who you are, Agent Tubb. For instance, you're well known for shooting first and asking questions later."

"Damn skippy."

"So, I won't make any sudden moves."

"You smart, boy."

"But I need to reach in my back pocket and pull something out to show you. It's proof how I know you're a shoot-first-ask-questions-later man. It's from the future, this thing that I'm about to show you. I think you're really gonna like it. Just take it easy." He slowly reached around.

Earl took another step forward and aimed for the head, ready to kill. "*Slowly.*"

Charlie said, "I'm going *slow*. You think I want to get shot?"

"I *don't* think, son."

Charlie pulled out a stack of trading cards and held them up.

"Sorry," Earl said. "I don't trade baseball cards anymore. Unless you got a deck of naked lady cards in your hand there, I ain't interested. My last deck got all stuck together."

Charlie threw them at Earl's feet and said, "They are Section Eight trading cards."

Without taking his pistol off the time traveler, Earl knelt down with overweight man's difficulty, picked up a few cards, and immediately saw his very own trading card staring back at him. In it, Earl stood in the classic Han Solo blaster pose, black vest included, with his arms out like he was ready to take flight.

Earl slowly looked up. "This is the coolest goddamn shit I have ever seen in my life."

*

The black four-door vehicle cruised. Red Tie drove as usual. M.C. Niggy-Niggy Nuts scribbled away in his rhyme pad from the passenger seat, lost in his own world and mouthing the words to rhymes that were already written in his pad. Red Tie looked over and shook his head at the up-and-coming rapper. "So, where do you want me to drop you off?" Red Tie asked bluntly. "How about The Village projects? Maybe you'll fit right in there with that up-and-coming Zoo Gang that's been taking it over."

"You're just mad because you *wouldn't* fit in there like I would," M.C. Niggy-Niggy Nuts said, scribbling rhymes. "Them cats will recognize game when they see it, just like all the rest. And soon, you will too."

"Good! Dropping you off as soon as we get out of these fucking backwoods. Let's get this goodbye bullshit over with pronto."

"Maybe when I get there, I can get a spot in the line-up on the next J.K. McCoy and the Homicide Squad album."

"That album sucked, dude."

"Pump the breaks on that shit right now."

Red Tie hit the brakes with a skid.

"I didn't mean to *actually* pump the breaks on the car. I think you might want to invest in a hip-hop slang dictionary like I did."

Red Tie pointed ahead.

M.C. Niggy-Niggy Nuts looked.

The vehicle's headlights shined on a small, Asian man standing in the middle of the road wearing a Michael Jackson jacket. It was Ginsu!

"What the fuck?" Red Tie asked. "Where the hell did he just come from?"

"Not sure," M.C. Niggy-Niggy Nuts said. "Dig the jacket though. You know, one of the dudes from 2 Live Crew is Asian, right? Fresh Kid Ice. Wonder if he knows him."

The Asian man began to walk straight in the direction of the headlight beams.

"Uh," Red Tie said. "He's coming this way."

"I see that. Maybe he wants a ride back to Neverland Ranch to return that jacket."

With just feet between him and the hood of the car, Ginsu stopped, unzipped two zippers on his jacket, produced several throwing knives, and leaped into the air with a, "Hi-yahhhh!"

With the high-pitched wail of two little girls, Red Tie and M.C. Niggy-Niggy Nuts both screamed.

Moments later, the slaughter was over.

With bloody hands, Ginsu whipped out his time-travel cordless and dialed into the future.

Hammer, chilling in his lion's den lair and watching *Exterminator II* on an old television set, answered his ringing brick phone. "Sup? Ginsu? What's the latest? ... I see ... so you got it? ... No trouble? ... Good-good. I knew you'd come through. Time to move onto the next phase of our mission." Hammer reached forward and picked up a small stack of Section Eight comic books from the desk.

"Check this shit out, G-su. Got me a small stash from Kimbo's comic book collection. Been getting high and shit and reading up some on this Section Eight. Turns out, back in the day, some asshole made some comic books about them under a ghostwriter name. The dumb muthafucka who wrote the shit even put in a possible location for the entrance to their secret base located at the old drive-in in town. There's a secret way to get in, so, listen closely."

Minutes later, Hammer stood before the Mad Dogs, a team of three roughneck ramblers from the deepest parts of the East St. Louis ghetto streets. Each Mad Dog sat on their own modified-for-battle four-wheeler as Hammer addressed them on their mission. "Thank you for coming. I have a little mission for you men that might be quite enjoyable for you all."

Hammer looked at the first in the line-up who was Rumble, a muscular brawler with two chains, homemade brass knuckles, and a large, metal pipe attached to his four-wheeler. A trash can lid with an anarchist symbol painted on the bottom was held in his massive hand that he used as a shield. "Rumble," Hammer continued. "I want you to knock that muthafucka down and out. It's what you are known for and it's what you do best. But don't go knocking his head clean off though. Just put his punk ass down for the count."

Hammer looked at the next Mad Dog, Boomer, who was a disillusioned patriot after losing four fingers, his left eye, both eyebrows, and his testicles in war. Black military fatigues and a backpack full of explosives was his choice of gear. Covering his scarred face was a red snow cap pulled over his head with the eye holes cut out. "Boomer," Hammer continued. "Once the target is down, I want you to do what *you* do best, and that's blow that goddamn punk the fuck up. Got it? *To pieces.*

I want Charlie Jones blown to little, itty-bitty, bloody pieces. It shouldn't be any sort of a problem for a man like you."

In an Australian accent, Boomer smiled behind his red ski mask and said, "It'll be my personal pleasure to boom his ass into a thousand-piece human puzzle for you, mate."

Hammer looked at Third Degree, the last Mad Dog in line, who specialized in burning shit up with his homemade flamethrower from behind the safety of his bullet proof, metal gear armor. A gallon of gas in a portable, plastic container was attached and dangled from his hip and half his body was burned from past fire injuries. "And Third Degree," Hammer looked. "Burn his ass when they done. Collect all these little, itty-bitty pieces of Charlie Jones, sweep and put them shits into a muthafuckin pile and then flame the shit to a crisp."

Third Degree smiled, his burnt, scabby lips cracked and bled from the joyous expression of his firebug ways.

"Payment," barked Boomer down the line. "We don't fuck shit up for free, Hammer. You got the goods, eh?"

Hammer said, "The goods, that's all I have." He clapped once.

Reggie roller skated into the meeting with a large, travel-size ice chest in his grasp. He skidded to a halt and placed it on the ground.

Hammer leaned down and opened it, revealing three kilos of cocaine, a six pack of Welch's grape soda and a box of chocolate donuts.

The Mad Dogs were very pleased.

*

With Charlie's futuristic blaster riding shotgun in the passenger seat and Charlie Jones handcuffed in the back, Earl piloted his Section Eight cruiser on the desolate backroad, and the two men talked. "That's one bonafide tale of sadness you got there, Charlie Jones," Earl said, looking in the rearview mirror. "But you gotta understand something though. I have orders. I'm supposed to haul your ass in, not help you on some rogue cause to avenge the death of your future woman."

"I'm not asking you to help me. Just let me go."

"No can do. Earl Tubb hasn't lost a fish on his hook yet, and I gotcha right through the gills, son. How do you like that fishing reference, boy?"

"Look, man. I gave up the chance to travel back in time to save my LaQueefa before she was even attacked, but I chose to risk it all in order to save my city instead. This Zoo Gang you have going on around here, well, in 2037, my brother is the leader of them, and they are on the verge of terrorizing the entire city of East St. Louis. They already have the entire city, including the police department, gripped in fear as it is. If they acquire a batch of that serum from the Men in Black in this timeline, they might never be stopped."

"Never say never." Earl picked up the CB and called in. "Section Eight from Earl, come in." He looked back in the rearview mirror. "You know them Section Eight trading cards that you had? I gotta keep 'em by the way. They contraband." Earl pushed the CB again. "Section Eight, come in please."

Again, no radio response.

Earl put the CB handle back and said, "Dispatcher must be taking a shit. Anyway, what else do you know about Section Eight? Seems to be an awful lot, considering we a secret organization and all. So, if they got trading cards on us in the future, what else they got? T-shirts? Grade school lunch boxes? What, man, what?"

"A TV movie was made and aired through a hack on the television networks, but it was only shown to the public once. Rumor is the film print was destroyed after it aired, and the film hasn't been seen since. Nobody even knows who made it to begin with."

"Who played me? Was it Burt?"
"Burt?"
"Reynolds?"
Charlie couldn't remember. "Yep. It was Burt."
"Hot damn, I knew it! Anything else?"
"A comic book was written."
"*Hymph.* Reading, huh?"
"Yeah, *reading*. But it only lasted a few years. I read the last four issues while I was in the service. My lieutenant, who claimed he was former Section Eight, let me read his copies. He even claimed to know the writer personally. Who knows? Regardless, Section Eight has their fifteen minutes of fame in Rockwood and then it's all over ... according to the last issue."
"What happens in the last issue?"
"You really wanna know, Earl?"
"Hey, it's *Agent* Tubb, and I'm asking the questions here."
"So, yes?"
"Quit playing mind games with me by trying to get me to agree with you on something random and just tell me what happens in the last issue of that comic book already!"
Charlie leaned close to the steel cage that separated them. "... Section Eight falls because of you."
"Yeah, right."
"It's true. It happens on the night a time traveler shows up, but his mission gets unintentionally thwarted due to a good-intentioned moron. That moron character was *your* moron character, *Agent* Tubb." Charlie leaned back, looked out the window and shrugged with, "According to the comic book anyway."
Earl didn't respond. He sucked through his teeth at Charlie in the rearview mirror, thought a moment, picked up the CB handle again and called in. "Section Eight, this is Earl. Come in please."
No response.

Earl tried again. "Section Eight, I need you to getcha ears on and answer me. Pinch that loaf and let's go. Come back." He looked at Charlie in the rearview, put the CB back on the radio clamp and said, "What a bunch of *Twilight Zone*, prediction horseshit. Comic books don't predict Earl Tubb's future."

Up ahead, the Men in Black's car was parked in the middle of the road with the doors and trunk fully open, looking like it had been left ransacked and abandoned.

Earl leaned in. "What do we have here?" He slowed the patrol car to a stop, put it in park and said, "Wait here, Kyle Reese." Earl exited the vehicle. He whipped out his large flashlight (that doubled as a single-use mini shotgun he made himself), and approached the stranded vehicle. Shining the shotgun flashlight inside the vehicle's cab, Earl spotted the Men in Black, dead, with one of them dressed like he was trying to be black. "Well, I'll be dipped in shit," he said.

Seconds later after a quick inspection of the crime scene, Earl was back in his patrol car. "It's them two Men in Black dickheads alright. They're dead as yesterday. Looks like one of them was even having an identity crisis and thought he was black."

Charlie exhaled heavily with, "And their serum?"

"If they had any on them tonight to begin with, shit's gone. Not a drop in the vehicle."

There was a moment of silence.

"So, tell me," Earl said. "If somebody was supposed to take out Section Eight tonight, the same way it went down in the comic, who does it exactly? Don't tell me it's that Switchblade piece of shit. Can't be. Not while he's in The Hole anyway."

"You really wanna know?"

"Let's not play this game again, son."

"It was an Asian man in a Michael Jackson jacket."

Earl roared with laughter.

Charlie was unfazed.

Earl finally settled down. "*Shieet*, boy," he said. "We Section Eight around these parts. The best in everything we do. Highly trained, well hidden, and always on the lookout. And ain't no little Asian runt from the future gonna be the downfall of one of the baddest groups of colorful super soldier-type characters this side of the Mississippi. You can count on that shit, son."

Chapter Eight
Easy Peasy Japanesey

Gripping a bloody Section Eight flag in his palm, Ginsu rode the Section Eight elevator back to the surface at the abandoned, Rockwood drive-in. He exited the phone booth and scanned the area. To the left, he spotted a billboard for Boar's Whores Galore on the side of the road. He glanced at his watch. With Boar's Whores Galore only being a mile away, and with a little time to spare before the jump back home, Ginsu proceeded to the bar to see some live-action, eighties nudity.

*

Minutes later, Earl and Charlie pulled up to the secret phone booth/elevator, and the vehicle's headlights revealed a sign of the worst: red stains all over the interior of the phone-booth with a bloody trail leading out.

Charlie said, "Told you."

Earl hopped out of the cruiser. He opened the back door, quickly uncuffed Charlie, handed him back his blaster rifle, pulled his own pistol and said, "Stay here, *Quantum Leap*. Watch my six and guard the cruiser."

Earl stepped up to the elevator and observed the bloody mess. "Goddamn sumbitch!" He looked at Charlie. "I'll be right back. Don't move." Earl threw himself into the elevator, punched the numbers, gave the command, "I'll take a Pepsi," and down he went, leaving Charlie all alone on the surface.

Off in the distance, Charlie could hear hair metal blasting through the trees. He magnetically slung his weapon across his back, brought up his forearm, hit the button for the holographic bounty screen and spotted where Ginsu was. He shut off the hologram, looked up at the Boar's Whores Galore billboard, shifted his head with a quick crack of the neck, and began walking directly toward the music. Time was running out. And when Charlie got to Boar's Whores Galore, he was going to smash Ginsu's face in, take his stash of serum then call it a day. But only a few steps into his journey, the sound of four wheelers roared in, and within seconds he was surrounded by the Mad Dogs. Before he even had time to react, he was knocked to the ground and his weapon flung far out of reach.

Boomer yelled, "Fuck orders! Let's have a little fun with this prick first! I feel like having some fun!"

Charlie tried to get up, but was instantly clipped by the corner of Third Degree's four-wheeler, which sent Charlie flying through the air. He landed in the overgrown brush on the side of the road, tumbled into the woods then came to a stop by slamming into a tree and dislocating his shoulder. Lying on his back motionless, in excruciating pain, everything went double-vision and fuzzy for Charlie. He looked up at Rockwood's two out-of-focus full moons. Then he heard the four-wheelers park on the side of the road and shut off. Three voices approached, coming through the brush.

"Got the gasoline, Third Degree?" Rumble asked.

"Got it!"

"I'll chain his ass to a tree, mate." Boomer added. "Who's down for a friendly little wager, eh?"

Then Charlie passed out cold.

*

On the lower level of the Section Eight base, Earl observed the carnage everywhere. Technicians, secret agents, even the janitor, were all dead and bloody from random knife slashes. Blades were left in multiple victims, many throats were cut, and in the break-room, the perpetrator had farted in the microwave and cooked it, making the crime scene almost too much to bear from the stench. Earl braved the scene anyway, pinching his nostrils along in order to block the smell, his space revolver cocked and ready. He stepped over a torso that was missing every limb, then entered Tinker's station. Tinker was dead as well, strung out on the metallic table with half his face melted from whatever gadget the Asian perpetrator used against him. Earl was horrified. He looked down at his Pac Man watch and back to Tinker. "Shit, Tinker. You won't be able to help me celebrate when I finally beat Pac Man. You got robbed, son."

That's when a beep emitted from the Section Eight central computer.

Earl quickly made his way over to the panel and hit the answer button. On the large screen above appeared a young man wearing head-to-toe red, ice skater, speed racing spandex with a W.B. logo on his chest. Earl looked up at the image and said, "WindBreaker, we got trouble! Where are you right now?"

"Canada, operating on a mission within the Section Eight multiverse and fighting my arch enemy, The Speed Demon, *as usual*. I caught him this time. But that's another tale for another time. I received the distress signal, that's why I've contacted you. What's happening down there?"

"Oh, it's bad as shit, WindBreaker. *Bad as shit.* How quick can you let it rip and get your fast ass down here?"

"Once the proper Section Eight escorts show up to haul Speed Demon's slow-poke ass away to the nearest Section Eight holding facility, I'll leave. I'm two thousand three hundred and seven miles away. It'll take me about ten minutes to get there after a quick multiverse jump that only I can pull off using my special abilities."

"No restroom stops."

Earl shut off the call. He reached forward and hit the security cell cameras in The Hole. Frank

"Switchblade" Butz was long gone, along with all the other villains, all twelve cells empty.

Earl shook his head. "I'll be a sumbitch."

*

Almost passed out, beaten to a bloody pulp, maybe even close to death, Charlie dangled helplessly upside down from a tree limb, his body bound and wrapped tight with a twenty-foot dog chain as the Mad Dogs continued to pound on him and have their fun.

Rumble, wearing his trademark, steel-toe combat boots, delivered a brutal roundhouse kick to Charlie's face that spewed blood all over the tree he was hanging from and sent him swinging.

Boomer walked in the background with Charlie's large, Cable-inspired blaster and admired it. "Bloody fucks, mate. You got ya 'self an excellent little boom-boom maker here, Charlie Jones, if ya don't mind me saying so m'self. You mind if I keep it after they get done beating your ass to death over their stupid-ass bet?" Boomer quickly cocked the large cannon and without hesitation shot a laser blast right under Charlie's head.

The explosion rocked Charlie's world and showered him from below and pelted him with dirt and gravel.

"Goddamn it, Boomer!" Rumble yelled. "You almost shot him *and* me! Don't go ruining the bet, you fucking prick!"

Boomer leaned back with the futuristic weapon in his grasp and laughed out loud like a maniacal douche, his shoulders bouncing with every *ha*. "*Mwahahahaha!*"

Third Degree looked down at his watch and chimed in. "You have two minutes left, Rumble. If he's still alive after two minutes, you lose *all* your share of the chocolate donuts."

Rumble turned to face Third Degree. "I haven't lost me a beat-them-to-death bet with you yet, and I don't intend to lose this one either." He pointed angrily at Boomer and shouted, "As long as Boomer stops interrupting me by shooting that goddamn blaster gun!"

Boomer abruptly shot again, this time right over Third Degree's head and cut the tree he was leaning against in half.

Third Degree jumped away as the timber fell and crashed. He shouted, "You crazy, Australian fuck! Knock it the fuck off, man!"

Boomer laughed again. "Piss off, mate!"

Rumble shook his head at Boomer's stupidity but couldn't help but chuckle at his craziness. Rumble reached inside his cargo pocket, pulled out a set of extra-thick brass knuckles and put them on. He approached the dangling Charlie and smiled. "Bet we can wrap this up in under a minute. Can't lose no bet against Third Degree. He ain't getting *my* chocolate donuts." He reached forward and grabbed Charlie by the hair then drew his brass-knuckled fist back. The brass knuckles that were drawn back began to electrify in the dark with random spurts and sparks of energy. "You like?" He asked Charlie. "Made 'em myself. Electrified brass knuckles, Charlie. Say goodnight." *Whap!*

The blow put Charlie out for the count. Maybe for good. A white light appeared before him as his soul slowly left his body. Everything around him became a magnificent golden light, brighter than anything Charlie had ever seen before but was still very easy on his eyes. His pain was also gone. He began floating upward, slowly at first before building speed faster and faster towards the light at the end of the quickly forming tunnel. Was this a trip to heaven? If so, he was ready. Ready to see LaQueefa waiting on the other side. Once they embraced, he would never again let her go. Almost there!

And that's when Charlie sprung up in his old bed with LaQueefa sleeping quietly next to him. The décor of the room was familiar, as it was their place exactly two years prior. Covered in sweat, Charlie began to pant from the dream.

LaQueefa, usually beautiful, but instead wearing a green mud mask on her face with cucumbers over her eyes, woke up too. She removed the cucumbers, looked at her man in distress, sat up next to him, and with a loving hand tried to rub the tension away from his clammy back. "Are you okay, Charlie? You're sweating."

"I'm okay, I think."

"Another dream?"

"Yeah. It was just a dream. Fucking weird one this time. But it was just a dream."

"Of course, it was just a dream, baby. We are here. I'm here. Everything is okay. We're safe."

Charlie looked at LaQueefa with a smile and a nervous exhale. "Just felt so real this time is all."

"I told you not to eat before bed."

"I think that's an old wise tale, baby."

LaQueefa smiled. "Well, the dream is over now." She grabbed her cucumber slices, leaned back, and got comfortable. "You want to lay back and tell me all about it?"

Charlie declined to lay back. "I was near death. I had lost you to a vicious gang attack. I traveled back in time in order to avenge you by trying to steal some super-human serum from some Men in Black." Charlie put his head down. "...Only I failed. I failed the city, the mission, and I failed to avenge you, LaQueefa. I was near death from a beat down. That's when I woke up." He shook his head. "What a fucking nightmare." Charlie looked at his LaQueefa and then back to the wall. "I know it all sounds pretty stupid, huh?"

LaQueefa rubbed the top of Charlie's butt area and said, "No it doesn't, baby. It doesn't sound stupid at all. Sounds like a bad movie maybe. Nothing to worry about."

Charlie stared through the wall. "What do you think a dream like this could even mean?"

"Maybe it means you watch way too many fucked up movies while high, Charlie."

"Maybe," Charlie agreed.

"Or maybe it means that you can't do everything alone. You'll need some help if you want to come back to me."

Charlie smirked. "Come back to you?"

"Come back to me, Charlie."

"Yeah, I heard you. I ain't going anywhere, baby."

LaQueefa's voice screamed at its highest volume possible. "Come back to me!"

Charlie jumped off the bed and looked.

LaQueefa was lying in bed, back in her assaulted, turkey-shaped torso like before, looking up at Charlie with wide eyes and burnt bald spots, turning his dream into a sudden nightmare. She shouted again, "Come back to me!"

Charlie stepped back and freaked.

LaQueefa's voice suddenly became male with a redneck accent and shouted one last time, "Come back to me!"

Charlie regained consciousness back in Rockwood, Mississippi as Earl Tubb smashed the plunger of a needle straight in Charlie's heart and shouted, "Come back to me! C'mon, goddamn it! Come back to me! Live!"

Fresh from Section Eight's trademark Serum 13B shot to the heart, Charlie jolted back to life. He quickly shuffled up against a tree to regain his bearings then grabbed the needle and yanked it from his chest. The 13B healing process quickly took over, and Charlie's vision cleared in an instant. He spotted Earl Tubb in the darkness, kneeling on the ground where Charlie had just sprung back to life from. Then he spotted WindBreaker and Sam Dickey the Ninja taking out the Mad Dogs in the background with much glee, as if it were a game to them. Boomer had already bit the dust, decapitated from Sam Dickey's ninja blade, but Rumble was still up and trying to give WindBreaker a good fight. It was useless.

WindBreaker ran circles in a blur around the Mad Dog, and before anyone could blink, Rumble was stripped bare-butt naked from WindBreaker's lightning-fast abilities.

Streaking naked as a Sasquatch, Rumble took off running in the dark, back to the main road. He hopped on his four-wheeler and fired it up.

But before he could even get it in gear, a foot from WindBreaker knocked Rumble's naked ass off the ATV and onto the pavement.

"I give," Rumble shouted. "I give!"

Back in the brush, Third Degree quickly went for his lighter and the gas can attached to his hip.

Sam Dickey did a triple, ninja flip up onto a tree branch for safe distance, whipped out her blow gun, spit an actual laser blast from it, and nailed Third Degree's gas can which ended in an explosion that blew him into little, fiery pieces.

Once the explosion settled, Charlie looked at Earl in amazement.

Earl noticed the serum had taken full effect and Charlie's face and bodily injuries began to heal on their own.

Charlie let out a gruntish moan as the serum filled his veins with the good stuff. The adrenaline pumped, the pain-free nerve endings took hold, and the body high from it was like nothing Charlie ever felt before in his life. His tough guy demeanor disappeared and a giddy side began to peer through as the wave of super-human serum took him over from the inside. And damn it felt good.

Earl smiled at the realization on Charlie's face. "Shit feels good, doesn't it? Guess you needed my help after all. You can thank me later."

*

Back in the year 2037, deep within the Zoo Gang compound, Hammer Jones watched several of his gang members pour bags of gun powder all over a large pile of raw meat on the ground. Hammer looked down into the bear pit that housed about twenty bulldogs, one of every breed imaginable, and shouted, "*Whoof-whoof!*"

The dogs barked up at Hammer.

Hammer shouted back, "Y'all muthafuckas hungry?"

The dogs went apeshit, snarling and snapping at one another as they tried to get a spot up close for the meat toss feeding.

Excitedly, Hammer barked back with an imitation of the ninety's rapper, DMX, with, "*Arf! Arf!* Where my dogs at?"

The dogs barked back louder.

Hammer laughed and said, "Throw down the fucking meat, man."

The gangsters began to throw down the meat.

The dogs tore into it with violence, snapping and attacking one another over the raw meal. Several began to fight on the spot.

Hammer looked at one of his gangsters with a grin and said, "Look at them fucking dogs go at it, man." He pointed at three bulldogs to his side that were chained to the wall. "Don't forget to feed my personal dogs, Rerun, Roger, and Dwayne. Extra gunpowder. And chain 'em up in my office when you're done with them."

Kimbo approached the scene with his timid, skinny jean, tight-butt walk. He looked into the dog pit, adjusted his nerd glasses, cautiously took a few steps back and said, "Uh, Mr. Jones. Boss. Um, Hammer. It's almost time to pull Ginsu back through. You said you wanted to be there for it."

Hammer looked at his Rolex watch. "Shit. Thanks, Kimbo. Go ahead and get the time machine elevator fired the fuck up. I'll be there in two seconds." Hammer looked at one of his meat toss soldiers and gave him a finger point to the chest with, "And you? Get on the loudspeaker and tell everyone to get their asses over to the penguin exhibit. Tell them to wait there for me. It's go-time!"

One of the dogs from below began to yelp from a fatal attack on its throat by another.

Hammer looked down and smiled. "Look at them fucking dogs, man."

*

Hammer entered the bear cave and walked over to Kimbo's setup in the corner. Kimbo typed away on his computer as soft rock played from his monitor's speakers at low volume. Hammer stepped next to Kimbo. "Fuck you listening to now? *Gilligan's Island* on wax?"

"It's 'Daniel' by Elton John."

"Yeah, well, shut Elton John the fuck up about his little butt buddy while I'm around."

Kimbo reached forward and decreased the volume.

Hammer continued. "How much time we got?"

Tapping on the keyboard and focusing on the screen in front of him, Kimbo said, "Any second now, boss. Any second."

Hammer almost drooled. "C'mon, Ginsu. Bring daddy the serum."

The time-travel elevator began to vibrate, and the crack between its sliding doors glowed bright as if a light was trying to escape from inside. A loud pulse of energy hit and rippled the entire room in a wave.

Hammer put up a protective hand to shield his face.

Then it was over.

Kimbo tapped a few more computer keys, hit enter, and the smoking elevator doors opened.

Out stepped the short, Asian assassin, Ginsu, along with a tall, long-legged blonde stripper from Boar's Whores Galore that he fell in love with while there. With his hand on her waist and his other hand clutching the metal container of Buzz Benny's experimental serum, the two stepped out of the elevator and greeted Hammer.

Hammer was beyond thrilled. "Goddamn, Ginsu. You came through once again like a true ninja warrior."

Ginsu handed him the container and then dropped the bloody Section Eight flag at Hammer's feet.

Hammer gladly accepted them both. He opened the metal container, took a whiff of the contents inside and jerked his head back with a quick shake of the head. "Goddamn, that's some funky smelling shit. Beyond horrible. Worse than anything I have ever smelled in my entire muthafuckin life. If they were to take a crack head's vagina and bottle it, it'd smell better than this shit, yo." He handed it to Kimbo. "Put it in some needles and let's start injecting my chosen, lower-level followers with the shit ...*immediately.*"

Kimbo, holding his breath from the fumes, recapped the container. He began to walk out but struggled along as his weakling arms tried to carry the heavy load. He stopped at the door and turned. "What about one for you, boss?"

"Are you crazy? Let's see how the stanky shit works on the others first. I ain't the righteous type, nigga."

Kimbo turned and left.

Hammer turned back at Ginsu.

The blonde honey on Ginsu's side just couldn't take her eyes off her new man as she looked down at him with carnal lust.

Hammer smiled at the lovers. "What's your name, honey?"

The blonde continued to stare at Ginsu and said, "Whatever this sexy little thing wants my name to be."

Hammer was proud of his soldier. He looked down at Ginsu. "Guess you want to kick back now? Take a break? You know what? You got a bad bitch right there. And you deserve a little break, G-su. *My* room is *your* room. Use it. I just put in a dope-ass water bed and shit. Black light. Go play plumber and lay some pipe on this fine-ass dime piece."

Ginsu bowed, and then him and his nameless woman walked out.

Hammer walked over to the metal prison mirror that was bolted to the cave wall. Candles burned from both ends and threw Hammer's reflection back at him with a golden aura. He picked up the cordless hair clippers from the shelf, put the clippers to the side of his head and said, "My time is *now*." He fired up the clippers.

Hair fell in clumps by his shiny, black, wrestling boots.

*

Back in Rockwood, Charlie, who was completely healed by the Serum 13B, sat on a tree stump and fussed with his holographic, wristband projection device. The screen was malfunctioning and glitchy.

WindBreaker said, "I'm pretty good at tech stuff. I can take a look at it, if you'd like."

"You're a scientist?" Charlie removed the hologram projector from his wrist and held it up. "You look more like a speed skater with running shoes on instead of ice skates."

Within a microsecond, WindBreaker took the object from Charlie's hand and was back in his original position ten feet away and already tinkering with it. He looked at it and said, "Crude device, but with future knowledge used to build it. Impressive, but unfortunately made of junk."

"It'll do," Charlie said. "Improvise, adapt, and overcome, right?"

"Isn't that an old Marine Corps. saying?"

"Yeah. How do you know so much about technology and how the hell do you move so goddamn fast?"

"I was a scientist working on trying to reduce the space between myself and the physical world, but on a molecular level. Basically, trying to bind the atoms within my brain to a smaller scale within the physical world, which would almost allow me to teleport to an object that I'm thinking about with just the speed of thought."

"So, you aren't actually running? You're teleporting?"

"Yeah, but without disappearing in the process. I should be called Teleportation Man, but Earl here recruited me and insisted I was called WindBreaker instead and act like a rip-off of the Flash."

Earl stepped up and into the conversation. "I like the name WindBreaker. Now be quiet, WindBreaker, and try not to let one rip. I need to talk to our time-traveling guest here a second. In fact, head into town. Grab some food. We gonna need our energy." Earl looked up. "Want anything, Sam Dickey the Ninja?"

Perched in a tree high above, with her ninja bow cocked and ready, Sam Dickey slowly scanned the area and said, "Like, I ate at the mall with Sean, Brie, and Dustin tonight. But Tommy showed up and made a total scene. He's really, like, turned Loserville since I broke up with him for Randy. But Tommy just can't compare. Like, Randy is *so* bitching!"

Earl looked up with sarcasm. "Like, *I* care." He looked back at WindBreaker and pointed. "Grab me a couple hotdogs from Chuck's Thunder Dogs Cafe. Better make it one. Started a new diet." Earl looked at Charlie. "Want a dog?"

Charlie adjusted his battered clothes. "Nah."

Earl pointed at WindBreaker. "Grab some ketchup!"

WindBreaker tossed Charlie his holographic wrist projector and in a "flash" was gone from sight.

Earl giggled. "Named after a fart. Huh-huh. Rookies." He walked over to Charlie.

Charlie strapped his wristband device back on, fired it up and a holographic map of the area emitted before him. He reached forward, slid around the interactive sliders, hit a few buttons, then shut it off with an angry, "Fuck! Little bastard is gone!"

"Who?" Earl asked.

"That little Zoo Gang fuckface that came here from the future! The one you said couldn't take out Section Eight all by his lonesome. Well, he did! And now he's taken that entire stash of serum from the Men in Black back to 2037 for my fuck-face brother and his stupid gang." Charlie stood and walked over to the burnt-to-a-crisp Mad Dog, Third Degree, and kicked his smoking corpse. "All because of these three assholes here, not to mention *you*, Agent Tubb, my plan has fallen apart!"

"I had orders, and the personal dilemma of the man on the other end of them orders won't have shit to do the fact that Earl Tubb *always* catches his fish. So, don't be too hard on yourself. But you might need some more help ... from *me*."

"You've done plenty already. Anyway, I work alone."

"Alone, huh? Sounds to me like you've had help along the way, whether you like it or not."

"It was never my intention. Besides, this shit is too personal for anyone else to get involved with any further."

Earl sympathized. "I hear you, son. I once lost a good friend. He got a switchblade thrown into his forehead right in front of my very own eyes. Died right in my arms. Been playing cat and mouse with the prick that did it ever since. I catch him, they lock him up, he escapes ... every damn time. Even shoved the prick in

The Hole this time. Still got out. But now that Rockwood's Section Eight is pretty much destroyed, there can't be no locking him up anymore. I think the puke face bastard needs to go for good. As in d-e-d dead. You know he shit on my desk once?"

Charlie stood and began to walk back to the main road without a response.

Earl yelled up, "Sam Dickey, watch that naked one WindBreaker tied to the four-wheeler. Arrow his ass if he moves!" Earl headed for the road after Charlie.

Sam Dickey followed from high above, jumping from limb to limb in the darkness without making a sound. She spotted the naked Mad Dog passed out cold chained to his ride. She perched low on her branch and drew back the arrow on her bow, ready to kill.

Charlie stopped in the middle of the road, pulled out his time-travel phone from his utility pack, held it up and began to pace the area.

Earl asked. "Whatcha doing there, Charlie?"

"Reception. Looking for a good signal."

"Signal? Reception? That a cellular phone? You selling drugs, Charlie?"

"We all have cell phones in the future."

Earl shook his head in disgust. "A future full of drug dealers, huh? Damn, that's sad. Y'all *do* need some of Earl's help after all."

"We *really* don't."

Earl looked hurt at the comment then shrugged. "Never say never."

Charlie ignored the comment. He finally caught the signal from Vanguard 1, the satellite that Rudy Ray hacked into for their communications, and said, "Okay, I found something. I better split before I lose the signal."

"No long goodbyes, huh?" Earl asked.

"Not for me. I need to get back to my own timeline to stop Hammer from tearing my city apart."

"Might be easier for you with that Serum 13B in your veins now. And that's the *real* shit too, boy. The real deal. Not like that synthetic bullshit them Men in Black assholes were pushing. You're welcome for that, by the way. Nothing like a little *help*, huh, Charlie?"

"I suppose a little never hurt anyone." Charlie dialed on his phone and after a couple of rings, Rudy Ray answered it. "Uncle Rudy Ray, it was a total bust ... I was held up and then fucking ambushed. The serum is gone. ...I will ...Tuck modified the suit? ...What does it look like now? ...The Punisher issue #34 suit but with full flight capabilities? ...Good, because we're gonna need it ...Right ...Give me just a minute and then pull me back through." Charlie hung up his phone with a mentally exhausted exhale and looked at Earl.

Earl approached. "Time to click them heels, huh?"

"There's no place like home. The odds are against me, but the city needs my help. Now, more than ever."

"We could always use you too, Charlie. *Here*, that is. As it stands, there's only a few Section Eight members left standing. How about we form our own squad? A Section Eight spinoff! We can call ourselves Tubb's Howling Commandos or some cool, original shit like that."

"As enticing as that sounds, I'll have to pass. The vengeance for my dead LaQueefa is in East St. Louis 2037, not here and now. But I do owe you big-time for saving my life. And for the Serum 13B. I'll never forget it."

"Well, that serum I shot you up with should help you out plenty. You'll heal fast as shit with it. Shame I couldn't give you a cool, robot hand like me, but ya gotta lose a limb first."

"That's okay. I have a metal man suit waiting for me back home." Charlie's phone began to ring. "Supposed to be badass." He fished his phone from his pouch and looked at Earl. "Thanks again for your help. And as far as plans going to shit are concerned, I guess I can say it was a pleasure meeting a legend such as yourself during it all, Agent Earl Tubb."

Earl smiled. "Nothing cooler than a team full of colorful, superhero types to watch ya back, son. Trust me. And you're welcome." He held up the Section Eight trading card of himself. "And thanks for letting me keep this. I have a special place in mind for it, right next to the Luke Duke magnets on my refrigerator door."

"No sweat." Charlie magnetically strapped his weapon to his back

"Maybe I'll see you around, Charlie Jones."

Charlie nodded. He answered his time-travel phone and a ball of light quickly formed around him, which blinded Earl. Within seconds, Charlie zapped away at lightning speed and disappeared from the timeline.

Once Earl's vision returned, he held up his wrist and looked at Tinker's latest invention: The Section Eight time-travel device. "And maybe you can pay me back in person."

WindBreaker appeared on the scene, hotdogs in hand. "What's new?" he looked around. "Did that future guy leave?"

Earl continued to dwell on the time travel device.

"Hot dogs are cold from the wind burn, by the way," WindBreaker said. "Sorry. What's that thing?"

"Time-travel device."

"A time-travel device? And who put *you* in charge of a time-travel device?"

"Since most of Section Eight is dead, *I* put myself in charge of it."

"Time travel is nothing to play around with."

Earl knowingly nodded. "I have a little something I need to do real quick. I want you and Sam Dickey to wait right here and hold on tight to my wiener." Earl stood tall and adjusted his sagging trousers. "Alright, Frank Switchblade Butz. Time for the final round. And *this* time, it's for good." He held up a finger to the time-travel device. "*Ding-ding.*" And with the push of a button, Earl zapped from the timeline's existence.

Chapter Nine
Hammer Jean: The Legend of a Failed Wrestler

Back in 2037, over at the local East St. Louis news station, ESLN, a young kid entered the lobby and handed the secretary at the front desk a package wrapped in a plain brown bag. The lady took it and asked "What's this?"

The kid shook his head.

"Well, who's it from?"

"Dunno," the kid shrugged before turning around and walking out.

The secretary opened the package and inside was a VHS tape with Hammer Time written on the label. She picked up the phone, dialed and said, "Yeah, Cliff. You better get down here and pronto. I think I may have something big."

*

Across the city, television programming simultaneously went black before cutting back in with a headline across the screen that read Breaking News with Your Trusted State-approved Media.

People from all walks of life stopped what they were doing and leaned into the various television screens across the city in order to hear the latest lies the media was going to spin.

A young female reporter came on the screen, an ESLN logo was on the wall behind her and in the corner of the screen was an early mugshot of Hammer Jones. "Hello, East St. Louis," the reporter said to the camera. "I'm Cara Lane, and we interrupt your regularly scheduled broadcast to bring you this breaking ESLN report. We have just received possession of a videotape that was apparently sent to us by the local thug, and former failed bad-guy wrestler, known as Hammer Jones. We will run it around the clock. Brace yourselves. Roll it, Scotty."

Hammer Jones, with a fresh mohawk and spiked shoulder pads, appeared on screen. Sweating, wide-eyed and extra hype from all the cocaine intake he had in order to get pumped for the video, he looked dead at the screen and spoke with intensity. "Hello, citizens of East. St. Lou! Hammer Jones here! The most gangster muthafucka these streets have ever seen, in and out the ring! And I'm here to tell you that the days of me running blocks are long gone. I want the whole Monopoly board!" He showed off his biceps with a, "Oh, yeah!" He put his arms back down. "And I'll kill all of your asses just to get what I want. But this isn't a submit-or-else situation. Nah. Unfortunately for you, many citizens will have to die today. And Imma rule what's left over of you scared little bitches with an iron hammer, my own rules and shit, and with an army of beasts to back me up. The *real* King of the Ring, baby. The city will be mine! Yeah! *You* will be mine! Each and every one of you! And if you want to try and challenge me, I'll meet you in the ring any day of the week!" He raised his rusty hammer. "Hail, Hammer!"

Hammer quickly sniffed back. The leftover cocaine in his nostril hit a blood vessel and popped it. Blood oozed from his nostril as he continued, a little embarrassed. "Guess it makes little sense explaining my motive to a bunch of dead people, so I guess I better just go." He quickly wiped his bloody nose with his gang colors and then turned off the camera.

Reporter Cara Lane looked stone-faced into the camera at the home audience and simply said, "Terrifying."

*

Back at Rudy Ray's cave, Tuck Pendelton, with his legs sticking out, worked on the undercarriage of the van. Off to the side, random go kart parts were scattered about. Sitting at the cave's computer terminal, Rudy Ray was typing away. "You sure you know what the hell you're doing over there, Tuck?" Rudy Ray yelled over. "Can't have you fucking my shit up with a bunch of Jerry-rigged bullshit, my man."

"Trust me," Tuck yelled back. "Worked at the motor pool for a while. Learned from this one dude how to modify the shit out of vehicles before he got accused of a crime he didn't commit. For instance, I installed a ramp and mini go kart in the back of the van that Charlie asked for specifically. The go cart is equipped with—"

"Can it, Tuck." Rudy Ray spun around in his chair. "Charlie's coming back through."

Tuck started shuffling from under the van. "Good deal."

The room quickly lit up into a shining ball of light that disappeared just as quick as it came.

In the middle of the cave, Charlie stood before them, empty handed.

Tuck walked over and greeted him with, "Welcome back, Charlie. Another mission over and done with."

"Another mission I failed," Charlie said ashamed.

"Maybe you failed that little battle there," Tuck said. "But who gives a fuck? This war has just begun."

Rudy Ray chimed in. "And *this* war, little nephew, is far from over." Using a remote control, Rudy Ray opened the closet's steel door that concealed the new flight suit. The door opened slowly.

The sight of the new flight suit lifted Charlie's spirits quickly.

Rudy Ray smiled. "Let's suit you up."

Chapter Ten
2037: The Battle of the Lou

Hammer Jones and about twenty of his serum-infected army, who were now Sasquatch size and had mutated into gray skinned, pointed-teeth beasts, walked the city sidewalks. Like the mindless monsters they had become, the posse of beasts grumbled and grunted along behind Hammer in their shredded clothing that was now too small for their mutated bodies. People screamed in terror, scattered, and quickly cleared a path for the oversized mutants. Those who didn't, got snatched up and devoured on the spot. Exempt from taking the serum, the roller-skating Reggie weaved in, out, and around the mutated bangers but stopped at one point to whip out a can of spray paint to write ZOO GANG 4 MUTHAFUCKIN LYFE on a store-front wall. He never wrote the date on his graffiti. Why bother when it was "4 muthafuckin lyfe," right?

The gang made a hard-left down Puff Daddy Sucks Ass Avenue and headed straight for the police station.

Approaching the police station, they came to a stop before the building and Hammer turned around to face his monsters. "After we finish overrunning this bitch, we will immediately begin phase two. I want the heavy artillery set up on the second floor. Eight men on the lower level will help set up and provide security as Kimbo sets up the network. Use *their* computers. Where's Kimbo?"

The computer nerd Kimbo stepped away from the lumbering mutants who salivated over him, all of them mouth breathers and showing their alligator-looking teeth that were just dying to tear into some human flesh such as Kimbo's. Kimbo nervously gulped with, "Yeah? I'm here, boss. I'm here."

Hammer put a fingerless, spike-gloved hand on Kimbo's shoulder. "Now, Kimbo. I'm relying on you to hook up the computers while business is handled out here. Link up the office systems with our factions in Compton and Chicago. We need to be in touch with these muthafuckas at a moment's notice. And be sure to send them a like request for my Zoo Gang Facebook page. Got it?"

Kimbo nodded, "Sure thing, boss."

"Hold on," Hammer ordered. He pulled out his cell phone for a quick selfie, looked down, turned the screen sideways in order to get his shoulder pads into the frame, then snapped a shot. He thumbed the screen a few times then under his breath mumbled, "*And* send." He looked up to his mindless, mutated, mouth-breathing soldiers. "Just uploaded a new cover photo on Twitter. My last post about 'fuck the police' has already received two hundred and thirty-seven likes and shares."

The monsters roared in celebration.

Hammer was hopeful. "These social media numbers are proof of our expansion." A sinister grin slid across his face. He turned to face the police station, and with a quick motion of his hands, yelled, "Ever forward!"

The beasts rushed the building.

*

Back in Rudy Ray's cave, Charlie was walking around, trying to get used to the new suit's mechanics. "This is fucking nice. Heavy, but nice."

Tuck smiled. "You look like a tank with arms and legs, my man."

From his computer chair, Rudy Ray schooled Charlie on the latest suit. "The mechanisms inside that we attached to your body will cause the suit to respond to the actions of your muscles. Without them, you couldn't move the suit around. It's heavy as shit. I don't give a fuck how strong your ass is." Rudy Ray typed on his computer. "Data will flood your screen inside the helmet when called for. I can also insert anything needed during the fight from my end. I can even take over the suit from here if I wanted to. The two systems are linked. And don't you go worrying about the suit trapping any farts inside. Tuck drilled some holes in the ass."

Tuck thumbs upped Charlie.

Rudy Ray continued. "The small cannon welded to the forearm, the shit that kinda looks like Megatron, in fact, that's where I got the idea from. It emits a controlled burst of proton blasts. Ten rounds in that thing. Once you're out, you're out. But as long as the suit has power, repulsor rays can still be shot from the palms."

Charlie raised his robotic forearm and admired the ten-shot cannon attached. "How bulletproof is all this shit?"

"Very bullet proof," Rudy Ray said.

"But too many shots to the body and you'll end up like a human church bell," Tuck said. "Ears'll ring for hours."

Charlie raised a fist and admired the metal. "Punched in the face by an armored fist. That's gotta hurt, right?"

Rudy Ray spun around in his chair and faced Charlie. "A gauntlet to the face? Yeah, I'd think so. But just make sure your hydraulics don't get cut."

Tuck schooled Charlie on the rest of the updates. "Automatic nail gun attached under the forearm, thermal vision, cybernetic hearing and total access to every camera in the city, including the *Playboy Channel*! That was Rudy Ray's idea. The suit is also made with a unique vibrational property material. Even remote flight. Fuck, if you want, you can just pilot the damn thing from here ... if you wanna stay safe."

"I'm not trying to play a video game with this prick. I'm kicking Hammer's ass in person."

Tuck tightened down a few last-minute bolts. "Fuckin-a. Its molecular structure is also bound with an ionic energy of sorts." He tightened the last bolt. "Hit something."

Charlie lumbered over and punched the cave's wall with his oversized, iron fist and busted it to rubble.

Tuck smiled. "I think he likes it."

Rudy Ray said, "Let's try out levitate mode. The propulsion boots will do the job for you."

The suit's boots began to push at the ground with their small, concentrated stream of rocket propulsion and Charlie levitated high above, tilting wildly left and right before quickly learning how to steady the hoover.

Tuck looked up and yelled, "I think you might have it already!"

Charlie did a quick lap around the cave, spun into a twirl and shut off the propulsion boots. He slammed to the ground with a rumble and stuck the landing in front of Rudy Ray and Tuck perfectly. For the first time since the war, Charlie felt like a kid again.

Rudy Ray smiled. "You should be sealed in glass with a sign saying, Break Glass in Time of War."

Over at the computer terminal, a notification appeared on the main screen. Rudy Ray pulled his cell phone from his pocket and opened it. "What the hell?" He ran to his computer screen. "Guys, come over here."

Charlie and Tuck made their way over.

Rudy Ray looked up at the cave's main screen and typed. "I think it's begun."

The cave's main screen lit up and began running live news footage that looked like something out of a bad, sci-fi movie.

ESLN's Cara Lane, spoke from her little corner of the screen. "It appears that Hammer's Zoo Gang has not only taken over the city as promised, but in a strange twist of events that would only feel at home in a self-published novel's third act that stinks of desperation, the gangster's in Hammer's army have mutated into rather large monsters, attacking random civilians and ripping them to shreds on the spot. Many bodies are being found half eaten. Fires have broken out in various parts of the city, and the city police have been rounded up and taken away. Even the president herself has said that the city is burning from within and only God could help the sister city of St. Louis. It seems the Lou is on its own. I'm afraid we have been abandoned by all."

A rapid beep began to emit from the computer.

Rudy Ray responded on the keyboard.

A two-mile radius map of the surrounding area replaced the news footage on the large screen. Hundreds of little red dots were making their way through the sewer tunnels and straight for Rudy Ray's secret cave. "We have something on the way. A threat of some kind. How in the fuck does anyone even know my cave's location in the first place?"

Charlie said, "I bet that little karate fucker probably followed me here yesterday."

Tuck asked, "How serious does it look, Rudy Ray?"

"Serious enough to make this a priority at the moment. Charlie, it's time to put the new suit to the test."

The suit's helmet and faceplate quickly flipped from behind and slammed over Charlie's head. Its eyes lit up with a smooth, white glow. From the helmet's voice decoder came a robotic-sounding version of Charlie. "Found the quickest route through the tunnel," he said. He held his arms out and from the palms and feet of the suit came small blasts of propulsion that levitated him a few feet off the ground and into flight mode. He hovered for a moment, said, "I'll take care of this, Tuck, you take the van and meet me on the surface. And bring the Turbo Kart."

Tuck saluted with his socket wrench in hand and ran over to the van.

Rudy Ray looked at Charlie in hover mode. "Good luck. nephew. I'll stay connected with you here."

"Thanks," the robotic sounding Charlie said. "For everything."

Rudy Ray looked at his nephew. "You look badass, Charlie. A white Ghetto Blaster that flies! I like it. Characters develop over time, right? Besides, we've been shamelessly stealing y'alls characters for years instead of creating new ones from scratch. You might as well do the same, white boy."

Charlie gave a simple nod then flew away at high speed into the cave's connecting tunnel systems and out of sight.

Tuck, now armed with two belts of ammo crisscrossed across his chest and an M-60 machine gun in hand, hopped in the van. He slapped a red bandana on top of his permed mullet, checked it in the rearview mirror, then turned the key on the van. The engine roared. The fresh-cut panels on the sides of the van fell open and revealed two gatling guns that plopped out into position.

A large door hidden in the cave's wall suddenly opened to reveal a tunnel leading up to the surface.

Tuck flipped on the stereo and Link Wray's "Batman Theme" played loud.

Rudy Ray heard Tuck's song choice and shook his head.

Tuck kicked the van into gear, floored it, and was gone.

Inside Charlie's suit, he heard the sound of his uncle's voice coming in loud and clear. "Rudy Ray to Ghetto Blaster, do you copy?"

Flying along the dark tunnel system at breakneck speed, Charlie responded with, "This is Ghetto Blaster, I copy and read you loud and clear. A night vision scan of the area below me shows multiple people living under the city but no present threats."

"Those are the under dwellers of the city. Just ignore them. My scopes tell me the actual threat is coming from the west end. It appears to be a shitload of electronic rats that double as explosives. Either that, or it's actually a bunch of rats with bombs strapped to them. But that would mean that Hammer actually trained rats to take orders and attack, which would mean the rats could actually understand English, but that's too stupid to even consider."

"Not for someone like Tim Burton."

"English speaking or robotic, it matters not; don't let them reach the headquarters!"

"I see them up ahead."

"How about some theme music?"

"Fuck yeah!"

"Just speak the command to your suit. Its name is Leroy."

"Leroy."

"Sup, man?" the suit said.

"Play 'Staring Down the Demons' from that *Thrashin'* movie."

"... *Really?*"

No response from Charlie.

"You duh boss. Playing "Staring Down the Demons" by Animotion from the never officially released *Thrashin'* soundtrack."

The song began to play, and it fit perfectly. Charlie zeroed in on the incoming threat and took them out with ease by flying overhead and dropping random bombs from the ass end of his suit like deadly bird turds.

The explosions sent hundreds of rats straight to sewer hell.

Charlie continued in hover mode above and used his flamethrower wrists to light up the stragglers.

"Not bad, Ghetto B," came Rudy Ray's voice. "Not bad at all. I think you might have the hang of the suit already."

"I think so."

"Alright then, let's take it to the street."

Ghetto Blaster shot off.

*

Drinking a forty ounce and watching the news coverage on the mutant takeover from the comforts of his prehistoric chair, Hammer chilled without a care in the world, both feet up. On the desk before him was a sample of the stolen serum, glowing bright green in its glass container next to three plastic dog bowls. Randy, with tape covering his broken nose from Hammer's fist the day before, stood off to the side with Kimbo. Along with Hammer, they watched the news footage of the city getting destroyed by the soulless, mutated monster army. Hammer took his feet down, clapped his hands together once and said, "So, how do the two of you like my new world so far?"

Randy wasn't so sure.

Hammer could see this. "Ease up some, Randy. You lucky you one of the ones I *didn't* inject. But I can't have a bunch of lurking, Hulkish gangsters around me all day, you know what I'm saying? I need a council. And I saw something special in you. Or I *did*. Your eagerness to please seems to have vanished. Now, I'm guessing it must have a little more to do with just me smashing your big, wide, nigga-ass nose yesterday." Hammer opened the desk drawer and pulled a *Cobra Night Slasher* replica movie knife from the drawer and started to poke the top of the desk with it. "So, speak on it. You gotta problem, young buck?"

Randy shook his head and did a cool three-sixty with the expression on his face. "Yeah, Hammer. I'm cool with all this monster shit. I been down with you since I was a little kid and watched you wrestle at my old high school gym and on cable access TV and shit. You legend. And your legend grows."

Hammer grinned. "Had no idea you were a fan, Randy."

Randy casually put up his fist. "Hail, Hammer, right?"

A midget with a bald head and spiked, leather collar entered Hammer's domicile with three pit bulls attached to chains that were almost as tall as he was.

"I like the sound of that, Randy." Hammer said. "Y'all check out my personal dogs. Say hi to Dwayne, Rerun and Roger."

Randy and Kimbo both waved.

With the midget holding the chains tight, the dogs growled and snarled at them both.

Hammer laughed. "Now, the two of you get the fuck out."

Randy gladly left in a hurry.

"Kimbo!" Hammer said, halting him at the door.

Kimbo turned around. "Yeah, boss?"

"Are you sure this serum here has been filtered of all its impurities?"

"My read-out equipment for detecting Gamma radiation is junk to say the least. I wouldn't trust it, boss."

"Just tell me the results."

"I couldn't find any traces of Gamma radiation after the tests, but like I said, that doesn't mean much. Whatever happens is anyone's guess, and whatever happens will be irreversible. Just remember that. Don't ruin your new take over by risking ingesting something so foolish, boss. Just a little friendly advice."

"You have done well, Kimbo." Hammer waved his rusty hammer. "You may *now* leave."

Kimbo pushed up his glasses, hugged his butt cheeks tight, and ditty-bopped out.

Hammer looked at his dogs Dwayne, Rerun and Roger, who all sat next to one another and waited for Hammer's command. Hammer grabbed the serum from the table, took off the cap, poured a little serum in each dog bowl then placed the bowls on the floor.

The dogs began to quickly lap up the glowing substance. Slowly their muscle and bone structure began to grow as they each popped and cracked along, expanding outward, similar to that of a werewolf transformation, until each dog grew twice its original size in every way shape and form.

Hammer observed the mutation. "So, this is on some steroids times ten on-the-spot shit?" He held up the sample for a toast. "*That's* for me! Could have beat Red Rocket in the ring that night with some of this shit." He gulped it down.

*

Back in the secret cave, Rudy Ray located the Zoo Gang hideout. He alerted his two-man team. "I located the Zoo Gang hideout, which is located at the old city zoo. I guess we should have looked there first. Sort of a no-brainer, huh? I've locked their coordinates into both of your GPS systems. Meet on the surface and I'll do my best to guide you through the city."

Tuck responded, "I'm already on the surface and my van is crawling with these beastly pricks! But Tuck has something for their ass!"

Up on the surface, Tuck grabbed the steering wheel and shouted, "Hold on tight! It's Tuck time!" He jerked the wheel and sent his reinforced van rolling down the street, smashing and slinging the large, snarling mutated beasts off his vehicle and away from him in the process. On Tuck's last roll, the van landed on its side.

Shaken but far from damaged and done with, the mutants quickly formed into a pack around the van and closed in fast.

Tuck didn't even have time to assess the situation. Instinct kicked in, and he pulled the lever over his head. A kickstand-like contraption shot from the vehicle and flipped the van right side up. The gatling guns flipped out from the sides of the vehicle. Tuck hit the gas, spun donuts in place and fired from both gatling barrels without letting off.

Creatures screamed and tried to run for cover but were ripped to shreds. The buildings around them, every single one, were getting destroyed because of Tuck's guns.

Regardless, Tuck continued spinning and firing anyway until every last creature dropped to the pavement and every round was spent. When the donut-induced slaughter was finally over, Tuck stopped his spin, exhaled, and shouted, "Holy shit. *That* is what I call some fucking Tuck Time!"

Rudy Ray's voice came through. "It was quite impressive. You definitely get a spot on my team modifying vehicles and shit. Just need to lay off the bottle."

Tuck held up the fifth of whiskey from in between his legs. "I'll drink to that."

"I figured. Now, get your ass moving!"

Tuck put the bottle back and saluted. "Yes, sir!" He hit the gas and off he went, running over dead enemy for a bumpy exit.

*

In the parking lot of the old abandoned zoo, Randy was outside schooling some of the local kids of the neighborhood, who had gathered around to hear the tale of his drive-by initiation from the previous day. "You gotta cap someone if you wanna be down with the Zoo," he said through his nasally, broken nose. The tape on it had begun to show blood soaking through.

One of the kids looked up. "What's that on your nose?"

A kid answered, "It's a nose job, I think."

Another said, "My mommy got a boob job."

Randy halted them. "Wait-wait-wait. It ain't no muthafuckin nose job. My nose is fine."

A kid said, "It doesn't look fine to me. Blood."

"Don't worry about my goddamn nose. I'm trying to tell y'all about my initiation and shit, so gather around."

The kids formed a horseshoe reading circle around Randy and sat down.

Randy began. "So, we were driving down the avenue and shit, right?"

"What was you bumping?" A kid asked.

"We was bumping music, muthafucka. Now, shut the fuck up. We was rolling, right, and Hammer hands me this machine gun and says 'handle these niggas, Randy,' because he knows can't nobody get down with some gangster shit like me. Hey, kid." Randy pointed at the one with the jump rope. "Your mom named Sheryl?"

"Uh-huh."

"Tell her Randy says hello. But only if your daddy ain't in the room. Anyway, I cocked back, pulled the muthafuckin trigger and shot up the block, yo. Took out this bitch-ass breakdancer named Boogaloo who has been beating my cousin in all these dance competitions lately. Guess he won't be winning shit anymore," he laughed.

His audience was stone-cold expressionless.

"What?" Randy looked left to right.

*

A few miles from the Zoo Gang compound, Charlie finally made his appearance on the surface. He flew up from the tunnel system below through a manhole cover and knocked the sewer lid high into the air and sent it tumbling down the street. Hovering along the second story windows of the connecting stores and using the digital screen readouts inside his helmet, Charlie scanned and assessed the chaotic situation below. Beasts were attacking people everywhere. Random buildings were on fire. Screams filled the air. But to Charlie's left came the sound of screeching tires. It was Tuck in the van! He turned the curb with a furious skid and tried to shake off several mutants who held tight to the vehicle's sides. "I spotted you, Tuck!" Charlie shouted through his comm link. "Looks like someone is having a little trouble, huh, soldier? Nice van by the way, Hannibal."

Swerving back and forth and crashing through storefront displays of every kind, Tuck radioed back, "Fuck you and your snarky Tony Stark humor and get these fucking things off me!"

Charlie flew in and with his massive, gauntlet fists slugged several mutant beasts that were dangling off the side of the van and sent them down to the pavement in pain.

The beasts tumbled down the road. As soon as they were back on their feet, they attacked the random civilians standing by who were still dumb enough to be out.

The last mutant held tight to the roof of the van. It glanced down and peered at Tuck through the windshield with its long, lizard tongue and spiked fangs. Tuck hit the gas in a panic and screamed. "Fuck kind of enemy is this, Charlie?"

Charlie trailed behind. "It's one of them nameless, faceless armies like they slap in superhero flicks. Only these are mutants, not aliens."

"Good, because I don't believe in aliens. But do you know what I do believe in?"

"What's that, Tuck?" Charlie fired a few proton blasts from his palms that seemed to have little effect on the thick hide of the beast. "What do you believe in?"

Tuck replied, "I believe in Tuck Time!" then slammed the brakes on the van.

The beast flew off the roof, rolled down the street then quickly jumped to its feet and faced Tuck in an attack posture.

Tuck pulled from his pocket a little green Buddha on a string necklace and put it over his head and around his neck. He reached behind the seat then hopped out of the van.

Hovering above the scene, Charlie said, "Uh, Tuck. What are you doing? Get back in the van, man!"

The beast began to charge Tuck full throttle.

Tuck raised his weapon, the M-60.

Mindless and unafraid, the beast wasn't backing down. It closed in fast on Tuck with a humongous leap at the end.

Tuck lit it up, the belt clip wrapped around his forearm became smaller and smaller as Tuck put the beast down and emptied his entire belt of ammunition into the monster. When it was all over, and the rounds were gone, and the beast was finally dead, Tuck was left standing, covered in slimy, green blood from the mutated beast. He looked up at Charlie. "And *that's* how you do it old school."

Charlie yelled down, "And that's why I love you, Tuck! Now, wipe that shit off your face and let's head over to the zoo and play veterinarian. It's time to put down some sick animals."

Tuck threw the M-60 back in the van, used his snot rag to wipe the green goo from his face, put the van in gear, and side-by-side, the two took off through the battleground streets.

*

Inside the zoo compound, Ginsu's new woman watched from all fours on the water bed as Ginsu showed off his horrible moonwalking skills. Wearing nothing but his zipper jacket, high-top sneakers and a leopard print speedo, Ginsu slid backward across the floor as if it was ice. "Billie Jean" by Michael Jackson blasted from the room's stereo.

The woman said, "You *are* better than the real Michael Jackson!"

Ginsu began going in a circle with it, stone-faced and dead serious.

"Are you *really* the one who taught Michael Jackson how on your time travel mission?"

Off in the distance outside, Ginsu heard the sounds of Charlie's flight suit and Tuck's van going full throttle, coming at the compound with AC/DC blasting from one or the other's stereo.

Ginsu quickly pulled two butterfly knives from his jacket, flipped them open, and scurried over to the cave's window. Looking out, he immediately recognized the van from Rudy Ray's cave the previous day. Next to the van was a man in a metal, flight suit, flying by his side. Ginsu quickly hopped on the cave's window seal into a crouch position. And without saying a word, he leaped off the second floor and was gone from sight.

*

Outside, Randy stopped imitating firing an AK-47 for the children during his story hour when he heard the approaching vehicles. The *A Team* van smashed through the gated entrance at high speed and skidded to a halt.

Charlie landed right next to Tuck's driver-side door with a loud, metal *clank* on the pavement.

One of the kids looked over at the far end of the parking lot and pointed, "Gangster Randy, is that a superhero?"

Randy said, "Shut yo little ass up for a second." He whipped out his cell phone and dialed. "Ain't no such thing as superheroes, kid. What the fuck is the matter with you?"

Tuck yelled out his window at Charlie. "Guess he's calling for backup. You go on ahead, Charlie. Find Hammer! I got this here."

Charlie fired up his flight mode and into the air he went, over the concrete wall and into the main compound, out of sight. "I think I know where Hammer is located from a scan of the area," he communicated back to Tuck. "Are you sure you have things covered back there?" Charlie scanned the area below and saw movement on his radar. "About twenty armed men are heading your way!"

"Tuck Time, baby!"

"I guess that's a yes."

The bangers appeared on the scene and rushed the zoo's parking lot.

Tuck hit the gas, shot forward and advanced for the crew behind the safety of his bulletproof windshield.

Randy grabbed his AK-47 from the front seat of his car, aimed at the approaching van and riddled it with bullets to no effect.

Looking as if Tuck might ram the gangsters and just be done with them, Ginsu suddenly landed on his hood.

Tuck lost his beeline for the enemy and tried to shake Ginsu off with a rapid swerve.

Ginsu held steady. He hopped to the roof of the van, produced several throwing blades from his jacket and threw them straight through the roof of the van and into the cab, even striking one in Tuck's shoulder.

Tuck clutched at his bloody shoulder. He ripped the blade out with a large spurt of blood and screamed out his window in excruciating pain, "You little prick! Time for you to fly, motherfucker!" He pushed the red button on the dash, and the missile on the roof fired up. It took off, caught the back of Ginsu's speedo, and off he went for an explosive ride as the projectile hit the side of the zoo's wall.

Hostages, half of them naked cops, began to pour from the facility's fresh, rubble exit.

Sitting parked, Tuck threw Ginsu's blade down to the pavement and screamed, "How did you like that shit? You little dickhead." Holding his injured shoulder, Tuck smiled, then looked left and spotted every banger on the scene pointing an automatic weapon directly at him. "Oh, shit," he yelled before trying to roll up his window.

The shooting began. And it continued for a full thirty seconds before every last round was spent. Conserving ammunition was not in the Zoo Gang's vocabulary.

Once the hailstorm of bullets was over, Tuck was left sitting in the smoking wreckage with a few bullet holes in his body. He coughed up blood.

A banger in the crowd yelled, "He done for! Now, let's rip his ass apart!"

Another yelled, "Nah, man! Let's feed 'em to the dogs and shit! ...*Alive*."

The crowd screamed in agreement with their chains and spiked bats held high.

Hearing this, Tuck's eyes went wide.

The Zoo Gang slowly approached in unison then steadily gained speed into a full sprint.

"Well, kid," Tuck said looking in the rearview mirror. "Time to make your entrance!" Despite the two bullet holes in his leg, Tuck kicked the lever on the floorboard, and the van's back doors opened up.

From the back of the van came Boogaloo, strapped in a Mad Max-inspired go kart and completely controlling it by mouthpiece.

All the bangers stopped to get a look at the vehicle, which was not even close to being street legal, with its welded, steel cage protecting the cockpit and spiked hubcaps ready to cause serious damage. On top was another trusty gatling gun Tuck had attached, waiting to fire.

Boogaloo skidded to a stop and looked over at the gangsters. *The Turbo* was painted on the go kart's sides.

Randy couldn't believe it.

Using his mouthpiece, Boogaloo hit the gas, did several figure eights then slid to a full stop to face Randy and his gang in the near distance.

It was now a standoff.

Boogaloo revved his go kart's engine.

Randy yelled, "I already shot you once, Breaker! You ready for round two?"

With Tuck's good arm, he took control of the vehicle's machine gun system (hidden behind the phony headlights) and quickly locked and loaded both barrels at the gang. He looked out his window down at Boogaloo. "Well, kid. It's just me and you. Are you sure you want to do this?"

Boogaloo looked up at Tuck then slowly back at Randy with tearful vengeance in his eyes and said, "He took my moonwalk away from me, Mr. Tuck."

Tuck nodded. "Say no more, kid. You handle that prick that shot you. I'll handle the rest."

Boogaloo shouted, "Save Miracles N Shit," and both vehicles skidded off.

*

High off the effects from the filtrated, gamma-free serum, Hammer sat back and observed as the last of his mutation took over and pushed his now larger-than-life biceps out more and more. The veins along his arms and body became water hose sized as the serum pumped its enhancement elements throughout his body's system. He continued to grow and Hammer's shoulder pad straps finally popped and the shoulder pads fell to the ground. Now finished, Hammer sat and enjoyed the feeling as he observed his fists that were now double their original size. All felt good. But outside, the battle raged on. Hammer looked down at the dogs he experimented the serum on and smiled at the frothing, devil dogs, their muscle structures like something off of a Marine Corps' exaggerated bulldog logo. On their shoulders, Hammer had placed football shoulder pads that matched his own trademark ones, spikes and all. "How are you feeling there, Rerun, Dwayne and Roger? Good as me, I hope."

The dogs didn't even respond.

That's when Charlie bum rushed the scene and landed at the entrance with a massive *clank* that cracked the cave's stone floor.

Hammer stood up from his desk and smiled. "Hey, Charlie! What's happening?" Hammer clapped. "Get his ass!"

All three dogs went into a furious attack mode and lunged at the metal man.

Charlie simply unleashed the flamethrower option from his wrists and crisped the dogs to ash within seconds.

Hammer grabbed the large blade from the desk and held it up in a defensive stance.

Charlie's metal mask retracted back into its nanotech pouch behind his head; his eyes burned like fire. "You stole that fucking knife from me when we were kids. I looked for it for two months, you thief!"

"What?" Hammer asked. "You mean this Night Slasher *Cobra* blade here? The one you thought you lost? Yeah, I stole it, bitch. Of course. Fuck outta here." He used it to cut a slit across his own chest.

Charlie watched the wound rapidly heal as the veins along Hammer's body pumped with their exaggerated pulses of healing abilities and adrenaline.

Hammer absolutely loved it. "That is on some *Silent Rage* shit, my brother! Fuck Bane! C'mon, you pussy. Take off that gear and fight me like a man."

"And why would I do that?"

"Because your punk ass can't fit through these tunnels in that big-ass suit. That's why. Here. Take your knife back!" He threw the knife at Charlie's head.

Charlie's helmet quickly retracted, covered his face, and the knife bounced off and hit the cave floor. The helmet flipped back, Charlie looked around, and Hammer was gone from sight.

Making a break for it through the tunnel entrance that was behind his desk, Hammer laughed and yelled back at Charlie with, "Enjoy the booby traps, asshole!"

Charlie tried to give chase, but his brother was right, the suit wouldn't fit through these tunnels. He stepped back and began to remove it piece by piece and threw them to the cave's floor.

Rudy Ray's voice came through. "Don't get too cocky, Charlie. Hammer's genetic makeup now outmatches yours physically in every way. Proceed with caution, little nephew. This could end up being your last trip to the zoo."

Charlie threw the last piece on the ground then picked up the Night Slasher knife. He ripped off his shirt and entered the cave with caution.

*

Outside the dilapidated Miracles N Shit recreational center, the local news was covering the festivities of raising charitable donations in order to save the building from the evil, white contractors. There were various breakdance lessons, head spin demonstrations, and friendly competitions where the winner was based on audience reactions; but it was all in fun. "Despite there being a city-wide riot with mutated monsters attacking and killing random people," the reporter said into the camera, "it doesn't seem to have stopped any of the fun going on down here at Miracles N Shit. To the left of me, we have the parachute pants and bikini car wash, to the right of me, there's a puppet show of the movie *Breakin' II: Electric Boogaloo* happening, and standing just a few feet from me is Bongo, the rec centers mime and master balloon animal maker, who is entertaining the children with his latest creations." The reporter looked over, "Say hi to the audience, Bongo!"

Bongo the Mime smiled, tipped his black hat to the reporter, pulled out a new balloon, and started blowing.

The reporter went wide-eyed and smiled at the camera with extreme anticipation.

Suddenly, Randy drove onto the scene, completely out of control, and skidded straight for the puppet show with the many kids gathered around.

Boogaloo ramped onto the scene next inside his modified go kart, hot on Randy's desperate trail. His go kart hit the pavement hard which sent sparks flying high from its metal body.

Missing the kids by just mere inches, Randy swerved and took out Bongo the Mime on live TV.

Kids screamed and fled as Bongo's blood splattered the crowd.

Breakers scattered.

The entire crowd began to scream.

Boogaloo zeroed in on his terrified target and decided it was time to take him out. A green laser blast shot from the front of his go kart and hit the rear end of Randy's car and made it explode on site.

Randy tried to escape the flaming wreckage. While the clothes on his body burned, he crawled out, ran several feet, then hit the pavement as the flames finally took his life, right next to the news van.

The camera crew quickly grabbed some close-ups of the victim.

Boogaloo was pleased. Sitting parked by the crowd, he yelled out, "That was for me and my mother! Save Miracles N Shit!"

Someone shouted, "Hey, everyone! It's Boogaloo!"

Someone removed Boogaloo's helmet. "It is! It's Boogaloo, everyone!"

Several people unstrapped Boogaloo from the go kart's cockpit and hoisted him up on their shoulders. The crowd began to chant, "Boogaloo! Boogaloo!"

Randy continued to burn in the background.

*

Back at the Zoo Gang Compound, Hammer and Charlie brawled in the tunnel systems. They continued to trade blow-for-blow with neither backing down. But without a fatal blow or decapitation from the other, their wounds would just continuously heal from their serum enhancements in the pointless brawl. And they knew that. They continued anyway, letting out years of aggression on each other with each strike. Minutes later, with the *Cobra* replica knife in hand, Charlie stood in a defensive stance and said, "This could go on for a while. How about we have some fun before I end your life?"

With the large, rusted hammer by his side, the now massive Hammer Jones chuckled. "What do you have in mind, little runt?"

Charlie held up the knife. "Take it from me again, and stick it in me, and look me into the eyes as you turn it, and see what's going on there. Come on, Hammer. Let's party!"

"I can beat you, you movie-line-stealing cracker. Without that stupid metal man suit you left back there and with just that knife in your hand, what could you possibly do to me? Why don't you come show me what you got, bro?"

Charlie stood, unfazed.

Hammer continued. "Jump, Kermit. I'll whip your ass up and down these cave tunnels and back to the swamp with Miss Piggy for all to see, bitch. Just like when we were little, and I used to practice my lethal, signature, wrestling moves on your little bitch ass."

"We aren't kids anymore, Carlton. And this *ain't* the backyard."

Hammer's mood changed immediately. His smile disappeared, and he stepped forward. "Call me that again, bro. I fucking dare you."

"What? Carlton?"

"Yeah."

"Okay. And wrestling is fake too by the way."

"Say what?"

"Fake as you, Carlton."

In a rage, Hammer charged.

Charlie was actually taken off guard.

Hammer slammed into him like a linebacker, crushed all of Charlie's ribs on one side, and smashed him against the rock wall, which sent debris and dust high into the air and swirling all around them.

Charlie could swear he felt the earth shake upon impact. He hit the ground in pain. And before his healing process could even begin, the large, rusty hammer was swung and cracked Charlie right in the skull.

Charlie's head bounced off the rock floor. Healing properties or not, he was down for the count.

Hammer stood over him in victory. He pointed the Hammer at Charlie like a scepter as he spoke. "All who oppose the mighty Hammer Jones, will eventually kiss the floor. Where to start with you, Charlie? Where to start?" He began to walk back and forth. "First off, I never wanted a brother."

Charlie mumbled, "I did," through the blood coming out his mouth.

Hammer cracked him in the back with the hammer. "Well, I didn't, muthafucka! So, when mamma took you in after some stupid, cracker family left you on our doorstep, I naturally wasn't thrilled. I didn't even want to share my shit with my own kind, let alone some stray white boy like you."

Charlie managed, "You always were a greedy little motherfucker. Wouldn't share shit. And what I did have, you always destroyed. Always fucked up my toys." Charlie was able to raise up to his knees some, but with great difficulty. "I walked in on you one time, and you were literally sodomizing my Teddy Ruxpin doll while laughing your ass off. You even cut a hole in its goddamn ass, man. Are you really this crazy, Carlton?"

"My name isn't Carlton, motherfucker!" Hammer grabbed Charlie by the hair and held him up before him and got face to face. "It's Hammer!" he yelled. "Hammer Jones!" And with his massive arms, Hammer slung

Charlie through the tunnel's wall and down Charlie fell out of sight.

Charlie finally landed on a bridge that connected all the zoo exhibits down below him.

Hammer looked down at Charlie on the bridge and laughed.

Gangsters from below began to gather and look overhead at the action unfolding.

Hammer shouted down to them. "Come one, come all, watch Charlie Jones fall!"

The gangsters looked up and gasped at the size that Hammer had grown into. He was monstrous.

Hammer upped the show for his audience by jumping down and landing on the bridge and damn near crippling it from the weight of his impact.

The crowd was in awe.

The Hulkish Hammer, with his rusty hammer in hand, slowly approached Charlie, who was still laid out. "H-A-M-M-E-R, boy!" Hammer said. "I'm more than just a muthafuckin thug with a bad attitude! I'm now a god amongst men! A ghetto Titan on earth, mightier than Thor and twice as deadly in the ring as The Road Warriors were! I am Hammer Jones!" He faced the crowd and looked down. "Hail, Hammer!"

The crowd threw up their fists. "Hammer Time!"

Hammer looked back at Charlie.

Charlie was trying to sit up and slowly regain his bearings. "Hammer Time, huh?" he asked.

"That's right! Hammer Time!"

Charlie felt his internal healing process begin. He let out a slight cough. "Hammer Time? You *actually* ripped that off from a rapper back in the eighties? Talk about lame. Stealing tag-lines like that, it's no wonder your wrestling career never took off, Carlton."

The gangsters below giggled at Hammer's real name.

Humiliated, Hammer pointed at Charlie. "What did I say was gonna happen to you if—"

"Look, man," Charlie painfully wobbled his way onto his feet. "Knock off the routine. Because no matter how much you try and look cool, you'll always just be that failed bad guy wrestler that dookied in the tub once when we had to share a bath as kids."

There was an embarrassed silence, even from below.

Hammer broke it and played it off with, "I did that on purpose, bitch."

"Yeah. Sure. And did you and your pussy, bitch gang accidentally kill my LaQueefa?" Charlie lunged, kicked Hammer square in the face and sent him off the bridge down to his own gang's feet.

Charlie yelled down, "Or was her death on purpose?" He leaped off the bridge and landed in the midst of the crowd.

One right after the other from Hammer's gang rushed in and attacked but did little damage.

The Serum 13B enhanced Charlie, to put it bluntly, beat the shit out of each one as if it were a casual stroll. Noses were cracked, legs and arms were broken, and the Night Slasher knife slashed its way through multiple necks.

Several gangsters quickly advanced with thick chains and caught Charlie from behind in a bad way.

Charlie fell to his knees in pain.

The remaining bangers (that were still left standing) rushed in. In no time flat, a pile of criminal scum was on top of Charlie.

With Charlie now occupied under the huge mound of extreme body weight, Hammer took off running.

Charlie thrashed about and struggled. He sucked in his breath, held it, then with a thrust of adrenaline, quickly rose to his feet and threw his arms out with a yell.

Gangsters spun out of control as bodies flew up and away from Charlie before finally landing all around him like a human piñata of neon punks had exploded.

Charlie looked around and spotted Hammer running around the corner, back into the lion's den where their fight first began. Charlie took off after him.

Hammer entered his office. Kicking parts of Charlie's suit out of the way, he bolted for the desk and opened the drawer. Inside was a twenty-ounce metal container with the label reading Time Juice in black Magic Marker. He slammed the drawer and quickly took off down one of his various escape tunnels. When he stepped out the other end, he was in the time-travel elevator section of the zoo.

Kimbo was typing away on the computer.

Hammer yelled, "You got them coordinates locked in yet?"

"Yes, boss. It's all set." Kimbo held out his hand. "Time juice?"

Hammer handed him the juice. "Now, get me the fuck outta here for a while!"

Kimbo nervously got up to fill the tank on the side of the time-traveling elevator.

"And hurry!" Hammer ordered.

Charlie busted onto the scene through the side of the cave's wall, safely tucked back inside his flight suit and well protected from flying debris and rubble. "Not so fast, Carlton," he said in his robotic-style voice and holding up a palm that was armed with a glowing pulse just waiting to burst a round at its target.

Hammer looked at Kimbo, who was frozen stiff and hugging the canister of time juice. "Proceed, Kimbo."

Kimbo looked unsure what to do.

Hammer said, "Go ahead, Kimbo. Charlie ain't gonna shoot someone like you: an innocent." He looked at Charlie. "Are you, little brother?"

Kimbo moved behind the elevator where he felt safer, pulled the cap off the juice and began to pour it into the tank.

Hammer looked at Charlie and smiled. "What the fuck is your deal with me? Why can't you just leave me be?"

"My plan when I returned from the war was to just take my woman and leave, but you and your bastards killed her."

"Oh, yeah? Well, *I* didn't do that shit."

"Your gang. Your streets. Your fault."

Hammer started to walk his time-travel lair and preach. "I can't control all the crazy shit my gang does when they get high and shit. C'mon. Even a soldier boy like you knows that the frowned-upon shit happens when the boss ain't looking."

Charlie's mask retracted back so he could look Hammer in the face. "I look at the junkies, pimps, whores, I'm assuming you get paid off all the shit. All the drugs come through you, the weapons, the intimidation, all you, right?"

Hammer said proudly, "Damn right. Make some good jack off this shit too. Your brother from another mother done came up, and I didn't need no wrestling ring in some high school gym on local cable to do it neither."

"This culture belongs to you, bro. You set this tone."

"I didn't set shit! How in the fuck you gonna blame me for this culture? My entire life, I had violent gangster rap and fucked-up movies shoved down my goddamn throat. So, I played along. But as I knowingly became a product of my environment, that they purposely pushed onto me, I began to wonder just why these muthafucks running shit wanted us niggas to turn out so fucked up. Have you ever heard a Spice 1 album before? If anyone hates niggas, it would be him. And I listened to his ass way more than I would ever listen to any adult. But this culture, I didn't create it, *or me*. *They* did. But as time went by, and I realized just what the fuck they were doing to my people, I figured that if they gonna purposely turn me into a product of a fucked-up environment like I'm some kinda human experiment and shit, then I figured I'd *own that shit*. Then when I couldn't get any more gangsta, I'd take over and use their own monsters *that they created* against them with a few monsters of my own. All I needed was an army ... and I got it! Moral of all this, good things come to those who travel time and steal some super-human serum, Charlie."

"These mindless soldiers might look up to you, but only because they fear you. Well, I'm about to show them you are not only nothing to fear, but you are an absolute joke of a human being."

Hammer looked over at Kimbo, who had snuck back over to the computer terminal.

Kimbo gave him a thumbs up and hit enter on his keyboard.

The time-travel elevator doors opened.

Hammer launched his rusty hammer at Charlie's head.

Charlie's helmet quickly retracted. He fired back but missed when the hammer hit him square in his metal dome and flipped him backwards against the wall.

Before Charlie could even look up, Hammer was already in the elevator.

Hammer yelled, "Hit it, Kimbo!"

But before the elevator doors could close, the elevator exploded and blew Hammer out and back against the wall. He landed on the ground next to Charlie. He looked up, dazed.

Charlie's palm was smoking from the fresh proton blast that took out the elevator. "Your ass ain't going anywhere," Charlie said. He reached down, grabbed

Hammer by the mohawk, dragged him a few feet, then aimed his palm at the computer set up.

Kimbo ran away.

Seconds later, Charlie blew Kimbo's computer set up to smithereens with another proton blast.

Hammer looked up from Charlie's grasp and said, "How does your suit know when to fire?"

Charlie aimed at the wall. "Don't ask." He fired and blew a new hole into the cave wall.

The sun shone into the room through the fresh hole.

Kimbo quickly exited through it and was gone.

Hammer looked up at Charlie, who still held Hammer's afro mohawk tight in his iron grip. "All this bullshit is useless, Charlie. With both of us having healing factors the way we do, how the hell is either one of us ever going to win this battle?"

Charlie put his iron boot to Hammer's face and the flight propulsion shot out bare minimum and melted most of the flesh from his face.

Hammer screamed in pain. Seventy-five percent of his face showed skull.

Charlie dragged him through the rubble and looked outside. "How do I kill you? It's actually gonna be simple, Carlton." Charlie stepped outside and continued to drag Hammer behind by the hair.

Hammer, with his exposed skull, screamed, "Hammer, muthafucka! My name is Hammer! Hammer Jones!"

Charlie grabbed Hammer under the shoulders and lifted him the way a parent would do their kid, got face to face, then viciously head butted him with his metal dome.

Hammer went completely limp.

Charlie's faceplate retracted and he stared eye to eye with his adopted brother. "I have a question about pet ownership." Charlie looked down into the dog pit then back to Hammer. His face plate covered his face back up and through glowing eyes asked, "Can hungry dogs eat a hammer?" And with all of the power of the suit's strength, Charlie lunged Hammer down into the pit and cracked nearly every bone in his body.

Knowing he was done for, Hammer did his best to look tough as the snarling dogs slowly approached. He looked up and spotted Charlie and shouted, "Damn it feels good to be a gangster!"

The dogs attacked. It took a while. Hammer healed along as the dogs ripped and tore him to shreds. But the dogs finally got the upper hand, ate quicker than Hammer could heal, and the screaming finally stopped.

Charlie said, "Goodbye, brother. You always were an asshole, but I tried to love you anyway." Charlie flew off; mission accomplished.

Chapter Eleven
Some Assembly Required

Charlie landed in the zoo's parking lot next to a half-dead Tuck Pendelton who, covered in bloody gauze dressing, leaned against the disabled van with nothing but a Beretta 9mm pistol in hand. Parked next to him was Boogaloo, who had returned to help his father finish the job. Charlie's helmet retracted so he could get a breath of fresh air. "What's up, Tuck? Boog? Job's done on my end. Ready to call it a day?"

In the distance, the three could hear the mutated beasts from the city coming closer and closer.

Tuck stood as well as his legs would allow and cocked his pistol. "Sounds like someone is heading this way to give us some overtime."

The monsters appeared in the distance, coming in through the trees, surrounding neighborhoods and streets. They began to close in like zombies, slowly.

Charlie's helmet flipped back over his head, his eyes lit up and he said, "There's way too many of these things. I might be able to pick a few off from the sky, but in the end, they are going to overtake everything on the ground."

Boogaloo said, "And then they'll overtake the entire city, if there's anything left."

The beasts picked up the pace and started to jog.

Boogaloo gulped. "Um, Dad. What should we do?"

"We run and hide. Or we stay, fight, and die."

Boogaloo thought then said, "Let's go see mom in ghetto heaven." He revved his go kart.

"That's my boy!" Charlie lifted in hover mode.

Tuck spit some blood on the concrete. "Fuck it. Let's go."

Together, the three men advanced slowly as one, cocked back and ready to die.

The beasts picked up speed.

The space between the two sides grew shorter and shorter. The monsters shot into a dead sprint across the parking lot and straight for their three-man meal.

There was no surviving this battle, and the look on Tuck's face showed it.

The clash was almost there. Just ten more feet and...

Boom! A large beam of light hit the entire area and it knocked everyone and everything on the scene back and on its ass. The wind blew the trash in the area into a short-lived tornado of litter and debris.

When the light vanished and the trash finally dropped, everyone looked up.

Hovering high above on a jetpack with a gatling gun attached to its frame was Earl Tubb, Section Eight soldier from the past, there to save them all, and screaming at the top of his lungs like a *Braveheart* warrior. In his robotic hand, the severed head of Frank "Switchblade" Butz.

Earl threw Switchblade's head to the pavement.

Charlie dodged the severed head, steadied his flight suit then flew up next to Earl. "Good to see you, Agent Tubb! Never thought I'd need this much help, but as it turns out, I did."

Earl smiled and said, "Everyone needs a cool-ass team, Charlie." He hit a button on his time-travel device and a sparkling portal of golden light opened up underneath him on the ground below.

Everyone on the ground was floored (even the beasts) as Section Eight members from the past started pouring out left and right, one after the other and each one just as colorful as the next.

The only thing Charlie could hear was the sound of Rudy Ray screaming from his end, "*Endgame*, baby! Look at that shit! I told you it'd be cool shit, Charlie! Fuck yeah!"

Earl announced the arrival of each one as they came through. "First up, Sam Dickey the Ninja!

Molecular Man flying an actual G.I. Joe helicopter! Lizard Boy, Hugo Thunders! Lightning Bug in his power company's utility van! Sammy Comet with her Uzi and wearing her trademark cheerleader outfit! WindBreaker! Chuck Thunders and Rodney Tibbs in their stolen Duster! Lester Boone, rocking a Section Eight battle suit! Fucking cool shit, Lester! The Bronze Skateboarder from galaxies far beyond ours! And last but not least, LaQueefa the Street Samurai!"

LaQueefa, back from the dead and looking sexy as hell, in her afro puffs, skin-tight black one-piece and a samurai sword in each hand, stepped out from the portal.

Charlie looked down at his ghetto queen, who had never in her living years been that sexy before.

She looked up at Charlie in his hover mode and gave him a wink.

Time stood still for Charlie. But only for a moment; this was no time for a reunion.

Section Eight quickly scattered and formed a battle line and posed like action figures, ready to be played with.

Vehicles on the scene revved.

The monsters on the scene stood, formed a line of their own, then without hesitation, charged with a roar.

Section Eight charged too.

*

After the battle was over, and the city was saved, Earl landed his jet pack on the apocalyptic-looking parking lot next to his Section Eight soldiers—who were war-torn but still in victorious spirits as they administered first aid on themselves and each other on the smoking remains of the battlefield. Earl walked through the sea of dead monsters and thick goo, picked up Switchblade's smashed and bloody head from the pavement, and held it up. He smiled at Frank's head and then tossed it into the nearest public, trash receptacle. "And that's that. Rot in hell, Switchblade Butz. You damn pussy." Earl turned around and several Section Eight members were approaching.

One of them was Lightning Bug. Wearing his utility, electrician outfit, he holstered his jumper cables onto his large tool belt that was slam full of tools. "Thanks for including me in this, Earl. I shocked the shit out of at least twenty of these things." He looked around at the various dead. "Whatever the hell they were."

Earl nodded. He began to walk the battlefield remains; smoke rose all around from the dead.

Charlie landed next to Earl. His helmet flipped back. "It was damn good to see you again, Earl."

"*Agent* Tubb."

Charlie smiled. "It was damn good to see you again, *Agent* Tubb."

"I like your suit, Charlie," Earl said looking him up and down. "What do they call you here in the future?"

"Ghetto Blaster."

Tuck limped up, gun still in the hand of his injured and dangling arm. "Yep! East St. Louis' newest hero and ultimate badass original!"

Earl grunted, "Original? Uh, looks like a junkyard, Iron Man rip-off to me. But what do you expect when Brad McCormick is writing the goddamn story?" Earl spit on the ground. "Sumbitch needs to grow up." He looked at Ghetto Blaster. "But don't you worry, GB, my man. We're gonna change that shit. Right, Tinker?"

Tinker stepped through the portal and up to Earl. "That's right, Agent Tubb. I'm bringing all of Section Eight's technology here to the future just like you requested. I hope you know what you're doing."

"I do," Earl said with confidence.

Lab technicians, scientist, and We-Haul movers carrying equipment and boxes, all began stepping through the portal and gathered for instructions.

Tinker looked at his crew. "Where would you like us to set up shop, Agent Tubb?"

"Shit if I know. Haven't thought that far ahead yet."

Ghetto Blaster chimed in, "We have a kickass cave with computers and shit that could use a serious upgrade. How about there?"

"You heard the man," Earl yelled. "Start stacking all the shit up over there until I can locate a flatbed truck or some shit."

LaQueefa came up to Charlie's side. The samurai blades in her hands were blood soaked and her sexy face and afro puffs were spotted with blood.

Charlie's suit opened up and he completely stepped from the iron man shell with ease. He hugged his woman and she almost melted into his arms and became weightless. Finally, after this horrible past year for them both, the two shared a loving embrace and a kiss that seemed like it would never end. And that was fine with them both.

Earl said, "*Hymph.* They done caught the Jungle Fever. I can dig it. It *is* the future after all."

They continued to kiss.

Boogaloo, still in his go kart, finally turned his head. "C'mon, guys! Not in front of me! Gross!"

LaQueefa laughed.

Charlie looked at Earl. "I can't thank you enough for everything, Agent Tubb. You not only helped me when I needed it the most, but you brought my LaQueefa back to me."

LaQueefa and Charlie kissed again.

Earl said, "You can have your cake and eat it too; like you deserve, Charlie. Uh, I mean, Ghetto Blaster."

LaQueefa's eyes widened. "Is that your new nickname, baby?"

"Only when fighting supervillains. That's if Earl and his team will have me."

The various characters gathered around.

The Section Eight Martian with two heads, red eyes, and a neon green cape stepped up. "Not only do we accept you as one of our own," both of its heads said in unison, "but we *need* you, Ghetto Blaster. And considering the psychic signal that I am picking up from you with my special abilities, we sense that *you* need us too."

Earl detached the jet back from his back and it fell to the ground with a loud *clank*! "He's right, GB. If you're gonna continue to live a peaceful existence in this here crazy future full of drug dealers with cell phones, you're gonna need some help. Besides, them folks in Rockwood don't appreciate shit I do. So, Imma gets me a fresh start, somewhere where the people don't know about the time I shit my pants back in grade school."

It got silent.

Earl continued. "*Ahem-hem*. Time to set up shop! First thing we gonna need to do is move all our shit to the new headquarters GB graciously donated. Put in a big-ass table with chairs all around it. A big screen up on the wall. Maybe a spotlight on top of the police station that'll shine a big-ass eight ball in the sky when trouble strikes. All that good, original shit that I'm coming up with here on the spot."

Charlie looked at Earl. "Well, you can count the Ghetto Blaster in."

"Me too," said Molecular Man from his G.I. Joe tank made combat-battle ready for his small size. Next to him in the passenger seat was the red-headed Scarlett action figure.

"I'm in!" said one of the heads on the two-headed alien.

"Me too!" said the other head. They nodded at one another.

"I'll drink to that," the bloody Tuck said, sitting in the parking lot and holding up the last of his fifth before gulping it down.

Lester stepped next to Earl. "Gee, Earl. How many people did you pick up from your time travels?"

"All of them, Lester, my man. Section Eight's motto is Here to Save You All, and it's not just a slogan to old Earl Tubb. So, that's what I did. I took out Switchblade and then saved you all." Earl looked around at his soldiers. "And here we are."

Lester smiled, proud of his mentor and grateful for being saved from his untimely demise in the past. "You'll have to tell me all about this Section Eight stuff, Earl. Bet you gotta heck of a story to tell, huh?"

"Bet your ass I do, son. Someone should force that dickhead Brad McCormick to write the truth about me for once." Earl looked at the time-travel device on his wrist. *"And I'm just the man to do it."*

Chapter Twelve
The New Lou

Over at Miracles N Shit, the graffiti was nearing the end of its existence as the last of it was getting covered up by a fresh coat of paint by several teens who used paint rollers attached to extensions. "I can't believe we raised enough money to save Miracles N Shit," the one in the red leopard print attire and light blue sweat band said.

His buddy in the half-cut shirt and short, mesh shorts stopped rolling his paint, adjusted the dangling boombox earring hanging from his ear lobe and said, "I guess we can be thankful that Boogaloo's chase ended here and the news station's ratings shot up. Once that evil, white real estate dude saw just how committed we were to keeping the bad ones off the street and heard about the story of Boogaloo on the news last night, he had a change of heart. He's right over there."

Over to the side of the building, the old white guy was kicking it with several kids while wearing some breakdance attire and trying to learn how to moonwalk.

The painting teens nodded with a smile.

"Warms your heart, huh?"

Inside the building, sitting motionless in his wheelchair from the neck down, Boogaloo spoke with his mother and father who stood before him side-by-side and looked happy as ever, despite their son's condition. "It was really good how I helped in that battle, huh Dad?"

"Despite not having the use of your limbs, you came through like I knew you could. I never got to see you dance, but I *did* get to see you in battle, and your bravery had me in awe. I'm proud of you, Boog."

Boogaloo smiled. "Thanks, Dad. Maybe I can join Section Eight."

"Um. Maybe *not*."

They all three overly laughed at the bad comeback.

LaQueefa interrupted the moment. "Well, fellas. It's a beautiful day out. What are we gonna do with it?"

Charlie pulled out a hypodermic needle full of a glowing green substance. "Sorry, but I actually have a meeting, but before I go, we're going to watch our son dance, sexy mamma."

Boogaloo's eyes went wide.

Ten minutes later, breakdancers were gathered around as Boogaloo laid in the center of the floor, motionless, and looked up at the ceiling. A few feet away from his head was a double-sized boombox.

Charlie looked at the kid next to the boombox and pointed. "Drop the beat."

Everyone watched Boogaloo. Not a soul could blink.

The beat bumped. The snare slapped. The bassline kicked in and began to loop with the rhythm of a heartbeat.

Boogaloo said, "I feel a tingle in my arms, everyone. Oh, my god! It's a tingle! Oh, my god!"

The taekwondo instructor in his gi pumped his fist and said, "C'mon, Boogaloo! You can do it!"

LaQueefa and Charlie embraced tight.

The kid next to the boombox said, "C'mon, Boogaloo!"

The beat pumped harder.

Once the scratching guitar hit the track, Boogaloo shouted, "It's in my legs now, Mom! Dad! I can ... I can ..."

The breakers felt it coming and stepped back.

Boogaloo leaped to his feet and began to pop and lock like never before. "I can dance again! I can!"

The crew formed a circle and began to clap to the beat as Boogaloo tore up the floor.

LaQueefa began to cry in joy.

Charlie was never happier. The happily-ever-after ending he wanted had become his.

*

Back in Rudy Ray's cave, he and Tuck worked on repairing busted equipment and shot the breeze. An old table radio played something old school and funky. "Wish I could have been there," Rudy Ray said as he slammed a metal plate on the side of the van for Tuck to bolt down. "From the looks of you, I'm glad I stayed back."

Using his good arm, Tuck adjusted the sling on his left arm, lifted up the bolt gun, and fired a bolt into the metal plate. "All right, let go."

Rudy Ray did.

Tuck took a swig from a forty ounce of malt liquor. "It'll hold until I weld it back down."

The cave's computer terminal began to beep.

"Looks like we have some company."

Tuck and Rudy Ray casually walked over to the computer terminal and Rudy Ray hit the "access granted" button.

Down the hall, the elevator door opened and out stepped Earl Tubb in his Han Solo vest. Following behind was Charlie Jones, WindBreaker, Sam Dickey the Ninja (in aerobics attire), Chuck Thunders, Rodney Tibbs, and Molecular Man flying along in a nineteen eighty-three G.I. Joe Dragonfly helicopter that, much like all his G.I. Joe vehicles, he had converted to a functioning vehicle for himself.

Rudy Ray welcomed them. "Hello, squad. Welcome to the cave."

The squad stopped.

Earl shook Rudy Ray's hand. "Nice cave, Rudy Ray."

Rudy Ray said, "Thank you."

"Yup. Next to me having my very own trading card, this might be one of the coolest things I have ever seen." Earl stepped away from the squad and nodded in approval at the scene. "Yep. This cave is the shit. And it'll do. It'll do *just* fine." He turned to face the crew of super soldiers, "*Ten-hut!*"

The squad came to attention.

Earl pointed at Molecular Man. "You supposed to be standing at attention. Land your toy, Tiny."

Molecular Man landed his helicopter and stepped out of the cockpit and came to attention.

"Now, my name is Tubb. *Captain* Earl Tubb of the 2037 division of Section Eight, and I expect nothing but the best from each and every one of you. It's time for East St. Louis to have their very own Justice League. We'll slap a big round table in here, put in a mini fridge, pull shifts the way firemen do, and any time the signal I had Sergeant Kickass install on top of the police station hits the sky and we get the call, we whip that evil, villainous ass. The signal is an 8 ball. For Section Eight. That was *my* idea. Any questions?"

Not a one.

Earl's head raised proudly. "Let's get to work."

Rudy Ray asked, "What about your hometown, Earl? Will they be okay without you there to watch over them?"

"I put Switchblade in the ground and then put the word out that if anyone tried anything, I'd be there quick as shit to wipe up the mess. I have Lester, my main man, back home guarding the fort as we speak. Linked his skinny little ass up to my cool wristwatch that can make time-travel calls."

Earl's device he was referring to began to beep.

Earl looked down. "I'll be damned." He answered it.

A miniature holograph of Lester appeared in front of Earl and shouted, "Help us, Earl Tubb! You're our only hope!" Around Lester, maniacal laughs were happening accompanied by terrifying screams and multiple gunshots. A siren blared in the background along with what sounded like random car crashes.

Earl leaned in and whispered, "I'm giving my speech right now, man."

Lester shot his pistol at an off-screen target and a dead body fell into the holograph's frame by his feet as a man in the background ran by on fire.

Earl continued. "What could possibly be so important right now that you gotta interrupt the dream speech I waited my entire life to give? Wait. Is that the Rockwood Home for the Criminally Insane siren I hear in the background?"

"Yep! That's it. Sorry, Earl. But it's that Switchblade fella again. He's back!"

"Bullshit," Earl declared. "That boy ain't no Jason Krueger and shit. I took that boy's head myself."

"In the timeline *you* entered, but not the one during the Section Eight massacre, where he escaped with the help of that Zoo Gang assassin. Apparently, he done stole a bunch of Section Eight's serum here, drove a car into the side of the mental hospital, killed a bunch of guards, freed a bunch of patients and has been injecting them at random ever since! They are attacking and killing the entire town as I speak!"

Earl exhaled. "And I take it you can't handle this zombie apocalypse bullshit alone, huh?"

Lester screamed, ducked, and a body flew over his head.

Earl rolled his eyes. "I'll be right there. I have your time coordinates locked in and ready. And, Lester?"

Lester took a few shots and killed a man in the background then looked at Earl through the holograph. "Yeah, Earl?"

"We're gonna have to have a talk about scheduling interruptions in the future when I get there."

Lester's look showed shame, and then he ducked a flying trash can.

Earl shut off the call and said under his breath, "Goddamn it, Frank Butz, you fucking time-jumping cockroach you." He faced the squad. "Rudy Ray," he pointed. "Call the rest of the squad here. Looks like we gonna have to wait to redecorate."

WindBreaker asked, "Do we have a mission already?"

Earl got dead serious. "Yep. And its name is Switchblade Butz."

Using the clouds above the city for a screen, the Section Eight light shined high above.

THE END

COMING SOON

The Rise of Earl Tubb: Switchblade Part II

ABOUT THE AUTHOR

Brad McCormick is an American award-winning author and screenwriter. His many interests include a wide range of movies, music, and books that has influenced his unique writing style. Most notably, his interest in 80s Horror, B-Movies, and obscure straight-to-video releases have helped contribute to the tone of his narrative pieces.

Made in the USA
Monee, IL
15 January 2021